DARE TO LOVE

"I don't know what I want, except *you*," Jake finally admitted. He glared at her, as if angry she had forced him to this admission. "I want you, Kate Rose. And if you can't handle it, fine. Just say so. But if you can . . ."

He left the thought unfinished, waiting. Kate swallowed, intending to tell him where to get off. But she couldn't quite muster the words. Her lips remained clamped shut because she knew whatever came out of her mouth wouldn't be the truth.

"You want me, too," he guessed, coming to stand in front of her. She had a clear view of his denim-clad legs, but she refused to look up. "You do. You wouldn't have responded like that unless you felt the same thing." He squatted down in front of her, waiting until she reluctantly met his eyes. Then he whispered tautly, giving her no chance to squirm out of a direct answer, "You want me, and I want you. And I think we know where this is heading. Why don't we just admit it and stop torturing ourselves? I want *you*," he stated deliberately. "Now, tell me you want me, too."

BY CANDLELIGHT

Janelle Taylor

Zebra Books
Kensington Publishing Corp.
http://www.zebrabooks.com

Prologue

A Moment Long Ago . . .

The church sat on a rise at the forgotten end of town. White clapboard siding encased it, and five cement stairs capped by a railing that hung drunkenly amidst blistered, chipped paint stood out against a threatening sky so black it made the hair on Katie Tindel's arms rise just looking at it.

She squeezed Jake's hand to reassure herself, shivering, huddled within his navy blue and gold letter jacket. "It's so dark," she whispered.

"It's great, isn't it?" He grinned, bright teeth gleaming, blue-gray eyes dancing with excitement.

She caught the fever, smiling back. Jake threw his arm around her, and they ran up the stairs to the slanted porch, crowding together as a blast of lightning lit the sky, followed by a thunderclap that nearly deafened.

Jake's lips parted as they watched together. Katie could feel his heart racing next to hers. Her thoughts ran in a jumble of happiness through her mind.

Glancing down at her, Jake leaned forward and kissed her with lips that were cool and dry and curved with the beauty of this special time for them.

Rain poured. Buckets of it. A shimmering silver curtain that enveloped them both. The electric scent of ozone in the wake of another zap of lightning brought a sense of exhilaration that was inexplicable to anyone but those whom it touched.

Katie was not immune. She ran down the cement steps, lifting her arms to the heavens and her face to the rain's torrent. Jake laughed, ran after her, swept her up and carried her back to the church's front doors. He fumbled for the handle, still carrying her. Katie kissed his face, all over. The doors swung open, the lock picked by Jake earlier that morning. Just a small bit of breaking and entering— all for a good cause. Nothing the good Lord could blame them for, for this was their day. Their destiny. Their untouched future.

The church was empty. Abandoned. A For Sale sign swung forlornly at the end of the lane, nearly obscured by the current downpour. But it didn't matter. This, too, was *their* church. *Their* private place. They would lock up later, but for now Jake managed to pull the doors closed behind them while Kate's arms surrounded his neck and she held on for dear life.

"I love you," she whispered in his ear.

"I love you more," he answered automatically.

It was a game they played. They had played it all through this last year of high school, and now with graduation just around the corner, their love had reached a new level, a new distinction. The physical side had yet to be breached. They had waited for the right moment, and on this April night with a symphony of rain surrounding them they planned to pledge their love to each other solemnly and permanently, in a church, a secret "marriage" that his parents would never really allow.

With long, ground-devouring strides Jake carried Kate toward the altar. His steps were hollow. The room swirled with drafts from cracks around the windows. One pane was blocked by plywood; some caring citizen's attempt to keep the church from becoming the home of vagabonds and thieves.

The pews sat straight and rigid at attention—Jake and Kate's only witnesses. Setting her on her feet in front of the altar whose maple base was carved in a relief of autumn leaves, Jake cupped Kate's face in his cool, strong hands. They stared at each other, lost in their love.

"Look in the pockets of my jacket," Jake urged, and Katie dug inside to discover two white candles, two tiny crystal candlesticks, a book of matches and a Bible. Solemnly, silently, she handed the rich booty to her "husband-to-be," and Jake set the candles upon the altar, striking the match and lighting the wicks with a tiny gold and blue flame.

A wisp of smoke and the scent of candle wax. Kate slowly shed Jake's jacket and stood beside him in a short white satin gown studded with seed pearls in an all over design of rosebuds. She had saved her dimes and nickels all school year from the job she had taken at a local restaurant. College was a dim thought, distant and indistinct. Her love for Jake was bright and real, and she had searched long and hard for the perfect dress, finding it unexpectedly in a boutique that also sold used clothing. The dress had a history; the saleslady said it had been owned originally by a wealthy woman who had purchased it for her daughter's coming out party. The daughter had spurned the dress, and the mother had shoved it to the back of a closet. Finally she had rediscovered it and sold it second-hand. Kate had walked into the store the day it was draped across an antique rocker in the store's window. It still cost a small fortune. She had put down twenty-five dollars to hold it and paid off the rest over time.

Now, today, she wore it proudly as she stood beside Jake. His rain-soaked shoulders were broad beside hers. Glancing down at her own drenched feet, she silently bemoaned the destruction of her cream pumps. But it was worth it.

"I love you," he whispered, turning toward her, taking her hands in his.

"I love you more," she answered on a breath.

Swallowing, Jake took a small, crumpled paper from his pocket, and Kate listened as he "married" her with words of love and commitment. Her own avowal came straight from the heart, not merely memorized, but felt from the soul. They stared at each other in the silence that followed, candlelight flickering eerily over their faces.

She gazed at his strong jaw, the darkening of beard, the beauty of eyes a dusky blue that was almost gray. His brows were straight, his mouth unusually sensual in such a masculine countenance. A shock of hair fell over his forehead, the only boyish quality still left in Jacob Talbot's face.

He kissed her, and his lips felt soft, yet strong and determined. He loved her. He *loved* her. She could still scarcely believe her good fortune. She was poor and struggling and he came from wealth, but it didn't matter. He had chosen her and she had chosen him, and the world was theirs for the taking.

Outside again, the candles snuffed, their ceremony complete, they stood on the porch and listened to the rain. Four weeks till graduation, and someday, somewhere, a real marriage sanctioned by church and state.

But today they owned each other's hearts.

In unspoken agreement they ran for Jake's car, laughing

madly. As if the heavens were teasing, a deluge of precipitation pummeled the car, covering the windows with the visibility of a carwash.

Their plan was to drive twenty miles to the outskirts of Portland and rent a room at a motel. People knew them in their little suburb of Lakehaven far too well—at least they knew Jake. Talbot Industries was a huge Portland concern, and the fact that Jake's parents lived in the community west of the city, on the way to the coast, meant only that the local residents knew the Who's Who of their town even better.

But now in the steamy intimacy of Jake's sports car, a bit of high school rebellion and fantasy intervened. When he leaned forward for another kiss, Katie suddenly knew she wanted to make love to him here and now, with rain curtaining them from the outside world. It seemed more romantic. Juvenile, perhaps, but something to remember for years to come and chuckle about in old age.

And when she whispered her desire in Jake's ear, he grinned hugely, a flash of white that was his trademark—a smile as bright as Hollywood.

They relit the candles and placed them on the dash. Climbing into the backseat, Jake laid his jacket on the leather tuck and roll. The scent of vanilla wafted from the candles and mixed with his cologne as Jake made love to her awkwardly and tenderly, both of them giggling as they whispered their vows again and again, conscious not to rock the candles from their crystal candlesticks.

It was only much, much later, when her dreams had turned to dust and she was left alone, that Kate realized the tragedy of sharp memory. Yes, she remembered their lovemaking. Yes, it was etched forever in her mind. But it was painful and stabbing instead of soft and romantic, and it could never be forgotten, for those first awkward moments together, followed by lovemaking in more con-

ventional places, had produced a child. A daughter. April.
Named for the month she was conceived and a wedding
that never was. April, her lovechild. Hers and Jake's.

The daughter he had never learned he had sired.

Chapter One

Today . . .

"Try this one," the saleslady suggested, holding out a gilt and faux crystal atomizer for Kate's inspection. She spritzed a cloud of perfume somewhere near Kate's wrist. The scent rose up like fragrant mist from a lake, a soft, sweet faintly musky aroma that reminded Kate of something sad and long ago.

Jake Talbot . . . a forgotten wedding . . . gentle misery.

"No thanks," Kate murmured, swallowing.

It had been years. Eons. Several hundred lifetimes since she had seen or heard from him, yet reminders crept in like cold fog swirling around her. She would be doing something mundane and normal—like shopping—and then it would happen. Some memory would surface, swimming to the forefront of her mind to torment and hurt.

Yet why should it hurt now? she asked herself as she left the perfume counter and stumbled blindly through the store. Since Jake's defection she had lived a whole new life. She was no longer naive Katie Tindel. She was Kate Rose. Married, widowed and mother of a seventeen-year-old daughter whose dusky blue eyes reminded her of Jake, but whose sweet and slightly devilish character reminded her of herself.

Okay, that wasn't quite fair. Jake had been devilish, too. They had found each other in high school, and kindred spirits had bonded. But then he had left. Abandoned her. And she had been forced to grow up fast and discover the new life she was meant to have.

Now, thinking back, she still shuddered at the pain. Even before she had learned of her pregnancy, Jake had left her. He had taken off right after graduation for a trip to Europe, promising to call, write and bind them together legally. A real marriage, he had assured her. But then he had disappeared, and when Kate realized she was carrying his child, she couldn't live on dreams anymore.

Pregnant and lost, she had shown up on Jake's parents' doorstep. She hadn't known what to expect, certainly not a warm welcome, but neither had she anticipated the Talbots' frigid antipathy. Desperate to contact Jake, she would have walked through a lion's den to find him.

Unknowingly, she came pretty darn close when she met with Marilyn and Phillip Talbot that afternoon in late June. Her hand was lifted to knock when the door was suddenly thrown open, as if her presence had been expected and entirely unwelcome .

"Yes?" asked his perfectly groomed, tough-eyed mother.

Though Kate had been introduced to Marilyn Talbot once before, the woman chose not to remember her. Swallowing back the news that had forced this meeting, Kate said in a small voice, "I'm Katie Tindel. We met once before. I'm a friend of Jake's."

Marilyn had a snob's knack of looking down her nose. In heels, she was a couple of inches taller than Kate, and she used her height to her advantage. "Jake's not here," she stated firmly.

"Will he be back soon?"

Marilyn's lips pursed. Kate braced herself for the bellow of rejection she expected to blast her. She had known from the onset of her relationship with Jake that his parents would never accept her as his girlfriend. She wasn't in their league, and though Jake had scrupulously avoided the issue, playing light on his parents' disinterest in his girlfriend, Kate had easily picked up the vibes. She wasn't good enough, and that was that.

But now she was pregnant, with their grandchild. She desperately wished for Jake to magically appear, but it was not to be.

"I really need to see him," she choked out.

"You'd better come in," Marilyn invited stonily.

This was more than Kate had expected. With trepidation she crossed the threshold and followed Jake's mother along the thick oriental carpet runner that flowed into a mahogany-paneled den at the south end of the Talbot minimansion.

It was late afternoon, a rather wintry June day, which wasn't unusual for Oregon in the least. Summers started late, sometimes in the middle of August, but Septembers and Octobers were generally warm and gorgeous.

On this day rain pounded outside, and a maple tree limb slapped against the paned windows, its green leaves tragically ripped from the branch or shredded with each successive beat. Kate stared at the tattered leaves through a haze of self-involvement. She could scarcely keep her mind on the words issuing from Marilyn's mouth.

"You're very young," Jake's mother kept insisting. "It's silly to think there's anything between the two of you that would have any true meaning. Do you understand me? I'm not trying to be cruel."

Maybe not. But it sounded cruel. Beneath the polished voice lay an anxious desire to cut Kate out like a cancer. Kate was too intuitive to miss the real message.

"Jacob's in Europe for the summer," she went on, shocking Kate to her toes.

"I thought he was just supposed to go for a couple of weeks. He said he would call if things changed!"

"I'm sorry."

Kate couldn't take it all in. "When—when did this happen?"

"As soon as he got there. He had wanted to—get away."

Untrue! Kate's inner voice cried. He had *never* wanted to go in the first place! Marilyn was lying, forcing her will on both of them, dividing them like a knife.

Jake's mother sat primly on a peach-colored, velvet, wing-backed chair, her hands folded in her lap. Kate glanced her way and saw the clasped white knuckles which belied her composure. Tension was thick enough to almost see. Indeed it felt as if a mist had entered the room.

"What's your name again?" she asked with a faint gesture of apology. "I'm afraid I've forgotten it."

"Kate Tindel," she whispered. The room was cold. No, it was hot. Dear Lord, was she going to pass out?

"Miss Tindel, Jacob has responsibilities to his family. Surely you know that."

"I just want to talk to him," she said from far, far away.

"I understand, but it's just not possible. He's gone." She shifted in her chair, and just when Kate thought things couldn't get any worse, Phillip Talbot's large frame filled the open doorway. He was the epitome of a patriarch: broad chest, bulldog chin, steel gray eyes and hair streaked with silver. His mouth was hard and unsmiling, and Kate shrank inside her own skin. Marilyn, with her poise and haute couture, was bad enough; Phillip Talbot was pure iron.

Even in her distracted state, memory swirled. She recalled Jake relating the exploits of his black sheep older brother, Phillip, Jr., who was six years Jake's senior. Kate had never met him, but Phillip's wild ways and lack of responsibility had nearly gotten him thrown out of the family. As she watched Phillip, Sr., flank his wife, placing one hand on her shoulder as they both faced Kate—the enemy—Kate silently sympathized with Phillip, Jr., for running wild.

"Miss Tindel," Phillip, Sr., said to Kate, booming out her name with a familiarity that sent her nerves into overdrive. Clearly he had heard Marilyn address her before he had walked in the room. "Jacob is in Europe for the summer. After that, Harvard."

"Harvard?" She felt like a parrot, repeating everything, but it was all so foreign, so *wrong!* Jake didn't want to go to Harvard; that was his parents' wish. He wanted to stay in state, so they could be together.

"The point is, he's not coming back."

"You mean, he's going directly to Harvard after his Europe vacation?"

"He's not coming home at all," Phillip declared bluntly.

Kate wanted to cry. Her lips quivered, and she waited for the nightmare to end. They were serious. Jake was gone, and she knew without asking that they wouldn't tell her how to contact him.

Her heart beat at her temple. She should tell them. There was no other choice. They needed to know she was carrying his child.

"I'm pregnant," she said at the same moment Phillip Talbot informed her, "He's with his fiancée."

Kate blinked twice. Her mouth gaped open. A roaring in her ears. She saw the flicker of annoyance cross Phillip's face the instant before her knees gave way and she collapsed in a dead faint.

Later she realized she hadn't truly voiced her condition. The words had just reached her lips, about to be spoken, when Phillip Talbot, Sr., announced that Jake was with his fiancée.

Fiancée! The word had a dreaded ring to it. Kate hated this unknown witch as soon as she learned the woman existed. She instantly envisioned some man-stealing, cold-blooded vixen with long, red fingernails and lips that curved into a sneer rather than a smile.

But her hate was infantile and useless, an emotion she could indulge in because what she really felt was hurt and fear. Jake had hurt her. Crushed her. Stolen her faith in love and happiness. She was scared right down to her socks because she was eighteen, pregnant and with no family she could depend on.

A girl she knew had taken an apartment on the outskirts of Portland. Kate had already been spending more time with her than at home, and after that meeting with the Talbots she moved in with her lock, stock and barrel. Her parents never knew she was carrying Jake's child; she never told them. They said goodbye to her when she gathered her meager belongings, and their only subsequent contact with her was when Kate initiated it.

"You got a letter," her father mentioned to her on the phone later that fateful summer. "A couple of 'em. From Switzerland and some other Europe place, I guess."

Jake! Kate's initial thrill was instantly snuffed. A "Dear Jane" letter, no doubt. "Burn them," she bit out in a tight voice. She slammed down the phone, shaking all over, agonizing over what words he may have written. In a fit of emotion she drove to her parents' house that evening only to find her father had taken her at her word. Jake's letters were ashes. Well, so be it. It was better not knowing. When she left Lakehaven that night she didn't return for a long, long time.

But it was all so long ago . . .

Now, with a blast of August heat hitting her square in the face as she stepped out of the air-conditioned department store to the street, Kate watched gooseflesh rise on her arms. Memories of Jake still had the power to undo her. Ridiculous, but true.

Sweat dampened the armholes of her sleeveless, taupe linen dress as Kate walked determinedly through afternoon Portland shoppers. She clicked the remote lock for her vehicle, a Mustang Saleen, a sports car nearly as ridiculous as the one she and Jake had first made love in so many years ago.

Only hers was midnight blue, not black. She smiled grimly to herself as she climbed inside. These small things counted mightily.

Heat sweltered as she maneuvered into traffic and waited for the air-conditioning to blast away the stuffiness inside her convertible. Too much money, but Ben had bought it for her and she hadn't demurred. That's what happened when you married for money instead of love.

Not fair, she told herself. She hadn't married for money. She had married for—desperation. Pregnant, alone and a burden to parents who had never cared about her in the first place, Kate had taken a job at Rose Talent Agency that August as a part-time receptionist. The owner of the business, Ben Rose, was refreshingly, if bluntly, honest.

"You're pretty and you look like you might have a few brains inside that head of yours," he had assessed her. "You don't have to do much. But wipe that sadness out of your eyes. This is a happy place."

"I'll try." Kate was grateful.

"Don't try, do it."

He cushioned that remark with a quick smile. Charm was not Ben Rose's strong point; but he was magnetic in his power, and people turned to him as Kate soon learned.

She also learned that he liked her a little more than she felt comfortable with. Was this how he treated each new, feminine employee? No, she found out from the two women who also worked there. Ben was notoriously stand-offish with the "help." They both found it highly amusing that he was smitten with Kate, but Kate was in a quandary about how to proceed.

And then . . . he asked her to marry him. *Boom!*

It was after hours. Kate had worked at the agency a month to the day. It was September, and the agony of her secret pregnancy gnawed at her like a beast from within. Soon she would have to take some steps. Soon . . . But what?

She was seated at her desk, staring at the appointment calendar open to the date—September 5. A year earlier, Jake had first kissed her on September 5.

Ben Rose's slightly gnarled hand came into view. His hands showed his age, though he scrupulously dyed his hair a light brown that looked natural even when the gray showed through a bit.

She stared at his hand, so carefully placed in front of her line of vision. With a magician's flair he suddenly lifted his palm, and on the teak desk top glimmered a gold band studded with diamonds.

She glanced up, quizzically. He stared her down.

"The sadness is still there," he said. "I'd like to help take it away, if you'll let me."

"I'm pregnant," she said without a moment of thought. This time the words passed her lips.

His brows lifted. He considered. He was not, as Kate had believed, put off by the idea. He gave his quick smile and said, "I've always wanted a little girl."

And Kate broke into heartbreaking sobs to which Ben pulled her into the comfort of his arms. He stroked her head with the tenderness of a father, something she had never really known. Her own father was a selfish man who had resented having another mouth to feed besides her mother. It was the unspoken rule that she leave home right after high school. She hadn't told either of them about her dilemma.

She married Ben two weeks later, a quick ceremony in front of a judge. No candles, no church, no breathless romance. Kate would have none of it, which suited Ben Rose just fine.

So Katie Tindel became Kate Rose, and April Rose was born in January. Ben balked at the name. "April Rose is like Holly Tree, or Candy Barr! It's terrible."

"Her name is April," Kate insisted, for that was when she was conceived. "She can go by Tindel."

"No!" He nearly had a coronary over the idea. "I want everyone to know she's my daughter. She's no one else's. Do you understand?"

Kate understood implicitly, though she wasn't sure she liked the idea all that well. Ben wanted everyone to think April was his daughter, and if people believed she came into the world a few months too early, well, that was their problem. In time they wouldn't care; they might not even remember.

So April arrived in late January and was christened with a moniker that never bothered her. She was sweet and lithe and blase and possessed a smile as bright as Hollywood—just like Jake's. Sometimes it made Kate's heart break a little to be reminded of her first love, but there was nothing to be done about it. All that showed of Kate in April was a peeking dimple and light brown hair shot with streaks of gold. Her eyes were Jake's grayish blue ones. They gleamed with mischief and strength of personality. And there was no telling April Rose much of anything, Kate learned as her daughter grew up. She was her own person—to a fault!

Thinking of April reminded Kate that her daughter was supposed to show up at the talent agency this afternoon. In a strange parallel, April was working as a part-time receptionist at the talent agency as Kate had when she was still a teenager.

Life is a circle.

Hurrying, Kate parked the car in her designated spot in the one-time warehouse's underground lot. The elevator doors were open, and she pushed a button for the third floor. With a jolt and chug the old machinery lifted her upward. The bell dinged and the doors slid open, and Kate hurried down the newly redone oak floors to the heavy green metal door with the bold black and gold lettering that announced, ROSE TALENT AGENCY.

Grabbing the handle with both hands, Kate jerked hard. With a rumble the door reluctantly gave way, revealing the warehouse loft that had been converted into offices in Portland's once tawdry, now tony, northwest industrial district. It was her agency, and as she crossed the sanded and stripped hardwood floor, she didn't know whether to groan or smile at the wildly ringing phones and her assistant Jillian's bouncing, frizzy curls as she answered three lines in a row, "Rose Talent, please hold and someone knowledgeable will be with you in a heartbeat!" Unorthodox was the word to describe Jillian, but she was also loyal, efficient and a tornado in three-inch red pumps.

Kate signaled that she would be in her office, a cubicle in bright blue with a watercolor of the coastal town of Astoria adorning one wall. Jillian's curls bobbed as she caught the first line. "Good morning and thanks for waiting. You're a peach. What can we do for you?"

Discarding her short Eton, Kate ran fingers through her own shoulder-length, blond/brown hair. Summertime it was blonder; winter it could border on dishwater. Today it felt hot and sticky against the back of her neck, and she wistfully wished for a cool rain.

A frisson of memory made her shiver, and she glanced around superstitiously. Sometimes rain, or even the thought of it, reminded her of Jake Talbot and that silly wedding so long ago. A lifetime ago. She had been married—really married—a millenium since.

But like the musky perfume at the department store counter earlier, once in a while something reminded her. Some trick of her dormant brain. Some faint déjà vu. Then, like now, she would remember and wish she had been smarter as a teenager.

Fighting the memory, Kate hugged herself, rubbing opposite elbows briskly. Since Ben's death she had been more susceptible to this kind of thing. Funny. But just one more dish to add to a plate already way too full.

Her phone buzzed. Through the side of her office that was a window open to the main room she saw Jillian waving madly.

"What's wrong?" Kate asked into the intercom.

"It's Delilah. She's here and she's coming your way!"

At that moment a wild-eyed Delilah Harris rushed past Jillian's desk in a beeline for Kate's office. Groaning inwardly Kate grabbed for the tissues placed conveniently on her credenza just as her door flew open.

"They cut me out!" Delilah wailed, throwing out her arms. "They cut me out!"

"Who did?" Kate asked.

"Those—those cheerleader people. I went in this morning and they—they—"

"Here," Kate said, pressing the tissues into Delilah's hand.

Delilah sniffed and dabbed at tears that came way too easily. She was an actress/model and inclined to behave as she thought actor/models should. This meant hysterics at every conceivable occasion. Kate had worked at the talent agency since she was eighteen and had learned that although talented people could be high strung, they didn't have to act like two-year-olds.

Delilah had yet to learn that lesson.

"They brought in *real* cheerleaders!" she declared with affront. "Paid them nothing, and those smug little witches didn't care! They just smiled and jumped around like frogs! It was *awful.*" She broke into keening sobs.

Kate inwardly sighed. Since the agency had specific prices per hour, this, too, was nothing new to the industry. When companies could cut their advertising overhead, they did. Delilah's job was supposed to have been modeling for a catalog that displayed cheerleading uniforms, but her price was awfully high if you could get *real* cheerleaders for nothing.

"So, they sent you home. Did they sign the voucher for the work you did?" This was how the agency got paid.

"Yes . . ." Delilah valiantly swiped at some baby tears, thought about breaking into another storm of weeping, shrugged and handed Kate the copies of the vouchers with her hourly rate and signature along with Northwest Uniforms' client representatives' signature as well. Rose Talent Agency took twenty percent for setting up the bookings and networking with the companies that paid the best. Kate had learned her trade from Ben. His death six months earlier had sent ripples through the industry, and Kate was working hard to assure longtime customers that business would be "as usual." So far she had met with limited success, and her husband's once healthy business was starting to feel the pinch of slow sales. Kate had an appointment set up with her accountant because she had begun to grow nervous. Ben, for all his supposed wealth, had really owned nothing but the talent agency and the small house he had bequeathed to her and April. Now the responsibility for both lay on Kate's shoulders, and she had the squeamish feeling there was serious financial trouble ahead unless she improved business *pronto*.

"I'll talk to Northwest Uniforms myself," Kate assured Delilah. "Did they like what you did?"

Her lips curved into a sad smile. "They said I was beautiful."

"Well, there, then. It'll all work out."

"You think they liked me?" She was anxious.

Kate came around her desk and gave Delilah a big hug. "Of course they did. Why wouldn't they? They're just trying to cut costs. Now, go home. Pull yourself together. You've got an audition for Tender Farms tomorrow."

"That cheesy commercial for Thanksgiving?" Delilah made a face. "They put a live turkey on the table and expect me to *talk* to it!"

"It'll be fun," Kate said firmly, leading Delilah to the door.

"Do they bite? What if it bites me?"

Kate looked into her big blue eyes. *Save me,* she thought, but said merely, "Don't borrow trouble. Go home. Get ready. I'll try to stop by the shoot and see how things are going."

"I don't like animals," she stated just before Kate slid the door to the agency closed behind her.

"Whew!" Jillian declared. "Baby-sitting again."

Kate smiled. "It's a living."

"Better than when Ben was here," Jillian said blithely. Her disrespect for Kate's husband was legendary. Ben hadn't liked Jillian from the onset; she was too irreverent, too self-assured and way too outspoken. Ben Rose had been an autocrat, and Kate, who had married him out of desperation and a belief that she could fall in love with him, had spent the last seventeen years in a bit of a prison marriage. For April's sake, she had stuck it out. That, and the fact that it had seemed easier to stay with the status quo than sail the uncharted seas of divorce. And what was out there anyway? Kate had been abandoned long ago by the one man she had loved. She wasn't foolish enough to believe there would be another one. She had forced herself to forget Jake and had melted willingly into Ben's strong arms. Their age difference didn't matter. He loved her, and she was starved for love. If the passion of her relationship with Jake wasn't there, well, too bad. This was better. More mature. It was better for her and better for April. Period.

No regrets.

Kate thoughtfully chewed on her lower lip. She hadn't loved Ben, but she had hoped she would learn to. Unfortunately over the intervening years she had learned she never could. But he was good to her, if a bit overbearing, and he was good to April, too. And though these last few years Kate and he had been more like distant friends, he had left her the business, and Kate was humbled by his generosity.

Of course Jillian thought she should get out in the dating scene, but whenever the subject was broached, Kate merely smiled and shook her head. A man was something she definitely did not need in her life right now.

Now, as if on cue, Jillian started in again. "There's this guy I know—"

"No."

"—who is really cute and really nice."

"No."

"And I know you two would hit it off. He wants to meet you."

"Are you listening? No!"

"No, I'm not listening. I never listen. It's one of my most endearing qualities."

Kate laughed and waved Jillian away as she headed for her office.

"Where are you going?" Jillian demanded, following after her. "You can't get away that easy."

"Do I have any phone messages? It looked for a while like you were holding them off with a whip and a chair."

"Lots of messages, but nothing urgent. Come on, Kate. Come out with me and Jeff. You should meet Michael. He's great."

"I'm sure he's wonderful, but April and I have a dinner date. She's coming to work in a few minutes."

"April's a wonderful kid, but she's not the kind of companion you need right now."

Kate lifted her brows. "Oh, the kind I *need?*"

"That's right!" Jillian was undeterred. "You need a man, dear."

"I've got way too much to think about for that."

"How long's it been since you did the wild thing?"

"*What?*"

"How long?" Jillian insisted.

"Ben's been gone six months."

She arched her brows. "How long?"

"Six months." Kate's voice said the discussion was closed.

"Been a lot longer than that, I'll bet," Jillian singsonged on her way back to the reception desk. "I'm making us a date for next Friday night."

"Don't you dare!"

"It's practically done."

"NO!"

"Lighten up!" Jillian grinned and wiggled her fingers at Kate through Kate's office window.

Grumbling to herself about mutiny and how difficult it was to get good help these days, Kate actually stuck out her tongue at her friend which sent Jillian into gales of laughter. Kate was rescued from further abuse by the arrival of several young men in black silk shirts and slacks whom

Kate recognized as actors who were scouting new talent agents. Jillian turned her attention to them, and Kate heaved a sigh, watching through her office window. Their youth made her feel tired. At thirty-six she felt almost ancient in a business where appearance and presentation were everything.

Ben had been a dinosaur, but he'd had connections.

If I could bring in one new, really big account, it would convince everyone else that I can handle things, Ben or no Ben.

April suddenly appeared at Jillian's desk. The young men looked at her appreciatively. Slim and poised in blue jeans, a silvery blue T-shirt and clunky sandals, April epitomized the carefree loveliness of youth. She wasn't trendy in oversized and bulky clothes, nor was she wrapped in a skintight sheath. The way she dressed was perfect for the anxious, youthful, talented young people who entered the agency hoping to get a start. It was nonthreatening. No serious statement made about what one should look like. And April's comfortable ways helped ease tension. The fact that she was a teenager made them relax even more.

In a word, she was perfect—at least that was her mother's unbiased opinion.

Spying Kate, April grinned and waved. Her hair was straight, a couple inches longer than Kate's, which left it hanging just below her shoulders. Gold highlights, helped along at the salon, shimmered beneath the overhead agency track lights.

A smile as bright as Hollywood . . .

Kate's throat constricted briefly as she called, "In here, you. We've got things to talk about."

"Like what?" April asked, flopping into the chair Delilah had perched on so delicately half an hour earlier.

"School's right around the corner. Are you sure you can juggle a few hours to work every day?"

"I have so far," she pointed out, frowning at Kate.

"You're a senior now. One more year and then college. We've got to start applying to schools all over."

"Mom, I'm okay. I don't want to leave Oregon."

"You've got good grades. I'm just asking you to keep your options open."

"They're open, okay?" April half smiled. "But nothing's going to come along and change my mind. I'm all set, and I like working here. Besides, I need the cash. If you're going to pay someone, you might as well pay me."

"Okay," Kate murmured, feeling unsettled somehow.

"What could possibly happen to screw up my future?" April asked innocently.

Kate's heart somersaulted painfully. *You could fall in love with the wrong man!* "What about that Ryan?"

" 'That Ryan' is a friend, and he's going to college, too." April exhaled a long-suffering sigh. "You know that. You're just paranoid."

"You're right. I am. Where's he going to school?"

"I told you!" she declared in exasperation.

"Tell me again," Kate said with a sheepish grin.

April stared at her and shook her head. "I swear, whenever I talk about Ryan you go deaf! And you know what's weird? I actually think you like him. But you're afraid." She paused, her brows drawing into a line. "What are you afraid of?"

"I just want you to have a future," Kate revealed.

"Mom!" April laughed.

"I know, I know. You're right. Everything's going to be fine," she agreed without much conviction. "Tell me again, where's Ryan going to college?"

"Portland Community, for a start." April pushed back a swath of hair, a thoughtful gesture that sent Kate's motherly instincts on alert once again.

"Are you sure?"

"Of course I'm sure! He's not a loser!"

"I know he's not a loser. Did I say he was a loser? I just think college is really important, and I don't want anything to get in the way."

April regarded Kate seriously. It was unsettling, really, how little got past her. "I don't want to bring up a bad subject, but you didn't go to college," she reminded her mother softly.

"A mistake I don't plan on having my daughter repeat." With that Kate scooped up a pile of papers and began stacking them with more energy than necessary.

"Nothing's going to change my mind," April reassured her. "You've got to get over this paranoia thing before it drives us both crazy!"

Kate managed a laugh. "Okay. Now, go relieve Jillian. She's got some appointments to keep."

April rose to leave, then stopped at Kate's door. She hesitated a moment, then said, "I like that scent, Mom. Kinda musky. Kinda sexy."

Kate snorted. "The saleslady squirted me with it." She didn't add that it had brought back way too many memories.

"What's it called?"

"I don't know. She got me when I wasn't looking."

"Well, I think you should get some more. It's time to get out there, you know?"

Kate groaned. "Not you, too! Go away!" She shooed April from the room, and April grinned at her through the glass.

Kate shook her head at both April and Jillian. Inside, she felt a bittersweet sadness. They didn't know. They couldn't know. But there was no way she could jump into the dating scene and find Mr. Right. He didn't exist.

April changed places with Jillian, who signaled Kate that she was going to dial the phone and make a date for them both with Jeff and his friend, Michael. So doing, she waved to Kate before disappearing through the sliding front door.

"Everybody's a matchmaker," Kate muttered aloud.

Ten minutes later the agency door rattled open again, and a fortyish-year-old man, with a face that showed the weary lines of hard, fast living, walked up to April's desk and started a conversation. Something about his body movements bothered Kate. He was turned slightly, with dark hair growing down his nape in a thick pelt that seemed oddly familiar. Did she know him? She didn't think so, yet. . . .

She stepped into the outer room, just to be a presence. He glanced up, and she swept in a shocked breath. Déjà vu gripped her again. He reminded her of Jake!

With his gaze centered on her, Kate was hit by a cascade of feelings. So much like Jake, but not Jake. He seemed too old, too relaxed, too . . . derelict.

"Mom, this is Mr. Talbot of Talbot Industries," April introduced.

Kate gasped in shock. "Oh, yes?" she said faintly. *Mr. Talbot?*

"Uh . . . yeah," she went on, her brows drawing together at Kate's strange reaction. "They're looking for a spokeswoman to promote their new office buildings and well . . ." She broke off in consternation as Kate squeaked out a protest. "Are you okay?"

Kate trembled. *Talbot Industries . . . Jake's family's business . . . then who? Oh, God! Jake's brother!*

"I'm Phillip Talbot," the man greeted her, extending a hand, just as Kate's brain made the connection.

"Junior," she breathed before she could stop herself. Of course. Jake's older brother. The black sheep. The one whom she had never met because the Talbot family had closed ranks against her before she had ever had a chance.

His brows shot up. "Well, that's right," he said in amazement. "You know my family?"

"I've—heard of them," Kate murmured. The room reeled. This wasn't happening!

"Mom?" April said from what felt was somewhere far, far away.

Kate turned to her, feeling oddly detached from her body. It had been a day for thinking about Jake, and *now this!* Phillip Talbot, Jr. How strange!

With an effort she pulled herself together. There was absolutely no need to be upset. None at all.

"What can we help you with?" she asked him in a voice that sounded almost normal.

"Mom!" April broke in. "Mr. Talbot wants *me* to be the spokesperson for their company! Isn't that just incredible. Me! What do you think?"

Chapter Two

"What?" Kate stared at April in shock.

"Well, I'd like her to audition," Phillip Talbot, Jr., responded. "My brother makes all final decisions."

"Your brother?" Kate asked faintly.

"Jake's the man in charge," he explained with a touch of derision. "He only gave me this job because he can't be bothered, but don't worry. Unless I bring home a real dog, he'll agree."

"Do you mind if I sit down?" Kate asked. "It's been a long day."

She practically collapsed in one of the client chairs. April peered at her.

"Are you okay?"

"I'm fine."

"You're really pale," she said, concerned.

"I'm okay."

"You're sure?"

"April isn't—one of the talent here," Kate tried to put in.

"Mom!"

"Well, you're not. You're the part-time receptionist and you're only seventeen!"

April's mouth dropped open in surprise at her mother's attitude. "Well, I know, but does that mean I can't try out?"

Kate knew she was overreacting, but she couldn't help herself. "You've never shown any interest in modeling before."

"No ... but hey ..." She shrugged apologetically at Phillip.

"She can try out, can't she?" he pointed out reasonably. "What would it hurt?"

Kate just gazed at him blankly. His eyes weren't as blue as Jake's, and his hair wasn't quite as dark. But that smile lurked in there somewhere. April's smile.

She swallowed hard. This was *not* happening.

"Mom?" April asked, pleading.

Kate didn't know what to do. She wasn't ready for this twist of fate. She just felt so out of control. "I—whatever you want, I guess ..."

April jumped up and hugged her, then shook Phillip's hand, hard. "Thanks. I'd love to try out. Should I just come by the main office Tuesday, then?"

"Yeah, show up about ten." He glanced at Kate. "And send some other models along, too. Ones that look kind of like her. Like I said, my brother will make final approval."

Kate apparently managed to make appropriate noises because after he left April jumped into her arms in excitement. "This is so great!"

"I never knew you were interested."

"Well, if it just falls in your lap. I mean, c'mon, Mom! This is too cool!"

"What about school?"

"It's August!"

"But these shoots are weeks out sometimes. You could miss some classes."

"Mom!" April looked at her as if she had gone crazy, which perhaps, in these last few minutes, she had. "I can miss a class or two. This is work experience. I can make it up, and I'll get paid. A ton!"

"Oh, April . . ." Kate buried her face in her hands, annoyed to find she was quivering.

"What *is* it?"

"Nothing. I'm just—tired."

Two hours later Kate left the office. April, who drove Ben's car these days, a late model sedan that was the farthest from "cool" as it could be, would close up the agency and join her at Geno's, the tiny Italian restaurant near their house.

As Kate wheeled into Geno's parking lot, she sighed deeply, weariness creeping in like a silent invader. What she wouldn't do for some peace of mind. Since Ben's death it felt as if she were trying to keep too many balls in the air at once.

With determination to put her worries aside, Kate gratefully settled into a chair on Geno's back patio. Glancing around, she let the beauty of the outdoor dining area replace her anxieties. Geno's was one of her favorite spots. Square, taupe tiles and spouting fountains made the place seem like an outdoor Italian cafe—exactly as they were meant to. Kate ordered a glass of Chianti and sipped the rich, red wine while waiters hovered over glass-topped tables spread with white linen. The sun still beat down through a wrought-iron gate at the edge of the patio that looked over a tangled garden. More fountains lay behind its black, filigreed wall. The place was pleasant and close to the house she and Ben had shared in southwest Portland.

It was Ben's favorite restaurant. It was Ben's house. Kate had adopted everything, easily now; it had been much

more difficult in the beginning while she was still a teenager and her husband was already in his fifties.

Closing her eyes, she inhaled another breath and held
it. There were roses in the garden, but closer was the scent
of vanilla from the candles on the tables, whose tiny flames
flickered in a soft breeze.

Inexplicably, Kate wanted to cry. She felt the sensation
rush through her and the faintest dampening of her lashes
before she could get herself under control. Embarrassed,
she blinked several times and buried her nose in the menu.

Meeting Phillip Talbot, Jr., had jangled her nerves.
Thrown her world out of orbit. She was spiraling to some
unknown and unwelcome fate. With a concentrated effort
she pushed thoughts of him aside, but traitorous memories
of Jake popped up in their place.

They had made love the first time in his car. Silly, awkward and crazy, giggling all the way. Kate hadn't known
what to expect, and there was so much to feel and sense
that she couldn't have recounted the experience later if
her life had depended on it.

But that had only been the start.

For the next two months, while graduation set the wheels
in motion for their futures, Kate and Jake slipped away at
every opportunity to make frenzied love and vow anew
how much they loved each other, how they would always
be together. Always.

Their second attempt at lovemaking was at his house,
in the guest cottage at the edge of the property. Quiet as
church mice they crept into the one-room bungalow,
spread out a sleeping bag and explored each others' bodies
tenderly and thoroughly.

But it was on a weekend trip to the beach that Kate
really learned the true joys of making love. Jake sneaked
the key to his parents' oceanfront home. He lied to them,
telling them he was going with Phillip fishing off the coast

of Washington. Because Phillip showed no interest in anything besides wild women and drink, Jake's parents were delighted with the arrangement. They never questioned whether he was telling them the truth or not. Jake had never lied before, to their knowledge, so it stood to reason he wasn't lying this time.

But to be with Kate, Jake would do more than just tell a few fibs. So, on this day, they took off in his convertible, top down, hair flying in the wind, to make the two-hour trip to the coast.

A watery sun guided them through a coolish May day, casting shadows from the lines of firs that were silent sentinels nearly the entire route. Kate's teeth chattered; Oregon's springs were nearly glacial sometimes. But she didn't care. With brown-blond silken strands whipping around her face, and Jake's hand lying protectively on her knee, she knew an exhilaration and excitement she had never known before.

"I love you," she said.

"I love you more," he answered with a sideways grin.

The Talbot's beach home was a two-story cottage done in dark gray, naturally weathered shingles and trimmed with gingerbread in a lighter, almost silver, shade. It faced Seaside's prom, looking across the sidewalk that rimmed this part of the beach to a restless, white-capped ocean. Waves roiled in the distance, then pushed angrily forward to skim quickly across the silent sand. Kate watched this beauty of nature with Jake's arms surrounding her, her head resting against his shoulder, her hands tucked inside his jacket pockets. He smelled of musk until his scent was snatched away by the harsh breeze that hit them both in irregular intervals. When that happened, they inhaled salt-sea tang that cleared their senses.

It was as if they were both afraid to enter the Talbot house. They were cautious trespassers, but it was more than that. They hadn't been able to race off to a Portland motel for a honeymoon like they had planned the night of their "wedding." Jake had been caught sneaking out, and they had been forced to rearrange their schedule. Here, then, was a house with real beds and blankets and pillows—a place for serious lovemaking. Kate found it all a bit overwhelming. Lovemaking in Jake's car after their vows had been a sweet, fun consummation, but she hadn't expected bells to ring, so to speak. The night on the floor of the guest house had been another stolen, secret intimacy. This, then, would be like a honeymoon, and Kate couldn't help worrying that she would be lacking somehow, that Jake would realize he had made a mistake and simply leave her when it was over.

Oh, if only their marriage could be for real!

Patience, she told herself, snuggling inside his jacket lapels and hiding her face from the wind. She knew he would marry her as soon as he could; they had vowed as much to each other.

"Let's go inside," Jake suggested on a soft murmur, leaving Kate to wonder if he was feeling a little of what she was.

The cottage was cold. Kate rubbed her arms briskly as Jake, instead of turning up the thermostat, stacked an oak log on the fire followed by chunks of fir.

"Dad's big into fires at the beach," he explained, crushing old newspapers and shoving them around the pieces of wood. "We never use the heat unless we absolutely have to."

"I like it," Kate said, settling on an overstuffed red plush couch. The place was furnished Victorian, with ornately carved furniture upholstered in blood red velveteen. The windows were draped in heavy green velvet, and gold tassels sparkled everywhere. Dark wood paneling made the walls feel close, and a silk-draped chandelier, shimmering with tassels, hung overhead.

Catching her look, Jake glanced around. "This place was originally built at the turn of the century. It's gone through a bunch of changes, but Mom wanted to add some glamour." He shrugged. "I'd rather have a lodge cabin with stone and wood."

"Maybe a large fish mounted above the mantel," Kate said with a smile.

"Yeah! And a bear rug right here." He kicked aside the doilylike hooked rug and spread his arms wide. His gaze met hers. Messages passed. Kate's blood heated in spite of herself, and she couldn't help glancing away, her cheeks burning.

Then Jake was beside her on the couch. His fingers entwined with hers. No words were spoken. He kissed her, gently yet deeply, and before long Kate felt as if she were drowning beneath the sweet pressure of passion.

He led her upstairs, stopping every few steps to kiss her again. By the time they reached the top landing, she was clinging to him in earnest. Later, she would remember every rose and dahlia in the heavy wallpaper that covered the slanted walls of the upstairs master bedroom. She would recall the bright brass lamps, thick tasseled carpets, and smoothly curved wood dresser and nightstand, all covered with intricately crocheted doilies. Her mind's eye would remember the bedspread as a sheet of gold satin, the sheets a buttery cream color of the same material.

But when Kate first entered his parents' bedroom suite, it was within the shelter of Jake's strong arms, and all she saw was him. He laid her on the spread and rained kisses over her face until her own hands were reaching upward, pulling anxiously at his clothes.

He laughed, standing beside her, his jacket tossed haphazardly on the floor, his shirt untucked and askew from

Kate's tugging fingers. With a muscular twist he ripped off the rest of his clothes, lying down atop her while Kate wrestled with her own blouse and jeans.

"Wait, wait," she whispered.

"No," was his amused answer, and his hands helped divest her of her jeans and undergarments. Within minutes they were naked in each others' arms. Jake's hands caressed every square inch of her body; her own did likewise.

"My God, Katie," he whispered.

"Jake . . ."

No other words needed to be spoken. This time Jake's lovemaking was tender and serious, different from the laughter and wildness of their earlier consummations. Kate felt his hands caress her, his body possess her, and the rhythm of his movements kindled a response inside her as old as time.

"I love you!" she cried at the height of her passion.

Jake's answer was a groan of submission, and much later, when they had both descended back to earth, he answered, "I love you more."

Later yet, Kate would wonder about that hesitation. It had seemed so natural. He was, after all, in the midst of a climax. No woman could expect a man to keep his wits about him when worlds collide. Hadn't she learned she couldn't be responsible for her outbursts and behavior during that time?

And yet . . .

There was always a distance. As if he *knew* even then that he was destined to leave her. He made love to her with a passion and ardor that sent her senses spiraling, her blood pumping, thrills of submission tearing through her until she was lost and spent, totally a slave to sensation.

And yet . . .

Something had been missing. Or he would have never

run away to Europe instead of marrying the girl he had left behind.

"Would you care to order a bottle of wine?"

Kate jumped, the waiter breaking into her reverie. Her cheeks flushed. "Ummm . . . yes . . . actually, no, just another glass of Chianti," she amended, recovering herself.

Twisting the stem of her now empty glass, Kate chewed on her lower lip. Jake had always planned to leave her; she knew it now. She just hadn't known it then because he had swept her off her feet, bamboozled her with romance and a "secret wedding," drowned her fears with kisses and sex of the sweetest kind. She had been young. Naive. Guileless. Ridiculously susceptible to his charm and wealth.

Yes, she could say it now. She had been dazzled by the whole package that was Jake Talbot. Not that she had wanted to leech on to his fortune. More that it was so foreign to her, so out of reach, that it attained a mystery and glamour all its own. Oh, she had been dumb. Lord, it was enough to make her want to bury her head in her arms in embarrassment even now! Luckily Ben had come along and shown her what a real relationship was. It might not have been hearts and roses every day; her own heart couldn't quite be won. But it had been full of respect and stability, and those were qualities Jake could have never given Kate. He would have always looked at her as the poor waif; she saw that with the benefit of hindsight. But Ben hadn't cared about that. She had appealed to him, and he'd had the honor to make her his wife, pregnant or no.

She owed him a lot. Her life, no less. And so their love had been imperfect. So what? They had been partners. He had left her this business as proof.

So, what are you going to do about Talbot Industries, my girl?

Kate muttered to herself as the waiter gathered up the unused glasses and brought her another full one of deep red Chianti. Hadn't she just been wishing for that one big account to prove to all and sundry that Rose Talent Agency would keep right on without a hiccup?

But Jake's company? No! Never!

Yet . . .

She was just taking her first sip when April appeared at the edge of the patio, searching. Kate raised her hand, and April hurried over.

"How can you stand that stuff?" she demanded, wrinkling her nose. "I'd rather have a screwdriver."

"Really." Kate gave her a look. "And how are you so knowledgeable?"

"I'm not saying anything more. You'll get all worked up and you won't like Ryan."

"The soon-to-be college student," Kate said. "Ex-guitar player?"

"The guitar is his passion," April disabused, reading her mother too easily. "That bugs you, doesn't it?"

"No. If he can play the guitar, more power to him. I just like to think that my daughter's boyfriend is planning some diversity. Portland Community College is good."

"It's not like we're getting married tomorrow."

"I know. Thank God. I mean, hey, you're only seventeen." Kate grinned.

"Mom, what's with you today?"

"Nothing. Why?"

"You're just so—worked up." April wrinkled her nose in an unconscious mimic of Kate. When she chewed on her lower lip, Kate really recognized her own habits.

And what habits does she have of her father's?

"I hope your association with him isn't turning you into a raving alcoholic," Kate added mildly.

"Mom!"

"You are a little young."

"You're teasing me." April managed a laugh. "All right. I just tasted a screwdriver at Ryan's dad's birthday party."

"Last Saturday night," Kate confirmed, feeling a little miffed. It bugged her when other parents were lax on issues she counted important.

April read her mind. "I *sneaked* it, Mom! Good grief. Ryan's dad's even straighter than you! I keep telling you, you need to meet him."

"Oh, no. Not again," Kate groaned.

"What do you mean?"

"Jillian's been after me. Wants me to go on a date with Michael-somebody-or-other."

"Not until you date Ryan's dad!" April decreed. "His name's Tom."

"I'm not dating anyone."

"You should! Dad's been gone over six months. C'mon, Mom!"

Kate just shook her head. Though it had never bothered her before, hearing April call Ben "Dad" sent an uncomfortable stab through her now. She searched her feelings and realized it had to do with meeting Phillip Talbot, Jr. Any association with the Talbots bothered her.

If they only knew!

And what about April? Kate asked herself. When, when, if ever, was she going to tell her the truth?

"I want veal," April declared, staring at her menu. "But I'm not going to have it. Do you know what they do to those poor little baby cows? They kill 'em while they're just babies!"

"You've always loved veal," Kate pointed out.

"That's because I didn't know what it was! It's awful!"

"Why don't you have a steak?"

"I don't know." April sighed hugely. "I might just become a vegetarian."

Kate nodded. April was always trying on new hats. It was partly because she really cared, partly because she was searching for her own identity. Even at seventeen she was still so impressionable.

A lot like you, my girl. And look what happened. . . .

Kate closed her mind to that thinking.

By the time they had finished their dessert, Kate was feeling a lot more ready to face the future. Whether owing to the excellent meal she had just consumed, or her second glass of Chianti, Kate set down her napkin in a happier state of mind. She had just opened her mouth to say as much to her daughter when movement in her peripheral vision arrested her.

A man was standing at the edge of the tiled patio, scowling slightly as he searched the area. His familiarity turned Kate's body to water, and she collapsed back in her chair like a rag doll.

Oh, no! Jake!

Seventeen years and suddenly there he was. Older, yet just the same. How could she have ever mistaken his brother for him? The similarities were striking, yet far, far removed.

Could he . . . was he . . . looking for *her?*

As if in answer to her unspoken question his gaze touched on her. *My God,* Kate thought, dry-mouthed.

Shock waves reverberated; she saw him react with a slight start, his eyes widening a bit. Instantly she wondered how she had changed. Good Lord, seventeen years! Yet she could be back with him on the porch of the ramshackle church for the potency of her reaction.

She felt as if she were in a vortex.

"I . . . I . . . ," she murmured.

"Mom?" April looked concerned.

"Water. Could you—call the waiter?"

April glanced around. She didn't notice Jake. Why

should she? Kate thought half-hysterically. With a maturity that still astounded Kate, April stood up and signaled to a passing waiter.

"Water," she ordered.

In those few moments Jake suddenly got into motion, approaching them with ground-devouring strides that alarmed Kate through and through.

April saw him coming and hesitated, frowning a bit. She sat slowly down in her chair.

"Hello, Katie," Jake said in a deep voice that was still too familiar. It ran over her skin in an almost physical sensation, goose bumps rising on her flesh.

"*Katie?*" April asked, turning to her mom, brows lifting.

Kate couldn't find her voice.

At some level April recognized her mother's dilemma and took charge. "Are you a friend of Mom's? You look kind of familiar."

Oh, no! Kate thought as she witnessed Jake turn to give April a long look.

"You must be the daughter," he said, which sent Kate's heart into overdrive.

"She's . . . she's Ben's daughter. My husband's. My . . . deceased husband," she babbled.

"What's with you?" April asked with real concern now, leaning toward Kate.

"I don't know. I'm . . . I don't know."

"Did you come here to see us?" April asked Jake, her eyes still searching Kate's face.

"My brother, Phillip, told me he'd asked Kate Rose's daughter to audition for our company," Jake explained. He seemed to be having a little difficulty getting the words out as well.

"Oh," April said. "That's how you knew where we were." She glanced a little sheepishly at Kate. "I guess I told Mr. Talbot about our dinner plans when he was in our office."

"You guess?" Kate choked out.

"He said you were president of Talbot Industries," April informed Jake. "I didn't expect to meet you—so soon. I'm April Rose." She came slightly out of her seat to shake Jake's hand. Watching that contact between them made Kate's head swim.

"You—wanted to see us?" Kate managed to get past lips that felt slightly numb. They were all playing roles and acting with the emotion of mannequins. Jake was stiff and uncomfortable. April was confused. And she, well she was downright annihilated!

"I, um . . ." Shifting his weight from one foot to the other, Jake took a deep breath. Kate slid him a surreptitious look beneath lowered lashes, wanting to examine him without being obvious. He didn't notice. His jaw worked as if he were struggling to find words.

Time had been kind to him. Apart from the merest silvering at this temple, his hair was as dark and thick as ever, a rich brown that bordered on black. His mouth was still sinfully enticing. Unfair! She remembered kissing it with a fervor that sent emotion flooding her face now, and she mentally kicked herself for her susceptibility.

Lord, she was ridiculous!

"I wasn't sure you'd be right for the part," he said to April a bit stiffly. "I came to see for myself."

"I thought I was just auditioning." April turned to Kate for help.

"That's what—Mr. Talbot—said," Kate confirmed.

"Do you know each other?" April suddenly asked, as if the messages being sent along invisible lines between Jake and Kate had finally been picked up by her receptors.

After all, he had made the mistake of calling her "Katie." April was just catching up.

"We've met." Kate tried on a smile for her daughter. It felt awkward and quivering.

"We went to high school together," Jake added, his frown deepening. Clearly he had stepped into quicksand. Whatever he had expected to face with Kate and "the daughter," this hadn't been it.

Her heart squeezed. *Does he know? Looking at April, does he know she's his daughter?*

No way! Kate's galloping pulse was joined by a sudden rush of perspiration. If she didn't watch it, she would pass out right here and now!

"Really," April said, gazing from Jake to her mother and back again. "You didn't tell me that you knew Mr. Talbot," she accused Kate. "You acted like you'd never seen him before."

"You mean—Phillip? I hadn't met him until today."

Jake gave Kate a swift look. She read surprise in his blue-gray eyes. Had he thought she had set this up somehow? She didn't understand.

"Would you like a chair?" Kate asked, belatedly remembering her manners.

"I don't think so . . ."

"Oh, sit down!" April invited eagerly. "Please. If you want someone else, I don't have to audition," she told him with a little shrug, as if it meant nothing to her. "But my mom's agency really has some great people. Somebody will be perfect for you."

"That's not it," Jake demurred, and in another lifetime Kate would have been amused and even felt sorry for him. He had come here ready to slam dunk Kate and her daughter, thinking some nefarious plan was afoot, and instead he had been hit full force with April's openness and lack of guile.

Tough break, Kate thought with a bit of mean satisfaction. Oh, she could read him still. Funny how things came back so swiftly. He had probably heard what was up from Phillip and raced down to the restaurant, loaded for bear. No daughter of Katie Tindel's would ever work for a Talbot. No, no. She wouldn't have what it takes to play in the Talbots' major leagues. Uh, uh. She was a minor leaguer, just like her mother.

April actually pulled out his chair, and to be polite— manners were deeply ingrained in the Talbots—Jake reluctantly accepted.

Both Kate and Jake looked at April. Kate was afraid to examine him this up close and personal. He, apparently, felt the same. April smiled at them both, her perfectly readable face registering confusion at the way they were both acting.

The waiter spied Jake and cruised by quickly. "Something to drink?"

"Scotch and soda."

"Chianti," Kate said on the heels of Jake's request. "I guess I do want another drink after all," she said as an afterthought, though the waiter-couldn't have cared less.

"Italian soda," April ordered. "Raspberry."

He bowed and left, and as soon as he was gone, the tension escalated at the little table.

"It isn't that I didn't want you to audition," Jake said to April. Kindness touched his voice, and sap that she was, Kate felt her eyes suddenly sting with emotion. "I just, sometimes, follow up on what Phillip does."

"You don't trust him," April said soberly.

Jake half laughed and ran a hand through his hair. "I don't trust his judgment all the time."

Kate glanced to the side, focusing on the tile floor, listening to the clink of glassware and faint strains of violins coming from within the restaurant. She was melting inside. Disappearing. This feeling was terrible, like a tremendous hurt that was attacking her from the inside out.

"But it looks like he made an excellent decision this

time," Jake answered April honestly, his voice slightly rough.

"Really?" April was pleased. Boldly, she asked, "Why don't you get along with your brother?"

"Long story."

April waited, but Jake would say no more. Silence pooled amongst them. Kate remembered those long-ago references to Phillip, how he couldn't seem to get his life together. Jake had been the Talbots' shining star, and when they had thought she would tarnish his bright, gleaming future, they had pushed him toward a more suitable girl. And Jake, because he had wanted it just as much, had dropped the girl he had fancied in high school and married one of "his own kind."

"So how are your folks, Katie?" Jake asked, just as the silence was becoming awkward.

"They died a few years after graduation," she answered.

She could have sworn she saw a flash of sympathy in his eyes. Of course, he'd known all about her relationship— or lack of a relationship—with her parents. The reminder of how well he'd known her shook her composure further.

How's your wife? Kate wanted to ask. *Thanks for letting me know you were getting married.*

As if reading her thoughts, Jake suddenly asked, "The agency was originally your husband's, wasn't it? Are you running it by yourself now?"

Kate swallowed. "Yes."

Mistaking her reluctance for grief, Jake said, "I'm sorry."

"Oh, don't be," April answered before Kate could respond. "Really. It's okay."

Kate attempted another smile, failed miserably, and buried her nose in her wineglass. This idle chitchat made her nerves scream.

Jake downed his scotch and soda so quickly Kate wondered if he might have a problem. Probably not, she decided a moment later. After all, she was on her third glass of Chianti, and it wasn't enough by a long shot.

I fainted in front of your parents when I learned about your fiancée and suffered the embarrassment of having "Mom and Dad" drive me home. But you don't know that, do you? And you wouldn't care anyway . . .

"Well, I'll see you at the audition on Tuesday," Jake said to April, throwing several bills on the table and abruptly standing up. It was as if he suddenly could no longer stand their company. "It was nice seeing you again, Katie. Nice meeting you, April."

He strode away before either of them could respond with more than a murmur of goodbye.

"What the heck was that all about?" April demanded as soon as he was gone. " 'Katie.' He called you 'Katie.' Were you friends?"

"Acquaintances."

"You really made him uncomfortable!"

"I did?"

"Yeah, and you were white as a ghost. Something's weird here." April gave her mother a look that said, "You'd better come clean before I jump to my own conclusions."

"We—dated a little," Kate admitted, giving April just enough of the truth to appease her.

"Really?" She smiled hugely. "I get it. Still got a few feelings left, huh?"

"Not a chance!"

"I think she doth protest too much."

Kate rushed in, "It was over seventeen years ago. A few dates. Big deal. Don't start with me."

"Okay, okay." April lifted her palms in surrender. "It just looks like I've hit a hot button, that's all."

"I'm just tired of being the speculation of everyone's romantic thoughts," Kate muttered grouchily.

"Oh, my God!"

Kate half rose from her chair, glancing around for whatever new calamity was coming their way. "What?"

April held several bills in her hand. The money Jake had dropped on the table. "These are all fifties," she whispered. "There's over *two hundred* dollars here!"

Kate stared at the money. Emotion fired through her, hurt and anger and humiliation. Damn him! He thought he could buy himself out of guilt even after all these years.

I would rather chew off my leg than be beholden to a Talbot, she thought grimly.

Snatching up her purse, Kate bit out, "Leave it for a tip," then pushed back her chair and left before her astonished daughter could voice another thought.

Chapter Three

Jake stepped outside Geno's and gulped air, clearing the light-headedness that had hit him like a hammer. Night had fallen in a soft, dark curtain without his even seeing it. A breeze lifted his hair and fanned his face as he crossed the slate path to the parking lot. A grape arbor, loaded with purple fruit, hung over the trellis that guarded the entrance. Jake's shoulder brushed a clump of grapes, and they fell and rolled in front of his feet as he headed toward his black Bronco.

He felt sick. Dragging more air into his lungs, he tried hard to get his bearings.

Katie! My God. After all these years and with a gorgeous grown-up daughter!

He wanted to die. It was all he could do to make it to the Bronco. Fiddling with his remote entry, he realized his hands were trembling. With a groan he slumped a hip against the fender. He felt empty and used up.

Katie Tindel! No, Kate Rose. And April Rose.

There was something achingly familiar about April. Kate,

at a young age. Seventeen and in love. Jake's memories were thorn sharp.

He shook his head in bewilderment. After all these years and boom! There she was.

Phillip had taken him completely by surprise. Jake, who had known of Rose Talent Agency because Katie had married the owner, had been bowled over when Phillip announced, "I've found the spokesperson for Talbot Industries. She's the daughter of Kate Rose, you know, Ben Rose of Rose Talent Agency's widow. She's perfect. Absolutely. You need look no further, brother. April Rose is it."

"What?"

Phillip was enthused. "I'm telling you, she's the one. And I think the lady knows you. She said something like it. I don't know. But wait till you see her daughter. Man, oh, man. If I were ten years younger!"

"You mean twenty," Jake said repressively, absorbing the information with alarm.

"Yeah, I guess." Phillip was unconcerned. His taste in women wasn't limited to age, color or creed. He was an equal opportunity womanizer in Jake's biased opinion. "Anyway, you just wait. She's the one, I'm telling you."

Kate Rose's daughter. Katie's daughter. Ben Rose's daughter. Jealousy rose like a green monster, blinding Jake, reminding him of those heart-tearing moments following the truth about why Katie hadn't written him while he was away.

"She's married," his mother had baldly announced. "She married for money, just like she wanted to do with you."

"You're lying!" he had gasped.

"No." Marilyn Talbot was positive, and the fact that she wasn't reveling in the information was what convinced Jake she had spoken the truth. His mother had been clear that she had wanted Katie Tindel out of his life, yet she had enough motherly empathy to reveal the news without relish. She hadn't enjoyed it because she had known it would hurt.

And it *had* hurt. He had been unable to think. It was an effort to even breathe. He had come home from that blasted summer in Europe in a fury at his parents for lining up such an itinerary. What had started out as a three-week tour had turned into a lengthy stay with distant relatives and a "romance" with the daughter of some friends of his parents who lived on the east coast.

But it had been too late. Katie was gone and all he had were memories of her and the frustration of his expected engagement to Celia Cummings to fall back on. He had met Celia once or twice when he was a kid; he hadn't known she was part of the summer package. At first Celia was interested in the arrangement. Apparently she had been privy to the plans made by both sets of parents. But when she realized Jake's heart wasn't in it, she quickly became interested in a variety of suitors and turned to Jake as her surrogate big brother. He spent the entire time disentangling her from one rotten affair after another. He wrote Katie constantly, but it was as if he were sending messages in a bottle that bobbed endlessly and uselessly on the waves, never reaching a destination.

Celia ended up falling for an Italian lothario who called her *bella* and promised passion and adoration and endless love. When she learned he was married, she threw herself in Jake's arms and begged him to tell her parents that they were engaged since she suspected she was pregnant.

Fed up with the whole thing Jake finally took charge and told Celia's parents the truth. In fact, she wasn't pregnant, and Jake's interference was suddenly seen by Celia as a major betrayal! By the time Jake got back to the States, he was sick of the whole thing. Anxious, worried and about as eager as one human being can be to see another, he came home in search of Katie.

And then his mother dropped the bomb.

"I may have made a mistake," Marilyn admitted, looking unusually contrite. "I should have given her your address."

"You didn't give her my address?" Jake gaped at his mother, too stunned to feel real anger. That would come later. "You told me you did!"

"Well, I meant to," Marilyn excused herself, signaling to his father, who was staring into the cold ashes left over from the previous winter's fires. "But, we knew she was wrong for you. Right, Phillip?"

"That is correct," Jake's father said in his clipped diction.

"You're not serious! You didn't make this decision for me! I'm eighteen years old, damn it! You can't do this!"

"Don't swear at your mother." Phillip was terse.

Jake felt like running through every curse word he knew. He had to fight himself to stay in control. This was what had sent his brother spiraling into irresponsibility. He wasn't about to do the same. "I don't believe you did this. I love Kate, and I'm going to see her."

With that he headed for the door, with only a vague idea of how to find her. Kate had made it clear she wasn't living with her mom and dad a day later than she had to; the truth was, they were anxious to be rid of her as parental responsibility was way down the list of the Tindels' priorities. He knew Kate had probably taken off directly after graduation, but the only way to find her was to check with them.

"Wait!" his mother called as he headed for the door.

"Jacob, get back here!" Phillip ordered.

"You said you may have made a mistake," he bit out over his shoulder. "You sure as hell did."

"Jacob, she's married!" Marilyn cried.

His steps slowed but didn't stop. He ran onto the front porch, his ears ringing. With no clear idea of which way to go, he jumped into his convertible and raced into town, cruising the main streets, lost. Kate's parents' house was a rental several blocks away from the main street, yet he couldn't make himself stop there.

Eventually he pulled up to the curb a block away, gathering courage. He had never been a man who couldn't face challenges; exactly the opposite! But thinking Kate was married was more than he could bear.

He didn't believe it. It couldn't be true.

With lead weights seeming to anchor his feet, Jake crossed the weed-choked walk that led to Kate's parents' front door. He knocked loudly, over and over again. When a bleary-eyed man with three-days' growth of beard appeared, yawning and squinting against the daylight, Jake swallowed and asked, "Are you Mr. Tindel?"

"Who's asking?"

"I'm Jacob Talbot. I graduated with your daughter."

He snorted and gave Jake the once-over. Jake was used to people in Lakehaven reacting to the Talbot name, but Katie's dad didn't seem to care. In fact, that appeared to be his defining characteristic: he didn't care about anything.

"Kate's gone. Got married off to some guy with money. Hell, he's damn near as old as I am!" That choked a laugh out of him. "She always was ambitious, our Katie."

"Do you know the man's name?" Jake asked, feeling as if he were being pulled out of the picture, far, far away. Everything was distant and unreal.

"Rose. Uh . . . Mr. Rose. Don't know his first name. Owns a business in Portland with models." He barked another laugh. "Kate worked for him and now they're married. Got herself knocked up by him, and I guess he had to do the duty!"

This was more information than Jake needed. Reeling,

he left without saying goodbye. He couldn't remember the drive home, but when he saw his parents waiting for him in the living room, he staggered down a different hall, ending in the laundry room where Darcy, the daily help, looked on in dismay as he lost his breakfast in the sink.

That was the last foolish thing he did over Kate Tindel Rose.

Oh, he had done other foolish things, he reminded himself a bit harshly as he straightened from the fender. Lots of foolish things. Leaning his head back, he stared up at the black heavens pinpointed with billions of stars. After all, he had married Celia, hadn't he? Married and divorced her within eighteen months.

Now there was something to celebrate.

Climbing behind the wheel, Jake snorted in derision at the mistakes of his youth. He had headed for college after that dismal summer. Harvard, like his father and mother wanted. Majored in business. Took to school as if it were a battle to not only be won, but won at all costs. No mercy. No thought for anything else. His determined study habits decimated the curve in classes that relied on it. He provoked instructors to challenge him, then met the challenge. College wasn't an education; it was a test, a war. And he wanted to annihilate the opponent.

He burned through women, too. Relationships were quick and even more quickly forgotten. His brother's reputation as a womanizer was undeserved when you took into account Jake's ruthless pursuit of the ladies. He didn't care. Not at all. And in his second year of graduate school Celia came to rescue him and breathe a bit of humanity into his empty soul.

And Jake was starving for love; he could admit that now. He buried his head in the comfort of Celia's soft breasts and let her caress and embrace him. She was already through two marriages, but that didn't stop him. He married her, though his parents were now less than thrilled at his choice; our Celia hadn't performed with decorum over the years.

But that made Jake happy. Screw them all. He didn't give a damn. He actually toyed with the idea, in those heady days, of chucking the whole Talbot Industries job ladder and running off in his brother's reckless footsteps.

But Jake was too practical, deep inside, and once he was finished with his Master's and actually looking for employment, saddled with a wife whom he didn't really love who was interested in starting a dynasty of children, he woke up from his deep coma of misery and took a long look.

He didn't like what he saw.

Telling Celia he wasn't interested in having children sent her screaming into the arms of a younger man—a twenty-year-old with shoulder-length hair, soulful brown eyes and pectorals that made even Jake take a second look. Celia's "boy toy" promptly got her pregnant. She divorced Jake, married him, had a baby girl and lived off her family's money till Boy-Toy headed for greener pastures.

Jake bought himself a high-rise condominium in downtown Portland, started in the family business and discovered, to his amazement, that he had an aptitude and interest in it. His parents breathed a collective sigh of relief that their younger son was back on track, and Jacob Talbot skyrocketed through the ranks to take over the helm when his father bowed out in early May of this year.

So, here he was, running a mini-empire, seeking to keep his brother gainfully employed and his parents happy, and that was all he really asked. Everything had been going fine, too. He had even started dating a woman recently who worked for a local advertising agency which handled Talbot Industries' commercials.

How ironic that Phillip, in a quest to act responsibly,

had taken on the duty of finding the perfect spokesperson for the company's latest series of commercials. This was normally the ad agency's job, but Phillip had, for no apparent reason, taken an instant dislike to Jake's new date, Sandra, and suggested he himself search out some talent for the shoot. And then he had found April Rose, *Katie's daughter!*

Life was an endless circle.

As soon as Jake had made the connection, he had driven like a maniac to Geno's to confront Katie Tindel Rose himself. He'd had visions of storming in and telling her to get her conniving hooks out of his business. She might have succeeded in bamboozling old Benjamin Rose, but her tricks wouldn't work on him anymore. No, sir.

But then he had seen her and memory did a number on him. Suddenly he was a tongue-tied, lovestruck, moronic teenager with big, hang-dog eyes and a wagging tail. He could scarcely move, and now he wasn't certain if he had made a whole lot of sense. He'd had to concentrate on Katie's daughter to keep any degree of balance at all!

And what a beauty she had been. Fresh, insouciant, yet sweet and intelligent. Man, oh, man. Kate might be a gold digger with ambitions, but she had turned out one pretty nice daughter, Jake reluctantly conceded. April Rose was instantly likeable and memorable, and he understood completely why Phillip had chosen her.

So, now what? he asked himself as he drove to his condo, the lazy Willamette flowing by, glimpsed through stands of firs and houses crouched on the cliffs above the river. What was he going to do about Kate's lovely daughter? And where did that leave him with Kate herself?

Growling in frustration Jake turned into the underground lot, strode to the elevator, punched the up button and waited impatiently for the lift to come down to his level.

What he really needed was a stiff drink, he decided as the elevator sped upward, the doors opening with a soft ding as he reached the eleventh floor.

"Should I be upset that I was forgotten?" a voice greeted him as he stepped into the plush, gray-carpeted hallway.

Sandra Galloway stood outside Jake's door. With an inner groan, Jake remembered they'd had a date. "I'm sorry. Something happened . . . ," he apologized lamely.

"I was just about ready to give up."

"You haven't been standing out here the whole time, have you?" Jake felt terrible. He was over an hour late, at least.

"No, this is my first trip. I called a few times, but your answering machine isn't working. I just slipped a note under the door and was heading over to Piper's Landing."

"Give me ten minutes," Jake said with forced heartiness. The last thing he wanted was to see Sandra right now.

She followed him inside the condo, perching on the edge of a smooth black chair while he headed for the bedroom. He carried her image with him as he stripped off his jacket. Dark, petite and carefully groomed, Sandra projected the perfect image of a '90s businesswoman, at least to Jake's mind. Her brown eyes were watchful, her makeup so understated that only if you were "up close and personal," as Jake had been a few times, could you tell how beautifully and precisely it was applied. Her features were small, her body so trim it was almost sharp. Her quick wit was what had first interested him, but now, with the memory of Kate's smooth, softer curves and girl-next-door appeal still fresh, he couldn't find anything about her that he wanted to see again.

You're a bastard, he told himself, shocked that he could be so fickle. Things had just started getting interesting with Sandra. It bugged him that one quick collision with Kate Rose could destroy what he had with Sandra so quickly.

Maybe those days of his college affairs weren't quite past after all.

Piper's Landing was the seafood restaurant a parking lot away from his condominium complex, and Jake squired Sandra inside while he continually berated himself. Almost because he was losing interest he tried harder, hanging on Sandra's every word as she sat across a small table in front of the window. Blue-and-white-striped awnings hovered over the windows as the Willamette River sailed by slowly in the darkness beyond.

"So, I told them they'd have to come up with something better than 'It's where to go.' I mean, come on. What kind of advertisement is that?" Sandra complained. "It could be anything! I wouldn't want to go to a restaurant with that motto."

"It's like telling someone where to go," Jake concurred.

"Exactly!" Sandra smiled and reached a hand across the table to his. "I knew you'd understand. Those morons at my office are so dense!"

It was all Jake could do not to slide his hand from beneath hers. Irritated with himself, he ground his teeth together and determined to try harder.

"So, where were you?" Sandra asked casually.

Jake didn't want to get into it. "Following up on something my brother handled."

"What do you mean?" Her fingers rubbed his.

Trapped, Jake saw no way out other than the truth. "Phillip found someone he thinks would work for our spokesperson."

"Phillip!" she sneered, sitting back in her chair. As soon as his hand was free Jake stuck it beneath the tabletop. "He'll be the downfall of Talbot Industries."

"Why can't you two stand each other?" Jake asked without any real curiosity. Their antipathy was mutual and had been immediate. Sometimes it happened. Maybe it was because he, Jake, had shown an interest in Sandra and she in him. Maybe it was bad Karma. It hardly mattered, but Jake was searching for any conversation that would get him through this date. All he wanted was to be alone.

"Phillip's rude," she said, making a face. "He thinks I'm wrong for you."

Jake's brows lifted. "We've only gone on a few dates."

"It's been a little more than that," Sandra reminded him with a secret smile.

Jake silently called himself a bastard once again. They had been dating a little over a month, and yes, they had slept together a few times. If he were truly honest, the physical interest had been more on Sandra's side than his. He just hadn't cared enough to really pursue her. What he had wanted was companionship, and the time to really get to know her. But Sandra had come on like gangbusters. Maybe that's why Phillip resented her.

To Jake's relief their meals came before he had to answer. He had ordered a salad. He hadn't been hungry earlier; he wasn't hungry now. Sandra picked at her pasta, pushing the plate aside, a tiny frown darkening her brow.

"What's wrong?" she asked.

"Nothing. A long day."

"You seem so distant."

"Do I?"

Sandra gave him a look. "Why do I get the feeling you're keeping something from me. Is there someone else?"

Jake couldn't hide his surprise. "What?"

"Are you seeing someone else?" she asked tightly, as if he were totally dense.

"No."

"How come I don't believe you?" Sandra's dark eyes probed Jake's. Though he had spoken the truth, he wondered if she could read the turmoil of his thoughts.

"Make me a promise," she said suddenly. "If you fall

for someone else, or think you are, give me a chance. I know I'd be good for you. We're a team. I felt that from the start."

"Sandra, don't put more into this relationship than there is," he suggested softly, trying to be kind but honest.

"Oh, I'm not. I know exactly what I've got. Just don't count me out too quickly, that's all." Her smile was tight.

Jake didn't respond. Superimposed over her smile was another one in his mind. Kate's smile. Kate's mouth. Deep pink and curved with mirth. Like it used to be. Years and years—eons—ago. He thought of her lips, and desire rushed through his veins. A feeling he hadn't experienced in years! He sucked in his breath and expelled it slowly, bothered deeply by his roller coaster reactions.

"Promise?" Sandra warned.

Uneasily Jake realized he was seeing what Phillip had felt from the start when it came to Sandra Galloway. "I promise I'll be honest with you," he answered.

Her dark eyes studied him carefully. "Then everything's okay, isn't it?"

He nodded.

She seemed to want to say something more. Jake braced himself, realizing that their relationship had already subtly changed. Katie Tindel's fault, or his own?

Sandra dropped her combative attitude and slid him a sideways smile. "How about if we cut this short and go to your place?"

With a feeling of taking the first few steps down the gangplank, Jake stated firmly, "I can't tonight. I've got a ton of work and a lot of issues waiting for me. I'll have to take a rain check . . ."

Kate's coffeemaker dribbled a thin stream of coffee into the pot while the whole contraption audibly pumped as if in labor. It was seven o'clock in the morning, and her kitchen was bright with summer sunshine. She poured herself a cup, then looked up in amazement as April appeared from her bedroom.

"What are you doing up so early?" Kate asked.

"Coffee," April murmured, running a hand through her tousled hair. Kate grinned and poured her daughter a cup. It wasn't fair for someone to look so good in the morning. *Youth was dangerous,* she thought.

"I want to go to work with you," she said, stifling a yawn. "I want to get ready for next Tuesday."

"You don't have to be there until three."

"I know. I'm just preparing myself. I want to go with you to Delilah's shoot."

Kate held the cup to her lips, considering. "Don't get your hopes up too high, okay?"

"They're not. I know I'm just one of the sheep."

"Just checking."

April frowned in serious thought, holding her cup, but not drinking. She might ask for coffee, but she hadn't really gotten used to drinking it yet.

"What?" Kate asked.

"Nothing." She shook her head and turned back toward her bedroom. "I'll be ready super quick. Wait for me."

"That audition's five days away!"

"Just . . . wait for me."

Kate sighed. This was going to be a problem any way you looked at it.

While April took a shower, Kate sat at the kitchen table and reflected on the events of the night before. Sleep had been impossible. She had spent hours tossing and turning, running through the scenario with Jake a thousand times, only to run through it once again. Now, this morning, she recalled it again and shuddered. Why did he still cause so many feelings? Good Lord, it had been almost eighteen years!

April showed up in faded blue jeans and a soft yellow shirt that brought out the golden streaks in her hair. She slid into the chair opposite Kate's.

"Why are you looking so guilty?" Kate asked, recognizing all the signs.

Wrinkling her nose, April pulled out her wallet. No purse for her, just a small leather wallet to keep her bills and coins. Chapstick in her front pocket was her only traveling makeup.

"This," she said, tossing over a stack of fifties.

"Oh, no," Kate groaned.

"I couldn't leave it as a tip," she admitted. "I picked up Mr. Talbot's money."

Hot emotion raged through Kate's veins. She leapt to her feet, hands clenched, realized how ridiculous she looked, and sat back down, hard. April's mouth dropped open.

"Mom?" she inquired, perplexed.

"You can't take his money!"

"I'll give it back to him on Tuesday."

"No! Just—put it down. Now."

April did as she was bidden. Kate was shaking all over. She stared at the money as if it were about to sprout horns and attack. April said in a scared voice, "Mom?"

"It's all right. I just don't want—anything from him."

"I never intended to keep it. I was going to give it back at the audition. Maybe I can take it to him earlier," she said uncertainly.

"No! Don't—" Kate reached out a hand toward her. "He won't . . . he won't like it. He meant to leave it there."

"I'm sorry." April swallowed, truly worried.

"No, it's okay. It's just—" Kate drew a long breath,

knowing there was no way to explain. "I don't trust people with lots of money."

"Like the Talbots."

"Like the Talbots," she agreed. "Jake Talbot left that money on the table to make a point. He's got tons of it, and to him it's as unimportant as confetti. Might as well be used the same way."

"That's not how it was," April protested. "He just kind of dropped it, like he was in a fog or something."

Kate shook her head. "You don't know him."

"Neither do you," her daughter pointed out.

She was right. Kate didn't know him anymore. Her memories from those teen years hardly mattered now. How could they?

"Let's not talk about it anymore," Kate murmured, scooting back her chair. "You ready?"

Wordlessly April climbed to her feet, her worried gaze touching on the bills lying on the table; but she preceded Kate out the door to the car, and neither of them mentioned the money again.

Three hours later, as Kate headed over to Delilah's "turkey" shoot, she knew she would never rest until she had put those memories of Jake back in the bottle. Somehow they had become uncorked and the genie had escaped. Seeing him again had resurrected feelings she had prayed were long dead, and she suspected, with the sharpness of painful truth, that unless she trotted them out one-by-one, she wouldn't be able to get through these next few meetings with Jake.

Pulling into the lot, she urged April to go on ahead, and then she strolled across the hot concrete of the parking lot to a small park where ducks paddled lazily on a tiny man-made lake in the center of some developer's designed commons. Probably Talbot Industries, she thought with an inner snort. They were known for creating office communities, commercial buildings and even doing some renovation of historical sites at discounted rates.

But she wasn't feeling particularly charitable toward any Talbot right now, so Kate shoved those thoughts aside. Instead, she concentrated on the past. Closing her eyes, she leaned her head against the sun-warmed slats of a wooden bench and gradually thought back to that last year of high school when Jake Talbot chose her to be the girl he fell in love with. . . .

Chapter Four

Go Wildcats! Go Wildcats!

The chant blasted from the crowd of frantic fans. Pom-pons on sticks danced in navy and gold, shimmering in a frenzied wave as the fans of Lakehaven High crowed for their team. It was a hot night, made more so by the blinding stadium lights. Football players moved through patterns on the field while everyone else watched the clock count down until opening kickoff.

Katie Tindel squeezed through the crowd, smiling apologies as she made her way to the senior section. It wasn't exactly designated only for seniors, but woe be to any underclassman who inadvertently stumbled onto their territory. She had seen senior boys actually tote the interloper on their collective shoulders to be dumped unceremoniously with his own kind.

Senior year. School was almost a memory already. Fanning her hot face with her hand, Katie perched on the end of the row where her friends grudgingly made way. There was nowhere to sit. Everyone was here for the first football game of the season. And what did it matter that Lakehaven was ranked bottom of the league? They still had some great players, and that's what it was all about anyway.

"Look!" Andrea Walters pointed. "There's Jake Talbot. Number two!"

Katie squinted at the navy figures on the field. They all looked like Storm Troopers with their helmets on. She picked out number two, who was in a line of players sent out for passes. While she watched, he leapt up and caught a spinning football, making it look easy.

Andrea had subsequently moved on, pointing out other senior boys on the team. She was indiscriminate in her adoration of football players. Katie, however, held a special place in her heart for Jacob Talbot, and though he barely knew she existed, she still nurtured her secret crush.

"I thought you had to work," Andrea said, practically screaming in Katie's ear to be heard above the crowd, though they were seated right next to each other.

"I did. I do. I'm sick." She made a face, feeling like a traitor.

"Oh, ho! You're playing hooky!"

"I tried to get someone to replace me, but nobody was interested. I couldn't miss the first game!"

"You work too hard anyway. You deserve a break, and if they can't see that, just quit."

Katie smiled at her friend for her words of encouragement, but the truth was, it wasn't that easy. While Andrea's family planned to pay for her college education, Katie was going to have to earn her own way. For the last two years she had worked as a bus girl and some-time hostess at the Shoreline, a steakhouse at the south end of the lake. The lake itself was really a misnomer. In actuality, it was merely a wide bend in the Bryant

River and therefore had no real reason to be called a lake. The town of Lakehaven collectively turned a blind eye to this minor detail. The locals preferred to think they lived on the lake, and no one disputed them. The more chichi houses bordered the water, and Jake Talbot's home was a minimansion on the lake's northwest corner.

Once in a while Jake had appeared at the Shoreline with his parents. She had offered him a quick smile and even quicker service. Her reward had been a flash of his white teeth in a silent "thank you." She savored the memory as if it were a declaration of love.

Tonight, though, Katie just couldn't go to work. She had wrestled with her conscience when she had been unable to find a replacement, but in the end, she had called in sick. She had missed out on a ton of fun already, while her wealthier friends regaled her with the stories of their weekend exploits time and again.

What could one night hurt? she reasoned, although throughout the football game she glanced to and fro, afraid she might recognize someone who would guess the truth. Guilt. She was fraught with it.

With a sigh she glanced down at her right ankle, currently wrapped in an elastic bandage. She had twisted it the night before while at work, and a part of her wanted to use it as an excuse to stay home. But that wasn't the real reason. She just hadn't wanted to miss this game, and though, yes, her ankle hurt a bit, it wasn't as injured as she might want to think.

Pushing her uneasy thoughts aside, Katie concentrated on the football game. Against all odds the Lakehaven Wildcats appeared to be holding their own. The score seesawed back and forth until two minutes before the half when Jake Talbot caught a spinning pass and raced in for a touchdown ahead of a nipping opponent to pull the Wild-cats ahead.

The crowd leapt to their feet, stomping and cheering until the stands reverberated and Katie's own throat ached from screaming.

It was, however, the last perfect play of the evening. The second half slid into the Wildcats' normal routine of tired, battered play. Still, when the horn blew, Lakehaven had only lost by six points, and the festive mood remained as the stands slowly cleared.

Beneath the lights the crowd surged around the players. They had removed their helmets and were meeting the fans' questions earnestly. With their padding, they all looked like Arnold Schwarzenegger wannabees. Jake was no exception. His shoulder pads bulged, and the football pants hugged tightly, increasing the disparity between torso and legs in a thoroughly interesting way. Jake's hair stuck wetly to his forehead as he listened to the advice of a middle-aged gentleman who seemed determined to school him on the ins and outs of football.

"You gotta want that ball. Pull it into your chest. Cradle it. Love it. You gotta want that ball . . ."

Jake's gaze shifted briefly, catching Katie's eye. The faintest smile tugged at the corners of his mouth. Katie grinned. She could feel her cheeks redden with heat and silently bemoaned her expressive face.

"You listening?" the man demanded.

"Yes, sir." Jake was polite.

Since Jake hadn't dropped the ball, Katie couldn't see why the man cared. He wasn't the coach, but then, some people went nuts over football at any level.

The man clapped Jake on the shoulder. "Good game, son."

"Thank you."

Jake turned to Katie, glanced at the retreating man, then

shrugged as if to say, "It's all bullshit, but who cares?" Katie liked sharing in the moment. She was astounded that he seemed to be eager to talk to her, but before a word could pass his lips, another well-intentioned, middle-aged would-be coach jumped in with another round of advice. The crowd moved in closer, and Katie was forced to step back. She hung at the periphery of the fans. Other players began marching into the locker room to change, but Jake was still surrounded by adults and teens alike.

What was she thinking? There was no room in Jake Talbot's life for the likes of Katie Tindel. She was just too poor. Someday, she determined, when she had made it on her own, she would find a guy like Jake, and it wouldn't matter what their backgrounds were. She was determined for that to be her fate.

She wanted a guy like Jacob Talbot.

"Hey! Wait!"

She heard his voice and glanced around to see whom he was calling to. In amazement, she saw he was signaling her. With a few last words to the group still huddled around him, he sidled away, reaching Katie in a matter of moments.

"I didn't think I'd survive another post mortem on the game," he admitted. "So, where are you going?"

"Ummm . . . nowhere special." Katie linked her fingers together to stop her hands from quivering. They were such betrayers. She couldn't do anything without them giving her feelings away as they quaked and shook.

"You going to Trey's party?"

Trey was a member of the squad whose parents didn't mind having a bunch of the team over after the games. It was an open invitation, but Katie had never felt comfortable dropping in. Most of the kids who went were part of the wealthy, more popular set.

Not that she wasn't accepted by them, she reminded herself. For reasons she didn't care to speculate on, Katie

Tindel had been okayed. Her looks and figure had caught the eye of several of the more noted males of her class, and the girls had been forced to follow. A shallow victory? Undoubtedly, and one Katie was a bit reluctant to grab with both hands. It was safer to stay on the fringes, and until this moment, that's where she had happily been.

But Jacob Talbot was showing some interest, and Katie's senses whirled in spite of her general level-headedness. "I don't know," she told him, afraid to commit. She couldn't see herself just walking through Trey's front door, bold as you please. Besides, she would have to get a ride. She couldn't afford to waste her money on a car, which reminded her that Andrea was undoubtedly stewing right now, waiting for her to get to her Toyota for her ride home.

"Would you like to go? I can give you a ride," Jake said, as if reading her mind.

"Well, sure," she said, struggling to tamp down her delight.

"I've gotta change and stuff. I'll pick you up in about half an hour or so?"

"Great."

"Where do you live?"

Instantly Katie was sorry she had been so quick to accept. The idea of Jake Talbot pulling up in his black Corvette convertible in front of her parents' rental sent fear rushing like ice through her veins. She wasn't embarrassed exactly. It was just the disparity was so vast!

Still, there was nothing else to do unless she wanted to wait outside the locker room like a pathetic groupie until after he had changed. That, she couldn't do.

She rattled off the address as quick as she could, then headed for the parking lot. "My ride's waiting," she explained on a yell as she tore away. "See ya soon!"

If he thought her behavior bizarre, she couldn't help it.

She had to escape before his mind recognized the address as somewhere far less desirable than his own street.

Once home, she ran into more obstacles. Her mother and father were seated in the living room, mindlessly watching whatever came on the television screen. Katie tried to sneak through to her bedroom, but her mother looked up as she slipped past the living room archway.

"Why aren't you at work?" she demanded.

"I—got a replacement," she stammered.

Her mother nodded and turned back to the set. Her father didn't acknowledge her at all. Katie scurried to the sanctity of her room and closed the door. She didn't relate to her parents on any level, and neither did they relate to her. It wasn't teen rebellion on her part. It was more like they had so little interest in her well-being that she was as much a part of the furniture as a member of the household. How it had happened she didn't rightly know; but over the years the realization that her parents' feelings for her were lukewarm at best had seeped inside, and in consequence, she returned the feeling. Most of the time it didn't bother her that much. Only when she saw other parents interacting with their children, laughing and hugging and generally having a good time, only then did a deep pang of misery assail her. Each time that happened she vowed that when and if she ever had children she would give them everything, all her love, caring and worldly possessions. It would not be the same for her and her child. No way.

Now, she gazed at her reflection in her bedroom mirror. Her hair was in a ponytail. She brushed it down, but the line from the rubber band held firm. With an exclamation of disgust, she relooped the band, then examined her makeup. A dusting of eyeshadow and a bit of mascara. Summer had tanned her skin so that blush was beyond unnecessary. She added lip gloss, then surveyed her white tank top and denim shorts. Though she wore no socks, the elastic Ace Bandage showed above her white sneakers, and with a small cry of annoyance, she ripped off her shoe and unwrapped it. Minor discoloration still appeared on her flesh from the sprained ankle, nothing anyone would notice. On a lark she clipped on a tiny anklet which tinkled so softly that it sounded like an imagined Pan's pipe off in the distance. A bottle of cologne sat on her scarred vanity. Picking it up, she sprayed a flowery scent against her throat.

What are you doing? she asked herself. *Jake Talbot isn't going to look at you. He was just being nice. Why are you going to Trey's? You'll feel like an idiot. Don't go.*

Panic filled her. What would she do there? What if they all cut her dead?

But Jake had invited her. She was being paranoid for no good reason. Bolstering up her courage, she returned to the front room, and this time both of her parents turned her way, scrutinizing her from head to toe.

"Where are you going?" her father demanded.

"To a friend's house."

"Which friend?" This was from her mother.

"His name's Trey. He's on the football team." With a certain amount of pride, she added, "Jake Talbot's picking me up."

"Talbot?" Her mother gaped. The name was way too familiar in Lakehaven for anyone to miss.

Katie nodded happily.

"You're going on a date with one of the Talbot sons?"

"He ain't the one who landed in the drunk tank, is he?" her father sneered. "God, he's a wild one."

"He's on the football team," Katie said through her teeth. *Pride goeth before a fall.* Or something like that. She wished she had kept her date with Jake a secret; but no, she'd had to crow, and now her parents were avid with curiosity.

"Don't let him get anything," her father added, turning back to the television, and Katie was affronted.

"Get anything?" she demanded.

"You know what your father means. Young men have one-track minds, and especially young men with too much money."

"Only a fool buys a cow when he can get the milk for free," her father threw out over his shoulder.

Humiliated right down to the soles of her feet, Katie murmured a goodbye and slammed out of the house. Jake wasn't anywhere in sight, so she walked down the street a ways, just where she could keep her own house in view without actually having to be there. Plucking at some tall grass which bordered this side street into Lakehaven proper, she fought back a tide of anger. She had her own doubts, for crying out loud. She knew Jake Talbot couldn't be interested in her for Katie Tindel herself. That wasn't the way it worked.

But why not? her foolish, romantic heart demanded. Why couldn't he fall in love with her? She was a nice person. And yes, she was pretty. And she was fun and smart, too.

These positive affirmations made Katie feel marginally better.

His Corvette appeared on the street, top down, creeping along as Jake searched out her address. Quickly, Katie hurried forward, hailing him with one arm. Her ankle twinged without its wrap, but she barely noticed. Spying her, he swung to the curb and actually got out of the car to hold the door for her.

"Thank you," Katie said, surprised.

He laughed. "Well, I guess I could have pulled over and told you to climb over the top. I just didn't think you'd want to."

She laughed right back. "Chivalry is not dead."

His brows lifted. He seemed surprised by her choice of

words, and Katie inwardly congratulated herself that she hadn't resorted to silly high school flirtation lines, such as "Cool car!" or "I loved watching you tonight." She had heard her friends line up to deliver the same inanities time and again until she wanted to throw up. She had determined long ago that if ever given the chance, she wasn't going to blow it.

And this was her chance.

Jake softly closed the door behind her as Katie buckled up. While they drove to Trey's, Katie asked a few questions about football, a sport she knew just enough about to be dangerous.

"I'm a wide receiver," Jake explained to her query. "The quarterback has a choice of where to throw the ball. Or, he can hand off to a running back."

"How often does he choose to throw to you?"

"Depends on the other team's defense. If I'm open, and it's working, we might run the play a lot. But if they've shut me down, or the linemen can't protect the quarterback long enough for him to make the snap, then he'll pass off to a running back instead."

"Oh," Katie said, nodding. It made a certain amount of sense, but to tell the truth, she had zero interest in the game, really.

As if reading her mind, Jake shot her a sidelong look, his lips curving in what could only be described as a sexy smile. "You don't care, do you?"

"Not really."

Her candor brought another chuckle from deep within his chest. Katie glanced out the side, letting wind cool her hot face as the convertible traveled faster, away from Lakehaven's city center.

Trey's house was on the lake, near Jake's. As they passed through two brick pillars which guarded the drive, Katie's nerves stretched. What would they all think, when she appeared with Jake? It bothered her that she cared so much, but no amount of rationalization would tame her thundering heart.

Jake swung the Corvette into the semicircle in front of the two-story house and parked to one side. The house itself was a small manor built in the French chateau style. It was sided with flat gray stones, and white-paned, arched windows rose upward to a mansard roof. Katie let herself out of the car, conscious of her denim shorts and tank top. She had just expected to wear regular Lakehaven High gear. What if she were underdressed?

But no, Jake was in jeans and a black T-shirt that hugged his shoulders. They walked up the wide, brick steps together and rang the bell. Ten seconds later footsteps sounded, and Trey threw open the door.

"Welcome!" he called, his freckled face split by a wide grin. "The party's downstairs."

He didn't seem surprised in the least to see Katie, and when she descended the stairs after Jake, she saw that many of her classmates were already there. Nobody even noticed her arrival apart from a few hellos. She realized that she had made too much of the whole thing just because she felt somehow inadequate. She was the only one who seemed to worry that she didn't belong.

Andrea was there, and she detached herself from a group just long enough to dig her fingers into Katie's arm and drag her down a short hallway, away from the pool table and refreshments. "You're with Jake!" she declared. "My God! How'd you work that?"

"He asked me to come with him. I told you in the car."

"No, you didn't. You said Jake had asked if you were going to Trey's. That's all you said."

Katie shrugged. She could have reminded her that the reason she hadn't elaborated was because Andrea had changed the subject—a typical Andrea move. Andrea wasn't really interested in what someone else was doing unless it affected her in some way. In that respect, she was like nearly every other student at Lakehaven High.

"So, what gives? Are you dating him? I mean, is this a *date*?"

"Don't ask me. He just offered me a ride, and I took it."

"Oh, Katie, if you start seeing Jake Talbot, I'll just die! Everyone'll be so jealous. You know, as well as I do, half the girls here have chased after him at one time or another."

"You're making too much of this." She was starting to grow uncomfortable. Wouldn't it just be great if Andrea started the rumor that she was with Jake, and then Jake overheard? Like she had been spreading the news herself? She would die of embarrassment!

"Oh, there's Donna. Let's go tell her!"

Andrea yanked on Katie's arm, but Katie dug her heels in. "If you say anything, I'll kill you. He offered me a ride. Period. He's probably already sorry he did."

"Oh, come on. Don't be so dumb. This is big news!"

Swept along on the tide of Andrea's enthusiasm, Katie was passed from friend to friend, relating how Jake Talbot had asked her to be his "date." By the time she escaped and could search out Jake himself, she was terribly uneasy that he would get the wrong impression of her. Sure, she had a secret crush on him, but so did everyone else. She couldn't bear being one of the pack.

Jake was standing at the pool table, cue in hand. "Could I talk to you a minute?" she asked, when he had finished a shot.

"Sure." He regarded her patiently, leaning on his cue.

The guys had all separated to the pool table with an occasional foray to the trays of food, while the girls were hovering in small groups, just watching. There was no mixing. Though everyone seemed desperate to cross that invisible line, no one knew quite how.

"When you're done," she said, motioning him to continue.

"You want to be my partner?" Jake asked. "This is about wrapped up."

In truth Jake only had a few balls left on the table while his opponent still had a tableful. At that very moment his opponent sank the eight ball, disqualifying himself. He howled in protest.

Jake appropriated the loser's cue stick, and another set of guys stepped forward to play Jake and Katie.

Pool wasn't something she was good at. She had played a couple of times at a few arcades, but apart from knowing how to hold the cue, she was miserable. "You'll be sorry," she warned him.

"I don't think so."

When it was her turn, Jake leaned over and showed her which ball to select to try to get in the pocket. His arm lay against hers, his hand guiding her wrist. She could smell his musky male scent, a mixture of cologne and something uniquely Jake. The hair on his arm brushed against hers, a soft abrasion. She felt his hips glance against hers, and the sound of his breathing near her ear sent shivers along her skin.

Katie was so nervous that her hands began to shake again. She stopped and rubbed them together to calm herself.

"It's okay if you don't make it," he assured her. "I don't mean to put pressure on you."

"Oh, no," she said, when she realized he intended to back away. "I like having you teach me."

Their opponents both made a sound of amusement, but to Katie, they were just part of the wallpaper. With Jake's help, she sank her first ball. She clapped hands with him in a high five, his fingers hanging on a second longer than necessary. Katie was in seventh heaven.

After that, she couldn't remember much about the game. She struggled to sink more balls, failing more than winning, but Jake was there, his arms and body guiding her through each step. By the time they were finished, when Jake called the pocket and sank the eight ball, Katie had forgotten all her earlier fears. All she could see was Jake. If she had thought she had a crush before, she was rapidly spiraling into full-fledged love—and lust.

All the way home she was supremely conscious of his thigh next to hers. Just the sight of his arms, stretched out to grasp the steering wheel, sent thrills down her spine. His fingers were long and strong, flexing against the wheel, and Katie fantasized about what they would feel like caressing her.

She was losing her mind. She couldn't credit it. What was the matter with her?

At her house, he stopped at the curb. She let herself out only to find him right beside her. He walked her up the weed-choked walk to her concrete porch. It seemed so unkempt and unloved that Katie had to force herself not to spout excuses.

"Thanks for taking me. It was really worth skipping out on work tonight." She pulled a guilty face and shrugged, her smile sheepish.

"How many nights a week do you work?" he asked.

"Four."

"Both weekend nights?"

Her pulse began pounding in a slow, slow beat. The air was still hot, though it was closing in on midnight. The moon hung low in the sky, illuminating a patch of ground just outside of where her feet stood.

"Sometimes I can get off," she admitted. "If I find someone to work for me."

"What about next weekend? Maybe like, Saturday? We've got a game away on Friday."

"I could try," she said, fighting to hide her runaway eagerness.

"Okay." He grinned. She could see his features in the darkness. They both moved at the same moment, awkwardly, toward each other, and Katie's ankle slipped just enough to shoot pain up her leg.

Her involuntary gasp stopped him short. "What's the matter?"

"Oh, nothing." She was so frustrated! "I twisted my ankle a few days ago. I do it all the time. It just hurt a bit."

"Let me see it." He bent down to her slim, bare leg.

"No, really, it's fine."

She sucked in a breath when his fingers reached around her left ankle. Goose bumps popped out on her arms and legs. "It's—it's the other one," she breathed, feeling slightly faint.

Now his fingers probed her right ankle, and the tiny bells of the anklet tinkled in soft protest. "It's a little bit swollen, I think," he said uncertainly.

"It's a little bit green, if you look closely," Katie added on a breathless laugh.

"Better take your weight off it." Jake straightened just long enough to tug on her arm and help her sit on the step. He sank down beside her, and to her surprise, he propped her right leg over his and examined her ankle more thoroughly.

"What? Are you my doctor?" She laughed nervously. His hands were warm and gentle.

"I could be." In the semidarkness she could see his eyes crinkle at the corners with humor. When he turned to her, his blue eyes were a deeper shade in the darkness, but they caught the moonlight, glimmering like liquid.

When he leaned forward it seemed like the most natural thing in the world to move toward him. His arms encircled her; his breath feathered her cheek. When his mouth brushed across her skin, searching for hers, Katie's lips parted instinctively, eager for his kiss. For a moment he rubbed gently, back and forth, teasing her; then his mouth slanted down with searing intensity.

Katie's senses went wild. One moment she was afraid her fears would be noticed; the next she was in orbit! Her ears buzzed, and her heart galloped frantically, threatening to escape her chest. Her eyes drifted closed automatically, and her lips quivered as if she were about to cry.

Jake's kiss turned her legs to water; her spine lost its strength. When his hand caressed her cheek, holding her in place for another firmer, longer kiss, she could do nothing but lie quiescent in his arms. Yet, a furor of activity was taking place beneath her skin as her magnafoozled brain sorted through too much sensory input.

Slowly, ever so excruciatingly slowly, he pulled back. She could practically feel her lips sticking to his, as if they refused to let go. She didn't want him to leave. She couldn't bear it!

In the moonlight his face looked serious and unfamiliar and hauntingly sexy. "Was that your first kiss?" he asked.

Within his arms, she trembled like the proverbial leaf. Did she have to be so obvious? "No," she lied. "Maybe. Well, yes," she finally admitted.

He laughed silently, his shoulders shaking. Nervous giggles erupted from her mouth, and she buried her head in his chest, dying of embarrassment. "Don't tell anyone!" she cried, which sent them both into gales of laughter.

"It's our secret," he agreed.

"There just hasn't been anybody at Lakehaven—that's even close," she struggled to explain, not wanting him to think she was some kind of fanatical prude.

"I know the feeling," he admitted, beneath his breath.

"I'm glad you were the first," she burst out, then suffered another bout of embarrassment until Jake drawled, "So, am I . . ."

After that they kissed some more, until Katie began to worry that one of her parents might hear them and decide to throw open the door unexpectedly. Reluctantly, she pulled away a bit, and Jake let her go.

"Next Saturday," he reminded her. "I'll call you."

"Next Saturday," she repeated happily.

She spent the next week in a sort of anxious euphoria. Jake saw her in the halls and said, "Hi," whenever they passed. It wasn't much, but then, he was busy and what did she truly expect? She refused to tell her friends about their date because she didn't want them spoiling it somehow, so she wrote her feelings feverishly in her diary, circling the date of that first kiss with a red felt pen— September 5.

The only person she actually confided in was a girl a few years older than she was named Lisa, who was a waitress at the Shoreline. When Katie first approached her with working an extra night—not as a waitress, but as a bus girl—Lisa laughed out loud.

"Are you kidding? Ask Karen. I'm not bustin' my butt to clear tables. It's bad enough waiting on them." Seeing how crestfallen Katie was, Lisa, who was more bark than bite, threw an arm across her shoulders and said, "Oh, for pete's sake, I'll do it if you can't get someone else. What's so all fired important, anyway?"

The words tripped all over Katie's tongue. "I've got a date. A real date. With a boy from my class."

"No kidding. Who's the lucky guy?" she asked without any real interest apart from the fact that she had appointed herself Katie's "older sister" when it came to these things.

"Jake Talbot."

"Jake *Talbot?*"

"Yes," she said, surprised at Lisa's galvanic response.

Urgently, she declared, "Don't do it! Don't go out with him! I guarantee you, you'll be sorry if you do!"

Chapter Five

"What do you mean?" Katie asked, surprised.

They were in the middle of working, and Lisa glanced over her shoulder to see if the evening manager was anywhere in sight. However, for the moment the coast was clear.

"Do you know Jake?" Katie demanded as Lisa's brows drew together in a frown, as if she wasn't quite sure how to continue.

"I know his brother," was her surprising answer.

"You do?"

"Phillip and I—" Lisa hesitated, searching for the right words. Finally, she lifted one shoulder in a faint shrug. "We dated."

Read that to mean they had slept together. Katie wasn't completely naive. And from the way Lisa acted, it hadn't been all that wonderful of an experience. "You don't see him anymore?"

"Phillip doesn't hang around that long. He comes back

to Lakehaven every once in a while, but I don't think things are that great between him and his parents."

"Jake isn't like Phillip," Katie argued defensively.

Lisa gave her a knowing look. "They're all the same without their clothes on, honey."

This was more information than Katie really needed, and it left her feeling slightly unsettled. Still, nothing could dissuade her from seeing Jake on Saturday, and when Karen agreed to work her shift, Katie was free and eager and nearly paralyzed with anticipation.

Saturday night she couldn't decide what to wear. She knew next to nothing about their plans. Jake had called her once with vague information about getting something to eat and figuring the rest out as they went. He, apparently, wasn't exactly spreading the news around school, either, for by the time Saturday arrived, their date was still a very well kept secret.

It was still unseasonably hot. Katie's wardrobe was not extensive, so to compromise and still be ready for anything, she wore a pair of khaki slacks and a sleeveless white knit shirt. A black cotton long-sleeved shirt, cuffs rolled back, completed the outfit. She threw it over her arm to use as a lightweight jacket just in case.

There was still forty minutes to spare before Jake was due to pick her up. Nervous, Katie prowled around the house, stopping in the small kitchen and looking in the refrigerator. Apart from a storehouse of beer and some cheap wine, there wasn't a lot to eat. Her parents' tastes weren't extravagant, but they were certainly consistent.

When I graduate, I'm never coming back.

"Where are you going?" her father asked from somewhere behind her.

Katie's heart leapt. "I—don't know. To dinner somewhere."

"With that Talbot kid?"

"Jacob Talbot," she answered carefully, rebellion flashing in her eyes. If he said anything else disparaging about Jake's family, she would blow her top.

Her father merely grunted, swung open the refrigerator, grabbed a beer, twisted off the top and swallowed a huge gulp. He left a moment later for his beloved television, but upon his departure, Katie's mother took up the cry.

"When will you be back?" she asked, standing at the edge of the kitchen where the room bled into a dining room which the Tindels used as a storage room. The only table was a drop-leaf shoved beneath the kitchen window, and there were boxes everywhere. There was no such thing as family meals.

"I don't know what we're doing exactly."

"I want you home by eleven."

"Eleven!" Katie's lips parted. She never arrived earlier than midnight from her job. "How about twelve?"

"Eleven." Her mother was firm.

Katie was nonplused. Her parents had scarcely shown her as much interest as a mother cat since the time she was in junior high school. Before that, their parenting skills were perfunctory at best. Now, suddenly, they cared about propriety.

I will never treat my children like this! she vowed to herself as her mother trundled back to the living room to settle in beside her father.

Once again, she couldn't bear for Jake to meet her at the door. In a move that was to become the template for her dates with him, she headed outside early, eager to meet him without her parents eyeing her like a hawk. "Goodbye," she sang out, closing the door behind her at her father's, "You be good," and her mother's, "Be home at eleven, now."

She supposed she should be glad they didn't regulate every minute of her date, demanding to know where she was and whom she was with. Yet she had been on her own so long, cadging rides with other workers at the restaurant and working late hours, that this sudden change bugged her.

But as soon as she was out in the warm night air, the sense of freedom was like an elixir. She breathed deeply, sensuously, spreading her arms to the heavens as if she were a prisoner, newly released from some terrible, dank dungeon.

Jake pulled up moments later. The throb of the Corvette's engine and the sound of loud music heralded his arrival. This time she didn't wait for him to get out and hold the door. Grabbing the handle as soon as he came to a halt, she jumped inside.

"Let's go," she whispered, eager to put her unhappy life behind her.

"Sure. Is there a problem?"

"No." She wrinkled her nose at the lie. "Just my parents."

"Really? What's the matter?"

He pulled away and turned the nose of the vehicle east, toward Portland. With the top down, the scents and feel of the night rushed across her. She closed her eyes and breathed deeply, hoping against hope they were heading all the way into the city, because Lakehaven felt stifling and small, and she wanted to break free.

She shouldn't talk to him about her home life. It was so vastly different from his, she knew instinctively it might put the kibosh on their fledgling relationship. Still . . . "I can't wait to leave home. My parents—are ready for me to go."

He glanced her way. "What do you mean?"

"Are we going to Portland?" she asked, in an effort to change the subject.

"Do you want to?"

"Yes," she admitted. "I just want to get away."

"We can go anywhere you want."

She smiled at him, and he smiled back. Katie couldn't take her eyes off his mouth, and with an effort she dragged her thoughts away from the dangerous curve they had taken.

But Jake was unwilling to completely give up the topic they had begun exploring, and he asked, "Don't you get along with your parents?"

"In a word: no. They think I'm fine, I guess. But I'm more of a burden. They don't really have any—interest in having me around. I mean, it's not terrible or anything. They just have no interest in my grades, or my job, or my aspirations. You know?" she asked, cringing at how whiney she sounded.

"Actually, I've got the opposite problem. My parents want to run every part of my life. They've got me scheduled for Harvard."

Katie stared at him. "Do you have the grades?"

Jake seemed slightly embarrassed. He fiddled with the radio a moment before answering simply, "Yes."

She didn't have to ask if he had the money; the Talbots were blessed that way. And he probably had a few connections as well. It made the gap in their life-styles so wide that Katie was speechless until they reached downtown Portland.

It wasn't that she didn't have the grades; she had studied hard and worked like a trooper to pull herself ahead. But she would be lucky if she could afford a local community college. Her plan, vague as it was, was to work nights, probably at a Portland restaurant, and go to school during the day. There was no question of living at home; it was understood on both sides that she would move out. No, the best she could hope for was to find a roommate to share expenses.

"Where would you like to eat?"

Katie was too wound up to feel hunger. "Anywhere. Maybe somewhere more casual. I'm not all that dressed up."

"There's this little cafe by the Willamette. . . ?"

"Perfect."

The "little cafe" turned out to have a pricey menu. Gulping back her inhibitions, Katie ordered a large garden salad, the least expensive item she could find. When Jake looked at her askance, she hurriedly answered, "I'm not all that hungry." Since this was the absolute truth, he seemed to believe her. They talked about nothing. Later, Katie couldn't really remember what was said. But she fell desperately in love with him in a few short hours, and just knowing how tiny a chance there was for them to have any kind of relationship added another dimension to the evening, a bittersweet edge that left her aching for all the things she couldn't have in life.

Her melancholy mood wasn't lost on Jake as they drove back to Lakehaven, the night air playing havoc with her hair. Katie held it back with one hand, eyes closed, pretending to be absorbed in the soft rock music issuing from the radio.

"What's wrong?" he asked.

"Nothing. What do you mean?"

"You've barely spoken two words since we left the restaurant. Something's bothering you."

She grimaced and opened her eyes. He glanced her way, his jaw strong and hard, his expression guarded. Did he think she wasn't having a good time? she fretted. Good grief! She never wanted the night to end!

"I just wish—everything was—different," she struggled.

"Different how?"

"Oh, I don't know. You and me. When I think about

your family and mine . . ." Katie sighed. "It's just hard, that's all," she finished lamely.

Silence followed them for several miles. Then Jake burst out, "I don't want to go to Harvard. I don't want any of it."

Now it was Katie's turn to ask, "What do you mean?"

"It's their dream for me. It's not mine. I don't even know what mine is. When I'm playing football, or working in class, or whatever, I don't care. I'm just doing it, you know? But when they start talking about my future and taking over the family business, I get—uneasy."

"They want you to take over Talbot Industries?"

"They wanted my brother to," he corrected. "But Phillip will never stand working with my dad. I don't think I can either."

"So, what are you going to do?" Katie asked.

"I don't know. Maybe I should flunk out this year. That'll kill my chances!"

He sounded half-serious. "Oh, don't do that! You don't want to ruin your chances anywhere."

After a long hesitation, he sighed. "I know."

They pulled into the outskirts of Lakehaven, and Katie was filled with a sense of dread. It was such a letdown to return to her normal life. Cinderella after the ball. But they didn't seem to have any set plans, so when Jake drove aimlessly through town, Katie took the bull by the horns.

"Do you want to go somewhere? I'm really not interested in going home yet."

"What time do you have to be home?"

She couldn't answer. "Eleven" just stuck in her throat. "No set time," she prevaricated. Lie, upon lie. She was getting worse by the minute!

"Well, I have an idea what we could do."

He didn't say more than that. Instead he drove through

town and toward the north shore of the lake. Instantly Katie became alarmed. Were they going to *his* house?

As if reading her thoughts, he said casually, "I thought we'd go canoeing on the lake. It's dark, but . . ." He left the thought unfinished.

"I would love to!" she breathed.

The Talbot's house was set back from the road. There was a short drive to one side which led to a guest house. Jake pulled his car to a halt in the turnaround to the left of the guest house, backing in so the Corvette faced toward the street. He and Katie climbed out of the car, and he took her hand as he led her down a flagstone path that circled the guest house and meandered down to the waterfront.

A canoe was beached next to a vacant boat slip. Jake quietly slipped it into the water, then motioned for Katie to climb inside.

It was all she could do not to upset the balance of the craft. She held on to the sides while Jake situated himself in the stern, dipping the oars in the water and gently, almost silently, sending them away from his parents' property.

"They might object to me taking off without lights," he explained. "We'll keep close to the shore, just in case there's another boat."

"This is fabulous," Katie said, watching the draping limbs of a willow tree pass by, a dark sentinel to their passage. The dank scents of water and wet vegetation were their own perfume, and Katie drank deeply, her senses overwhelmed.

I love you, she thought.

"I love it," he said, and she started, thinking for a moment that he had said those three little words! "I want to have property on water someday," he added, reminding Katie what he had really meant.

She had to be careful that her fantasies didn't run away with her.

"Do you want to live here?" She dipped a hand in the water. It was surprisingly warm, but then the temperature had been hanging in the upper eighties and nineties for a while. Soon enough, however, fall would hit like a hammer. Indian summer only lasted so long.

"No. I want to get away from Lakehaven. Maybe Portland. A place on the Willamette."

"A houseboat?"

"That'd be fun for a while," Jake conceded, cocking his head as he thought it over. "Where do you want to live?"

"Portland, I guess," she agreed. Before she realized it she was telling him her plans to find a roommate and go to a community college. "I'll have to work, of course," she said quickly, not wanting to dwell on their economic differences more than she had to. "But I kind of like working at the Shoreline. It's great experience, and the customers are nice."

"I wish we'd known each other before. Here we've gone four years to high school together, and this is our first real date. Why is that?" he asked rhetorically.

Katie linked her fingers together over one knee, carefully keeping her balance. "Maybe because you never looked at me before," she said lightly.

"Maybe." Her words didn't put him off. He rested the paddle, and they drifted lazily, bobbing near shore.

There was a lot unspoken. She could feel him assessing her through the darkness, and it sent a frisson of awareness down her spine. Slowly, he picked up the oars, and she realized he was turning them around, heading them back toward his parents' property.

She wanted to protest. She didn't want the night to end. But her heart gave a little jump when he said, "It's almost midnight. I've got to be home."

"Oh!" Katie sucked air between her teeth as Jake docked the canoe. He jumped lithely to shore, pulling the craft into the boat slip.

"You all right?" he asked, helping her from the canoe.

"Yeah, fine. Probably time for me to get home, too."

"How's the ankle?"

"Oh, great." She had forgotten about it this past week. Now she turned her right foot inward and rotated the joint, showing him how much better it was. It was still kind of stiff and there was a twinge of pain, but it was definitely on the mend.

To her surprise, he bent down and captured her sandaled foot. It was a reprise of the week before, and Katie held her breath, wondering what would happen next. Once again, his strong fingers probed her flesh, and once again she felt goose bumps. Then he rose to his full height, standing in front of her in the waning moonlight. His hands cupped her chin and he kissed her. Katie's lashes fluttered closed. She had dreamed of this. Had gone over last week's kiss so many times that if it had been written on paper, it would have shredded from overuse. His lips slanted down on hers, and her hands clutched the fabric of his cotton shirt as she met that hard mouth. Her senses swirled. She had never felt anything like this before. It was so consuming, so wonderful, so all out soul-drowning that she felt like an addict, wanting more, more, more!

When the kiss finally ended, he dragged her close. His heart thumped against hers. She kissed his chin and jawline without being asked, and his groan of need was like a flame to her already overheated senses.

"What are you doing to me?" he asked, bending his head down to capture her lips again.

"What are you doing to me?" she countered.

"I don't know . . . I don't know . . ."

"Do it some more," she whispered.

"God, Katie. *I want to!*"

She knew it was dangerous. She was asking for something she shouldn't be. But she couldn't help herself, and when he tugged her hand, urging her down to the grass beside him, she simply melted like wax.

He kissed her and kissed her, and when his hand dragged her knit shirt from the waistband of her pants, she didn't stop him. Neither did she when it stole upward, beneath her top, to cup one aching breast in his palm.

"Katie . . . ," he murmured. "Katie . . ."

Lisa's words floated through her mind, those clucking, mother hen comments about the Talbots. But Lisa had meant Phillip, her desire-drugged mind protested. This was Jake. Jake, Jake, Jake! The man she loved. She refused to listen.

Besides, it was too pleasurable for words. Her conscience shut down, and she breathed a sigh of pure pleasure. Her hands began an exploration of their own, running down his back and tugging his shirt free as well. Her fingers slid upward against the smooth muscle of his back to his broad shoulders.

His fingers unclipped the front closure on her bra, spilling her breasts into his warm palms. Gently he massaged her flesh, his breath hot against her mouth, his lips achingly demanding.

They were lying on the ground with Jake's chest half-atop hers. In the heat of the moment he rolled onto her, his legs tangling with hers. In that brief, hot instant, she felt his male hardness, and her splintered brain reconnected. My God, what was she doing? Remembering her father's admonitions, she felt shocked and embarrassed. Good Lord, she was asking for it! No, *begging!*

In response she simply shut down. Her hands stopped moving. Her body froze. Her parted lips slackened in shock, unable to return his urgent kisses. Her whole consciousness narrowed to the feel of his arousal against her, and the knowledge that it would take so little—so very little—to make love to him.

But her good intentions vanished moments later. His mouth slid down her neck to her bared skin, leaving a moist trail against her skin as it traveled to her breast. His tongue circled one nipple, and ripples of awareness moved beneath her flesh.

Her fingers clutched his hair. She wanted to drag his hot, seeking mouth away. *No!* She wanted to cradle him close. As his lips clung to her nipple, sucking hard, her nails raked his scalp. Her back arched in hot response, and she silently begged for some nameless fulfillment.

Were those mewling sounds issuing from her lips? Katie was too dazed to know. "Jake . . ."

Urgently he drew her hand down to him, and Katie felt the thick bulge of his manhood through the confines of his jeans. Her fingers probed carefully, but a tingle of fear remained. This was wrong. She knew it instinctively; but curiosity held her in its grip, and when her fingers encountered the zipper, his groan of submission spurred her on.

"Katie . . . ," he murmured brokenly, making her feel inordinately powerful. *She* was doing this to him.

Then suddenly his fingers were at her waistband, popping the button, sliding down the zipper, slipping inside to slide over the thin protection of her panties.

Alarm bells went off inside her head. "I can't!"

His groan was a denial, his fingers anxious and searching. She felt her own slickness and was appalled, then was relieved when he seemed to come to himself, for he abandoned his exploration.

She just wanted to kiss him and kiss him. Fervently she let her lips caress his face and neck. Jake's expression was tense and hard, and she really didn't understand what was wrong until he climbed full atop her.

"You're driving me crazy," he admitted thickly, his body trembling.

Good, she thought, and when he thrust against her through her clothes, she clung to him, distantly aware that her body was responding to his hard rubbing in a thoroughly enticing way. She wanted to strip them both of their remaining clothes and drag his hot body to hers. She wanted him.

But Lisa's warning held her in its grip, and she balled her hands into fists, fighting her own urges.

Jake suddenly rolled off her, his breathing harsh and ragged. His eyes were closed, his mouth a thin line. Katie swallowed, afraid she had done something seriously wrong. Oh, God! Did he think she was a slut? She had only wanted to love him a little.

"Jake?" she whispered, afraid, her heart still raging ahead in a wild beat.

"I'm sorry," he said, sounding stunned by his own behavior.

Relief swept through her. "Oh, no. It's okay. I thought you were mad at me."

"Mad at *you?*" He opened his eyes to stare at her.

"I didn't mean to—I don't know—" Heat flooded her face, and she gulped against a hot throat.

"Oh, Katie." He leaned toward her, his breath hard, his nose nearly touching hers. "I've never come on to a girl like that before. I know you won't believe me, but it's true."

"I do believe you!" She knew his reputation as well as anyone, and Jake Talbot had been indifferent to the girls at Lakehaven High. She was just thrilled he wasn't indifferent to her!

But it was scary how quickly passion could claim one's senses. She hadn't believed it was possible. She had never suspected that *she* could behave blindly and recklessly. She had felt so sure that a boy would never be able to talk her into sex. No way. But now she knew that at least with Jake Talbot, very little persuasion would be necessary. . . .

Almost without volition her hand reached out to stroke his cheek. She wanted to wipe away the anxiety she saw in his shadowed gaze. "I'm not sorry," she whispered. "But I think I'd better go home."

To her amazement and delight, he covered her hand with his own, then turned it over to press a kiss into her palm. Then he leapt to his feet and hauled her up beside him, his smile a flash of white in the darkness. His mood was infectious, and Katie smiled right back. Those three little words trembled on her lips, but she held them in. She couldn't tell him, yet. It was too soon. But would she ever be able to? She was just so afraid something would happen to keep them apart, and she couldn't bear the thought.

Their evening ended without further incident, with Katie successfully sneaking in after curfew. Later in bed, she relived every moment, every feeling. Lying on her back she stared at the ceiling; then she flipped over and buried her face in her pillow, grinning like an idiot, full of excitement about the future.

Over the next several weeks their relationship became the news of the school. One moment she and Jake were secretly smiling at each other; the next they were the rage of the rumor mill. Andrea grabbed Katie in the hall and propelled her to the girls' bathroom.

"You're with Jake! I knew it! Why didn't you tell me?" She sounded hurt. "I asked you at Trey's."

"We weren't together then. We're just—dating."

"Nobody's dated Jake Talbot. Not really. Oh, sure, Debbie Hawes was with him that one time, but that hardly counts. She forced herself on him and he took advantage."

Katie had forgotten the Debbie Hawes rumor. Now it

came back sounding ugly and sordid. "He took advantage?" she repeated.

"According to Debbie, it was the best night of her life. But he never cared about her." Andrea shrugged it off, unaware of Katie's growing uneasiness. "So, tell me, what's going on?"

"We—um—went to dinner," she answered distractedly, disturbed by sudden images of Jake in the arms of the notoriously buxom Debbie, writhing together. "And then we went canoeing."

"Canoeing! At his place? Then what?"

Her avid interest penetrated Katie's fogged brain. "I went home," she finished, leaving Andrea looking disappointed and unsure whether Katie was really playing square with the facts.

For her part, Katie just wanted to run somewhere and hide. As luck would have it the first person she saw was Debbie Hawes herself, and even though the girl was hanging on another guy's arm, her face turned up adoringly, all Katie saw was her silvery blond hair and the way her breasts thrust against her gray, deep V-necked sweater, offering an expanse of cleavage that Debbie was inordinately proud of.

She felt sick. The rest of that week, she berated herself for her ridiculousness. So what? Jake was his own person. Everyone had skeletons in the closet. So he hadn't mentioned Debbie. Big deal. Though it might look as if he had lied about never having any sexual gropings, he could have simply forgotten.

Yeah, right.

Nevertheless, she cheered for him at Friday night's game, her heart swelling with pride every time he got his hands on the football. She was going to have to pay more attention, she determined. If this was what he did, she would become an expert on football!

The season waxed on, and though she and Jake kept up a consistent dating pattern, apart from a few pecks on the cheek, there was no more amorous kissing. Katie couldn't help worrying about what that meant. One moment she was scared of him thinking she was too easy; the next she feared he wasn't attracted to her! It was a painful autumn, and as they moved into winter, she decided to work up the courage to talk to him about it.

Now people accepted that they were a couple, yet it was no more true than it had been in September, at least from Katie's point of view. What were she and Jake doing? Was this going to go on indefinitely?

Though she hadn't confided in Lisa again after that first time Katie didn't feel comfortable talking to her classmates about Jake. Screwing up her courage, she approached Lisa one Friday night while they were both arriving for their shift at the restaurant.

"You know I'm kind of dating Jake Talbot," Katie said by way of broaching the subject.

"Oh, yeah? Haven't slept with him yet, have you?"

"No!"

"Keep it that way."

"I am so tired of everyone reducing everything to sex!" Katie declared.

"Yeah, well, that's the way it was with me and Phillip, okay?" Lisa grabbed her Shoreline apron and tied it on as she stalked away.

That wasn't what Katie had wanted to hear. Grabbing her own apron, she dogged Lisa's heels until they were standing on the back deck of the restaurant which in late November was empty of customers and whose tables were stacked against the railing in a forlorn, forgotten row.

A stiff, chilly wind grabbed at them. "I didn't mean to bring up a bad subject," Katie apologized.

Lisa turned around. She wasn't that much older than

Katie, but her face already reflected a weariness of life that spoke volumes about her experience. "People like the Talbots don't look at people like us. You're just setting yourself up for a major fall. He'll hurt you. He'll use you first; then he'll hurt you. And don't believe anything he says, 'cause he'll lie, too."

"Jake isn't like that," she couldn't help defending, again.

This time Lisa didn't argue with her. She just eyed her in that way adults do when they encounter the folly of youth. Katie didn't like the feeling at all; but she had brought up the subject herself, and unless she wanted to back down now, she needed to make her own point.

"Nothing's happened like that," she told Lisa. "In fact, apart from one time when we kind of made out, he's left me alone."

"Kind of made out?" she repeated sardonically.

"That's all it was. But he apologized anyway, and now I don't know, I think he's afraid to make a move."

"Is that what you want?"

"I don't know!" Katie declared, throwing up her hands. "I just want *something* to happen!"

Their manager tapped on the french doors leading to the deck, frowning at them standing in the frigid night air. Lisa gave him the high sign, then turned back to Katie for a last piece of parting advice. "If you're smart, you'll stop seeing him right now. Believe me." To Katie's mutinous face, she added on a heavy sigh, "All right, fine. You're not going to. I can see that. Then, you just need to communicate your feelings. Tell him. The worst thing he can do is break your heart. But we can all get over that, right? Right."

Well, she had asked for that, she supposed. And though she had ignored Lisa's earlier warnings, she did heed her suggestion now. The very next time she was alone with

Jake, she broke right in with, "We need to talk about our relationship, if there is one. I mean, I need to know."

She could have maybe picked a better time and setting, but she had jumped in before her nerve broke. They were in his Corvette, driving to yet another party at Trey's. This had become a familiar pattern, and though Katie enjoyed being Jake's date and pool partner, it didn't offer a lot of private time, something Jake seemed to be scrupulously avoiding. So, when Jake said slowly, "What do you need to know?" Katie closed her eyes and drew a long breath, prepared to lay her cards on the table.

"I've been thinking about that night we went canoeing," she told him. "And . . . and what happened afterward."

His hands clenched the steering wheel, but he remained silent, waiting. When it came for the turnoff to Trey's, he shot right by, and while Katie watched in amazement, the last landmarks of Lakehaven disappeared behind them as they headed west, toward the coast.

Of course, he might turn off at any time. The Pacific Ocean was still about a two-hour drive. But he seemed rather intent. And where was there to stop between here and the coast, anyway? The road to Seaside was mainly two lanes, and one had to pass through the Coast Range before reaching the nearest beach town. Still, there wasn't a lot in between apart from a few forlorn roadside restaurants and gas stations, and though Katie recognized Jake had veered away from Trey's to give her his full attention, she had the distinct feeling they were on their way to the Pacific.

"Are we going to the beach?" she asked.

"Do you want to?"

"I have to be home by midnight," she said. She had gotten away with coming in late that first night. Her mother wasn't particularly vigilant where it came to her daughter. But Katie had chosen to keep some semblance of curfew in effect, though Jake hadn't exactly shown any interest in pushing the envelope, either.

Until tonight.

"We can make it to the beach, walk around for an hour, and still be home by midnight," he said.

"Okay."

"What were you getting at?" he asked, when she subsided into silence.

"I don't know. I just wanted to clear the air, I guess. Since that time, we haven't really—kissed—or anything." Her throat was parched with fear, her last words almost a squeak.

"Well, I didn't want to—I didn't want you to think that I was—you know—"

"Forcing yourself on me? It was hardly like that!"

"God, Katie, you just looked so scared," he expelled, as if he had been carrying around a ten ton weight.

"Scared! I was shocked. I couldn't believe I could feel that way. Well, I guess I was scared," she amended, "but I was scared of myself, not you! I've been worried you weren't really attracted to me."

"What?" He threw her a look of pure disbelief.

Laughter bubbled up into Katie's throat. "You never kissed me again like that except for a little brotherly peck! What was I supposed to think?"

"You had a pretty clear idea how I felt that night!" Jake pointed out, sounding as relieved as Katie.

"Did I?"

"You can't be that naive. You have to know that I wanted to just go for it! Generally speaking, I have more control."

"Really." She looked at him through the corners of her eyes.

"Really." He was emphatic.

"What about—Debbie Hawes?" she asked, knowing she was treading on thin ice, but desperate to hear the truth.

Besides, they might as well examine every issue between them once and for all.

"Debbie Hawes!" Jake muttered something beneath his breath, then stated flatly, "I never touched that girl. It was all in her head. She just made it up to say something, and I'm sick and tired of having it follow me around!"

Katie felt like a heel. "Sorry."

"No, don't worry about it. It's all over. You just wonder sometimes, what people are thinking."

"You know something?" Katie admitted. "Lately, every time I looked at her, I just felt sick. I didn't want you to want her and not me."

"God, Katie," he muttered, his jaw set. "I want *you*. Believe me."

"I want you to," she whispered.

Jake's hand reached across and covered hers, and they sped through the blustery night to the beach.

An hour wasn't enough time to do anything, but Seaside, in November at nine o'clock, even on a Saturday night, wasn't exactly a hubbub of activity. Shops were closed, and the promenade, which ran north and south along the beach, was drenched and slippery. After a few moments of standing in the slapping wet wind, they climbed back into the comparative warmth of the Corvette and cuddled as best they could, given their dropped-back, bucket seats.

His mouth was in her hair, and her ear lay over his heart. They kissed and caressed like two people starving for each other. Katie's bliss was pure and complete, and when Jake's deep voice whispered, "I love you," she shot back, "I love you more," so swiftly that they both collapsed into near hysteria.

"You're the only thing I want," he told her urgently, and Katie answered, "I feel the same way."

"So, what are we going to do?" he asked. Clearly the

question had been rolling around inside his head for some time.

"Just be together?"

"I don't want it to end," he muttered fiercely, as if he, too, had recognized that the disparity in their lives could tear them apart.

"It won't," she assured him with more passion than conviction.

"Graduation is six months away. I don't want that to be an ending."

She was ecstatic that he was thinking ahead, that their love for each other was strong and deep, and that Jake felt it should last much longer than high school. "It won't be an ending if we don't make it one," she assured him eagerly. "All we have to do is make it last!"

Thoughtfully, he tucked a strand of hair behind her ear. "Then, we'll make it last," he said, leaning in for another kiss, his voice so determined that Katie believed anything was possible. . . .

Now, however, she knew how hollow those promises had been. They had lasted throughout senior year, but then, once they had made love in the back of his miserably small convertible—and a few more times, for extra measure—those vows turned out to be as substantial as melting snowflakes. Jake had left her, and Lisa's words ended up haunting her for a long, long time.

Opening her lashes, Kate was surprised to realize it was still sunny and hot, and she was still thirty-six years old with a teenaged daughter and a difficult client somewhere in the adjacent building. Ducks paddled desultorily on the pond, and the world was just as it had been before her reflection.

Still, where Jake Talbot came in, Kate's resolve was solidified. No matter what happened with April's audition for Talbot Industries, she was not going to let him get to her in any way, shape or form. He was her past. A very distant, unimportant, best forgotten past.

And when are you going to tell him about April?

With a shudder, Kate rose from the bench, not liking her thoughts at all. The time would come, but it wasn't today. Today she had work to do, and as she examined the height of the sun, she realized she had better stop lollygagging around and get to it.

Chapter Six

"Oh, my *God!*" Delilah cried, jumping back from the table, hands pressed to her lips. "He tried to bite me! Did you see that!"

"He just stretched his neck," the director said in a long-suffering tone. "Turkeys do that."

"I can't—do this!" Abruptly she burst into tears.

Kate gazed anxiously at the cameraman who looked more amused than upset. The director, however, stuck two fingers in the collar of his shirt and jerked it away from his neck in frustration.

The turkey commercial was not going well.

She had come inside the building to find that her absence, though noted by April, who had wondered what had taken her so long, had not mattered at all. Delilah was being her usual difficult self, and Kate was fast losing patience with her at every level.

"Can I do something?" April whispered as her gaze followed the director.

"Just smile and be pleasant."

"Maybe I could talk to Delilah. You know, make her feel better, or something."

Kate half laughed. "Good luck."

"Let's try it again," the director said, heaving a sigh. "Max is a good turkey. He won't bite you. Just look him in the eye and say, 'Only the plumpest turkeys are from Tender Farms, so—'"

"—keep the weight off and you won't be picked.' I *know.*" Delilah looked mutinous. She finger combed her hair and inched up her chin.

Uh oh, Kate thought, stepping forward. "Could I get anyone something to drink? It's pretty hot in here."

The cameraman looked grateful. The director shot her an annoyed glance, then stopped and shrugged. "That'd be much appreciated," he admitted.

April smiled. The turkey chose that moment to go into his gobble-gobble routine, stretching his neck and wad- dling around the table. Delilah shuddered, but April walked up to him, looked him dead in the eye and said, "Hey, Max, only the plumpest turkeys come from Tender Farms, so keep the weight off and you won't be picked."

"You're hired," the director declared ironically, to which Delilah stamped her foot. Her face turned red with fury.

"Put that damn turkey back in position!" she shrieked.

Although resenting her tone, the director pointed for the cameraman to get back in position. The company's gofers quickly put the turkey in the center of the table. Delilah gazed in steely-eyed determination at her nemesis, who cocked his head, looking for all the world as if he were actually listening. This time she repeated the lines letter perfect.

"Cut!" the director called, amazed. "How was that?" he demanded of the cameraman.

"Good. Real good." He nodded.

"Take a break. We'll check it, but I think we're done."

Kate and April exchanged glances. Generally filming commercials required a ton of takes because anything could happen to just one print. But Delilah had ticked them off well and good.

"You want a job?" the director whispered at April. "You know something about talking turkey." He smiled.

"Ummm . . . thanks."

Delilah glared at her and said frostily to Kate, "I'll need an advance."

"We'll talk at the agency," was Kate's response. It was Rose Talent's policy never to advance monies to the persnickety talent. Bad business. Wait until the client forked over the money before paying out earnings. Delilah knew the rules; she was just flexing her political muscles which were flimsy at best.

With ill grace Delilah flounced out the door. By all rights she would be crying at Kate's desk before the day was over.

Kate and April followed after her, and the rest of the afternoon at the talent agency turned hectic. Kate was just about to call it a day when her phone rang and she heard from her accountant, Billy Simonson.

"Could we meet for a drink?" he asked.

Since Billy was happily married and a rather distant friend, Kate knew what having a drink together meant: bad news. Rose Talent Agency's finances had been shaky since Ben's death. Customers were afraid of change.

"What are you going to tell me?" Kate asked nervously.

Billy didn't bother making her feel better. "As you know, there are some financial issues we should go over."

"Things haven't gotten worse, have they?"

"There's that balloon payment ahead, Kate. You remember we talked about that."

"Yeah . . ." Kate was fairly adept at understanding financial statements. She knew there was a balloon payment for a loan on the business, but she had been determined to pull things together to keep operating soundly so she could make it. Now, she realized she wasn't exactly certain when it was due. "How soon?" she asked, in growing alarm.

"Not till the end of next year, but Kate, given projected revenue, I don't think you're going to make it."

"I just need a few more accounts," she murmured. *Or one really big one. . . .*

"Yeah, I know." There wasn't a lot of hope in his voice.

"I'll meet you at six at that cafe near your office," Kate told him.

"I'll be there," he responded grimly.

April stood outside the glass wall that divided Kate's office, talking with Jillian. She looked up and waved happily at her mother. Kate smiled back, but it felt forced.

I should keep Jake's tip money, she thought with a spurt of resentment, then was ashamed the thought had even crossed her mind.

Jake closed his eyes as he ran on the treadmill. Talbot Industries had recently added an exercise room complete with weight training machines and a juice bar. Jake himself wasn't much for indoor workouts. He preferred to run along the paths of several of Portland's parks; but today it was too blasted hot, and he was feeling strangely itchy and uncomfortable.

And he knew what the reason was. It had a face. And the face was Katie Tindel's.

Kate Tindel Rose, he corrected himself, stabbing the electronic button on the treadmill to increase his speed.

He didn't want to think about her, but she had occupied his thoughts almost nonstop since last night's encounter. He had gone to bed with her in mind and had spent a tense, restless night while his brain struggled to relegate her to some back corner where she had rested until he had seen her again. Then, this morning, while he was shaving, he had seen her face superimposed over his own image in the mirror.

Growling beneath his breath, Jake ran until sweat poured down his brow in rivulets. He swiped it away with his arm, realizing there was no way to outrun his memories. In fact, there appeared nothing left but to wallow in them awhile. Maybe then he could put some perspective on the whole thing.

With that in mind, he picked through the rubble inside his head where his memories of that long dead relationship lay. He recalled quite vividly that first time they had collapsed together on the sweeping back lawn of his parents' house. His body had been on fire, and had she not drawn back, he would have "gone all the way," to put it in high school lingo. He had felt no compunction to stop, and his heated desire had surprised him, especially since he had thought he was the master of his hormones since passing through junior high. He had congratulated himself, in fact, that he was in control of his sexual needs. As much as sex interested him—and it interested him a lot!—Jake had steered clear of involvements with females. A part of him had always known it would only create problems if he actually got entangled with one.

That didn't mean he hadn't groped around with some girls at summer camp. Hell, no. But when it came to Lakehaven girls, he was cognizant of the pitfalls like his brother never had been.

So, when Katie Tindel caught his eye, he had been foolish enough to believe she was a passing thing—nothing more than a momentary lapse. He liked her. He liked her company. She was certainly pleasant enough. And she was light-years smarter than the rest of the girls in his crowd.

He had asked her out on a whim, then been taken by surprise by her candor and humor. Still, he hadn't understood what was happening until that night by the lake shore. His blood had thundered in his head, his body on fire. Her skin had been so soft and pliant, and her lips trembling and sweet. He had brushed away her shirt with no effort at all, his mouth capturing one pert nipple in a hot suckling that brought her hands digging into his scalp, her body arching in surprise.

He thrust against her hard, time and again, uselessly through their clothes, mindlessly in his heated state. His tongue found the cavern of her mouth, and he pushed eagerly inside, matching his body's movements and undoubtedly making all kinds of desperate sounds in the process.

He even grabbed her hand to help in his own pleasure, a memory that had the power to dig at his conscience and embarrass him even now! Her tender, exploratory touch drove him wild, and he pushed himself on her like a rutting bull, wanting nothing more than to drive inside her warm sheath, consumed by images of how slick and tight and hot she would be.

He hadn't wanted to quit, and when he dimly realized her hands had stopped caressing him, that they had tightened into fists, the rest of her body following suit, as she strove for control, he only doubled his efforts. He didn't want to think. He wanted to make love. Fast and furious and damn the consequences. But his drugged conscience finally awakened and when he realized what he was asking—no, *demanding!*—he rolled away from her, consumed with guilt. Then, and only then, did he realize how far he had gone, how fast.

God, what a lack of control! Unbelievable!

Jake shook his head. Even now, years later, and in the midst of intense exercise, memories of those moments with

Katie had the power to bring on a physical reaction. If he didn't watch himself, he could have a hard-on to beat all hard-ons, right here! Checking his pulse, Jake pulled his thoughts back to a safer level.

But it was the night they had driven to Seaside and back that their relationship had taken a leap into hyperspace. While he had been torturing himself with the memory of his out-of-control behavior, Katie had apparently been worrying that he didn't want her. What a joke! He had backed off because he had been afraid he had scared her. She had taken it as a rejection.

Straightening it all out had been such a relief. He had dragged her into his arms, fighting the confines of his Corvette, but not caring in the least. From his heart the words had sprung forth, "I love you," and she had answered back in kind. He had clung to her like he never wanted to let her go, which wasn't that far from the truth, and it was after that night that they began making plans for the future.

But what do you know at eighteen? he asked himself now. Nothing. Not a damn thing. It was all misdirected feelings and vague notions of what the future would be. But it was powerful, nonetheless, and in those months between Christmas and graduation he had spent every moment he could with Katie Tindel, whispering plans for the future, kissing and touching and thrilling each other. They had discussed having sex—mature teenagers that they were then! he thought sardonically—but had decided to wait until they were "married." Since that was bound to be a long way off, they had circumvented the real thing with that silly wedding of their own.

But before that there had been a few little hurdles as well. His parents, for one. He had been reluctant to bring Katie home to meet them; he knew what their reaction would be. On Valentine's Day, though, he did the deed, and it was a fiasco from start to finish.

Katie had to work that night until eleven, so Jake planned to surprise her directly after school to give her her Valentine's gift. He drove her home most days anyway, but this afternoon he detoured away from Lakehaven High and headed east on Sunset Highway, toward Portland.

"Where are we going? I have to work at six," she protested.

"I know. It'll be quick."

It was the dumbest idea, really, since the temperature was in the mid-thirties and the skies were overcast and threatening rain, or maybe even snow. But Jake didn't think about that. It was Valentine's Day and he was with the girl he loved, and too bad about the weather.

He turned onto a two-lane road that meandered off the main highway into some rolling hills. Phillip, his brother, had told him about the old barn that was nearly condemned on an abandoned piece of property next to a small creek. Phillip was adept at finding out-of-the-way places to party.

So, Jake squired Katie up a gravel-strewn path to where the gray, dilapidated building sat like a tired, forgotten soldier. For a moment they both stared at the structure in mutual worry, but then it was Katie who shrugged and said, "It should be on a postcard," tugging Jake's hand and dragging him the last few steps to where they squeezed inside the lopping barn door.

The smell of musty hay and dirt greeted them, but the air was dry and the timbers seemingly firm. At least when Jake tested their strength they didn't groan and creak and act like they were about to collapse.

Katie looked down at the sack he toted in his left hand. "What's inside?" she asked.

It was dangerous. Jake had once again pressed his older

brother into service, and Phillip had done the deed with a knowing smile plastered all over his face. Reaching in the sack, Jake withdrew a bottle of champagne and two plastic cups. Katie looked at him askance.

"I hear it's terrible stuff," he admitted, following up with a bouquet of roses that he suddenly lifted from the rustling bag and presented to her with a flourish.

"They're beautiful!" she sighed, her eyes meeting his gaze above the bouquet, joy glimmering in their amber depths.

"You're beautiful," he rejoined.

"No, you're beautiful," she teased, and he grabbed her until she was laughing and writhing to get away from him as his fingers tickled her all over.

"Uncle! Uncle!" she cried, gasping for breath.

He released her ever so slowly, then poured them both a glass of champagne. They sipped it and discussed how champagne, wine and alcohol in general tasted like lighter fluid; then they exchanged their glasses for each other, falling into each other's arms as if the whole thing had been orchestrated from the start.

It was a quick event, all told, since Katie had to get back and they could easily freeze to death if they remained outdoors much longer. Plus, there was only so much making out either of them could stand without any real fulfillment, so they hurriedly left as daylight began to wane.

But when they got back to Lakehaven, Jake was unwilling to let her go. "Come to my house," he begged, and since he had never invited her before, Katie blinked at him several times, clearly unsure how to take him. "My parents will love you," he lied.

"Look how I'm dressed!" She gestured to her jeans and navy turtleneck sweater. His letter jacket completed the outfit as she had adopted it over the past few months, a move he heartily endorsed. He liked seeing her in it. He wanted the world to understand. She was his, and that was that.

"They're not going to care," he assured her.

He drove right to the house. The last time they had been on the property was when he had borrowed the canoe. His parents were rabid about him keeping up his grades, and their focus had narrowed to which college he would be accepted into and what courses would be best for him so that he could assume the role of president of Talbot Industries one day.

"Oh, Jake, I don't know . . ."

He overrode her protests by simply ignoring them. He didn't want to give her up. He wasn't willing to, just yet. She hung back as they stood on the porch together and Jake searched for his key. In one of those frustrating moments he couldn't immediately find it, so he growled an expletive, then yanked her close, his face buried in her hair.

Her arms slipped around his nape, and he kissed her neck and face. "I love you," Katie whispered, her mouth hot on his. "I love you more," he muttered back, holding her close, fighting the temptation to run his hands beneath her ribbed sweater and massage her breasts. It was torture, this frantic, quick rubbing of each other's flesh when nothing more could come of it. Yet, it was a sweet kind of madness, and when he pulled her hips up close to his, pressing his hardened sex against her in a way that left no doubt about his feelings, Katie's soft sigh of regret was like a flame to dry tinder. He wanted her. He *wanted* her.

And then the door swung inward.

It was so unexpected they both jumped, still locked in a tight embrace. It was his mother, staring at them with an expression of horror, until her manners took over and she said in her brittle way, "Well, Jake, why don't you and your—friend—come inside out of the cold . . ."

It had been a stupid, stupid thing to do, but in retrospect he wondered if he hadn't flouted convention on purpose, just to get a rise out of his folks. At the time, though, he was a slave to raging sexual needs, and they were all tied up with Katie. Now that he was at the house, he just wanted to be alone with her, but he was forced to sit in the living room with his mother across from him, Katie at his side. His father had parked himself in his den and seemed oblivious to their arrival.

When his mother looked inquiringly at Katie, Jake made the introductions. "Katie, this is Marilyn Talbot, and Mom, this is Katie Tindel."

"How do you do?" Marilyn said, to which Katie made appropriate responses.

Though Katie sat next to him on the couch, there was too much space between them. Jake chafed. With a familiarity he shouldn't have revealed, he moved closer to her, taking her hand with his. It showed a united front, and though Katie was dead quiet, Jake sensed that his mother got the message.

He couldn't remember the conversation, something about where Katie was going to college and what her parents did for a living. She was careful in her responses. Her father worked as an independent logger, and her mother filled in as a part-time checker at a grocery store.

"Maybe your father would like to meet Miss Tindel?" his mother suggested to Jake, and before Jake could protest she had risen stiffly from her chair and crossed to the den door, rapping twice, loudly.

His father appeared, a scowl on his features. He detested being disturbed when he was working. But when his mother whispered something about "Jake's girlfriend," Phillip squinted a glance in Katie's direction. He managed to cross the room and shake her hand, then pour himself a drink before he disappeared back into his lair. His mother, taking note, poured herself a heavy splash of scotch, something Jake had never seen before or since.

It felt like ages before Jake could herd Katie out of there, and then when he managed it, he said, "Come on," and dragged her toward the stairs and up to his bedroom.

"Jake!" she hissed, hanging on to the rail.

"Just for a minute," he insisted.

"Your mother'll call the cops!"

"Stop being paranoid."

He damn near had to haul her over his shoulder in the fireman's carry, but finally he got her safe inside his bedroom, shutting the door gently behind them.

"Do you want her to hate me?" Katie demanded.

"No. I just want to be alone with you for a couple seconds more."

And he wanted her to see his room, though he wouldn't have been able to admit it. Why, he couldn't say; but it was the only part of the house uniquely his, and he wanted Katie in every facet of his life.

Nervous as she was, she managed to glance around, noting the myriad of Little League baseball trophies, the football helmet given to him at the end of this season, and the books and paraphernalia he had amassed over the years. Her fingers touched on a picture of him holding up two, thirty-pound salmon.

"Fishing trip with my dad and Phillip."

"Looks like fun."

"All they did was fight."

Something in his tone arrested her, and the way her gold eyes looked into his soul was the real reason he loved Katie Tindel. She understood. They might be from two different worlds, but she understood him like no one else.

"Come on," he said, leading her back out of the bedroom and down the front stairs.

His mother waited in the entry hall, unsmiling and hold-

ing her drink between clenched fingers. Katie glanced
nervously at Jake, and he clasped her hand within his. They
stopped in front of his mother. He towered over her; but
she was on a level with Katie, and her austere, judgmental
regality made Katie lean toward him in support.

It ticked him off. This, then, was what was wrong with
his relationship with his parents. He wanted to yell at his
mother and tell her, "This is the girl I'm going to marry,
so stop being such a bitch!" He managed to hold his
tongue with an effort; but it put a pall over the ride back
to Katie's place, and when she began to climb from the
car, he grabbed her arm, holding her still for a moment.

"My mother's always like that," he apologized urgently.
"It's not you; it's her. She doesn't know how to unbend,
and I'm sick of it. It won't matter for us."

"Won't it?" She shed his letter jacket, laying it over the
passenger seat, a move packed with meaning.

Jake's jaw hardened. "No, it won't. You'll see."

Her lashes fluttered, hiding her expression, but he knew
she didn't believe him. He wasn't certain he believed it
himself; but come hell or high water he was damned sure
he was going to marry Katie Tindel, and Marilyn and Phillip
Talbot could just get over it!

That meeting made Jake realize more than ever that he
was fighting an uphill battle. Spring break arrived, and he
spent every moment he could with Katie, though with her
job and his parents' demands on him, that time was more
limited than he would have liked. But then the weeks
started counting down to graduation, and with each passing day came a fever of anticipation mixed with dread.
Changes were in the air. Serious changes.

And somewhere in there Jake conceived the idea to
"marry" Katie Tindel in the old, forgotten church.

It was a chance comment by his mother to a friend that
put it in his head. He was home, locked in his bedroom

where he spent most of the few hours he was forced to be at home, if he could, though Darcy, the Talbots' maid-cum-cook, had informed him in her sympathetic way that his presence was expected at dinner. A command performance, Jake knew, for when his mother decided to stand on ceremony, the rest of them had to salute and fall in line.

A couple Marilyn had known before she was married—Celia's parents, as it turned out—were visiting the West Coast for business, and she had made certain they stopped in Portland before their return. They were staying at one of Portland's nicest hotels, and they arrived in Lakehaven via limousine, an ostentatious touch that amused and delighted Marilyn.

As Jake headed downstairs and tried to slip past the living room where the adults were enjoying the cocktail hour, he overheard his mother say in an aggrieved way, "I wouldn't have allowed that wedding to stand. It wasn't legal, in the eyes of the state, so those two kids were just living together, no matter what you call it. Marrying each other doesn't count. You must have someone legally certified to perform a marriage."

"Oh, you're absolutely right!" Celia's mother gushed. At the time Jake had only known her as a rather round, easily swayed middle-aged women with too much money and too little sense.

"I told Dorothea if she wanted grandchildren who weren't bastards, she was going to have to force a wedding. Reciting vows of love is all well and good—" Marilyn's voice was withering—"but it doesn't stand up in court."

"What did Dorothea do?"

Marilyn snorted, her voice trailing away as she walked across the room. "Told her daughter she wouldn't get a dime unless she moved out or married him proper. They were married within a month."

The other woman sighed. "Still, it's kind of romantic, don't you think?"

"Silly vows of love by candlelight? It's for children with no sense."

His mother's words haunted him as Jake sat down at the table for dinner. He was the first one into the dining room, and he stared at the crisp white linen, fine china and crystal candlesticks. The candlesticks had been his grandmother's, a delicate woman who had shown a quirky sense of humor even as she was dying. She was the only person in the family Jake had ever really related to, unless you counted his brother, who had his moments now and again.

As he stared at the candlesticks, the wheels began turning in his brain. Candlelight, weddings, Katie in his bed once and for all. . . .

Then his brother suddenly strode into the room.

"Phillip!" Jake declared, surprised. He had been banned from the house, the last Jake had heard.

"The proverbial bad penny," Phillip responded insouciantly. "Think the folks'll care that I dropped in? What is this? Some special dinner?" He frowned at the elegant table array.

"Mother has friends from the East Coast." Jake shrugged. He was inordinately glad his brother had decided to show up, especially now, when the evening had looked like a big yawn before.

"Hey, Darcy!" Phillip called. "Why don't you set another place? I'm starved."

Jake lifted a brow of amusement. As Darcy complied, shooting anxious glances over her shoulder as she expected Jake's parents and guests to appear at any moment, Phillip lounged in the chair across from his brother. He looked like hell. His eyes were red-rimmed, and his waist was thickening. He had once been a fit, fairly handsome male, but already years of wasting his life had taken their toll.

At that moment the entourage entered the dining room. Marilyn couldn't quite conceal her gasp of horror at sight of her eldest son. Celia's parents hovered behind the Talbots, peeking over their shoulders, eager to see what calamity had befallen their friends. Phillip scratched his ear and said, "I'm Phillip Talbot, Jr., the uninvited guest. Could I get a drink, do you think? Or would that make everything even worse."

"You might have called," Marilyn managed, her lips tight. She seated her guests, ignored Phillip's request, then managed to monopolize the conversation with one brightly introduced topic after another.

Phillip didn't even care. He ate the succulent prime rib, potatoes and vegetables as if he hadn't seen food in a year, which was highly unlikely given the state of his girth. When a delicate, creamy flan was served, he wolfed it down. Jake's father eyed his son with displeasure that bordered on revulsion, and at that moment Jake almost envied his older brother's complete lack of social conscience. Wouldn't it be nice to flout convention, just once? To be out from under the thumb of parental expectation?

That's when the idea took root. The idea of a secret marriage appealed to him on many levels. He loved Katie and wanted to make her his wife, but he knew they were both too young. His parents, of course, would have a collective coronary at the idea, but that wasn't even the issue for Jake. He wanted to be able to provide for her, to be his own person. If that took a few years of college first, so be it.

But Katie Tindel was going to be his wife.

"Hey, Phillip," Jake said, corralling his older brother as soon as they could escape the dinner table. "Got a minute?"

"Bring a snifter of brandy to the back porch, and I've got an hour. In fact, bring the whole bottle. By the way, how was the champagne?"

"Gross."

Phillip clapped Jake on the shoulder, chuckled heartily, then headed out the back door while Jake went in search of the brandy. Luckily, his parents were touring the house with their guests, so he sneaked a half-full bottle and a crystal snifter off the corner bar, thrust them under his jacket and joined his brother outside.

It was a chilly spring night. Phillip, however, didn't appear to feel the cold as he lounged on the rattan outdoor furniture his mother had artfully arranged for this occasion.

Jake handed him the bottle, then the glass, to which he poured himself a healthy dose. "What is it?"

"This girl I'm seeing. Our parents would never give her a chance."

"And?" He gazed at Jake over the rim of his glass.

"And I'm going to marry her."

Phillip wheezed out a laugh. He practically buckled over in amusement. "You got a lot to learn, little brother," he advised. "You don't have to marry 'em."

"This girl's different," Jake explained tersely.

"They all are," he muttered ironically. "Trust me, I know."

Jake's envy of his brother died a quick and permanent death. Phillip saw issues only in terms of himself, and it didn't look as if he were likely to change. If Jake planned to "marry" Katie, he would have to find a way to handle it all on his own.

He came up with the idea of the old church when he happened to drive by that section outside the city on a windy day in late March. The church itself was locked up, but Jake figured it wouldn't be hard to break into. This wasn't his forte, generally speaking, but he was willing to step outside himself in the name of love.

When he outlined his idea to Katie, her eyes filled with glistening tears. "I'll get a dress," she whispered, and they set the date for a Saturday afternoon the following month.

The date dawned dark and gloomy, but with that feel of a storm approaching that makes one almost welcome it. The future had arrived in force, and Jake, dressed in a pair of black cotton slacks and a white shirt, threw his letter jacket on over the top to make himself appear more casual. He didn't want to have to explain things to his mother, should she somehow catch him on the way out.

But it was his father who arrested him as he stood with one hand twisting the front doorknob. "Where're you going?" Phillip, Sr., demanded.

"Out." Jake shrugged as if it were of no consequence. A faint *clink* sounded inside his pockets as the crystal candlesticks within knocked lightly against each other.

Jake swallowed. Two pilfered ivory candles and a book of matches rounded out the booty. Distantly, he remembered he needed to filch a Bible as well, but now it looked like the gig was up anyway.

"Just out?" his father questioned.

"I'm going to see Katie," he mumbled.

"Who's Katie?" his father asked, catching his mistake instantly as he said, "Oh, that girl."

"Yeah."

They stared at each other, both waiting for the other to offer more. Eventually Phillip sighed and gave Jake a desultory wave of goodbye. Jake headed for the bookcase, grabbed the family Bible, then let himself out into a wild, rain-driven afternoon and the promise of a wedding to the woman he loved. . . .

* * *

Now, heaving a sigh, Jake hit the automatic stop button
on the treadmill and turned from a fast jog to slow walk,
then eventually a dead stop. He glanced around the exercise room as he swiped at his sweating chest and neck,
glad that no one was paying any particular attention to
Talbot's president.

Grimly, he headed to the showers to wash up. He recalled
that wedding to Katie Tindel painfully. It was excruciating
to remember how long and hard he had worked on the
vows he had uttered that day. Now, as he remembered
pulling that crumpled piece of paper from his pants pocket
and reciting solemn words of love and commitment while
candles flickered and the rain beat outside, he felt almost
ill. He had been so callow. So *green!* He had loved her with
all that he was, his heart hers for the taking.

And she had taken it and stomped on it well and good.

Muttering an oath beneath his breath, Jake tossed off
his workout gear and stepped under the shower's hot,
needle-sharp spray. Never, *never,* would he allow any
woman to treat him like she had. He hoped, with a passion
that wasn't altogether healthy, that she and her lovely
daughter stayed out of his way.

He wanted nothing to do with either one of them.

Chapter Seven

Jake finished redressing and was leaving the exercise room when he ran into Phillip, who was just entering.

"Working out?" he asked his older brother sardonically. He knew Phillip's habits, and it was a pretty good bet he had never even seen the working side of a treadmill or weight machine.

"Nah. Well . . . yeah, maybe." He shrugged, glancing down at his gut. "Probably be a good idea."

"So, what are you doing?" Jake couldn't help asking. Phillip wasn't known for slaving away at the office. He didn't even have a specific job. Jake's father had just made it clear that as long as Phillip wanted it, he was to have a job with Talbot Industries. Jake complied, but it wasn't easy explaining what Phillip's function was to the other employees at the best of times. Today, while he felt unsettled and uncomfortable, Jake couldn't help needling Phillip a bit. After all, Talbot Industries had over a thousand hard-working employees who earned their pay. A loafing member of the Talbot family did not sit well with anyone.

"I'm getting ready for those auditions next week," Phillip answered.

"They're not till Tuesday," Jake responded irritably.

"What's that supposed to mean?"

Jake opened his mouth to tell him, then thought better of it. Phillip wasn't interested in becoming a full-fledged, functioning employee, so Jake would be just wasting his breath. Instead, he changed the subject. "We're meeting with Marcus Torrance and the other developers from Diamond Corporation this afternoon. Did you want to be there?"

Phillip hesitated. "Diamond Corporation?"

"The company that wants to do a joint venture on that property by the airport. Miniwarehouses. That kind of thing." Jake sought to jog his brother's memory. It was a multi-million dollar deal that had been in the works for months.

"Oh . . . yeah . . ." Phillip seemed to be off on his own train of thought. It irked Jake that he couldn't keep his mind on anything but the damned audition. "No, you go ahead," he said, unaware of Jake's growing impatience. "By the way, Pam's looking for you."

Pam was Jake's secretary. Nodding to Phillip, Jake headed down the dark green carpeting that led to the elevators. When he returned to his own offices, Pam looked up in relief. "There's some problem at the Beaverton strip mall. Sabotage."

"Sabotage? What do you mean?"

"I don't know. An officer called, and Gary wants you to get down there right away."

Gary was the foreman at the job site. Normally he handled all problems on his own. This, however, sounded more serious than most. "I've got that meeting with Diamond Corp. at three. Call Gary and tell him I'll be there as fast as I can, but I can't stay."

"Will do." Pam swung around efficiently in her chair and began dialing Gary's cell phone number.

Jake slipped into his own office. The place was accessed through double doors and was a masterpiece of natural cherry paneling and recessed lighting. His desk sat in front of the window, his back to a tremendous view of the Willamette River and four of Portland's downtown bridges. He glanced at his calendar and noticed a date with Sandra set for Friday night.

Groaning, he wiped a hand across his face. The last thing he needed was another verbal fencing match with her. Worse yet, he would have to dance his way around his disinterest in taking her to bed.

From that same, newly sensitive part of his mind rose the memory of making love to Katie in the confines of his old Corvette convertible. He recalled their limbs entwined and cramped, the smooth texture of her skin, her trembling sighs and choked giggles. He remembered slipping her ivory dress up long, creamy thighs and her fumbling fingers at his belt.

And then the moment of supreme surrender, when they had both trembled on the brink of fulfillment the instant before he had plunged inside her, covering her soft gasp with the fervent possession of his mouth. He had moved inside her in a dream, his senses thick, his body picking up a tempo as old as time itself. She was lush and womanly and all his, and with each movement they had cried out their love and passion until he had felt the rush of pure desire and spilled his seed inside her. . . .

Realizing his eyes were squinched shut, his hands clamped over the arms of his desk chair, his jaw hard as steel, Jake slowly lifted his lids, shocked by the power of his memories.

His black mood darkening further, he buzzed Pam on

the intercom. "Cancel all engagements for me this weekend," he ordered in a tight voice. "I'm going to the coast."

Billy Simonson wore a look of perpetual worry, his face long and hangdog. "A lot of your business departed with Ben," he reminded her. "You've got to come up with new clients or scale back."

"Scale back?" Kate murmured, not liking the sound of that.

"I know you don't have a lot of overhead. You're just a small operation. Ben piled a load of money into that business over the years and it managed to squeak by, but you've got your work cut out for you. It's been six months since his death. I don't mean to scare you, but you've got to do something or it's going die out from under you."

Kate considered in silence. Rose Talent Agency had once been a bustling establishment; it still was fairly healthy. But Ben's illness had forced Ben to turn his attention away from keeping it perking along, and Kate hadn't had the control to change things until it was too late. She had spent the last few months searching for a new account. A big account. Something to bring them back. A company that would hire exclusively from their agency.

But it had all been wishful thinking. She refused to consider Talbot Industries. Jake Talbot would never get into that kind of relationship with her. She would have to work on someone else from some other company. Barring that, it would be nice to have one of her actors or models suddenly shoot into fame and bring in hefty commissions.

Kate drew a breath. "I know it's bad, but just how bad is it?"

"Your house is paid for. Ben saw to that. And right now the business is surviving, but you're not going to have much to live on unless you improve sales."

"Isn't that the nature of business?" Kate questioned ruefully, wishing she had paid more attention while Ben was alive. That wasn't quite fair, however, since her husband hadn't exactly been forthcoming about the details.

"I'll do what I can," she murmured as they parted. Billy's assessment only intensified the feelings she had already had about the business.

It was a joke, really. Everyone thought she had married a rich man old enough to be her father. The latter might have been true; the former was far from the truth. Ben had been successful in a moderate way, and that had been okay with Kate. She hadn't wanted a man loaded with money. The Talbot family had cured her of that! She had only wanted someone to love and take care of her and her daughter. Ben had done his best to provide that. It was her fault if the relationship had been less than storybook perfect, not Ben's.

She picked up some groceries and headed home, sighing as she saw April's boyfriend's beat-up cream-colored Chevy parked in the driveway. Ryan was a nice kid, but Kate couldn't help being nervous. After all, she had made critical mistakes at April's age; she wanted better for her daughter.

"Hello, Mrs. Rose," Ryan greeted her when she walked in.

"Hi, Ryan. Want to stay for dinner?"

"Sure." He blinked several times, surprised because Kate wasn't known for inviting him to stay. She spent most of her time being polite and hoping he would just go home.

While Kate put together a salad and baked chicken, Ryan and April snuggled on the couch and laughed as they channel-grazed on the family room TV. *Ben would have had a fit,* Kate thought. As much as he had embraced April as his own, her arrival into the teen world had been a shock. Ben's autocratic nature had reared up and given full play.

April had ignored him.

Kate glanced at the money—Jake's money—now stacked behind the telephone at the kitchen desk. It irked her that he could throw bills down without a qualm. Worse, she knew April was right; it had been an unconscious thing. He hadn't meant to make a statement. He had just been in a fog.

Thinking about him caused a shiver to slide down her spine. Kate finished the meal and called Ryan and April to dinner. The three of them sat down, and Kate surreptitiously examined her daughter's boyfriend as she ate. He was about six feet tall with thin, straight, longish hair. His interest in guitar consumed him, and he possessed a pair of sorrowful, deep brown eyes to match his musical soul.

You've grown cynical, my dear.

Yes, well . . . that was true. But the pitfalls of parenting loomed dark and deep. She was happy he was planning to go to college. She hoped to heck he didn't change his mind.

Her glance darted once again to the money. What would Jake think about Ryan?

Of course, a better question was what would he think about having a daughter he had never been told he had sired?

"What's the matter, Mom?" April asked.

"Nothing. Why?"

"You're grimacing."

Kate swallowed, carefully schooling her features. "I'm just thinking about some things," she offered lamely.

"You know how I told you about Ryan's dad? He's looking forward to meeting you."

"April!"

She shrugged sheepishly. "He's a really nice guy."

Kate stared at her daughter in horror; then her gaze drifted to Ryan. "I'm sure he is," she said tactfully. "I'm just not interested in—dating right now."

"That's cool," Ryan agreed, tucking into his chicken.

"No, it's not." April threw him a dark look which he missed completely. "You've got to give yourself a chance, Mom."

"I don't need a matchmaker," Kate said sternly.

"But, Mom—"

"Nope." Kate wagged her finger at her daughter. "I'm not interested."

"You should be."

"Let me rephrase that: I'm not ready."

April clamped her lips shut. Her thoughts churned so hard inside her head, Kate could practically see them at work. "When was the last time you really felt something for someone?" April finally delivered. "I know you and Dad appreciated each other, but it wasn't there, was it?"

Kate was appalled that her daughter could read her so clearly. "I don't think Ryan needs to hear this."

"I don't mind," he said unhelpfully.

"Don't you want to be in love?" April asked her, her tone urgent and serious.

This was getting way out of hand. "Who says I wasn't?" she retorted.

"I know you weren't."

"Since when are you such an expert on romance?"

"Mom . . . ," April chided.

Kate couldn't think of an answer. It didn't seem right that her daughter was so on the mark, and it still wasn't any of April's business anyway!

"I just know that you were missing something," April went on doggedly. "And you know it, too. So, I think you should get out more. Try to think back to when you felt so excited to be with someone that you couldn't think of anything else." She gazed thoughtfully at Ryan, who seemed miles away from the conversation.

Kate remained silent. The last time she had felt anything like that was with Jake.

Jake, Jake, Jake! Everything comes back to him.

Kate opened her mouth for another volley of arguments, then closed her jaw again, more thoughtfully. What was she fighting? What did it matter?

"Okay," she conceded.

"Okay?" April couldn't believe her ears.

Kate nodded.

"You mean, okay, you'll go out with Tom—Mr. DeSart?"

Kate smiled in surrender, then said, "So, what do you think about that, Ryan?"

He started, then glanced up. After a moment of heavy concentration, he said, "Cool," and that pretty much decided it.

Jake's shoes crunched on broken glass as he walked with Gary through the vandalized rooms of the strip mall. Someone had broken through the back windows of several stores, stolen merchandise, then hacked away at the fixtures. The officer in charge, Detective Marsh, was convinced it was the work of juvenile delinquents.

"If they'd just planned on robbing the place, they would have slipped in and out, but they took an axe to that counter and broke out the lights and mirrors." Detective Marsh gazed tiredly around, as if he had seen it a thousand times before, which he probably had. "Vandalism. It's probably kids."

Jake was silent at the sight of the destruction. Talbot Industries had built the strip mall last spring and had filled up each store with reliable tenants. "It's senseless."

"Everything kids do is senseless."

Jake didn't entirely agree with the detective's cynical assessment, but he wasn't about to argue. He found the whole scene depressing.

Phillip pushed his toe against some splintered glass lying on the floor. To Jake's surprise—which was unending when it came to his brother—Phillip had decided to join him on this foray to the damaged strip mall. His face was grim, and he seemed even more disturbed than Jake.

"You never know what kids'll do," he said after a long moment.

Detective Marsh silently agreed, and Jake glanced at his watch. "Thanks," he told the detective, then headed outside to his waiting Bronco. All he wanted to do was clear out of here and head for some peace of mind at the beach.

But Gary, his foreman, caught up with him before he could escape. "A mess, isn't it?"

"Yeah. What do you think happened?" he asked the older man.

Gary shook his head. "I don't know. It's like someone's mad at us."

"At us?" Jake questioned, though he knew what Gary meant. If it had been random theft and vandalism, it wouldn't have been so targeted to the fixtures that were part of the building itself. None of the merchants' inventory seemed to be damaged, which was certainly strange. Generally perpetrators weren't so discriminating.

Phillip crossed the lot in their direction, and Gary's expression darkened. He had no use for the "playboy executive," a tag Jake had once overheard him use when referring to Phillip. Though Gary was scrupulous about keeping his thoughts to himself around Jake, he had been known to grumble once in a while to others, so his feelings about Phillip were no secret.

"Have we got any angry tenants?" Jake asked the foreman as Phillip joined them.

"What?" Phillip gazed at Jake as if he had gone mad. "What do you mean? You think someone did this to *us?*"

"It's a theory," Jake stated flatly.

"I don't know of anyone in particular," Gary said slowly, his brow furrowed in thought.

"Nobody's after us!" Phillip declared. "The damage was done to the tenants!"

"The damage was done to the fixtures. And I might buy it if whoever did it had a grudge against *one* tenant, but look around you." Jake swept his arm to encompass the length of the strip mall. "Some ten stores and nearly every one of them's been hacked at."

"And robbed," Phillip argued. "That's their inventory, not ours."

"What was really taken? All total, the thieves got away with a couple of thousand dollars of stuff, tops," Jake pointed out. "But the damage to the property—it's into the tens of thousands."

"All covered by insurance."

"It's malicious intent, Phillip," Jake told his brother in a tone that brooked no argument. "And if Detective Marsh is worth his salt, he'll come to that conclusion, too."

"Well, maybe it's one of the tenants themselves," Phillip huffed, unwilling to be wrong.

"No way." This was from Gary.

"What makes you so sure?" Phillip demanded.

Gary shrugged. "They're just trying to make a living, like the rest of us. Why would they hack up their stores? It's not like insurance money's going to get them anything better." He gazed back at the wreckage. "It's flat out mean, if you ask me. And a heck of a clean-up job, too," he added.

Jake nodded grimly. "We're going to have to start on repairs right away."

"Got a crew already scheduled," Gary assured him.

"Let's just pray this is the last of it," Phillip said before he headed for his car.

Jake and Gary watched him leave. Instead of giving Jake hope that his brother was finally coming around, Phillip's interest in the sabotage bothered him. It didn't jibe with everything else.

With an effort he shrugged off the niggling worry. He shook hands with Gary, glad someone was completely trustworthy, then headed for the meeting with the principles from Diamond Corporation regarding the joint venture between Diamond and Talbot to build miniwarehouses. Diamond's offices were located in downtown Portland about seven blocks from Talbot Industries. For reasons he refused to speculate on, Jake swung off the freeway and cruised through the northwest industrial district until he passed the building where Rose Talent Agency was housed. He drummed his fingers on the steering wheel as he waited at a light, his thoughts distracted. Kate managed to keep occupying his mind all right, and it bugged him to no end. Even in the face of looming business problems, he could count on memories tweaking his brain.

Despite all his vows to the contrary, he toyed with the idea of stopping in to see her. Then he wanted to kick himself.

What in God's name would he say? *I can't get you out of my mind. I've been thinking about you constantly. You're still as beautiful as I remembered and I want a second chance.*

Jake drew himself up short. A second chance? Not in this lifetime! He must be starved for affection to be thinking such thoughts! She was just another woman from his past, like all the others he had burned through in college, and he would be damned if a little misty nostalgia was going to get to him.

Growling under his breath at his own susceptibility, Jake yanked the wheel of the Bronco away from Rose Talent Agency and Kate Rose. He was through romanticizing about her. He was through being an idiot.

It was time to switch his brain back to the job ahead, and then a weekend by himself at the beach to put everything else back in perspective.

On Friday evening Kate found herself wishing she hadn't been quite so hasty. A date was the last thing on earth she wanted. She *wanted* to get out of town. She *wanted* to get away.

But instead she was pacing her kitchen floor, waiting for Ryan's father, Tom DeSart, to appear.

April was thrilled and hovered around Kate like a yenta. "This is a new start," she told her mom, examining Kate's choice of dress critically. Kate wore black slacks and a cream-colored, short-sleeved top. Her hair was up in a casual bun which April wanted to get rid of. "You don't have to look so much like a grown-up," she complained.

"I like being a grown-up."

"Yeah, but Ryan's dad . . ."

Kate stopped in the midst of threading the loop of a brushed silver earring in the shape of a sunburst through her pierced ear. Something sounded fishy. "April," Kate warned.

April made a face. "Well, he's a little unconventional."

"You're scaring me."

"No, no. Nothing bad. He just likes to dance, and he's really big on the tango."

Kate lifted her brows. "Well, okay, as long as he doesn't expect me to be Ginger Rogers."

"He's into the arts, y'know. Like that's why Ryan's so big with the guitar. His dad paints and lectures on art appreciation."

"It sounds like the evening's going to be more interesting than I expected."

"He's got a ponytail," April added, as if she had dropped a bomb.

Kate threw back her head and laughed. "Oh, my God. A ponytail! That's it. The date's off!"

"I just wanted to warn you," April grumbled a little, though the dimple in her cheek deepened as she fought a smile.

"It's just a date," Kate assured her, waving her daughter's worries away. "To be honest, I'm relieved. I was worried you'd hooked me up with a suit."

"If you want a suit, look no farther than Jacob Talbot! I mean, you were involved once and he's gorgeous!"

Sometimes April's innocent comments cut like a hot knife through butter. "We just knew each other in high school. That's all," Kate muttered repressively.

"Yeah, but, so what? Oh, wait . . . is he married?"

"I . . . I don't really know," Kate realized with a funny little jump of her heart. "I just assumed he wasn't. He was engaged once, I know."

"He didn't seem married," April mused.

"Well, I don't care if he is, or he isn't." She gave April a knowing look and added, "Now, there's a man who's *definitely* not my type."

"Oh, come on, Mom!"

"I mean it. Tom DeSart with the ponytail is just fine, thank you very much."

"You dated Mr. Talbot once."

"What is this? I thought you wanted me to fall head over heels for Mr. DeSart."

"I'm just saying, keep your options open. You never know what can happen," April pointed out patiently.

"Ain't that the truth," Kate muttered, slipping on the other earring and surveying herself in the mirror. She had on a bit more makeup than normal, and her golden eyes were shaded and hinted at secrets. April quickly pulled down a few tendrils of Kate's carefully scraped back hair.

"Hey!"

"You've just got to loosen up a bit." She met Kate's eyes in the mirror, examining the soft curls that wisped against her mother's neck. "Isn't that better?" she asked anxiously.

"Yes," Kate admitted with a reluctant smile.

The front doorbell chimed, and April jumped to answer it. "He's here!" she sang out.

Kate's jittery nerves kept right on jittering, but when April admitted Tom, she breathed a sigh of relief. He was five foot ten, tops, and his expression was calm and benign. He was about as unthreatening as a person could be, and after delivering April a hug, Kate climbed in beside him in his rather dilapidated Jeep.

"Did you get the same pressure I did to go on this date?" Tom asked with a smile.

"Yes!" Kate expelled, glad he had brought it up first.

"I told 'em I'd humor 'em. I figured you'd be an uptight businesswoman," he explained.

"Just about *out* of business," Kate murmured.

Tom was quick on the uptake. "You got money problems?"

"My accountant just gave me a talking to, and I have to increase sales. Easy, right?" she asked ironically.

"Hardest thing on God's green earth. I sell watercolors, and it's about all I can do to keep this thing runnin'." He affectionately patted the dashboard of the Jeep. "I'm always takin' it out to some godforsaken strip of country, and it's startin' to get tired." He shrugged. "But it's what I do."

"As long as you're happy, that's the main thing."

"Yeah, I am." He slid her a thoughtful look.

They ate dinner at a small cafe, and Kate noticed Tom carefully avoided all forms of red meat. He also stayed away from chicken and fish, and finally admitted he was a true vegetarian. Their conversation ranged from politics to their children, but no topic was dug into with gusto.

As the evening ended, Kate stuck out her hand to say goodnight, and Tom seemed relieved at the handshake. "I'm seein' someone," he admitted. "She's an artist, like me, but I just haven't introduced her to Ryan yet."

"No problem," Kate said, taking no offense.

"The kids were so gung-ho about us havin' a date that I couldn't say no. And I'm glad I didn't," he added. "But I thought you should know."

"This was fun," Kate assured him. She was relieved that this one date wasn't going to turn into a complicated thing. "Could you do me a favor?"

"What?"

"Maybe you ought to tell your son about your friend, so my daughter will get off my back."

He laughed and nodded. "You're a good lady," he said.

Kate smiled and waved as he drove away. She stood on the front porch letting the warm wind blow at her chignon, wishing for something she couldn't name.

Inside, she fixed herself a cup of tea and waited for April to get home from the movies. A feeling of melancholy stole over her. Okay, so she wasn't inherently suited for Tom DeSart, big deal. There were other men out there. And who needed a man anyway? She certainly didn't.

Plumping the sofa pillows with more energy than finesse, Kate prowled the room, but her sad mood wouldn't lift. Once again she felt like getting away, but it was easier said than done. She didn't want April to stay home alone. She might trust her daughter, but she had heard of too many teen parties that started innocently enough with just a few kids, then turned into raging bashes. However, Jillian would probably come house-sit if she asked. She had done so at a moment's notice in the past.

But where can I go?

The beach. She hadn't been there in over a year. Longer perhaps, since it hadn't been Ben's favorite vacation spot by a long shot. Ben had preferred dryer climes and resorts laced with golf courses. Oregon's beaches were notoriously overcast every season, and in the winter, wet and stormy.

But it was August, the one month of the year you could almost count on the weather. And what did she care anyway? If the rains came, so be it. She could stay inside her motel room with a good book and make a couple quick trips for razor clams and Dungeness crab.

By the time April showed up, Kate was decided. "Jillian's on her way over," she said. "She's going to house-sit while I take a trek to the beach, unless you want to go with me."

"Tonight? Is Tom going?" April asked.

"NO!"

April pulled back a bit at Kate's reaction. "Uh oh. The date was a disaster?"

"No, no. We're just not that compatible. We're too different, but we had a great time."

"Really?"

"Yes, really. But believe me, that's it," Kate said firmly.

"Oh, Mom, give it a chance!"

There was no talking to her. "Yeah, well . . . ," she murmured. She would wait until Tom talked to Ryan before she told April that Tom was seeing someone else. "So, how about it? You want to go to the beach?"

April glanced at the clock, squinching up her nose in a familiar gesture that meant she was about to let her mother down. "I'd kind of like to hang around here," she admitted. "Jillian doesn't have to come over."

"I think I'd feel safer, just the same," Kate said dryly.

"Nothing would happen!"

Kate half laughed. "Jillian's desperate to do a favor for me because *she's* trying to set me up on a date with a friend of hers. I swear, between the two of you I don't get a moment's peace!"

"Who's her friend?" April asked suspiciously. "You didn't like Ryan's dad, did you?"

"I told you, he was great. Stop fussing." Kate uttered a sound of frustration. "This is your last chance. I'm heading for the beach."

"This is weird, Mom. You never just take off at a moment's notice."

"Yes, I do. Jillian's come over here before in a flash."

"Not for a weekend to the beach!"

Realizing there was no way to explain, Kate hugged April and gave her a kiss, then reached for her carryall. "I'll call and tell you where I am as soon as I get there. And you be good," she added with mock sternness.

"If I can't be good, I'll be careful," April replied insouciantly.

"Oh, April . . ." Kate gave her a look and headed out the door.

Chapter Eight

Dark waves swept over the beach to end in white, frothy edges. Pinpoints of light dotted the jut of land at the south end of the beach where megahouses were currently being built. Seaside, Oregon, had been a vacation resort at the turn of the century, gradually diminishing in desirability as it grew shabbier and shabbier. Its neighbor to the south, Cannon Beach, sprang up to become the beach of choice. Trendier, it was the place to go during Kate's youth, its shopping and brighter look drawing huge crowds while Seaside seemed like a forgotten and less-loved stepsister.

But in recent years there had been a rejuvenation. Seaside's famed "turnaround," the landmark end of the Lewis & Clark trail, was still a popular place to visit. Shops were sportier, newer, dressed up. Real estate skyrocketed, and the once boiling carnival-like atmosphere of corn dogs and kiddie car rides and Coney Island sideshows had slowed to a simmer of taffy shops, espresso stands and just an occasional bumper car ride or go-cart track.

Kate stood on the promenade near the turnaround. The

night was cool but bearable. People milled around the swing sets on the beach or sat by fires they had built in pits they had dug into the sand. In her line of vision a couple lay on a blanket about fifty feet away, occasionally leaning close to cuddle and kiss, then lying back to stare at the stars.

Kate had driven to the coast in a near daze, the two-hour trip seeming almost instantaneous. She had surfaced on the edge of town when she had connected with a snarl of Friday evening traffic as vacationers surged through the streets. It had never occurred to her that she might find it difficult to rent a room, but after passing several No Vacancy signs, she realized how naive she had been.

She had rushed out of Portland with no thought except escape. Now she rued her impetuousness. She supposed she could drive south, toward Cannon Beach, but she imagined it would be much the same thing. She had parked her Mustang in a lot behind several shops, lucky to find a parking spot at all; then she had strolled toward Broadway, the main street which ended at the turnaround.

Now, backtracking, she weaved her way through the crowds to a burger spot which played 50s' music and seemed to be a shrine to Elvis. It sported sliding glass doors street side, pushed wide tonight so that the noise and smells from outside mixed with the sounds and scents of frying burgers and french fries on the inside. Kate grabbed one of the cafe tables near the sidewalk, luckily vacated just as she had walked in. Holding the plastic-coated menu before her eyes, she decided she wasn't hungry at all, but since she was occupying space, she told the gum-popping waitress she would take a Coke and curly fries.

She wished April had joined her. It was all well and good to get away from it all, but she was feeling decidedly lonely right now. She didn't want to think about work, and she didn't want to think about the future. April was about to start her senior year, and when that was finished, what then?

The curly fries were delivered with a hurried thump, the Coke with a little more care. Selecting a french fry, Kate squirted some ketchup in the grease-spotted paper tub that housed her fries, dabbed desultorily and munched without much real enjoyment. Idly, she watched passersby. Unbidden, memories of the night she and Jake had pledged their love to each other swirled inside her head. It had been inside his sports car, parked not two blocks from here. She remembered fogging up the windows while they kissed and cuddled and petted and generally acted like romantic idiots.

Of course it had been nearly Christmas, and the weather had been frigid and stormy. They hadn't actually gone to the Talbot's beach house then; that had come later. But it was a momentous night in spite of that, for their feelings had been placed on the table once and for all. It had been the beginning of the end.

The beach had always held a special significance for her; she could see that now. And whenever she had felt the urge to come here, she had been secretly glad Ben didn't want to join her. Seaside was hers and Jake's, and though it was a silly, romantic fantasy she couldn't quite shake; it was hers and hers alone. And she wanted it to remain that way.

She would come here about once a summer. All the while April was a toddler and into elementary school, the two of them would manage to sneak a weekend at the beach together. They were some of Kate's fondest memories, although now she could admit there had always been that element of "Jake" that had been a part of it, too. It was like a pilgrimage, a trek made to the memory of April's father, Kate's one-time love, and if she had spent too much time standing on the prom outside the Talbot's house, remembering, at least no one knew about it but her.

And it wasn't like she still loved him or anything. Heavens, no! But it wasn't possible for her to completely burn those memories of him out of her brain, so once in a while she wallowed in them. Big deal.

However, tonight she felt differently. She had *seen* Jake again, for pete's sake, and consequently thoughts of him and the time they had spent together at his beach house were very close.

Kate paid for her food, then made her way back toward the turnaround. Lights illuminated a swath of beach, but Kate couldn't help glancing south down the prom to where she knew the Talbots' house stood. With the escalation in real estate prices, the property had undoubtedly zoomed in value. It had been worth a small fortune even in her youth, beachfront property selling for a premium.

Lifting her face to a soft breeze, Kate made herself concentrate on dollars and cents, refusing to remember how she and Jake had spread a blanket on the sand just outside his parents' house so many years ago.

Well, a lot had changed since then, hadn't it?

Tucking her hands inside her lightweight jacket, Kate strolled down the promenade, her heart beating a rapid tattoo as she passed the low river-rock wall that ran the perimeter of the Talbot property. A wrought-iron gate opened to a flagstone path which led to the wide front porch. River-rock columns held up the roof which sloped skyward to those upstairs rooms where she and Jake had made love.

Stop it! Kate berated herself, infuriated. Trips down memory lane were just fine, but she had about had her fill. Just because she had laid eyes on Jake again for the first time since she was eighteen didn't mean the earth had stopped spinning. It was bound to happen eventually, wasn't it?

They lived in the same city, for crying out loud, and they each ran a well-known business. Okay, hers wasn't even an iota as well known as Talbot Industries, but that didn't mean Rose Talent didn't have a name. Heavens, no. There wasn't a talent agency in Portland with a better reputation. She was just in a temporary downturn, that's all. It didn't mean she was completely down and out.

So, it had been just a matter of time until she and Jake crossed paths. Actually, it was a miracle it hadn't happened before. Portland wasn't that big. The situation was as simple as that.

As Kate stared upward to the wide dormer that opened onto the master suite of the Talbot beach house, a light burst on. With a gasp, Kate shrank into the shadows. Someone was there! As she watched, a dark form stood in relief against the yellow, rectangular square of light. A familiar silhouette. Jake Talbot, himself!

Instantly Kate wanted to hide. She was standing directly in front of his house, bare and distinguishable, she was certain. She turned to and fro, feeling like a criminal. Where? Where? Without conscious thought she turned to the beach itself, half running, half stumbling down a weed-choked path that bumped over uneven sand hills. The flat stretch of damp sand, compacted by the ocean, seemed far away.

She ran like the devil himself were chasing her. Realizing how ridiculous she was behaving, she muttered, "You idiot!" beneath her breath at the same moment she began to slow her steps. Her lungs were bursting. Thinking of what her sudden race for the beach might have looked like to the man backlit in the window, she groaned in self-disgust, then lost concentration just long enough to miss a step. She tried to catch her balance, failed, and a second later her right ankle buckled.

"Uh!" Kate grunted in anguish as hot pain shot up her

leg. She crumpled facedown in the sand with a moan. She had twisted her ankle again, and she could tell she had really done it this time.

She lay still then, feeling her heart beat in her sprained ankle. It was a familiar, dull ache that brought with it a host of other memories. "Oh, God," she murmured, covering her head with her arms. She wanted to laugh. She was so horribly *stupid!* But the sound that escaped her lips was more like a sob, and she prayed to everything holy that no one had seen her demented dash, and that she could somehow rise up and hobble back to her Mustang unaided.

But as each second ticked by she felt her ankle grow tighter and tighter within her shoe, and she recognized with miserable defeat that she was going to need some help.

Jake swirled a snifter of brandy absently between his palms, staring into its amber depths. He was annoyed at himself. He had run out of Portland as if he'd had a pack of dogs at his heels. What was this sudden aversion to seeing Sandra? And when had he been unable to face a situation?

The answer: never. He had always been the one to address each problem as it arose. Not like Phillip.

He sighed, swallowing a deep gulp of the fiery liquid, grimacing as it burned its way down. Phillip was the one who had turned him on to brandy that night on the porch so long ago. Maybe they were more alike than he wanted to admit.

His meeting with the principles of Diamond Corporation had gone well. Marcus Torrance, the company's president, was a no-nonsense individual who liked to keep meetings short and concise. This suited Jake just fine, and they had concluded their business in record time. Then, thirty minutes after shaking hands with Marcus, Jake had been on his way to his condo to change clothes and pick up his bag. However, Phillip had caught up with him at his designated parking spot, and Jake, who had dealt more with his brother at Talbot this past week than in all the time they had hitherto worked together, was in no mood to be slowed down.

"What?" he had demanded, when Phillip straightened from his position of lounging against Jake's car.

"How did it go with Diamond Corp.?"

"Fine." Jake's brows slammed together. He didn't understand Phillip at all. "I asked you earlier if you wanted to join us."

"I know." He nodded as if he had been giving it serious consideration. "I feel I should—get more involved now."

Catching the aroma of liquor, Jake asked with a sinking sensation, "When did you start drinking today?"

"I've had one drink." Phillip was affronted. "I came to ask you if you wanted to join me for another."

"No, thanks. I'm heading to the beach."

"Tonight?" He gaped. "What about Sandra?"

"What about her?" Jake demanded.

"I thought—she gave me the impression you were getting together tonight."

"You talked to her today?"

"She's involved with the Talbot ads. I talk to her damn near every day," he added without much enthusiasm.

"Your choice," Jake reminded him. He waited a moment, but Phillip seemed in no great hurry to be on his way. It occurred to Jake that his brother may have had a few more drinks than "one." "Can I drop you somewhere?"

"I'm just heading over to the Gemini Bar." He hooked a thumb in the general direction of the street.

"Catch a cab home," Jake suggested.

"Always," his brother said, lurching away from Jake's Bronco. He managed to walk fairly steadily in the direction of the bar, but it didn't mean he was sober. Consequently, thoughts of Phillip had occupied Jake's mind almost all the way to the beach.

Okay, that wasn't entirely correct, he reminded himself with a painful little dig of conscience. *Kate* had occupied his thoughts, though he would give a hell of a lot not to admit it. His worry over Phillip had actually been underneath those recollections of his long lost love, and of the two subjects, Jake would have much preferred to think about Phillip.

But what did it matter now? The beach house had welcomed him like an old friend, and Jake had felt a sense of relief and well-being sorely missing in his life these days as soon as he had crossed the threshold. He had tossed his bag on the bed in the master suite, then searched out the liquor cabinet and discovered an unopened bottle of Napoleon brandy—his father's weakness as well.

Now he knew he needed to find himself some dinner; he had subsisted on the brandy from the moment he had arrived, and if he didn't get some food pronto, he was going to crash face-first to the floor. So much for worrying about his older brother's drinking problems!

Still, he wasn't really ready to move yet. It was a quiet pleasure to stand in the dark at the window watching the ceaseless waves. Cracking open a pane, he let a bracing August breeze snatch at his hair. Salt tang tickled his sinuses. He breathed deeply, swallowing, closing his eyes briefly.

Enough, he warned himself, setting the snifter down a bit unsteadily. It wasn't like him to indulge like this. Not Jacob Talbot. Not anymore. Circumstances had forged him into a harsh corporate executive with no close friends. He could be accommodating if it suited him, but he could be as unforgiving as a North Sea storm as well.

He knew it and didn't care. He didn't—in fact—care about much of anything. So, why was he having these yearning, nostalgic thoughts about Kate Rose? And why was he worrying about Phillip, who certainly wouldn't appreciate his little brother offering advice and solutions about his wasted life? And why, oh, why, had he suffered an attack of conscience over Sandra? It wasn't like *she* didn't know the score herself. One of the aspects of his personality she liked best was his hard shell; she had said as much, in so many words.

Maybe it was a combination of everything: Sandra, Phillip, the multi-million dollar deal with Diamond Corp., the robbery and vandalism at the strip mall. It was certainly enough to keep his plate full till the next millennium. Still . . .

It's all Kate . . . his conscience warned him. Emitting a frustrated snort of acceptance, Jake faced the truth. It was all fine and good coming up with other excuses, but meeting Kate and her daughter had really put him in this blue funk.

Because he didn't want to concentrate on Kate, he shifted his thoughts to her daughter. April Rose really did have what it took to make it in the modeling/acting business. He was no expert, that's for sure, but some people just came across that way and stuck in your mind long after seeing them the first time. She possessed that quality. He was completely aware of why Phillip had jumped in feet first, promising her way too much considering she had no training and no experience.

Okay, they hadn't seen her on film yet, but Jake would bet she would knock 'em dead anyway.

And how's it going to feel seeing her at that audition? Will Kate be with her?

His gut tightened instinctively. Flipping on the light, he tucked his hands in the back pockets of his jeans and stared into the inky night. His eye caught movement. Below, on the prom, a figure backed away as if burned from the yellow patch of illumination that hit the sidewalk. The figure then tore off toward the beach as if the hounds of hell were snapping at its heels.

Troubled, Jake frowned. Was someone watching the beach house? Was this somehow connected to the sabotage going on at Talbot Industries? A long shot, he supposed. Or was it. . . ?

He wasn't consciously cynical, but from years of seeing the avaricious side of people, Jake had developed a theory that nobody did something for nothing. Vandalism was certainly a common enough crime, but there had been something personal about the way the property had been hacked at, as if robbery wasn't the prime reason for the crime. Juvenile delinquent be damned; Jake was certain an adult fueled with a certain amount of fury had done the deed.

"I'd like to catch the bastard who did this," Gary had muttered when he had called later to report that the clean-up crew had arrived.

"You and me both."

"You know what you said, about someone being mad at us? Well, y'know I've had some other things happen on some job sites. Little stuff. Missing tools. Air let out of the tires and such. I didn't think too much about it 'cause stuff happens, but now I don't know. You think it's coincidence?"

Jake said succinctly, "I don't believe in coincidence."

"Me neither." Gary was grim. "Maybe someone *is* after us."

"Maybe . . ."

"But the tenants aren't mad. They're happy. Love the place!"

"Then it's someone else. Someone with a bone to pick directly with Talbot. We're a commercial contracting company," Jake said slowly, trying on the idea. "We've developed our share of land. Maybe we've inadvertently stepped on some toes."

"Like who?"

"Other companies we've outbid. A neighboring property who doesn't like what we've done. Environmentalists . . ."

Gary went defensive. "We've gotten every permit. Talked at meetings to every hothead. We've been okayed by environmentalist groups, *everything!* You can't tell me there's somebody out there targeting us."

Jake had smiled to himself at his foreman's loyalty and belligerence. "Detective Marsh will probably be forced to give up his pet theory of 'kids' and look at the facts. The police will sort it out."

Now, as he watched the figure scuttle away to the beach, the whole conversation with Gary flooded back. For a heartbeat he considered; then he clambered down the stairs, taking them two at a time, racing outside in hot pursuit of the skulking figure.

There was no sign of the intruder when Jake hit the prom. He kept right on, straight for the beach, a host of dark thoughts attacking him as he considered what he might do if he actually caught this culprit. Jake wasn't afraid, but his mood was tense and unsettled enough that he knew he had better be careful or he might compound the problem.

He silently cursed his sneakers which had filled up with sand the instant he tore onto the beach. He would never find the perpetrator! The beach was miles long, dark, and surrounded by grassy sand hills which gave perfect shelter for anyone wishing to hide. His steps slowed automatically, and he was more than a little miffed at himself for letting imagination carry him away. It was probably just some idle tourist. Good grief, he was chasing shadows!

At the edge of the sand hill lay a collapsed figure.

"Hey!" he called, moving toward it cautiously. Maybe it was someone other than the person standing outside his house.

Muffled sobs ceased at the sound of his voice. Pure silence followed except for the soft rustle of the breeze against the stiff, waist-high beach grass.

"Are you okay?"

No answer.

"Did you fall?"

When once again there was no reply, Jake leaned over the person who he guessed was a woman by the long hair that caught the wind and whipped like a curtain around her. He touched her shoulder, and she recoiled as if bitten.

"Look, I'm not going to hurt you. Do you need help? I could call someone."

"I'm fine. Go away," a muffled voice ordered.

Jake normally would have taken that advice with relief, but there was something so helpless about her that he couldn't in all conscience just up and leave her alone.

"Are you crying?" he asked softly.

"No. I'm just . . . breathing hard."

Since this was patently untrue, Jake grinned to himself. Maybe it was the brandy. Maybe it was being outside and enjoying the coolness of an August night on the beach. Maybe it was, oh, hell who cared! He sank down onto the sand beside her and said, "When you feel like sitting up, I'm ready to listen."

It was better than thinking about his own problems.

Chapter Nine

Unbelievable! Kate wanted to weep with frustration; but she was already weeping with misery and disgust, and anyway, there were no more tears left. How could she be so unlucky? What had ever possessed her to stand outside Jake's parents' house?

You deserve this, a voice inside her head told her.

She wanted to argue. She wanted to evaporate. She wanted to die with embarrassment. *Maybe you could,* she reasoned. She certainly felt like some kind of death had occurred because she felt rocky, light-headed and uncertain of anything except that she was an utter fool who would never escape this situation with even a modicum of pride.

She couldn't lift her head. Why did he have to sit there? She felt his presence as keenly as if their bodies were fused together. Oh, Lord, deliver me, she prayed impotently.

Time marched on.

Kate's hands dug into the cold sand. She couldn't look

up. She couldn't face him. And her ankle throbbed as if someone had tried to rip it off her leg.

Her face was wet. Tears were drying on her cheeks, but not before sand stuck firmly in their tracks. Oh, why wouldn't he leave?

"I'm fine," she struggled to assure him. "I just want to be left alone."

"Katie?" Jake asked in disbelief.

She shrank inside her own skin. For a wild moment she thought about bluffing, but the situation was bad enough as it was. Brushing a hand over hot, sand-dusted cheeks, she managed to lift her head and offer him a lopsided smile. "Hi."

"What are you doing here?" Jake sat up straight, his eyes glaring at her through the darkness. A light from down the beach diffused his outline. She would have rather it had been pitch-black so she wouldn't have to see him at all.

"I was just walking, and I stopped outside your house."

"Why did you run away?" he bit out, confusion quickly turning to suspicion.

"I didn't," she lied. "I just left, and then I—"

"You ran away," he corrected harshly. "I saw you."

"I was just walking along the prom."

"You saw me in the window," he guessed, too clever by far.

"Yes, but—"

"And so you took off. What are you afraid of?" His face was stern.

The ache in her ankle made her feel dull and stupid. For a while embarrassment had put her pain aside, but now her injured ankle throbbed like a heartbeat. "Nothing," she bit out through clenched teeth.

"Did you come to see me?"

"No!"

"Oh, I get it. You didn't expect me to be there, and then when I was . . ." He let her draw her own conclusions, and he was too close to the truth by far.

Kate sighed. "Don't make more of this than it is," she declared, feeling light-headed.

"I won't," he assured her, climbing to his feet. Staring down at her, she saw his lips compress. With extreme reluctance he offered her his hand, as if mere contact might contaminate him.

"Don't bother," Kate said. "I'm just fine."

"Call me crazy. I don't feel right just leaving you here on the beach." He reached for her hand, and Kate childishly tucked hers inside the pocket of her jacket. The movement jarred her ankle, and she winced involuntarily.

"What happened?" Jake asked at once.

"Go away!"

"You hurt yourself," he realized, talking more to himself than her. "Good God, how fast were you running? Didn't you look at the terrain?"

"Oh, yeah. I stopped and checked the ground because—you know—I'm just so cautious and careful and I knew you'd want a full explanation should I happen to run into you!"

"You've hurt your ankle," he realized when Kate winced again as she jerked away from him.

"It's not your problem!"

"It's that same ankle, isn't it?"

The knowledge that they shared this from their past turned them both silent. Kate lay her cheek against the sand and simply relaxed. Her muscles felt loose and useless. She had no strength.

"You were running away from me, weren't you?"

His voice was soft, as if he didn't even want to utter the words. Kate swallowed hard. He made it so difficult!

"You couldn't face me," he added, ruffling her feathers with his superior tone.

"I just didn't want to deal with you, okay? I ran off. So, sue me. You didn't have to chase me down like a criminal!"

"I didn't," Jake denied shortly. "Let me see that ankle."

"No." Stubbornness came awfully natural to her, Kate realized. She knew she would die of embarrassment all over again when she was safe and alone; but recklessness had invaded her soul, and she suddenly wanted to give Jake Talbot the rough side of her tongue. "I don't need your help."

"Oh, really?"

He was so damn sure of himself! "Really. I do this all the time."

"What? Run pell-mell in the dark across uneven ground?"

"Twist my ankle," she retorted evenly. "As you well know."

"Then, why don't you let me look at it?"

She responded with silence. She would rather crawl back to the Mustang than have him touch her.

"You're just feeling like an idiot," he offered dispassionately, as if he were some noted psychologist, "and now you won't allow anyone to help you."

That stung. "I just don't want *you* to help me."

"I'm all you've got."

"I don't need you!"

"Fine!" Jake released her. "Prove it, then."

Kate was instantly wary. "What do you mean?"

"Get to your feet."

"Oh, for God's sake!"

"What is wrong with you?" Jake demanded. "I'm offering help that you desperately need, and all you can do is snipe at me. What did *I* do to you?"

The shock of that statement swept her breath in so fast

she felt she might choke. But the belligerence and self-righteousness of his stance suggested he was perfectly serious. He really didn't know how much he had hurt her! Had that whole secret marriage meant nothing to him? A lark? A moment in time? A way to get a reluctant virgin into bed?

No . . . she would not believe that.

"You didn't *do* anything." Kate struggled to her feet. Jake automatically put out a hand to help. Pain shot up her leg. She gasped and sucked in air, new tears starring her lashes. She clung to him in spite of herself.

"Here," he said, slipping an arm around her waist. "Lean on me." His body was tense, his words clipped. He didn't like this any better than she did.

Berating herself for her rashness, Kate did as she was told, letting Jake take the bulk of her weight as they eased their way up the uneven path to the prom. She felt zapped. Spent. All her energy had melted away, and there was nothing to do but get through this with some bit of dignity—if there was any left to be had.

At the prom Jake kept right on going, pushing open the wrought-iron gate that led to his property. Kate stopped short. "I don't want to bother you."

"You're not going anywhere with that ankle without help," he pointed out. "Come on inside."

There was nothing to do but acquiesce. She let him guide her toward the stairs, conscious of his warm skin and hard body. She remembered his chest, its width and strength. Nothing seemed to have changed over the years as Jake felt as if he were made of iron.

She wondered what he thought of her. Did she seem the same? Or did he even notice?

Get over it, she told herself sternly, but her senses wouldn't listen. They were on overload, conscious of the feel of him and his masculine scent mixed with salty sea air, an aroma more potent than any bottled cologne. His deep breathing was like the throb of music, something she felt within herself, and she couldn't even bear to look at him, knowing even a sideways glance might bring those blue-gray eyes to gaze searchingly into hers. No, it was better to stare straight ahead and concentrate on the pain in her ankle. Thinking about Jake Talbot's proximity did dangerous things to her.

"Here," he said, guiding her through the front door to the couch arranged in front of the fireplace.

Kate swept in a breath. It was just as she remembered it. Victorian. Except . . .

"You've got the same furniture," she said, thinking aloud, "but all the doilies and froo-froo are gone."

"We took it down."

"We?" She dared a glance at him as she sank into the cushions. Bad idea. Those eyes did her in. Quickly, she glanced away.

"Phillip and I. My mother and father sort of—stepped out—of everything. Turned over the business to me and the house to both of us. Phillip wants to sell the place, but I don't know . . ."

"Phillip—doesn't own any part of the family business?" Kate asked.

"He works for Talbot Industries, but he and my father have never gotten along that well." Jake was brusque. "You remember."

"Yes. I just thought things might have changed."

"They have," Jake agreed, then added with an ironic smile that could have meant anything, "and they haven't." He bent down by her feet, and Kate grew alarmed.

"What are you doing?"

"Taking your shoe off."

"I'll never get it back on! It'll swell. Maybe I should take it off later, when I'm back at my—my room."

"Where're you staying?"

"Umm . . ." Her mind went blank. "That place—one of them—by the turnaround."

Jake threw her a knowing look. "You don't have a place to stay yet, do you?"

His mind-reading abilities might have impressed her if she hadn't realized how completely obvious she was. Good Lord, she might as well display a neon sign! She was no good at deception, at all.

Were her feelings as obvious? She prayed they weren't.

And what are those feelings, my girl? she asked herself.

Jake lifted her foot, and Kate opened her mouth to protest. He looked up, silently asking permission. She clamped her mouth shut. Why did she feel his touch as if it were burning right through her sneaker? It wasn't fair. She shouldn't care! He had hurt her so badly, and *after all these years* it shouldn't matter anymore!

Carefully, he eased her sneaker from her ankle. Even so, Kate had to suck in a sharp breath at the pain.

"You okay?" Jake asked, giving her a quick look.

She nodded. Her foot throbbed. Biting into her lower lip, Kate ignored both her ankle's hard ache and Jake's surprisingly gentle touch. Grabbing a moss green throw pillow, Kate clenched her fists into its soft velveteen folds, fighting every feeling coursing through her.

When he slipped off her sock, Kate dared a glance at her foot. Swelling had already submerged her ankle bone. Discoloration would not be far behind.

"You really did it in," Jake said with a hint of admiration. "I haven't seen that nasty of a sprain since that last time, in high school."

"High school," Kate breathed out.

"Mmmmm . . ."

Clearly he didn't want to talk about that time any more

than she did. Gently Kate moved her toes, sending needles of pain up the side of her foot.

At her unconscious moan, Jake said, "You should see a doctor."

"No, it's fine. All a doctor will do is wrap it up, tell me to keep off it and suggest I be more careful next time."

Her leg was stretched out straight; Jake still holding her heel. Kate longed to yank her foot out of his contact but wasn't quite sure how to do it without looking like a total ingrate.

It felt like an eternity passed before he pulled the pillow from Kate's clutching fingers and settled her foot against its soft velveteen fabric, balancing both pillow and heel on the coffee table. Then he stood back, staring down at her foot. Kate did the same.

Time ticked by . . .

It seemed predestined, she thought ironically. She had torn out of town to escape thoughts of him, then had chosen the beach—Seaside—the site of some of their most tender moments. It was as if she had planned it, at some level. Running *toward* him instead of running away.

"Want a cup of tea?" he suggested as he moved to the kitchen.

"Maybe the phone book?" Kate countered. "So I can call a motel?"

"You could stay here," he pointed out the obvious.

She had expected it. Had *wanted* it, at some level. But it was impossible. "Oh, sure," Kate snorted, but her heart began a steady, heavy beat way out of proportion to his casual invitation.

"I promise I won't attack you," he said dryly.

Kate's head whipped around in surprise, but he was out of sight. She wasn't quite sure how to take that comment. "I don't think it's a good idea to stay here with you," she muttered.

"What?" he called from the kitchen.

"Nothing."

"You can have one of the bedrooms downstairs," he yelled to her, opening and closing cupboards somewhere out of her line of vision.

"I'd rather go somewhere else," Kate responded loudly, wondering if he could hear her. Everything felt like such an effort. The truth was, she would *love* to curl up in bed and have someone bring her a cup of tea.

Someone other than Jake.

She was still sitting with her foot propped up when Jake returned with the hot mug. Kate gratefully accepted it and willed herself to relax when he chose the chair adjacent to the couch to sit on. He was as tense as she was, however; he was perched on the edge of his chair, his hands gripped onto his knees.

"I guess I will need some help getting to the motel," she admitted. "And my car's parked downtown."

"Give me the keys and I'll bring it here."

"Ohhhh . . ." She couldn't make these decisions.

"You can't just leave it in town."

"Jake, I don't know," she moaned, too emotionally weak to think clearly.

"Just stay here," he said, as if it were the most natural thing on earth.

For an answer Kate reluctantly dug into her coat pocket and produced her set of keys. Jake's warm fingers took them from her. He asked for directions to the Mustang, then headed for the door, looking unfairly sexy and masculine as he added with his trademark smile, "I'll be right back."

As soon as he was gone Kate collapsed against the cushions, wishing she were less sensitive to him. Deliciously, she recalled his every touch, then buried her head in the couch and groaned out her frustration, furious with herself.

Why couldn't her date with Tom have turned out better? She should have *demanded* Jillian set up an evening with her friend Michael rather than waiting until next Friday. She needed diversion. She needed a different man in her life. She did *not* need Jake Talbot!

Whatever possessed you to stop in front of his house, then?

With painful self-realization, Kate confirmed what she already knew: she still cared.

"Damn," she muttered, her voice muffled in the cushions of the sofa.

Okay, so what? she reminded herself. So what? A few residual feelings—big deal. It was natural. She hadn't seen him in over eighteen years, yet there had been a lot of stuff unresolved between them. Just willing it away didn't work, she reasoned. Maybe confrontation would put things in perspective. Maybe they needed—no, *she* needed to address the issues that had plagued her since that awful time when she had learned he was engaged to someone else.

And when do you tell him about April?

Kate drew an unsteady breath, lifting her head from the couch and feeling like an old, old woman. One thing at a time, she reminded herself. Rome wasn't built in a day.

To the empty room, she muttered, "You are going to hate yourself tomorrow . . ."

Jake walked steadily up the promenade to Broadway. A breeze fanned his hot face, and he felt curiously disjointed and out of sync.

What was it about Katie Tindel that stirred his senses? Whatever it was, it had always been there. Like something beneath his skin. Something that couldn't be dug out without major surgery.

She was the last woman on earth for him. The absolute last. She had run away and married a man over twice her age for security. That was a fact. If he, Jake, had stuck around, she would have married him, undoubtedly for the inheritance sure to come his way someday.

But she had cared about him; he knew that, too. There was only so much faking a person could do. It was just that other motivations were deeper and more important to her, obviously. In the end she had shown her true colors.

"Eighteen years ago," he breathed in disgust. Why did he keep rehashing it all as if it were yesterday?

Her car was parked a couple of blocks off Broadway. Jake found it without really trying. Unlocking the door, he slid behind the wheel, pushing back the seat to accommodate his longer legs.

Closing the door, he felt enveloped by her scent. His mind cast back to that juvenile time they had first made love after their "marriage." He had believed in her so much!

The convertible purred to life, and Jake maneuvered through the late evening throngs down the road that ran parallel to the prom until he found his driveway. He parked the midnight blue Mustang behind his Bronco, suffering a strange kind of déjà vu, though they had never driven their own cars to the beach before.

Maybe it wasn't déjà vu, he decided, shrugging as if to physically throw off the feeling. Maybe it was a glimpse into "what might have been." Either way, he didn't like it.

With purposeful strides he walked through the back door into the kitchen, stopping short at the archway to the living room. Kate lay on the couch, her eyes closed, her breathing deep and even as if she had collapsed into a deep sleep.

For long moments Jake waited in the doorway, leaning a shoulder against the jamb. She was beautiful, he thought dispassionately, not wanting to feel a thing. Time had been more than kind to her. She had blossomed. Grown into a woman twice as attractive as her naive younger self.

Maybe it came from leading an uncomplicated life, he thought wryly. His own had certainly taken a few twists and turns he hadn't expected or wanted.

He poured himself a cup of tepid tea from the pot and zapped it in the microwave. Quietly he walked into the living room and stretched out in the adjacent chair, resting his cup on the overstuffed arms.

Kate lay with her head on another of the moss green pillows, a change from his mother's fussy decor. Her lashes caressed her cheek. One hand was tucked beneath her chin, and when she sighed her breasts moved beneath the dark blue turtleneck sweater. She had tossed her jacket over the back of the couch, and he realized how small she was.

One more thing he had forgotten.

Frowning, he glanced at the empty fireplace. It was too warm for a fire, so instead he struck a match to the wicks of two long, tapered white candles resting on the mantel. He half expected a musk and vanilla scent, then shook himself out of his reverie.

That, too, was the past.

When he glanced back, Kate's eyes were open. She looked startled.

"You fell asleep," he said unnecessarily.

"Did you—already get my car?"

"It's out back, parked behind mine."

"Oh, brother." She sat up, swiping at blond-streaked strands that had tangled over her eyes.

Unwillingly, Jake felt a strong, male attraction to the sight of her. Clamping his jaw, he glanced away, toward the flickering candles.

"I've got to go," she said, "or I really will spend the night."

"I thought you'd already decided to!"

"I know, but, well, I can't." She cleared her throat, inhaled a deep breath, expelled it and added, "You know why."

Her candor surprised him. "I do?"

"Don't play dumb."

"I'm not," Jake admitted honestly. "I'm just, not quite sure what you mean."

"Take a wild guess."

She was dead serious. Her amber eyes stared at him with challenge. Jake wasn't used to being put on the spot so thoroughly, and he didn't like it one bit. "You mean because we were once lovers?" he asked carefully.

Kate looked away, as if he had hurt her horrifically. "It was a whole lot more than that to me. Then," she added meaningfully. "Once upon a time."

"We were kids."

"We were *infants,*" she corrected angrily. Was her anger directed at him or herself? He couldn't tell.

"We were old enough to know better," he replied softly. He wasn't sure he was ready to have this conversation. He wasn't sure he would ever be.

"I don't want to talk about this," she said, echoing his thoughts. "But that's why I can't stay."

"It shouldn't matter after this long," Jake said, thinking aloud.

Her cheeks pinkened. "You're so right," she muttered.

"Then, why don't you make it easy on both of us and spend the night. I promise I won't do anything to make you—uncomfortable."

"Are you kidding?" Kate's lips quivered. Jake was mesmerized by how they looked. An insistent little thrum started somewhere inside him, the harbinger of sexual desire. Irritated, he tightened his own lips to dampen the sensation, unconsciously hardening his expression.

Kate didn't miss the change. One moment he was almost approachable, scarily close to the Jake Talbot she remembered, endearingly boyish. The next he looked like an angry stranger, and that, she decided, was what he was.

"I'm already uncomfortable," she admitted with a little catch in her voice.

"Sorry."

"It's just that there's too much history, y'know?" she struggled. "I feel like I'm in a dream."

"A nightmare?"

"I wasn't going to say that," Kate said, her voice thready. "Why does it matter so much?"

"I don't know," she answered.

She could scarcely keep her eyes on him. His profile was so familiar. It made her throat ache. She was torn between the desire to scream out all the hurt and anger that had been her companion all these years, and to reach out her arms to him and drag him close. Some crazy part of herself wanted to draw her fingertip down the lines of discontentment that bracketed his mouth, to erase the unhappiness she witnessed. Here was Jake Talbot, a man of privilege if she had ever met one, yet he seemed miserable and a bit lost.

Kate shook herself awake. Lost? Was she out of her mind? She couldn't think of another person on the planet more goal-oriented than Jake these days.

She was letting nostalgia rule her, and it was downright dangerous.

"I don't want to make a federal case out of it," Jake said. "If you want to stay, you're welcome. We can figure out what to do about your ankle tomorrow. For tonight, I'm dead tired and you look done in." His gray-blue eyes regarded her seriously.

She nodded. She felt done in.

He waited an extra beat, then asked in a voice that said this was the final time, "So, what do you want to do?"

Chapter Ten

Kate lay beneath the fluffy cream comforter on the guest bed and stared through lacy window curtains to an ink black night. Her ankle was a dull ache that kept her fitful and awake. The fact that she had buckled under and stayed at Jake's house was another factor to her sleeplessness. She should have said no. She should have insisted on a motel room.

But, as they say, it was no use crying over spilt milk, even though it felt as if there were a lake of the stuff on the ground!

Jake had brought her bag in from the car, and she had changed in darkness to her sensible cotton pajamas. Still, she felt naked and exposed, and she held the comforter up to her chin, looking for all the world like a frightened virgin in the reflection of the oval mirror above the vanity at the far side of the room.

Okay, that image was a blur, sharper in her mind's eye than the one actually reflected in the mirror in this semi-darkness. But Kate knew how she felt, and her uncertain emotions had turned her into an anxious insomniac all evening. Now, flinging back the covers, she limped barefooted to the window, wincing every time her right ankle briefly took her weight. Beyond the window she caught a glimpse of a quarter moon riding low in the sky, intermittently obscured by swiftly scudding clouds. It was a beautiful August night; she was just too unnerved to really appreciate it.

She had called April before she had retired, itchily aware that Jake stood on the far side of the kitchen, acting as if he were completely deaf to her conversation. Like, oh, sure, he couldn't hear her stiltedly try to explain to her daughter where she was staying and why!

"Where are you?" April had demanded to Kate's vague report of spending the night at a friend's beach house.

For an answer Kate had repeated the Talbots' telephone number, adding hastily, "It's just down the prom," while she glanced over her shoulder to Jake.

"But whose house is it?" April wanted to know. She was not a child easily put off, and Kate ground her teeth, completely aware that she had fostered this take charge, responsible side of her daughter, even prided herself on it!

"It's a long story."

"I'm not going anywhere."

With a feeling of facing the firing squad, Kate revealed on a sigh, "It's Mr. Talbot's house. I twisted my ankle, and he saved me."

"Mr. Talbot?" April questioned. Kate could hear the smile in her voice.

"Yes," she said repressively.

"Which Mr. Talbot?"

"Are you even going to ask me if I'm okay?"

"Are you okay, Mom?" April inquired dutifully, her voice full of mirth.

"No, I'm not. My ankle hurts and I may never recover."

"I'm sorry." April was instantly contrite, and Kate wanted to bang her own head against the wall. She was taking out her feelings on her daughter, and it wasn't fair. "Have you seen a doctor?" April worried.

"Not yet. It was kind of late, and oh, I don't know, things just happened. But it's fine, really. Just kind of painful. I twisted it enough when I was younger to know I'll live." She shot another look toward Jake. His back faced her, and he was pretending to sift through some mail which had apparently accumulated since he had last been to the beach house.

"Which Mr. Talbot?" she asked again.

"You might have to guess on that," Kate sidestepped.

"Oh, he's right there? The younger one. The one you like."

"I don't—!" Kate bit off her denial.

"It's a good thing Ryan's dad and you didn't hit it off," April drawled, "otherwise I'd worry his heart might be broken!"

"You have no idea what you're talking about!"

April's laughter set Kate's nerves on edge, but she had to concede that she was right. She had asked herself if her feelings for Jake were so obvious; April's reaction was answer enough.

"I'll see you Sunday," Kate rang off; then she stood for a moment uncomfortably waiting for something else to happen.

"You're staying the weekend in Seaside?" Jake questioned, still thumbing through his stack of envelopes. Kate realized he had sorted through the small grouping several times, never looking at one item too long or with much interest. So, he definitely had been eavesdropping. She hazarded a guess on what that meant and decided it was better not to think about it. Too much supposition could make a person go crazy!

"Well, yes, I guess so. That's what I first thought, before I hurt my ankle."

He looked up at her then, and Kate sucked in a breath and turned away from the beauty of his eyes. She was so ridiculously susceptible.

"Tomorrow we'll see a doctor," he said, his proprietary manner getting under Kate's skin.

"Don't worry about it," she answered shortly and had hobbled off to bed before she could skirmish with him further.

You really are touchy, she admonished herself now, rolling her shoulders back several times, wondering why she couldn't shake the feeling that she was somehow to blame.

With determination, she tried to concentrate on her problems at work, but the thought of cornering new accounts—businesses that would turn to Rose Talent before other agencies—seemed like an impossible task tonight. Maybe she had given herself too much credit, she fretted. Maybe she didn't have what it took to survive in the world of business. She certainly didn't have the formal education, although Ben had been an excellent teacher in his own fashion.

Sighing, Kate pushed her hands through her hair in frustration. She couldn't think about the business now. It took too much effort, and she just wanted her mind to shut down and let her sleep.

Thinking another cup of tea might be the ticket, Kate teetered her way through the darkness in the direction of the kitchen—and ran straight into a warm, hard body!

She screamed, choking it off when she realized it was Jake's strong arms steadying her. "My God, you scared me! I thought you were an intruder!"

"Sorry." Jake sounded amused. "I was just . . . I couldn't sleep."

"Why didn't you turn on a light? You nearly gave me a heart attack!"

"I said I was sorry. I was trying not to disturb you. With that ankle, I figured you'd be horizontal for the night."

"Oh." Kate's heart rate slowly returned to normal. "I couldn't sleep either," she grumbled.

"I could make some more tea."

She realized then as he switched on the lights under the cabinet that Jake was helping himself to another brandy. Catching her look, he asked, "Or, would you like something stronger?"

"Apart from wine, I'm not much of a drinker."

"So, that's a no?"

Kate hesitated. She wasn't completely against the idea of anesthetizing herself with a stiff shot of brandy.

As if reading her mind Jake suddenly smiled, a boyish flash of white that had the susceptible portion of her mind fantasizing about capturing his mouth with her own. "I could add some honey to it," he coaxed.

"Sure," Kate agreed recklessly.

Jake did the honors, pouring brandy into a coffee mug and adding a dripping spoonful of honey. Kate tentatively tasted the concoction, half choking at the spirits.

"Okay?" he asked.

"Fine." Her voice was a croak. Clearing her throat, she tried again, "It's good."

"I keep thinking I ought to make a fire, but it's really not that cold," Jake said, easing toward the living room. His eyes were on Kate as she limped after him, but though she knew he wanted to offer help, he wisely kept quiet.

"Make one anyway," she heard herself say.

"Really?" His brows lifted.

"I mean, if you want to. I don't want to tell you what to do."

Jake snorted, an ambiguous sound. Still, he took her advice to heart, bending down to his task. His broad back and muscular arms were in her line of vision, and she forced herself to look away as she positioned herself on the couch once again. It wouldn't do to get too comfortable with him, not when her antennae were attuned to his every movement. Ridiculous! She wanted to kick some sense into herself, but it was no use. A quick mental check made her realize she was thoroughly enjoying herself, and that ticked her off all over again!

A glance at the clock told her it was two o'clock in the morning. "Why couldn't you sleep?" she dared to ask as he set a match to the crumpled-up newspaper surrounding chunks of driftwood.

"I don't know." He glanced her way, shrugged, and said with unexpected candor, "I guess 'cause you're here."

"Me?"

"You know what I mean."

Yes, she knew. She just wanted to hear him say it. "I guess we're both uncomfortable being together," she admitted, picking her way carefully.

The crisp crackle of flames and scent of burning oak filled her senses. As if by magic, Kate's anxiety and inhibitions began to melt away, and she sighed, cradling her mug of brandy and honey. Oh, she was in dangerous territory now, but her conscience couldn't rally her flagging defenses.

"It's because of our shared past," Jake said. "Neither one of us can forget it."

"Well, yes, but it was a long time ago."

"Apparently not long enough."

"What we had—bothers you?" Kate asked tentatively.

"Not bothers. It's just—*there.*" His profile was to her,

the glow of the fire reflecting in yellow and scarlet against his face. "It wasn't like some passing crush with us. You were my first . . ." He stopped himself before he trampled into dangerous territory. "We practically married each other."

"Practically," Kate agreed. "But it wasn't—real."

"Well, not exactly . . ."

He glanced her way to regard her seriously. His eyes stared into hers as if he could find the answers in them. Kate wasn't entirely certain he couldn't. After all, she had been thinking of practically nothing else since the moment she had run into him again—even before that! "If we'd actually been married," she said lightly, sidestepping a bit, "I wouldn't have married Ben."

"You didn't waste a lot of time waiting for me," Jake pointed out dryly.

"You were engaged to be married yourself, as I recall."

"Not immediately."

"Darn close."

Their eyes dueled. Kate would not back down. Her heart began beating fast and light, and her hands—those betrayers!—had begun quivering wildly. This bugged her to no end. Why, *why*, did she have to express every feeling so visibly? Why couldn't she be strong and stoic and inscrutable, sort of like Jake!

"Well, it doesn't matter now," he pointed out, his voice noticeably cooler.

"That's true." Kate tucked her hands in her lap to quell their trembling. "So, did you ever get married?"

"Not right away, but yes . . ."

"To the woman you were engaged to?"

Jake couldn't possibly explain all the twists and turns his relationship with Celia had encountered. It felt like a long, protracted illness with deep lapses into comas before he had fought his way back to health. "Yes," he admitted.

"Your mother once told me she was more suitable for you than I was," Kate admitted softly, pretending the hurt wasn't there. "At least she inferred it."

"She's good at that." Jake's voice was clipped, as if he hated admitting Marilyn Talbot's faults. "Anyway, she was wrong. She might even admit it now."

"Hah!" Kate disagreed. "I was not good enough for her favorite son. You can't convince me she's changed that much."

Jake rubbed his nose and sighed. "My mother has some strong opinions, none I really subscribe to."

"So, I'm right, aren't I?"

"No one appears to be suitable for me," Jake said dryly. "She even realizes that Celia and I were a terrible match."

"So, Celia—your wife?—was no good either?" Kate probed, surprised.

"Exactly."

"You poor thing. Must be tough being so impossible to live up to."

Jake shot her a sideways look, gauging her tongue-in-cheek tone. "I may stay a bachelor for the rest of my life."

"How long have you been divorced?"

"A long time. I was only married eighteen months."

Kate's brows lifted in surprise.

"Unlike you," he said, gesturing to her. "You were married, what? Eighteen years? And you have a daughter, too."

Kate's gaze slid away. Guilt, she thought uneasily. Her deception was as vast as the Sahara. She hadn't meant it to be; she had simply tried to survive during a terrible, terrible time of her life. But there was no way to tell Jake. He could only view her actions in their most negative light. Revealing the truth about April wouldn't work, no matter when, or how, she did it.

But she had to do it. Eventually. It was too, too unfair that he didn't know. And so he had hurt her when they were young. So what? He had a daughter, and he needed to know the truth.

"Kate?" Jake asked, witnessing her stricken face.

She made a sound of protest.

Instantly he was beside her, concerned. "Is it your ankle?"

"No," she breathed, swallowing.

He took her mug and set it on the table. "You look ready to pass out."

"I feel like I might," she said faintly.

"Put your head between your knees." Gently he pushed her neck down, but all she could feel were his strong fingers against her nape. "Maybe it's the brandy."

She couldn't bear him blaming himself. "No," she assured him. "I'm just—tired, I guess."

"Injured."

"Actually, the brandy helped." Her voice was muffled, coming from somewhere near the floor. Her hair had fallen forward, screening her face, and to her alarm he brushed it back until it lay on her shoulder. The intimacy was almost more than she could bear.

"Jake, I—" she began, only to inhale a sharp breath as he began to stroke her hair. Catching himself, he stopped short, dropping his hand. Slowly she sat up, but Jake was still seated next to her, so strong and male and sexy that her mouth felt dry and woolly and her heart beat in a strange, uneven cadence.

"What is it?" he asked, searching her face.

"Nothing."

"Tell me."

She shook her head. "You don't want to hear my problems."

"Sure I do."

Kate couldn't look at him. It distracted her too much. She didn't know how to scoot away, either. Because it seemed safest, she launched into her financial woes rather than address all the trickier issues that lay between them, issues he knew nothing about.

". . . and so when Billy took me aside today, it really hit home. I've got to do something, but I feel paralyzed." Jake didn't immediately answer. Instantly Kate was embarrassed. "Look, I know you've got some of my talent trying for that spokesperson position. I wasn't trying to push any one of them on you, especially April. I just needed to talk."

Jake was thoughtful. Kate cringed inside. She hoped he didn't think she had been begging. "We'll choose who's best for the position."

"I know, I know. Absolutely. You should." Kate rubbed her face. "I just heard myself and I sounded pathetic."

"You just sounded like you were working out a problem," he disagreed. "I know how you feel. I've got a few of my own right now."

"Would you like a sounding board?"

Jake hesitated. He didn't think he should really be discussing criminal activity directed at his company. "Not right yet," he said.

Kate couldn't help thinking he believed her unqualified to hear Talbot Industries' activities. It stung a bit, though she had no real reason to take offense. Still, it reminded her how unequal their positions were: in life, and the business world as well.

And it didn't help that he sat so close to her that she could feel the heat emanating from his body.

"Well, I suppose I should try to get some sleep," Kate murmured, picking up her mug of brandy and swirling the shallow remains in the bottom of the cup.

Jake didn't answer. Instead he lay his head against the back of the couch and stretched his feet out, crossing his ankles on the coffee table. It was much the same position Kate had been in earlier, when her foot had been propped on the velveteen pillow, but she doubted she had exhibited the same lazy sensuality as Jake did. It was effortless on his part, and totally unconscious. When he stretched, she could practically hear his muscles ease and lengthen like the sinews of a jungle cat.

It was too darn sexy by far!

Clambering to her feet, she nearly toppled over. Jake's hand shot out to steady her.

"Whoa, there."

"I'm okay," she assured him tensely.

"I just don't want you to fall."

"I won't fall," Kate declared, yanking her wrist from his grasp. Promptly overbalancing, she sat down hard on the couch. The tiny bit of brandy left in her cup plopped onto her pajama legs.

Jake had the indecency to grin.

"Well," she muttered, embarrassed. "It's your fault. You surprised me."

"My fault," he repeated.

She hid a smile, not wanting to give in. "Yes. It's all your fault, because I refuse to have it be mine."

He chuckled, the sound a deep rumble in his chest. Kate couldn't help her mouth curving in response.

"This reminds me of how you were," he admitted, still grinning.

That stopped her. "How I was?" she questioned gingerly.

"We used to laugh a lot."

"I don't anymore," she said quickly, unthinkingly. The topic was growing dangerous.

"That I believe. You're so serious now."

Kate opened her mouth to protest, but Jake's smile had been replaced by a thoughtful frown.

"Why did you marry him so soon?" Jake asked into the silence that followed. "Were you pregnant?"

"P—pardon?" Kate choked in shock.

"Your father said you were. He alluded to it, anyway."

"My father?" Kate whispered. "You talked to my father?"

Jake nodded.

"When?"

"When I got back from Europe. You'd already married Rose by then. I thought maybe you married him because you were pregnant. Sorry," he finished. "Never mind. It's none of my business."

She realized distantly that he thought she had been pregnant with Ben's child. She should have been affronted, but she couldn't be—not knowing what she knew to be the truth.

Clearly Jake felt he had overstepped the boundaries of decency, however, for he added tersely, "You married him because you loved him. I'm way out of line."

"It doesn't matter now," Kate murmured.

"I've always wanted there to be some other reason, I guess. It's no excuse, but there it is. I'm sorry."

"Don't worry about it," Kate negated. She couldn't stand to hear him apologize for his behavior when she alone knew how unfair she had been to him. "Why did you want to see me when you got back? Where was your fiancée?"

"Celia? She stayed in Europe. We weren't together at that time," he added for clarification. "I mean, not as a couple."

"You were engaged, though."

He gazed at her closely. Their noses were nearly touching. The intimacy wasn't lost on Jake, whose focus narrowed on Kate's face. Her lips trembled ever so slightly. "Not then. I was only thinking about you," he admitted with a self-deprecating twist of his lips.

She couldn't hear this. She knew better. "You sure had a funny way of showing it."

"I wrote you, but you never wrote back."

Kate inhaled a swift breath. "I never saw the letters. I told my father to burn them. You were *engaged!*" she hissed to his tortured look.

"No . . ." He seemed shattered that she had never seen his words. "I called your house once, but your mother said you were gone. No phone number. Just that you were gone."

"Jake . . . don't . . ." She couldn't let him turn this back on her.

"As soon as I got back I came looking for you, but you were married. And pregnant," he reminded her.

"But you were engaged," she insisted again.

He shook his head.

Her lashes swept the hill of her cheek, dark and lustrous. Jake remembered their moments together, here, at this house, and though he struggled to remain emotionally neutral, desire burned, compelling and deep. As if in a trance, he watched his own hand reach upward and slowly brush aside the curtain of her hair so he could stare at her profile directly.

"Don't," Kate said, swallowing.

"Don't what?"

"Don't do that."

"Okay."

Moments ticked by. Kate could feel the heat of his breath stirring her hair. Her insides were jelly. She and Jake were locked in silence. Unbearable, yet dangerously enticing. If she turned to meet his gaze, she would be lost; she knew it. She stared at the fire instead; but its embers throbbed, and her blood pulsed in hot response.

"I'm going to kiss you," he muttered, his voice a rush, as if he couldn't bear it, either.

"No," she murmured, as his lips brushed her cheek. Her breath swept in in a gasp. She half turned, unable to help herself, and his mouth searched for hers. Her lips parted in eagerness against her will.

His kiss was like liquid fire. She met it with the surrender of a drowning person clutching a lifeline. His tongue touched delicately, asking permission. She was weak, wanton, melting. Kate sank into the cushions and Jake came with her, his body half lying across hers, his kiss deepening as his tongue took over, thrusting inside the hot cavern of her mouth.

It's just a kiss, she lied to herself, allowing more. His hands gripped her shoulders, tense. As long as he just kissed her she wouldn't move, she argued with her drugged conscience.

But it was more than a kiss. It was an invasion. His mouth slanted hard on hers, his tongue a plundering invader that made her blood sing. A soft moan issued from inside her, encouragement for Jake. His palm cupped her jaw, held her tight. As if she would try to escape this sweet assault!

"Jake," she murmured.

"Don't," he whispered right back, dropping soft kisses on the edges of her lips.

"Please . . . don't," she answered, almost laughing at how soft, desperate and nonsensical they sounded.

"I can't help it." His hand convulsively slid down her neck to her shoulders, gripping her as if indeed he could not stop himself. Kate was shattered, begging her body to reject this seduction, but feeling every part aflame and eager.

He shifted position, pulling her toward him until they were propped on their sides, facing each other on the couch. She gasped when his hand slid over her hip to pull her leg over his.

"This isn't right . . ." Kate struggled to shake her head, but it only seemed to burrow her closer to him. "I can't, Jake."

"Why can't you?" He doubled his efforts, his mouth desperate and hot against hers. She lay limp in his arms, unable to fully resist, unwilling to take another step toward loving him.

"It'll hurt me too much," she choked out.

"Why?"

"There's been no one but Ben since . . ."

"Oh, Katie . . ."

His whispered endearment of her name nearly did her in. Gently he pushed her backward, downward until her shoulders touched the cushions. His mouth never stopped its raining kisses. His tongue lightly thrust between her lips, then pulled back, a teasing instrument of pleasure that worked like magic.

Kate's hands discovered a will of their own, traveling up and down his back, kneading and tracing the muscles she could feel beneath his shirt. The hot possession of his body atop hers was a thrill she had forgotten in the length of her lukewarm marriage. She *wanted* him! She wanted him to take her. And the hot scenes of passion flashing through her brain both shocked and incited her.

"Jake . . ."

"Don't talk." His muscles fit atop hers beautifully. She could feel his hardness, and it was sheer joy. Kate shifted frantically, afraid to think, wanting this more than she had wanted anything in her life.

Then pain shot from her ankle up her leg. She jerked involuntarily. Her leg was twisted beneath them, and she couldn't stop a groan from escaping her lips. Jake went stone still.

"Kate?" he asked, concerned.

"My ankle."

He shifted away swiftly with a muscular twist, and Kate felt bereft. When his fingers explored and found the pulsing pain in her ankle, Kate jumped again. "Sorry," he whispered, gently moving her foot.

Her sleeping conscience awakened. Heat invaded her face, and Kate squeezed her eyes closed. "Oh, my God," she murmured, struggling to her elbows.

Jake glanced up from her foot, his eyes still drugged with desire. His gaze dropped to her lips. It was almost more than Kate could bear.

"Don't look at me like that," she whispered.

"I can't help it." His voice was low and slightly rough with unfulfilled need.

"I can't do this! I don't know what's wrong with me."

"Why can't you?"

"Because it's not right!" She sat up fully, forced to clutch his arms to maintain her balance.

"Nothing ever felt so right," he disagreed tensely.

"You left me eighteen years ago!"

"And then you left me," he argued. "It was a lifetime ago, Kate."

"And that makes it okay?" Passion bordered on anger. She felt poised at the brink.

"We were kids. We were stupid and naive. And the whole thing was great, but it was a fantasy. You know it as well as I do."

He couldn't have hurt her worse if he had tried. "It meant something to me," she breathed. "Something incredible!"

"It meant something to me, too, but hell, it all blew up just because I was gone a few months. Let's face it. It wasn't this fabulous love affair of a lifetime. It didn't even last one summer!"

"That's because you stayed in Europe the whole time!"

"You couldn't even wait till I got back!" Jake nearly yelled at her. "We're talking a few weeks, and you hauled

off and got married. You really know the meaning of loyalty, don't you? It nearly killed me, Kate!''

"Don't turn this around on me!"

He swore beneath his breath, dropping her as if she
burned. As he paced the room, she could see the fury he
was fighting, but she knew it was only sexual frustration.

"I'm not going to be your bedmate tonight, for old
time's sake," she said flatly. "I'm sorry if I gave you the
wrong idea."

His hands clenched. "Thanks for reminding me what
this would be. For a second I thought it might mean something else."

Kate ground her teeth together. She wasn't the foolish
girl she had once been. "Like what? A second chance?"

"Maybe."

Oh, she wanted to believe him. To trust her feelings and
damn the consequences. But too much time had passed
for that. "Tell me, Jake, would I be the only woman in
your life?"

"*What?*"

"Do you really want a second chance with me, Kate Rose,
your ex-lover?"

"I don't know what I want!" he admitted half-angrily.

"I know what I don't want," Kate retorted. "I don't want
to be someone's sometime lover."

He made a sound of disbelief. "You really have a low
opinion of me, don't you?"

"Do I? Are you seeing anyone else?" Kate asked.

"What the hell are you talking about?"

Kate clenched her hands to tighten her own resolve.
Jake was ridiculous if he felt he could make her believe
he had been pining away for her all these years. He had
been callous before; he would be again.

"Are you seeing someone else?" she asked tightly.

"If you mean, have I dated, well—"

"I *mean* are you currently seeing someone. A woman. A date. A lover."

"I've dated a lot," he insisted through his teeth. "Of course I have!"

"But right now." She pinned him down, knowing she had hit a sore spot. And it cut deeply. Incredibly. Ridiculously! What had she expected? That now, since they had met again, he would renounce all other women in his life because of *her*?

When he remained silent, as if unable to form an answer, she said, "Well, I guess that's my answer."

"No, it's not," he bit out. "I didn't know I would see you this weekend. I didn't clear the boards on the off chance we'd run into each other. I didn't even know I *wanted* to see you until you showed up." Jake uttered a sound of disgust. "So, no, I didn't tell every woman I know that I was suddenly unavailable. That's not how it works."

"Well, that's how it works for me," she said, knowing she was being unreasonable and not caring. "I can't kiss a man like I kissed you just now unless I'm interested in only him."

"What if you just learned it?" he questioned, giving her a sharp glance.

Kate narrowed her eyes, sensing the trap. "Are you trying to say that you kissed me and suddenly you knew it was me you wanted, only me?"

"What if I said yes?"

"I'd call you a liar," she answered instantly. "And you're really good at rhetoric. Answer a question with a question and never say a damn thing."

"I don't know what I want, except *you*," Jake finally admitted in an outburst. He glared at her, as if angry she had forced him to this admission. "I want you, Kate Rose. And if you can't handle it, fine. Just say so. But if you can . . ."

He left the thought unfinished, waiting. Kate swallowed, intending to tell him where to get off. But she couldn't quite muster the words. Her lips remained clamped shut because she knew whatever came out of her mouth wouldn't be the truth.

"You want me, too," he guessed, coming to stand in front of her. She had a clear view of his denim-clad legs, but she refused to look up and meet his gaze. "You do. You wouldn't have responded like that unless you felt the same thing." He squatted down in front of her, picking up her limp hands, waiting until she reluctantly met his eyes. Then he whispered tautly, giving her no chance to squirm out of a direct answer, "You want me, and I want you. And I think we know where this is heading. Why don't we just admit it and stop torturing ourselves? I want *you*," he stated deliberately. "Now, tell me you want me, too."

Chapter Eleven

Doctor Phelpman examined Kate's ankle with the gravity of an oncologist about to deliver bad news. Expelling her breath, Kate hadn't even realized she had been holding it until the doctor removed his glasses and absentmindedly polished them, as if searching for the correct words.

"You've given yourself a sprained ankle," he said soberly. "Strained the ligaments. Possibly torn them a bit."

"I've done it before," Kate told the gray-haired man. He was a local, semiretired GP who came in on Saturday mornings to this small Seaside clinic.

Jake had insisted she see someone and had rooted around through the local directory until he had learned about Dr. Phelpman. He had driven Kate to the clinic this morning over her protests that she would be fine.

Now she felt compelled to convince the good doctor that she was healthy as a horse.

"Might want to have it X-rayed," he suggested gravely.

"I'll give it some thought, when I get back to Portland."

"Hmmmm . . ." Clearly he didn't trust her to make an educated decision.

Damn Jake for bullying her into this, Kate thought unkindly. Why couldn't he leave well enough alone? He had certainly managed to keep his hands off her last night after she had turned down his open invitation to have an affair.

Good Lord! Just recalling those heated moments sent blood rushing to her face. Under Dr. Phelpman's critical eye Kate pressed her palms to her hot cheeks. She felt like a child in trouble, and that irritated her all the more.

"Thank you," she told him as she hobbled out of the back room. She had refused crutches, and she could practically hear him tsk-tsking her as she headed for the waiting room.

There sat Jake, his denim-clad legs stretched out negligently in front of his lean body, his hair slightly ruffled from the sea breeze that had met them as they left his house this morning. He glanced up briefly, his brows quizzical. Kate barely refrained from glowering at him as she headed outside.

"I'm not your problem," she bit out, shaking off his arm as he attempted to guide her toward his Bronco. It was all she could do to climb inside, the vehicle's tires being too high for her to gracefully heft herself upward. That ticked her off all the more.

"You could use a little help from your friends," Jake observed with a slow drawl.

She snorted in response, and that, as they say, was that for a while.

Staring out the window at the passing landscape, Kate knew she was acting utterly childishly, but she was too afraid of her own wants to react with adult sense right now. It would be so easy to be swept into an affair with Jake

Talbot. Every cell in her body was screaming at her to give in.

Now, tell me you want me, too?

The night before when he had demanded a response to that, she had simply refused to answer. The heat of his stare had felt like it burned through her skin, and coward that she was, Kate had been unable to meet his steely gaze. She had wanted to answer in kind. The words had quivered on her tongue. But if she had admitted how she felt, he would know he had her, that she was his and *had always been his!*

Instead she had let the silence answer for her, and both of them had returned to their respective beds in an unrestful state of mind.

She didn't want to care a whit about him. Okay, she could accept that she was attracted to him. He was, after all, a very attractive man. But did she have to want him so much? So much that it was like a craving eating away her insides? So much that her head was full of aching fantasies every blasted moment she was with him?

You've got to leave now, she warned herself.

When they arrived back at the house, Jake came around Kate's side of the Bronco, offering a hand. It seemed churlish to sweep him away again, so she leaned on his strong arm as she descended to the ground. His muscles were hard and tense. Butterflies quivered in her stomach. Drawing a breath, Kate hesitated a moment, balancing herself.

"I hate feeling so helpless," she admitted.

"No kidding. I never would have guessed."

Kate groaned, glancing away. "I know I've been impossible. I just—don't know what to do."

"A shrink would say, 'Go with your feelings'."

"How do you know?" Kate asked.

"My ex-wife spent a lot of time on the psychiatrist's couch."

"Oh." She didn't know what to say to that. It had never occurred to her that Jake's marriage had been less fulfilling than her own.

He helped her inside, and either she was wearing down or she was listening to her own silly heart again. Whatever the case, Kate obediently let him park her on her favorite spot on the couch.

"I should get that room at the motel," she called loudly as Jake retreated to the kitchen. "Really. Thanks for everything, but I need to leave."

"Same song, second verse," was his muttered response.

He returned with coffee this time and a tiny pitcher of cream. Her hands reached for the steaming mug as if she and Jake had been partners and played out this scene time and again.

"I don't want you to leave," he said.

"Oh, Jake," Kate murmured in protest.

"What's wrong with a weekend together? We're not hurting anyone. We've got a lot to talk about. Years of information." He swirled his coffee, staring into its depths as if the secrets of the universe were written there.

"You're just trying to come up with something."

"Darn tootin'," he agreed. "I don't want to think about tomorrow. I just want today, and I want it with you."

His words were sharp daggers to her heart. Honesty could be so tough. But what had she expected? Some lie about his wanting her to be the one and only woman in his life? Those dreams died years earlier when she had realized he hadn't meant those words even then.

"I'm not made for quick affairs," she whispered.

"How do you know that's what it would be?"

"I just know."

"You're scared."

"Absolutely!" she agreed. "I've got a life that I love,

and a teenage daughter whom I love even more. I've got a job and a reputation. I've got a future."

"You act like seeing me will bring on the apocalypse."

"I haven't dated enough to be so casual about sex," Kate said seriously.

Jake gazed at her with a certain amount of frustration. He didn't know what he wanted, and he was trying so hard to play square. If he were smart, he would walk away from any part of her. She had screwed up his youth royally, and he should have learned from his mistakes.

But he sure as hell was a lot more attracted to her than he had ever been to Sandra.

"It isn't just about sex," he pointed out.

Kate's gorgeous amber eyes stared right into his soul. She was so prickly, so careful. Where others would just shrug their shoulders and say, "Why not?" she insisted on treading as carefully as if she were walking through a mine field.

"Then, what's it about?" she asked.

Tough question. "Being with someone who interests you."

"I could almost buy that, if it were from someone else, Jake."

"What are you so afraid of?" he demanded, his frustration leaking through.

"History repeating itself," she answered in a jiffy. "You hurt me so badly.

"I hurt *you*?"

Kate set down her coffee cup and pressed her hands together. "You don't understand."

"I don't understand," he agreed heartily. "I've never understood how you could swear your love to me at a church altar and then marry someone else within months."

"You're twisting that around. How many times do I have to remind you that you got engaged."

"Not before you got married."

"I didn't get married till late in the year."

"I didn't get engaged until I was out of college."

Kate's mouth opened in outrage. "Liar!"

"I'm telling the truth."

"You got engaged in Europe that summer!" she denied hotly.

A distant door cracked open in his mind. A door to a room full of ugly thoughts that he had slammed shut so long ago. "My mother lied to you," he realized with a tiny dart of anguish.

And Kate finally heard what he had been trying to tell her the night before, words she had stubbornly refused to comprehend: he *hadn't* been engaged. He had merely been finishing out his parents' wish for him to stay in Europe. He had come back expecting to be with Kate, and she had already married Ben. He had returned just a few weeks, or days, or *hours,* too late!

As she witnessed the truth dawn on Jake, she experienced her own latent shock and denial. She wanted to disbelieve, but there was no mistaking his reaction to news so old it shouldn't be able to hurt anymore. But it did hurt. How thin were the threads of someone's life that they could be torn and restitched so completely? She should be angry with Marilyn Talbot for ruining her life with Jake. Instead she felt numb.

And Jake experienced a similar rush of feelings. He stared at the ceiling, as if expecting divine intervention. He wanted to rail and shout and smash his fists into the wall. Instead, he tightened down his resolve and muttered harshly, "It doesn't matter."

"Doesn't it?"

"No." He shook his head. "If it had mattered, you would have waited."

I couldn't wait, she thought, half expecting him to leap

to the truth. She had told him she had gotten married in the fall, and he knew she had been pregnant by the time he returned. If he calculated the time, he would know April was his—unless he thought she had started an affair with Ben almost the moment he departed.

Gazing at him helplessly, Kate half hoped the truth would connect inside his head. Her heart thundered in expectation, deafening her.

But Jake didn't make the jump. Drawing a deep breath, he murmured, "I'd just like to see you again, that's all."

Kate struggled with her conscience. Telling him about April was something she had to do, and now would be an opportune time. But she felt weak, and his words made her sound like the perpetrator instead of the victim, a role she didn't want at all.

"Jake," she murmured, chewing on her lip so hard she tasted blood.

"What?" He was distracted, lost in his own thoughts.

"Jake, I feel—sick," she whispered.

That caught his attention. Quickly he sat down beside her, his gaze scanning her face. "You look pale. Do you feel dizzy?"

"No, it's not that kind of sick. I mean—"

"What?" he asked.

Sick at heart, she wanted to say.

"What?" he whispered, his voice changing tone as he, too, felt their proximity.

"All those years . . ."

He nodded, misunderstanding completely, yet picking up the yearning in her tone. To Kate's shock he cupped her chin and touched his thumb to her lips, rubbing gently. "Don't worry so much."

"I can't help it."

"Come here," he invited, drawing her mouth to his.

Kate should have resisted. She tried to talk in order to

do so, but mumbled syllables were crushed beneath the sweet persuasion of male lips. After that she went quite still, a small, breathless, traitorous sigh escaping despite all her will to the contrary.

And when Jake's kiss deepened into a persuasive insistence, Kate's eyelids fluttered closed, and her head lolled back. Later, she couldn't remember being eased to the couch, or quite how her blouse was found much later in a pool of light silk on the floor beside her. All concentration followed the path of Jacob Talbot's lips as they plundered the warmth of her mouth, trailed the trembling arch of her throat to capture one taut nipple through the sheer satin lace of her bra in a hot pull that sent fiery tingles shooting to the core of her femininity.

With a quick flip of his thumb and forefinger, the clasp on her bra was dispensed with. He brushed the garment away and sucked again on nipples erect from his pleasurable ministrations.

That nearly shocked her back to her senses. It dumbfounded her how she could react to Jake this way, when she had never felt the same thing with Ben. She had almost forgotten what it was like, but he was helping her remember double-quick now!

"Jake," she pleaded, tugging fretfully at his thick hair, seeking to lift his head from the source of this pleasure.

"Kate," he responded on a sigh, his breath cool against her wet skin.

"This isn't fair," she moaned.

For an answer the devil moved downward, wetting a trail down her abdomen to areas she knew she couldn't bear having explored! She yanked more violently on his hair and nape and shoulders, her fingers digging frantically. Jake refused to heed her as his fingers undid the snap on her jeans and systematically pulled downward, dragging her panties along as well.

"Jake, please!" Kate gasped, then gasped again as his mouth found the heat of her pleasure center, shocking her to absolute stillness.

Her bones melted. She simply had no substance. The fight went out of her in a rush of air, and her back arched as if she had been doing this for years instead of mere moments.

Her head thrashed on the couch, but Jake's exploration was tender and well-rehearsed. Had she been in control of her wits, his very expertise would have turned her off, but Kate was lost in a spiral of sensation that was wickedly self-indulgent. One instant, she was afraid to move; the next she was digging her nails into his back and climaxing with such a rush she cried out in a muffled scream.

She collapsed back, spent. His hands took up where his mouth left off, but when he started to strip off his own clothes, her head thrashed against the velveteen pillow.

"I can't! I can't! I'm sorry," she whispered, stricken.

He glanced at her, in the act of removing his shirt. "Sorry?"

"Oh, my God. I can't go on. I'm sorry! Oh, no, I don't believe this!"

Kate pressed her palms to her eyes, gulping, embarrassed to the pit of her soul when tears sprang out of nowhere, seeping through her fingers to run in rivulets down her cheeks. Her chest heaved.

"Katie," Jake said softly, shocked.

"I can't! I shouldn't have. I don't know how it happened. It's all my fault. I've never, never, *never* . . ."

"It's okay." He got the message, slowly buttoning up his shirt.

"No, no." She peeked through her fingers, abjectly miserable. "I've never been a tease, and after that—it's just not fair."

"It's okay," he assured her.

"My God!" Kate made a sound of humiliation and inhaled a shuddering sigh.

"That good, huh?" Jake managed.

She shot him a look. His face was angelic, and she realized with a rush of relief that he was hiding a smile. She wanted to cry all over again.

"You don't play fair," she murmured.

"I know," he admitted, shame-faced. Only it was all an act, and Kate, who was rapidly becoming aware of her nudity, grabbed up her clothes and struggled to put them on before another unexpected episode suddenly took her by surprise.

Jake brushed her hands away, refusing to let her put on her armor. "I like you like this."

"Oh, Jake, let me go."

"I can't," he said simply. "I want you to stay."

"Your powers of seduction are many," she murmured, cheeks flaming.

"I wish . . ."

In lieu of finishing his sentence, Jake seemed to come to his senses and allow Kate to redress. She felt his gaze on her several times, but he didn't actually speak until she was completely clothed—and then she cut him off.

"Kate—"

"You wish what?" she asked.

He hesitated. Her heart started pounding, and goose bumps rose on her flesh. For some reason, she thought he was about to say something momentous.

He gazed at her seriously, and Kate couldn't help lifting a hand to his cheek and stroking his beard-roughened skin. Jake shifted his lips to her palm, kissing her, and when he was about to answer the phone rang shrilly making them both jump.

Jake rose to answer it, and Kate collapsed against the

cushions, feeling as if she had run a marathon. She wished she understood herself—and him—a little better.

"Phillip!" Jake said tightly, clearly as undone by his brother's poor timing as Kate was. "What do you mean? When did you talk to Marsh?"

His attention was riveted to the phone. Kate waited, growing slightly alarmed at his change in demeanor.

"Damn it," Jake whispered under his breath. "Okay, okay. I'll be there tonight. No, wait . . ."

He stood tensely, his back to her. She could almost hear him calculating as his head half turned her way. "Tomorrow."

Whatever Phillip answered had no effect on Jake, who finished with, "I'll call him from here. Stop worrying. No, it'll be fine." He shook his head and asked in a lower voice, "What's with you? It's no surprise that he's changed his opinion. I knew it wasn't kids." After a moment, he added in frustration, "For God's sake, you act like someone's blaming *you!* Forget it! I'll deal with it as soon as I get back."

He hung up the phone with Phillip's voice still squawking from the receiver. Shrugging a bit, he said apologetically, "A few problems at work."

"The ones you didn't want to share with me."

He half smiled. "Yeah, those."

"You don't seem too concerned."

"I'm not—yet." He threw her a sideways glance. "I'll tell you all about it if you promise to stay another night."

"Blackmail. Coercion. Unfair advantage."

"All of the above," Jake agreed, watching her.

Sighing, Kate acquiesced, knowing she should be more careful, but sick and tired of listening to her conscience. "One more night," she agreed and wondered why it sounded like the death knell.

* * *

They barbecued hamburgers and drank beer which went right to Kate's head. She sat in the kitchen while Jake walked back and forth from the barbecue which stood on the small deck at the side of the house. The luxury of being waited on was a new experience for Kate, who had spent years being partner, wife and sometime slave to her husband. "I could get used to this," she admitted as he handed her a paper plate with a charbroiled burger face-up on a bun. The aroma sent her saliva glands into overdrive.

"I could, too," Jake admitted in a reflective murmur.

Kate munched on her hamburger, swiping at her chin with a napkin as juice dribbled from the sumptuous ground beef. "How embarrassing."

"What, are you kidding? I'm just glad I didn't burn them to hockey pucks."

"Are you trying to tell me you're normally not this handy in the kitchen?"

"Anything past the barbecue is way too tricky."

"So, what do you do? Go out for dinner every night?"

"Pretty much," he admitted.

"You're kidding." Kate saw dollar signs burning up. But he was a Talbot after all, and he didn't have a family to support.

"I tried a cook/maid for a while," he said with a shrug, "but she was always fixing something exotic and inedible."

Kate grinned. "No gourmet tastes, either?"

"Not a one."

"Meat and potatoes all the way?"

He lifted his hands in surrender. "Guilty as charged." He picked up his beer and took a long swallow, eyeing the bottle as he asked casually, "And your husband? What was he like?"

She didn't want to talk about Ben. Not with Jake. "Pretty much the same," she muttered dismissively.

"Meat and potatoes all the way." Jake met her eyes.

"Yeah."

"Was he good to you?" Jake asked after a pause.

"He left me the business, and he treated April like a princess."

He nodded, hearing the closure in Kate's voice but ignoring it in true male fashion. "How has April handled his death?"

"Fine, I guess. Death's always scary and upsetting, but she's coped."

Jake frowned. "Losing a parent, though."

"They weren't all that close," Kate revealed, then could have kicked herself for saying too much. "She's a teenager, and Ben never understood."

"Understood what?"

"Why she was moody, or not interested in talking about business, Ben's favorite subject. He fussed over what she wore and what she said. It just all bugged her." Kate nervously twisted her beer bottle atop the table. "She was devastated when he died," she admitted.

It was a milestone. She hadn't thought about Ben's death in relation to April that much because April had been unusually quiet. Kate realized her error too late. Maybe because she had known Ben wasn't really April's father, she hadn't given April's feelings the same merit she might have otherwise, and since April didn't ask for help, the issue had simply been shoved aside.

"She wants me to date again," Kate said, beginning to see new reasons for April's interest. She missed having a father. Maybe Ben wasn't perfect, but he had been the only father she had known. She wanted Kate to have a partner, and she wanted to be part of a family again.

"You mean you haven't been?"

"It's only been six months."

"Were you in love with him?"

This was getting into tricky territory. "That's kind of personal, don't you think?"

Jake inclined his head in agreement. "I don't know what it is. I can't talk to other people like this. Maybe it's because we grew up together; or something, but you're easy to be with. If I step over the line, just tell me."

"You constantly step over the line," Kate said, remembering those intimate moments on the couch.

"Hah. You just don't want to answer."

"What?" Kate asked, losing track.

"Were you in love with your husband?" he repeated patiently.

"When we got married?" she stalled.

"Ever."

She choked out a tense laugh. "This conversation is way too dangerous. And you and I are too comfortable with each other," she added. "But it's false. I just know it."

"What do you mean?"

"I mean, we'll get back to Portland and this will be over, and we'll be strangers."

He didn't deny it. How could he? A whole other life awaited them both, and so they were spending some intense hours together. It didn't change anything for either of them, no matter how much they might want to believe it did.

Kate felt a sudden chill. Excusing herself, she began to clean up the kitchen but stopped, frozen in mid-dishwashing, when she felt Jake come up behind her.

"We've got unfinished business," he said quietly. His hands rested lightly on her hips as his breath fanned her neck. He brushed her skin with light, nuzzling kisses.

Kate felt herself begin to respond to his persuasive mouth. She closed her eyes and swayed, but all the words they had spoken jumbled together in her head, making her feel uneasy. What had they really discovered this weekend? Nothing they didn't already know. They were simply two people who were chemically attracted to each other, but who lived in two different worlds.

"I can't let you seduce me," she said in a thin, unhappy voice. "I won't be able to live with myself if I do."

"Ahhh, Kate," he sighed.

"I know you think I will, give in, that is, and you're probably right. Enough pressure and everything goes back to the way it was in high school. But you hurt me. You may not have meant to, but you did, and I barely recovered."

"With Ben Rose."

"I made a choice," she said unevenly. "For better or worse, and it was mostly okay. Ben was good to me. And that's the bottom line."

"But you're blaming me for something that happened when we were kids."

"Of course I am! In my heart, we were married, Jake. We had a ceremony in a church with candlelight and vows—vows that *I meant!*"

"I meant them, too," he declared.

"You left me. I thought you were engaged."

"And you married someone else!" he interrupted harshly. "For God's sake, Katie, if I can forgive you that, can't you forgive me for going away for a few months? Because whether you like it or not, that's all I did. I didn't marry Celia for years, and then it was just because the timing was right. You and I—that's all that was wrong. Timing. We had bad timing because we were too young."

"I know, I know . . ."

"And my mother's interference didn't help. I'll take the blame there, but there's nothing more to say. It doesn't matter anymore, Katie," he added persuasively. *"Now* is all there is."

She swallowed. "Jake, there's something I've got to tell you."

"I'm listening."

"When you talk about bad timing . . . I, well, there were other things, too."

"Mmmm . . ."

He was nuzzling again, and Kate struggled to keep a clear head. It had been her saving grace for years. She prayed for it now. "I needed you home that summer. If you'd been there—but you weren't. And then your mother said you were engaged. Jake, please," she begged, no proof against such persuasive appeal.

"Please, what," he murmured, deliberately misunderstanding as he slowly turned her toward him.

"You're not listening, and there's something . . . something . . ." She gulped as his lips caressed her throat, his body pressed warmly against hers. ". . . something I have to . . . say."

"Go ahead and say it," he whispered, but his mouth had traveled downward as his hands sneaked beneath her sweater to roam up her bared back.

"I can't," she expelled, collapsing against him in total surrender. Her brain shut down. She gave in so completely that when Jake swept her into his arms and carried her upstairs to the room they had occupied so long ago, it seemed not only right, but preordained.

I love you, she thought, knowing it was true, knowing it had always been true.

"I want to make love to you," he muttered harshy against her mouth as eager hands stripped her clothes.

"I want you to," she whispered back, her own hands just as eager.

"No second thoughts," he warned.

"No second thoughts."

"Kate . . ." Desire throbbed in his voice, but it was a last question, a plea that she play fair.

For an answer she dragged his mouth to hers and plunged her tongue inside. With a groan, Jake hauled her body tightly to his, fitting her feminine contours against his masculine ones until there was no room for anything between them except physical love.

Their clothes were dispensed within a fever of desperation. His tongue entangled with hers, their breath warm and mingling. She felt his hands slip down her rib cage and over the curve of her hips, drawing her body hard against him. She felt his hardness and suddenly longed to be possessed by him once more.

With a moan that verged on a plea, she clung to him, her fingers exploring him as completely as his explored her. Jake groaned then, low in his throat, her touch having a direct effect on him. She nuzzled his throat with her tongue, tasting him, and it was this final coaxing that tore through the last shred of his resistance. No more waiting. He brushed her hands aside, held on to her hips and thrust inside her as if he had been waiting for years to thoroughly possess her. And Kate responded eagerly, urging him on, her own needs rapidly escalating out of control. She matched his rhythm as if they had practiced daily, not waited for eighteen long years to find each other again. When Jake stiffened in surrender, desire sizzled down Kate's nerves. Her body reacted simultaneously in a sweet, convulsive response that had every muscle pulsing with pleasure. Crying out, her fingers dug into his flesh, Jake's answering groan a signal that he, too, had reached the same, soul-shattering climax.

She was floating somewhere, languid and replete. Jake lay atop her, his heart pounding wildly against hers. She caressed his hair, his face, the muscle of his back and hips.

Her face turned to his in love, and Kate rubbed her lips against his warm flesh.

Distantly, she realized a bell was ringing. Jake's telephone. *No,* she thought selfishly when he stirred to answer it. Her eyes feasted on him as he dragged himself to his feet, gazing down at her in unfettered male splendor.

"Don't get it," she whispered, throwing out an arm to drag him back.

"I have to."

"Hurry back," she urged.

She had no idea how ravishing she looked, her hair fanned out wantonly against the pillow, her slim, toned body open for the taking. Jake leaned down and kissed her on the mouth, then headed downstairs to catch the call.

Moments later she heard his tread on the stair. He entered the room, still gorgeously naked.

"It's your daughter," he said solemnly. "She wants to talk to you . . ."

Chapter Twelve

Kate dragged Jake's shirt tightly around her, clamping the unbuttoned sides together with one arm. "I—um—don't know . . . ," she muttered to April, the receiver cradled between her ear and shoulder. Upstairs she could hear Jake moving around, dressing probably.

"It'll just be overnight," April went on eagerly. "A bunch of kids are going; and Brad's mom and dad are chaperoning, and they're serious campers. I've already told Jillian all about it, and she thinks it would be okay."

"She does?" Kate was distracted.

"Oh, yeah! It'll be fun!"

"You said Ryan's going, too?"

"Mom, don't go into overdrive. Nothing's going to happen. There's a whole group of us. Please say yes. Please, please, please!"

Kate was too shattered by her own recent experience to think clearly. "Uh . . ."

"Please!"

"Let me talk to Jillian."

April quickly put Jillian on the phone, but when the conversation was over Kate could scarcely remember a single word. Yes, Jillian believed it would be fine for April to go on the camping trip; that much Kate recalled. The words themselves receded to a dull hum, however, while every squeak and groan from the floor above her head was recorded in her mind as if on tape.

What is he doing?

"Well?" April demanded, snatching the receiver back from Jillian.

"I suppose it sounds all right." Were those footsteps on the stairs? Good Lord, was he coming to the kitchen? She felt next to naked in the scant protection of his shirt. Why hadn't she taken the time to get dressed?

You slept with him!

"Oh, Mom. Thanks a ton! I love you so much!" April cried jubilantly.

"I love you more," Kate answered automatically, just as Jake stepped into the doorway. He froze at the sound of her words, and Kate wondered wildly what had possessed her to repeat that phrase at that moment! It wasn't as if she and April played that word game; they never had. Undoubtedly, it was provoked by her intimacy with Jake, and now he was staring at her as if he couldn't bear to hear that particular phrase of endearment again.

"Hi," Kate murmured, swallowing hard as she hung up the phone. "April wanted to go on a camping trip with some friends."

"You let her?" Jake asked absently, his thoughts obviously far removed from the issue as well.

"It's chaperoned."

"You have a pretty close relationship with your daughter," he observed.

I love you more . . .

Kate nodded.

Jake eyed her body language, the arms tightly wrapped around her waist, her averted profile, the tension that emanated from her in waves. The glory of their lovemaking had been replaced by the realities of the outside world. He wished fervently that they'd had a bit more time to adjust.

"Kate—"

"Jake—"

They spoke together, in a rush. Jake pointed at her to go first. Clearing her throat, she said, "I don't want to act like a scared rabbit, but I think I'd better head home tonight."

"*What?*"

"I can drive with this ankle," she said, anticipating his first objection. "It's just a throb, and it's wrapped well enough to be as comfortable as possible."

"You just said your daughter's going on a camping trip. She won't be there."

"That's not why I'm heading home," she said in a low voice, bending her head a bit.

"I know why you want to leave," he stated flatly.

"Jake . . ."

"You lied to me."

Kate lifted her gaze in affront, her amber eyes wide. Jake's attention shifted to her sweetly familiar face with its pert nose and unfairly sensual, pink lips. He felt crazy and possessive and anxious to make love to her again!

"I didn't lie to you!"

"No second thoughts?" he reminded her sternly.

"I'm not having second thoughts!" she declared heatedly. A moment later she added more truthfully, "I'm way past that. I'm on to third and fourth thoughts."

"Oh, Katie, don't leave now. The sun's about to set. You don't want to drive at night, and I don't want you to go."

His passionate demands worked on her senses. "Jake . . . ," she murmured uncertainly, turning her back to him.

He couldn't stand it. He wrapped his arms around her and fitted his body tightly against hers, reveling in the feel of soft, feminine curves and the scent of lavender in her hair. "Come out on the porch and we'll sit in chairs and drink tea or coffee or brandy or whatever. We've got another night. I don't want to waste it."

His voice throbbed with persuasion, sending off an answering beat in her bloodstream. Kate lolled her head against his shoulder, her emotions raw. What she wanted from him she couldn't name; she was afraid to. But when he tugged her hand it wasn't to find the porch; it was toward the stairs. She gazed at him and silently shook her head. His gaze darkened, clinging to the lush beauty of her exposed legs and her breasts which peeked through the open throat of his shirt.

Because she couldn't help it, Kate stifled all the clamoring doubt ringing in the back of her head and let his will prevail. When they got upstairs together their hands worked quickly to divest each other of all garments; then they tumbled into bed as one, pushing the real world aside until the morning light.

Jake ran on the beach until his lungs burned and his body was soaked in sweat. Morning sunshine drifted over the cool gray beach. Far down the prom toward the turn-around a few brave souls were up this early as well, one even daring to bring a kite.

Bending over, Jake gulped air, propping his hands on his knees. His chest heaved. He had a long way to go still, but he was anxious to get back to Kate.

Straightening upward, he shook his head, raking his hands through dark, wet hair. He had left her cuddled in bed, her own blondish hair fanned out around her on the pillow, her face clean and devoid of makeup, her prudish pajamas lying in a forgotten heap on the floor. He had possessed her so thoroughly all night long he was torn between embarrassment and pride. It wasn't his way to lose control. He had been half-afraid she would leap up and cry, "Enough!" then disappear from his life forever.

But Kate had seemed to want him as much as he had wanted her. Languidly, her golden eyes half-closed, her arms reaching for him, she had invited him to her again and again, accepting his physical needs eagerly, and satisfying a few of her own. Even now, recalling her little sighs of pleasure and pleading moans, Jake determined he was just as anxious to be with her again as he had been last night!

With an effort he pushed his heated thoughts aside for the moment. He could feel his sweat drying on his skin, cold from the ocean breeze which buffeted briskly from the west. Dropping to the sand, he managed forty push-ups before he leapt back to his feet, running in place to keep his muscles hot.

He felt great. No, fabulous! The urge to throw back his head and howl at the heavens was so strong he had to clamp his lips together.

He and Kate were made for each other.

Jogging back toward the house, Jake ignored the little voice inside his head that reminded him how little he knew about her. Okay, there was high school, but lifetimes had been lived in between. Kate was a mature woman with a high-school-age daughter of her own, and a long-term marriage behind her. She was new to dating since her husband died. A neophyte. That was attractive about her, too, Jake had to admit, though he sounded like a neanderthal. In this day and age when men and women alike were supposed to be free to discover whom they loved however they chose to discover it, he still wanted someone fresh and untouched. Unfair, especially since he hadn't been exactly circumspect in his dealings with the opposite sex. For that reason, Kate shouldn't have to, either.

But Kate's relative inexperience was an aphrodisiac to Jake. He could admit it. Sandra Galloway's "around the block" attitude, be it in love or business or life in general, was a turn off. Sandra was so forward and confident and used to running the show that the softness and sensuality Jake had found in Kate were missing altogether.

Grimacing, Jake reminded himself that he had been perfectly satisfied with Sandra before—or at least he had told himself as much. But he wasn't satisfied now, and even if Katie decided to walk out of his life tomorrow, he knew he couldn't go back to Sandra the same way.

Thinking of Kate made him anxious. Picking up the pace, he ran at full sprint through the heavy sand until he reached the prom in front of his house. He jumped the low, wrought-iron gate and took the porch steps two at a time, slamming into the house like a hurricane.

"Whoa!" Kate cried, shrinking against the wall to the kitchen, his startling entry taking her by surprise.

"Sorry!" He cleared his throat. His blood thundered in his ears. "I just decided to race back."

"I guess," she murmured.

He sensed instantly that something had changed. The blistering heat of the night before had been replaced by an arctic chill. "What's wrong?"

"Nothing."

"I didn't mean to scare you."

"No, I'm fine."

Kate wore jeans and a bulky, cream-colored sweater against the morning's chill. Her feet were bare, however, one wrapped in its stretch bandage. Her hair was pulled into a loose ponytail, making her look closer to a high school kid herself than the mother of one.

"I should have asked you to go with me, but you were sleeping so soundly."

She gave him a look that could have meant anything. Unable to stand the sudden distance between them, Jake crossed the room, reaching a hand forward to caress her cheek. "I'd hug you, but I'm covered in sweat. Oh, hell . . ." He did it anyway, relieved when Kate squealed in mock horror, her laughter making it seem that everything was all right again.

"I wasn't sure where you were," she admitted in a muffled voice against his sweatshirt.

"You thought I left you?" he asked, appalled. "Are you kidding? After last night?" She blushed, turning away from him to hide her expression. Jake placed his hands on her shoulders and turned her right back around. "If I stayed another minute I would have been all over you again! I didn't want you to think I was a sex-crazed maniac—even though I am," he amended, "at least when it comes to you."

"I'm not—normally so—" Kate couldn't come up with the words.

"Eager?" he suggested.

"I mean, I was married and we . . . I can't believe myself!" Her hands flew to her cheeks, and fresh color pinkened her flesh.

Jake grinned. "It was great, huh?"

"Oh, Jake. I feel like I'm living somebody else's life. This isn't me, Kate Rose. I've got responsibilities and a certain reputation."

"Reputation?" he interrupted. "Lady, stop worrying. Nobody's going to know about this. It's between you and me. Period."

"In some ways, Portland can be small community," she

went on doggedly. "I'm just not used to this, and I'd die if I thought . . ."

"If you thought . . . ?"

"I'm just not comfortable with the idea that people might know I've been with you, that's all." She turned from him and walked through the kitchen to the back door and out onto the deck, arms crossed tightly around her waist, her back to Jake.

Her innocence endeared her to him all the more. He knew so many women who weren't shy in the least. Many bragged about their conquests. Jake didn't enjoy that characteristic in either a man or a woman. Katie's very fear for her reputation just resolved him to protect her and keep her all the more.

"Your secret's safe with me," he said, following her out to the deck. "Just don't tell me you want to quit right now. I don't think I could."

She bent her head. Golden-tinged strands fluttered in the breeze. "You probably think I'm being ridiculous."

"I think you're being smart."

"Really?" She half turned, her face in profile.

"Don't feel bad about last night," he whispered to her, wanting her to revel in this exciting new development as much as he was.

"I know this isn't the time, Jake, but I meant what I said before."

"About what?"

"I can't be a sometime lover."

Her face so near to his was a distraction he could scarcely cope with. She had turned him into a randy teenager, and it was pure hell to try and act like an adult. "So, what do you want?" He would give her anything, anything at all!

"I don't know!" she burst out unhappily.

"Then let's take it one step at a time."

"But . . . the other women . . . that you know. I really

don't want ... I just couldn't cope ... with that." She inhaled deeply and let out her breath, as if she had just come to a monumental decision. "I'm sorry."

"There are no other women in my life. Not since you entered it," he stated firmly. He turned her toward him, brushing thick blondish tresses away from her face. Her eyes regarded him solemnly. "You're all I want."

His words turned her to butter. She believed him, heart and soul, yet she knew she should hesitate, take her time. But lovemaking had scorched her soul and turned her into a hopeless, love-craving mass of jelly! For all her words, she couldn't have walked away now if she had been forced to.

"You're all I want," she admitted right back, her voice small and thready.

Jake swept her close, then dragged her upstairs to the shower, stripping off her clothes along with his own. They made love again beneath the biting hot needles of water, and when they were done, Jake dragged her back to bed to spend a luxurious, hedonistic morning touching and discovering and murmuring sounds of pleasure.

It was only later that she realized neither of them had once spoken of love. Of course it was too soon; she was no fool. Yet, she loved him. She always, always had. She hated herself a little for being so easy, so sappy, but it was the plain and honest truth—a truth she had hidden even from herself.

And if Jake had murmured words of love, she would have shouted back the same to him. Yet again, would she have believed those words if he had uttered them so soon? Wasn't it better to hope that a natural declaration would come in time? When their love had grown and become indispensable to both of them?

But what if that day never comes?

That, Kate couldn't think about, and as their day of

physical pleasure waxed on, she decided she wouldn't be able to think about it for a long, long time to come.

It was evening as they stood by her Mustang, kissing their goodbyes. "Here I worried about April taking off on this camping trip, and look at me!" Kate muttered, shaking her head.

"You're an adult. You can make those choices." He shrugged. "When you're a kid, most of the time you make the wrong choices, so that's why you need to protect her."

She had certainly made the wrong choices as a kid. April was living proof of her most shattering error, though she would never change having her for anything.

"See you back in Portland," Jake said, closing her door for her and waving goodbye.

Kate smiled uncertainly and backed the car down the driveway. Her ankle felt tight but comfortable enough. Her heart, however, seemed to fibrillate with anxiety.

She sensed, though she would do nothing to stop it, that she was headed for serious, soul-destroying trouble.

All hell broke loose on Monday. The office was a madhouse, and though Jillian attempted to keep everything under control, Kate had to help her with the phone calls. The good news was the business appeared to be on an upswing; the bad news was Delilah started making demands.

"You know we can't advance payment," Kate explained patiently. "If we did, we could be left holding the bag."

"Well, what do I pay you for, then?" Delilah asked haughtily.

"For getting you the auditions and singing your praises and keeping you working!" Kate retorted, bugged. Delilah would have never pulled this with Ben. She knew the nature of the talent agency as well as anyone, better than most, really.

"I'm moving to L.A.," was Delilah's next declaration.

"Well, then, I wish you the best." Kate held out her hand for Delilah to shake. It wasn't unheard of for talent to take off for the bright lights; it was a natural step. Whenever it happened, Kate truly wished them well. Never mind that ninety percent returned within six months, disheartened and disappointed. Once in a while someone actually succeeded.

Delilah stared at Kate's outstretched hand as if she didn't know what it was for. She managed a limp handshake. While Kate smiled a goodbye, she left as if in a trance.

As soon as she was gone, Kate heaved a sigh and collapsed in her chair. "Baby-sitting," Jillian had called it. Just another part of the business.

At lunchtime Kate slid a glance to her phone, her thoughts on Jake. He had been in the back of her mind all morning, and for some dumb reason she had expected him to call. When she had left Seaside they had made no direct plans or rules about what came next. Truthfully, in the harsh light of this morning, she wondered if she had dreamt it all! She had been unable to sleep all night, the night before, and consequently she now suffered a faint headache.

"He's not going to call you," she muttered to herself fiercely. "He's got a job, and a busy schedule. So do you."

When the phone rang she jumped, punching the button before Jillian could break in. "Rose Talent," she announced, waving Jillian away through the window. Jillian shrugged and turned back to some paperwork.

"Hey, Mom," April greeted her. "Wanna do lunch?"

Kate's racing heart began to slow. She mentally kicked herself for being such a dolt. "It's been crazy here. Why don't you come in and we'll make it a quick one at Lacey's."

"I'll be there in twenty."

Lacey's was a small cafe wedged into an alley between two brick buildings. The restaurant had been blocked off and covered with a skylight; its kitchen several of the rooms in the building on the left. Tables were kept in the alley itself, and the alley was heated by panels suspended high overhead to make the dining spot a year-round establishment. Its most convenient feature, however, was that it was two blocks from Rose Talent Agency.

Kate picked up the menu absently, wondering why she felt so let down. *Whatever do you expect?* she asked herself.

"Just water," she told the waiter. Inside, she could feel the germ of regret taking hold. During the heat of passion it was easy enough to tell Jake she would have no second thoughts, but as hours passed and she reviewed her weekend with her ex-lover, Kate couldn't help thinking she had made a mistake.

It was unlike her to be so out of control. Whatever had possessed her to embark on an affair with the one man who could really hurt her? Love was no excuse. Her feelings could do her in way too easily. She should have been smarter. Taken things slower.

Fools rush in . . .

"You could argue that it's been eighteen years," she said through her teeth. She was flat-out angry with herself.

April appeared in a rush. "It's impossible to find a parking place. I nearly got in a fistfight with a guy who tried to steal it from me."

"A fistfight?"

"Okay, I was exaggerating, but he did make a rude gesture at me," April declared, eyeing her mother.

"Just don't tell me you made one back."

"No. I was polite. I *told* him what I thought of him!"

"April!"

"I just said that I didn't think he was being fair since I

had my blinker on and I was pulling into the spot when he started backing up like it was his." She cleared her throat. "Or something to that effect," she admitted in an aside.

"He probably didn't realize you were there," she said, sounding like an authority.

April bristled. "Why are you taking his side? What's eating you?"

Kate snatched up her glass of water again, feeling itchy and quarrelsome. "Nothing."

"Oh, yeah? You wouldn't tell me about Mr. Wonderful last night," April said. "I told you all about my camping trip, but you were mum on the subject of Mr. Talbot, the younger."

"There's nothing to tell," Kate muttered repressively.

"You were pretty clear that you and Ryan's dad didn't work out, but you haven't said the same thing about Jacob Talbot. What gives?"

Kate narrowed her eyes at her daughter. "I don't think I like this dating thing."

"Oh-ho. Did something go wrong?"

"No."

"Did something go *right?*" she asked, a slow grin stealing across her lips.

"April," Kate warned, losing patience.

"When you feel like talking about it, I'm all ears." With that April bestowed her smile on the waiter, who reacted as if she were royalty and stumbled all over himself to help her.

Kate just felt tired. She knew she was being unfair to her daughter, but she had no intention of describing her love life in detail to anyone—and especially not Jake's daughter.

Her chest ached. A weight lay somewhere inside in the vicinity of her heart. Worse than worrying that she had made a mistake in rushing this relationship was the knowledge of the secret she bore. She had to tell him, and soon, or what was already an impossible situation would become catastrophic, and her worst fears would be realized.

Tomorrow, she thought. April's audition was tomorrow, and she would go with her daughter to Talbot Industries and figure out how to approach Jake. It was the right thing to do.

Tuesday morning dawned gray and hazy. It seemed like the clouds couldn't decide whether to form or drift away into a melting fog. Kate pretended that it was a normal day, and that she was just going to work, but she dressed with extra special care. Her dress was a button up the front denim worn without stockings, her shoes strappy sandals of soft brown leather. Her ankle was still bruised and swollen and she had to baby it, but there was nothing to do about that but wait until time healed the damage. She concentrated instead on the rest of her appearance, fussing in the bathroom longer than usual. For a final touch she twisted her hair up and secured it with a comb, then touched on makeup until her amber eyes shone like molten gold.

Now, staring at her reflection, she was surprised at what she saw. Even when she had gotten ready for her date with Tom DeSart, she hadn't looked so, so *sensual!* A weekend in bed with Jake Talbot had irrevocably changed her, and she wasn't sure how to feel.

"Oh, that's not true," she admonished the image in the mirror. She knew exactly how to feel. Terrified! They had made love over and over again, missing both an extraordinarily beautiful sunset and sunrise, according to the local papers, with neither of them caring a whit. Kate had been giddy with joy, though she had carefully kept her feelings close to her heart. With good reason, it turned out, when late Sunday afternoon she had suggested it was about time to head back to Portland and Jake made no demur. She realized then, that he had been waiting for her to make that decision. Their weekend together was over. Time to get back to reality.

It shouldn't have bothered her, but it did. And then when she had arrived home and there was no message from him, doubts had crept in on little feet, treading endlessly across her brain, giving her no peace. Then Monday had arrived and not a word. Now it was Tuesday, the day of April's audition with Talbot Industries, and Kate was a mass of nerves.

Was it just a quick physical thing? Maybe he wanted to expunge the past in the most celebrated way? Was I too forward, too easy, too eager?

"Oh, God," Kate muttered now, snatching up her purse and heading for the kitchen. Worried and anxious, she blanked out her mind and forced herself to concentrate on the task at hand.

"Wow," April said, her gaze skating appreciatively over Kate from head to toe.

"Wow, yourself."

April wore a short, straight black skirt and a white shirt that nevertheless made her look very feminine. Her hair was smooth and straight, and her skin glowed with the beauty of youth.

"You look . . . healthy," Kate commented.

"Whoa, hold down the compliments, Mom. I might get a big head!"

"You also might want to change that shirt. The camera hates white."

"What do you mean?" April glanced down at her apparel.

"White washes out color. It's too bright under the lights."

"Oh."

April hurried to change, and Kate sipped on a cup of coffee, fighting the nerves jumping around in her stomach. April returned with a dusty blue blouse that highlighted her gray-blue eyes.

"Dynamite," Kate told her, and they headed for Talbot Industries.

The corporate offices spanned a block and a half with room to grow. Steel girders stabbed into a gray sky, silent sentinels to the newest addition still under construction. Inside, they were escorted down a hall to an elevator that led them to the third floor. Here an anteroom opened to a room that had been equipped with a camera and rows of chairs where Talbot Industries' employees would hold the audition. The talent—a group of men and women from different agencies around Portland—were scheduled to arrive one after another in fifteen-minute intervals. Kate normally did not attend these kind of cattle calls, but this was her daughter they were interested in—and *they* were Talbot Industries.

Her pulse jumped erratically, but a quick reconnoiter of the area showed Jake to be missing from action. However, Jake's brother, Phillip, greeted her with a hearty handshake.

"April's got a good chance. She's got my vote."

Kate sent him a fractured smile. She wasn't certain what she thought of Phillip, and now, with the memory of her wild weekend affair filling her head, she was almost afraid to meet his gaze. As if he would know, and condemn, or something!

"You really think she's good enough?" Kate murmured.

"Oh, yeah. Absolutely."

Phillip hugged her as if they were old friends, and Kate

caught a whiff of alcohol. It was one o'clock in the afternoon. It appeared Phillip had to have been enjoying his lunch hour in more ways than one.

Kate stayed in the anteroom with April. Several young actors walked around, talking overly loudly and trying to impress anyone they deemed an employee of Talbot. April's eyes were rounder than usual, but she maintained an outward calm. In fact, she was better off than her mother, Kate realized ruefully, feeling her own pounding heart and trembling fingers, although she was nervous over other reasons than the audition.

As if he had heard her thoughts, a side door suddenly opened, and Jake strode through. His hair was combed in place, and Kate couldn't help noticing how its faint curl crept in where it curved near his ears. Without warning she remembered what it felt like to run her fingers through its thick pelt. Memories of kissing his beard-roughened cheek, and glorying in his murmured sighs and moans of love, filled her head.

But today he looked grim and purposeful, his gray-blue eyes alighting on April, though he flicked a quick look in Kate's direction. Kate's throat went dry. He smiled, seemed about to say something, then glanced behind him to where a petite brunette, slim and businesslike, followed him into the room.

This was no secretary, Kate realized, reading the body language, and from the way her hand touched his forearm lightly, this was also no mere business associate.

With difficulty Kate tore her gaze from the woman, only to realize that Jake had caught her staring. Heat flooded her cheeks.

"Hello, Katie," Jake finally addressed her.

"Hello, Jake." She had almost said *Mr. Talbot* because Jake sounded so familiar and for reasons she didn't want to examine too closely, she wanted to keep things formal. But then, he had called her Katie, hadn't he?

The woman focused on her with an intensity that spoke volumes. With feminine insight Kate realized the brunette was highly interested in Jake but concerned he didn't feel the same. This improved her mood enormously.

"Hello, Mr. Talbot," April chimed in, her smile a bright reflection of his. Kate's heart jumped. Their resemblance was so obvious she expected everyone else to see it, too!

"Hi, April." He shook her hand and said, "Good luck. Don't let the team of interrogators inside there put you off."

"Interrogators?" she asked, taking him seriously.

He grinned. Kate was no proof against that smile. She had to turn away to keep from adoring him. "Just some Talbot employees looking for the best person for the job. They're pussycats, really."

"You're April Rose," the woman said. April looked at her quizzically. She went on, "I'm Sandra Galloway of Turner and Moss Advertising. I understand Phillip felt you might work as the Talbots' spokesperson."

Phillip, who was leaning against a wall nearby, whipped around at the mention of his name. The scowl that crossed his face when he realized Sandra was talking about him was downright scary.

"Our agency came up with the copy for the series of commercials, and frankly, Miss Rose, we pictured someone older," Sandra continued.

"Oh." April gazed at Jake, whose own face had darkened at her terse words.

"Nothing's decided," he said.

"I'm just saying—"

"Keep it to yourself, Sandra," Phillip interjected. "You're not the boss, even though you like to think you are."

"Phillip!" Jake warned, annoyed.

Sandra, realizing her mistake, gave April an apologetic shrug. "It's up to Talbot Industries, of course." She walked away smartly, but as she passed Phillip, she inhaled deeply and lifted her eyebrows in silent judgment of the odor on his breath. Then she passed back through the door to the auditioning room.

"I'm nervous," April whispered to Kate.

"So am I." Her gaze surreptitiously followed Jake, who was now speaking in low tones to Phillip. Phillip apparently heeded whatever he was saying, because after an unsteady moment, he followed after Sandra.

Jake turned back to April. "Too many chiefs," he said by way of explanation. "Hang in there."

Then he was gone. April slid Kate a look. "I forgot to bring him his money!" she realized with a start.

Kate's mind's eye remembered the bills stacked behind the kitchen telephone. "You can do it later," she assured her.

"Mom?"

"Uh huh?" Kate's heart nearly broke at the terror she witnessed behind her daughter's calm exterior. "It's a cake-walk," she whispered in her ear.

"I'm scared."

"It's okay."

"Do you think that woman's going out with Mr. Talbot?" she asked.

Before Kate could answer, the door opened and April was ushered into the audition.

Chapter Thirteen

Kate paced around the anteroom. She was nervous as a cat waiting for her daughter. It was one thing having clients audition for parts, quite another to have it be her child.

When April reappeared she seemed slightly dazed. "They asked me so many questions," she admitted. "I don't know how I did."

"You're always great. You're a natural."

April smiled at her gratefully. "That's a mom talking."

"Of course it is. I am your mom."

April was barreling out the building, but Kate hung back, hoping to connect with Jake. As if surfacing from a fog, April suddenly said, "Oh, you want to see him, don't you!"

Having her mind read made Kate want to negate everything. "No, it doesn't matter."

"Yes, it does! You really like him." She slid Kate a devilish look. "He is kind of cute for an old guy."

"An old guy!" Kate choked on a laugh.

"Well, what are you both? Thirty-six?"

"We're not quite ready to be put out to pasture, thank you very much!" Kate declared, pretending offense.

April ignored her. "We can wait here." She paused by the exit door to the elevators. "He should be coming out soon."

"No, he's busy."

April finally picked up Kate's tense vibes. Reverting to her earlier question, she demanded, "And what about that witch he was with? She wasn't any better while I was auditioning. Kept giving me the old evil eye. Luckily the Talbots ignored her." April sighed and made a face. "I don't think she likes me at all." She slid a glance her mother's way. "Or maybe it's you that got her all worked up."

"You're imagining things," Kate declared, throwing open the door to the outer passage. "Come on."

"Don't you want to wait?"

Kate had already concluded that hanging around hoping for an iota of Jake's attention was an ill-conceived idea. If Jake wanted her, he knew where to find her.

On the way back to the office, she sighed to herself, realizing one of the reasons she had exited so hastily was to avoid dealing with the issue of April's parentage. She had sworn to herself that she was ready to tell him the truth, but it just wasn't so. She could tell herself to come clean with the truth till kingdom come, but it wouldn't make her do the deed any faster.

"You're awfully quiet," April observed as they headed up the clanking elevator to the third floor of their building and Rose Talent Agency.

"I've got a lot of things on my mind."

As soon as Jillian saw them, she jumped up from her chair. Her frizzed hair bounced with excitement. "I've got that date all set," she informed Kate. "You, me, Jeff and Michael. This Friday!"

"Jillian, you didn't!"

"Hey, I managed the baby-sitting last weekend, didn't I? Well, didn't I?" she demanded to Kate's look of consternation.

"Yes . . ." Kate threw a glance at April, who lifted her hands as if to say, "Don't look at me."

Jillian continued, "And you promised to pay me back by going on a date. Well, this Friday's the date, and unless you've suddenly developed a raging social calendar, you're on, my dear!"

There was no way to get out of it. Kate was well and truly stuck. And it was impossible to tell Jillian that she had fallen in love over the weekend—or maybe never fallen completely out of love—with Jake Talbot.

April, however, had no such qualms. "Mom's got a crush on Jacob Talbot."

Jillian stared. "Say what?"

"April," Kate began, her tone long-suffering.

"They were classmates together, and they've recently found each other again."

"I will go on the date with Michael," Kate stated firmly. "I could use an evening away from this obnoxious child."

April hooted with laughter. "She's soooo touchy!"

"Are you sure?" Jillian asked.

"Positive."

Jillian regarded Kate thoughtfully. "Well, okay, but if you change your mind . . ."

"I won't."

"Then we'll see what develops," was all Jillian could think of to say.

Jake called just before five. When Jillian, waggling her receiver aloft, pointed knowingly to Kate through the window of her office, Kate's skin feathered in anticipation.

She knew without being told who was on the other end. Carefully, lest he realize how much one simple phone call meant to her, she answered, "Kate Rose."

"Hey," Jake said quietly, a smile in his voice.

"Hey," Kate answered, feeling ridiculously happy.

"How about dinner?"

"Tonight? Ummm . . . okay. I've got to arrange things with April. Where?"

"Do you know Piper's Landing?"

"Sure." The restaurant was renowned for its seafood, and though Kate had never been there herself, she knew exactly where it was located.

"I live really close to Piper's Landing," Jake revealed. "Right next door, actually. I might run a bit late here, but I'd love to meet you for dinner. How about around six?"

"Sure. I've got a lot of things to finish, too. I'll see you at six."

"I've wanted to call you," he revealed, then stopped himself, as if rethinking what he was about to say.

She didn't care. Just knowing she was in his thoughts was enough. "I've wanted to call you, too," she answered back.

"Tonight," he told her, extra meaning in his voice, and Kate murmured a goodbye with a soft smile spreading across her face.

She replaced the receiver thoughtfully, trying to tamp down her runaway elation. He had chosen Piper's Landing because it was next to his place; he had let her know what his intentions were without really saying them. If she had wanted to back out of another evening of lovemaking, he had given her an easy route to splitsville. But no . . . just thinking about the evening ahead left her throat dry.

When April gathered up her things and gazed at Kate expectantly, Kate inwardly groaned. They had driven downtown together today because of her audition.

"Can you take my car home tonight?" Kate asked her. "I—um—have a dinner date downtown."

"How are you going to get home? With who? Mr. Talbot? Oh! Will he bring you home?" The questions came thick and fast. "Sure, I'll take the car. Where are you eating? No, don't tell me. Save it for later when I can debrief you in person."

"April!" Kate laughed.

"Is this love?" Jillian interjected as she got ready to leave the agency herself.

"I can tell neither one of you has enough to do if all you can think about is my social calendar," Kate grumbled good-naturedly.

"It must be," Jillian mused to April.

"Can I make dinner for Ryan tonight?" April asked her mom, her quick mind thinking ahead to an evening alone with her boyfriend.

"I guess so." She felt a tinge of uneasiness, although she knew from experience that if a couple wanted to make love, they would find a place, even if it was the backseat of a car. . . . "I won't be long," she added repressively.

April rolled her eyes and deadpanned, "Then we'll be quick."

"Please, April," Kate said on a deep sigh.

"I'm just kidding. You worry way too much. Ryan and I are really good buddies."

"That's what I'm afraid of."

Kate paced around the office after April and Jillian left, stretching the kinks from her shoulders in an effort to release tension. She wasn't used to this single motherhood. Ben had always been there to help out, and now, when she was discovering a new life of her own, she didn't want to suddenly think of April as an encumbrance.

How do other people do it? she wondered.

She was still ruminating on the situation when the phone

rang after hours. It turned out to be Rachel, one of the
agency's models who was also in her mid-thirties, and who
was checking up on her last audition. Kate assured her
that everything had gone well, then asked as an afterthought, "You have a couple of kids in their teens, don't
you?"

"Oh, my God, yes! It's enough to drive you to drink!"

Since Kate knew Rachel had been divorced for a number
of years, she inquired, "What do you do when you have a
date or an evening audition? Do you leave them alone?"

"Well, yeah. It's only for a few hours."

"Do you let them have boyfriends or girlfriends over?"

Rachel made a sound of annoyance. "I used to make
all these rules, but they'd just break them, or lie. Now
we're just up front with each other and it works better.
You got a problem?"

"I'm just getting used to this single mother thing," Kate
admitted.

"April's a great kid. Don't worry too much, okay?"

"I won't. Thanks."

That snippet of conversation rolled around in Kate's
head all the way to Piper's Landing. There was deeper
meaning there, she realized uncomfortably. She trusted
April to be smart. Her daughter had shown excellent judgment so far, and there was no reason to expect her to act
differently just because Kate had begun dating.

But Rachel's words had reminded her that she herself
had been less than up front with April about one very
important issue: her parentage. What would happen when
she learned the truth?

Kate's hands were clammy as she walked into the restaurant. Realizing she was fifteen minutes early, she put her
name in for a table, then walked through the restaurant
to the deck outside. The sun had finally shaken off its
clouds, and heat had gathered over the city. Kate leaned

on a rail above the Willamette, closed her eyes and turned her face skyward.

"Hi there," a familiar male voice greeted her.

Kate lifted her lashes. Phillip Talbot, Jr., gazed at her through bleary eyes. He had an arm looped around the dock rail, and it appeared he might actually need the support.

"I came to see my brother," he revealed. "He lives right there." He pointed to the high rise condominium building next door. "Yup."

"He said he was working late."

"Oh, yeah. The Diamond deal." Attempting to snap his fingers, he succeeded only in losing his balance for a brief second before he caught himself. "Always another deal."

Kate was uncomfortable discussing Jake. She glanced at her watch, wondering if she could sidestep Phillip. She didn't want to reveal that they were having dinner together.

"You went to school with him," Phillip said. "You were the girl my parents abhorred."

Kate could only smile in agreement. She hadn't known Phillip was aware of her and Jake's previous relationship. She had kind of hoped it was a secret, but eventually secrets managed to work their way out no matter how hard one tried to keep them hidden.

"I was talking to Jake about you. He hates it when I butt in, but he's Talbot's main man, so he's important." Phillip's mouth twisted. "I've got to make sure little brother stays on the straight and narrow, you know what I mean."

"I guess so." Kate tossed an anxious look to the door. When could she politely sneak away?

"I mean, it's my livelihood, too, isn't it? It's my inheritance. Just think what would happen if it all suddenly went away. Where would Jake be then? Huh?"

Kate didn't know what to say to that. "Talbot Industries seems rock solid."

"Doesn't it, though." His lip curled, as if the very idea of his family business's success was grounds for disgust. "Well, we all deserve our portion, don't we? I mean, I may be a worthless excuse for a human being, to quote my father, but I'm still a Talbot, right?"

"Phillip, I don't think we should be talking about this."

"Why not?" he demanded. "You're Jake's precious Katie from high school. He's never gotten over it, you know. Oh, he can fool everyone else, but he can't fool me." He waved a hand dismissively. "We may look different, but we're the same inside. A lot the same." He nodded.

They're all the same without their clothes on, honey. Lisa's admonition floated across her mind, but Phillip was a far cry from his brother. They hadn't been the same when she and Jake were high school lovers; they weren't the same now.

Kate glanced around again, a bit helplessly, hoping Jake would materialize. But just as she turned, Sandra Galloway walked through the restaurant's back door, and the two women spied each other, straight on. Kate inwardly groaned. She didn't know what showed on her face, but the fulminating look that crossed Sandra's spoke volumes.

"Mrs. Rose," she said tautly. "Phillip, what are you doing here?" she demanded a moment later. "Jake has final say on who the spokesperson is."

"Hold on, there. I just ran into her," Phillip declared defensively. "This is no secret meeting."

"I never said it was." Sandra's lips tightened.

"Jake's got all the decisions. I know my place." He lifted his hands in surrender. "And it's always second best, isn't it?" he said in a soft, insinuating tone, his eyes drilling into Sandra's.

She didn't respond to what appeared to be an insult directed at her.

Kate's nerves stretched to breaking. She didn't want to have to explain her date with Jake to them, but it was looking more and more like she was going to have to. And she hated being the object of Phillip's speculation, yet what did she expect? With a jolt it occurred to her that maybe Jake had purposely invited them both to the restaurant. Maybe he had planned for them all to eat together, like one big happy family.

Sandra inadvertently disabused her of that idea seconds later. "Have you seen Jake?" she asked Phillip impatiently. "He's been tricky to catch up with all day."

"The Diamond Corp. deal," Phillip said. "Busy, busy, busy."

"He had a meeting with them last week. It must be something else."

Phillip's expression changed, as if she had reminded him of something he would rather not recall. "Well, whatever it is, I don't think it's any of your business," he added rudely.

"Excuse me," Kate murmured. She hurried away, but not before she heard Sandra say, "For God's sake, Phillip. You'd better sit down before you fall down!" and Phillip respond sardonically, "Your caring nature really touches my heart, Sandra, dear."

With relief Kate re-entered the restaurant and learned from the maitre d' which table was slated as hers. Unfortunately, her table had a wonderful window side view of the river—which tonight included Sandra and Phillip.

What was it with the two of them? Kate wondered idly. They acted like a long antipathy existed between them. She would be glad when Jake showed up and they disappeared. She just hoped the latter would happen before the former.

As if her thoughts had conjured him up, Jake suddenly

appeared at the maitre d' stand. Kate's pulse fluttered. He looked so handsome. It humbled her to know that the searching gaze he swept over the restaurant was meant for her. She felt lucky that he cared about her, and though she knew that wasn't exactly a healthy attitude when it came to love, she couldn't help herself.

She just hoped he felt lucky, too.

Lifting a hand, she caught his attention. He grinned, his trademark smile seeming to brighten the restaurant like no electric lights ever could.

He wore the same suit he'd had on earlier: dark and conservative with an equally conservative dark blue tie. But as he walked toward her he yanked on the tie and undid the top button of his crisp white shirt. Stuffing the tie in his pocket, he pulled out the chair across from her, his gaze sweeping over her in what could only be described as lust.

"I've been thinking about you all day," Jake admitted. "I really wanted to talk to you at the audition, but it was impossible."

"I've been thinking about you, too."

"It's bizarre, isn't it? After all these years." He shook his head, boyishly happy.

Kate was deliriously ecstatic herself. "Beyond bizarre. Pretty wonderful, really."

He reached across the table and clasped her hands within his. "Kate—" he began, when Sandra and Phillip ducked into the restaurant from the river side. Jake's brows lifted, and he shot a glance toward Kate.

She whispered quickly, "I saw them earlier. I think they were waiting for you. I just didn't want to—give you up to them."

His back straightened as Sandra and Phillip beelined toward them, but he didn't offer a greeting. He appeared as disinterested in meeting either of them as Kate was—which brightened her mood considerably.

"So, what is this?" Sandra asked with a brittle smile.

"Dinner," Jake responded evenly.

"Oh, dinner." Her dark gaze fastened on Kate a moment too long. Kate couldn't miss the jealousy, and without realizing it, she began to hold her breath, expelling it only when Sandra turned to Jake. "Remember our pact?" she murmured. When Jake's eyes never left hers, Sandra swung toward Kate and said with false lightness, "How quickly they forget. Are you seeing each other?"

Kate blinked, not certain how to respond, but Jake offered, "Yes, we are," into the tense silence that ensued.

"What pact?" Phillip asked.

"Jake knows," Sandra said, her lips tightening.

Phillip sent her a disparaging look. "Give it up. Little brother's moved on!" He barked out a short laugh. "Wait till the folks find out. The Old Man will have a coronary!"

"What does that mean?" Sandra asked, frowning in distaste at Phillip.

"These two are longtime lovers," he explained, sweeping an arm expansively in Jake and Kate's direction, brushing a woman customer's shoulder in the process. The woman gasped and recoiled. "Sorry," Phillip murmured, staggering a bit.

"Get a hold of yourself," Jake said flatly. "What's wrong with you?"

"Same old thing. I'm not as good as you, brother. I'm the black sheep bastard." Phillip managed a small bow in Kate's direction. "So long, fair lady. I hope your involvement with the Talbots is long and fruitful."

"Go home and sleep it off." Jake's voice brooked no argument. "And make sure you take a taxi."

"You know it's the only way I drive after a few drinks. See, I can be responsible." He lurched his way to the front.

Sandra glared at Jake, her expression partly mutinous, partly miserable. "When you're finished with dinner, call me. No, I'll call you," she amended, as if fearing Jake would never follow through. "Good evening, Mrs. Rose. I see now how little influence Turner and Moss had on determining who would be the best spokesperson for Talbot Industries."

Into the moody silence following her departure, Jake said, "Don't let them complicate things. Remember how we were at the beach."

"I remember." But it was difficult because now she knew about Sandra. "What was your pact?"

Jake groaned and closed his eyes. "She wanted me to give her a chance. She knew our relationship was ending, and she wanted to keep a foot in the door. She begged me to promise that if I started caring about someone else, that I'd come right out and tell her so she could—I don't know—fight for our relationship, I guess."

"And did you? Tell her?"

"It was over by the time she wanted the pact, and we both knew it. It was never a serious thing to begin with."

"Ahh . . ." Kate twiddled with her fork. "By that, you mean it was never a 'physical' thing?"

Jake's eyes regarded her steadily, as if he could see the torment in her soul. "I mean it was never a serious thing."

Kate nodded, every muscle tense, her insides aching with fresh knowledge that she was a fool to fall so hard, so fast. She had built up this relationship with Jake into something much more complex and meaningful when they, too, were really *just dating!*

"Sandra showed an interest in me, and I let her. At the time I was way too involved in the company. My father turned it over to me last spring, and I wasn't interested in meeting any women. I didn't have time for them. When Sandra took over as our liaison for Turner and Moss, we noticed each other," he admitted, making a rueful face. "It was simple. Easy. Sandra's smart and dynamic."

Kate nodded quickly, not sure she could hear any more. Her ears rang as it was from hearing Jake praise Sandra. She wanted to bury her face behind her hands like a coward, but instead she fought to appear normal and poised.

Jake went on relentlessly, "Then I met you again. You said you can't be just one on a list. You said you have to be the only woman in my life, the only one in my bed. Do you think I've forgotten that? I ran to the beach to avoid seeing Sandra, and at the time I had no clear idea that you and I could ever have anything together." He shook his head. "Just meeting you again was enough to end it with Sandra. I didn't want her company, and I didn't know what to do."

"It's all right." Kate's voice was a whisper.

"And then there you were. On my doorstep like a gift from the gods. Injured, no less," he said, gesturing to her ankle. "And all I wanted to do was take care of you. That's still all I want to do."

The lump in Kate's throat was like to choke her. She uttered a sound of protest.

"Please, Katie," he said, his voice throbbing with need. "Don't let Sandra, or Phillip, or *anyone*, be a reason to stop seeing me. I want you. I *want* you."

The burn of tears fought behind her lids. She glanced away, touching a finger to the corner of her eye, seeking to hide the sparkle of misery that wetted her lashes.

"Oh, Katie . . . ," he murmured.

"Don't, Jake."

"Give us a chance."

"I have to," she said, her voice breaking. "I don't have any other choice."

Relief flooded his face. He picked up her hands and kissed them fervently. Kate smiled through a veil of tears that simply wouldn't stem no matter how hard she willed them to.

"Come back to my place after dinner," he pleaded. "Don't say no. Let me show you how much I need you. Please, Kate . . ."

Chapter Fourteen

"I can't spend the night with you," Kate murmured, curling into the warmth of Jake's arms, loving the feel of her naked body touching his. They were in his bed: a huge expanse of mattress covered by ivory sheets and crowned by a black comforter and an assortment of king-sized pillows.

"Why not?" he muttered, absently tucking a strand of her hair behind her ear while his lips brushed her cheek.

"April."

He groaned and cuddled her closer. She ran a finger lazily through his slightly rough chest hair, enjoying the moment. "Don't leave yet," he begged.

"No, not yet . . ."

After long, tender moments of kissing, her mouth curved into a smile. "What?" Jake demanded.

"I can't leave anyway."

"Why not?"

"You've got to take me home," she reminded him.

"Then, you're never leaving. I decree that you're staying with me all night."

Kate shook her head, rubbing her face against his chest in the process. "My daughter's home alone with her boyfriend, ostensibly cooking him dinner." *My* daughter, not *our* daughter, her conscience reminded her with a little twinge.

"The trails of parenting," he said ironically.

Kate shut her mind to the pitfalls awaiting her over the April issue. She couldn't think about it now. She couldn't.

Jake's bedside phone buzzed, and he groaned in annoyance. He let the answering machine pick up, but when Phillip's voice came on the line, he snatched up the receiver.

"Hello?" His voice sounded curiously sleepy from their hours of lovemaking.

"You're in bed already?" Phillip questioned in surprise.

Jake could have retorted with, "You're sober now?" but decided against it. Put-downs were more his brother's forte. "What's up?" he asked.

Tactfully, Kate slipped out of bed and started putting on her clothes. Jake motioned her back, but she shook her head.

"I meant to tell you earlier. I saw the folks today," Phillip said casually. "I told them it wasn't working."

"What wasn't working?" Jake flipped back the covers and patted the mattress, but Kate grinned and headed for the living room.

"The job at the company. You said yourself the employees didn't appreciate me taking in a substantial income when I did next to nothing." Phillip's tone was light.

He had Jake's full attention now. Something was going on with Phillip, and it was time to find out exactly what. And yes, Jake *had* expressed those feelings. "So, what are you planning to do, quit?"

"I asked our father for a piece of Talbot. Something easily broken off."

"What?" Jake sat up straight. Talbot Industries was not easily divided, and several departments and properties helped support other ones.

"Now, don't be greedy, little brother. You know you've wanted to be rid of me for some time. Dear Old Dad's thinking it over."

"Well, I hope he comes to his senses. Phillip, you own stock. Part of the company's yours already!"

"Those shares are not under my control right now," Phillip reminded Jake tersely. "Father's got control."

"If you really wanted to sell them, I'd talk to Phillip," Jake said. He and his brother alike could never seem to call their father "Dad" or any other familial endearment. The man was too austere, too cold.

"A fat lot of good it'll do you. Nope, this is a better way."

"What part of the company are you thinking about?"

"Oh, nothing much. I've got some things I'm working on."

"Working on?" The undercurrents here were making Jake very nervous. His brother's interest in feathering his own nest could be disastrous for the company as a whole.

"Hey, I'd even take over that unlucky strip mall. Just thought you oughtta know I'll be out of your hair soon."

Though there had always been hard feelings between his parents and Phillip, and though a part of him was relieved at the idea of having Phillip's problems separated from Talbot Industries once and for all, Jake couldn't help questioning his brother's true motivations. Phillip was tricky. He didn't operate in a straightforward manner. Half the time there was a hidden agenda somewhere, but for the life of him, Jake couldn't see what it was this time.

"We'll talk about it later," Jake murmured, hanging up. Throwing on a pair of boxers and jeans, he walked barefooted into the living room where Katie was once more fully garbed in her denim, button-up dress and strappy sandals. Her hair was down now, however, after Jake had dispensed with the comb she had twisted it in to run his fingers through its silken strands. She looked so beautiful to him that he couldn't keep himself from hugging her close again, feeling her warmth against his bare chest.

"You're not making it easy for me to leave," she pointed out.

"That's the idea."

"Jake, please," she half laughed, as his lips trailed down the soft skin of her neck and throat.

His doorbell rang at that moment. Stifling a curse of annoyance, he glanced toward the entryway as if it were the door's fault itself that he couldn't continue his lovemaking.

"I'll get my purse," Kate told him, heading back for the bedroom as Jake, after a moment of watching the soft sway of her hips, answered the bell.

Sandra Galloway stood on the threshold. "Mind if I come in?"

Jake forced himself to be polite, though his first instinct was to shut the door in her face. Cutting through whatever she was about to say, he told her flatly, "Sandra, there isn't any pact between us. I'm sorry if I gave you the wrong impression."

"Oh, no." Her mouth drew down unhappily. "You were pretty clear. And I'm sorry I was angry, earlier."

"It's all right."

Jake didn't want to see her. He didn't want this conversation. He only wanted Kate. In his arms. Right now. For some reason it seemed imperative that they jell all the details of their relationship right now, though why that should be he really couldn't say.

"You didn't have to take me off the job!" Sandra accused, her dark eyes full of hurt. "I can still do it."

"What are you talking about?"

"When I got home, there was a message from my boss. I got the impression you'd called him right after dinner. Maybe even from the restaurant!"

Jake stared at her. "I didn't make a call. I've been— busy."

"Yes, I know. With Kate Rose." Her lips twisted. "You don't have to lie, Jake. I'm a big girl."

"Are you saying someone at Talbot asked to have you dismissed as liaison with Turner and Moss Advertising?"

"That's exactly what I'm saying."

"It's not true."

"Yes, it is," she argued. "I'm off the account."

Jake's gaze narrowed. He realized there were undercurrents he had paid no attention to until now. "Well, I certainly didn't ask to have you removed. It may have been Phillip," he added uncomfortably.

"Phillip! He doesn't have any control!"

"He could have called up and said he was me," Jake pointed out. "It's happened before."

"That bastard!"

"What is your relationship with him, Sandra?" Jake wanted to know.

She started. "I don't have a relationship with him."

"There's something going on. I don't really care what it is; I just don't want it to influence Talbot's business."

Her wounded eyes searched his. "That's the problem; you really don't care, do you?" Jake didn't answer, and Sandra made a sound of frustration. "All right, I met Phillip first, but it was nothing. When you and I got together, things *clicked!*"

Before he could respond she strolled over to him, sliding her hands down his bare arms. Jake's hands were in his pockets, and he waited in silence, uneasy. His ears were tuned to his bedroom. Kate could come out at any minute.

"Can't it be that way again?" Sandra whispered pleadingly.

Kate chose that moment to throw open the bedroom door. Jake's attention was diverted, and Sandra's eyes widened as she realized they weren't alone. Jake attempted to gently pull back, but Sandra, quick as a cat, kissed him hard on the lips. He froze, a vision of her bright red mouth imbedded on his brain. She released him just as Kate entered the room. "For old time's sake!" she declared, tossing Kate a bright smile as she twisted open the front knob.

Kate was frozen, one hand on the bedroom door, the other clutching her purse. Her golden eyes were wide as they surveyed the scene.

"You'll talk to my boss, then?" Sandra threw over her shoulder to Jake as she sailed into the outer hallway. "I'd hate to lose Talbot Industries."

"I'll take care of it."

The door shut slowly behind her.

Jake swiped at his lips with the back of his hand, removing the traces of Sandra's kiss. "It's about time you showed up," he accused Kate. "I was being attacked by a predatory female."

"Really?" She arched a brow.

"It was terrible. She had me by the throat. If you hadn't come in when you did, it would have been ugly."

Katie's pink lips curved into a smile in spite of herself. He knew just what to say to dispel her fears.

"It appears Sandra was taken off our account by mistake," Jake added. "Probably Phillip's doing."

"Why would he do that?"

"Your guess is as good as mine."

Kate gazed thoughtfully in the direction Sandra had exited. She didn't trust the woman, and why should she? Sandra had made it clear she wasn't giving up on Jake, and for all Kate knew, tonight was just a respite. She could start her campaign to win him back again tomorrow, although Kate reminded herself that Jake seemed less than interested in the fiery brunette.

With a sound of impatience, Jake crossed the room in ground-devouring strides, gathering her close. She could smell Sandra's distinctive feminine scent on his skin and see the faint remnants of blood red lipstick smeared at the corners of his mouth.

With her fingertip, she gently rubbed away the telltale signs. "She's branded you."

"God!"

Jake dropped Kate and scrubbed at his mouth. Kate started laughing. For that he pulled her into his arms, hauling her over his shoulder back to the bedroom. Kate grabbed on to the casing around the bedroom door. "Stop! No! You must take me home!"

"You're driving me crazy," he muttered.

"Jake, please!"

"Oh, all right." Reluctantly, he set her on her feet. "But I want to see you again tomorrow. Same time, same place." He pointed to his bed just in case she had missed his meaning.

"Tomorrow," she assured him, her eyes laughing into his. Could he tell how much she loved him? She had the feeling there was no way she could hide it.

The call came in at closing on Thursday evening. Kate was talking to Jillian, who had reminded her yet again about their date with Jeff and Michael the following night, when April, who had taken the call, slammed down the phone and shrieked with delight.

"I got it! I got it! Oh, geez. Oh, wow. I feel like I'm going to be sick!" Her eyes glimmered a bright blue, and her lips trembled. She started quivering violently from head to toe.

"Are you okay?" Kate demanded at the same moment Jillian cried, "The Talbot audition? You got the Talbot job?"

"Sit down," Kate ordered, leading her shaking daughter to a chair.

"Yes!" April gulped. "Yes!"

"That's fabulous!" Kate squeezed April in a bear hug.

"Oh, my God. Oh, my God." April collapsed in the reception chair like a rag doll. She gazed blankly at her mother, then started, as if a sudden thought had caused physical pain. "You knew already, didn't you?" she accused.

"What? No! Why would I know?"

"Because you've been seeing Mr. Talbot every night this week."

"Just two nights," Kate protested, but her face flushed in spite of herself. *Two wonderful nights,* she could have added. "He wouldn't tell me what was going on at Talbot. We don't talk about company business.

"What do you talk about?" Jillian asked, crossing her arms over her chest and lifting a brow.

"The weather," Kate declared flatly, to which they both laughed.

"I can't believe it," April said, pushing her hands through her hair. Her face glowed with delight. "I just can't believe it. They picked me. But I thought I was going to be too young. They picked me!"

"Of course they picked you," Jillian declared. "You're perfect."

"I'm supposed to be there Monday morning for the first day's shooting. Oh, gosh. What'll I wear? Do you think I should cut my hair?"

"No!" Kate and Jillian cried in unison. Kate added, "They like you just the way you are."

April leapt to her feet. "I've got to tell Ryan. He'll just die. I'm going to die right here! Oh, Mom!"

Kate's heart swelled with pride. April was so smart and so adult, and yet such a kid sometimes. She couldn't wait to see Jake tonight again and thank him for making her— their—daughter so happy. "Jake's coming over to our place this evening," she informed April. "You can talk about it then."

"I'm going to kiss his feet!" Her brow turned into little lines of worry. "Are you sure you didn't have anything to do with this?"

"Positive. We're just—dating," she said again, beginning to really hate that term. It meant everything from sharing a meal to sexual fulfillment these days. Guiltily, she wondered if she was destined to be swept aside afterward as easily as Sandra had been.

"I'll call off tomorrow night with Michael," Jillian said a bit reluctantly. "It's pretty clear you're 'taken.'"

Kate had been hinting around for just that, but Jillian's capitulation made her feel like an ingrate. "No, let's go. Just because I'm seeing Jake doesn't mean I can't have fun with some friends."

"As long as Michael's informed of the facts," Jillian said.

"Well, yes, that would be better." Kate dimpled.

"Don't worry. I'll take care of it."

Kate nodded. After all, she reminded herself, it was just one evening, and she had already told Jake she was busy on Friday. He had taken the news in stride, although maybe that was because she had mentioned it just after they had made the kind of passionate love that left no doubt about her feelings for him. His, for her, seemed just as strong. The only tiny bit of strangeness was that neither one of them seemed to be able to say those three little words that would have clinched everything.

"Oh, let's go home," April said, her young face dazed but elated. "I can't stand it. I seriously don't believe what just happened!"

"Believe it," Kate said with a grin.

When they got to the house Ryan was already waiting in the driveway, his body slouched insouciantly against his beat-up car. Kate regarded him tolerantly. Maybe it was having Jake in her life, but she didn't feel the same anxiety she once had upon encountering her daughter's boyfriend. Then, also, April truly had a cool head on her shoulders. Ryan wasn't about to talk her into anything she didn't want to be talked into.

It was just Kate's own old fears at work. Her mind still shied away from those awful months after graduation when she had learned she was pregnant, abandoned and virtually without any family support. Talk about the acid test into the adult world.

With a mother's ferocity, she vowed again that April would never suffer the way she had.

Jake stopped at the flower shop near his office. He bought a dozen yellow roses, then after some thought, purchased another dozen of red. The sweet, familiar scent filled his head, and he drew it deep into his lungs, hesitating long enough to have the salesclerk staring at him wonderingly.

He didn't understand himself. He was as lovesick as he had been eighteen years ago. His brain was full of images of Katie, and though he knew it was the height of ridiculousness, he couldn't—and wouldn't even try to—contain himself.

Throughout the day Kate entered his thoughts. On the

treadmill, at lunchtime, in the latest phone conversation with Diamond Corporation. And though he sensed with his own innate talent and business acumen that something was rotten in Denmark about that particular deal, right now he couldn't summon up the will to care.

It hadn't helped when Sandra had blown into his office while he was daydreaming away, his gaze aimed toward the hazy cobalt sky. It hung like a curtain over the slow-flowing Willamette, the river coursing directly through Portland's city center, dividing the west side from the east on its languorous way to the Columbia River. He had been entranced by the view, another symptom that something was definitely wrong with him, since normally all he could think of was Talbot Industries no matter how beautiful the vista.

"So you're using April Rose," Sandra said without preamble.

Jake sighed. For a woman supposedly grateful that he had gotten her job back for her, Sandra was awfully abrasive. "We decided to use April Rose as the spokesperson. Damn near a unanimous vote all around."

"Is Phillip jumping for joy?"

"You'd have to ask him," Jake informed her shortly.

Sandra looked like she had a lot more to say. In truth Jake wished she would just leave. He hadn't wanted her to be fired from Talbot's account at his brother's whim, but he had to admit it might be a lot easier if she weren't around so much.

"You never gave us much of a chance," she suddenly put in, and Jake inwardly groaned, realizing they were about to start Round Two.

"Look . . ." Jake hesitated, not wanting this. He felt guilty and angry, both at himself and her. Yes, he had been callous to drift into a relationship that he had sensed had no future, yet in all fairness to himself, Sandra had certainly pushed things forward at a quicker pace than he might have chosen.

"You were already seeing her, weren't you? That's why you ran off to the beach."

"I wasn't seeing her then," he disabused flatly.

"Well, it doesn't matter, does it? Since things have clearly progressed pretty quickly since then."

"Yes, they have." He met her gaze squarely. There was only so much sidestepping he was willing to do.

"So, she's the reason," Sandra said through tight lips.

Jake could have cured her of that opinion. But was it kinder to let her think she had been thrown over for someone else rather than explaining that he had never had serious feelings for her in the first place? There was no good answer during a breakup.

"That's it, then? I'm out?" she demanded.

Jake could think of nothing helpful to say. "I'm sorry."

As a placating answer, it had the opposite effect. Her reaction was galvanic. She stormed to his desk, standing quivering above it. Jake lifted his brows in expectation. "I should have stuck with Phillip," she blurted out furiously. "At least he was honest."

"Phillip . . . ," he repeated with distaste.

So that was the answer. Phillip and Sandra had shared a relationship first. He wasn't really surprised, and he didn't speculate on what that might mean; he truly didn't care. But after she stormed away, he had been left feeling depressed and deflated. It would have been nice if one of them had seen fit to tell him about their prior relationship. It was a wonder, really, that Phillip hadn't blurted it out during one of his drunken binges, but then, maybe he hadn't cared that much to begin with, either.

Which hardly flattered Sandra.

Jake had turned from that dissatisfactory scene to a meeting with Gary later in the afternoon. But during talk about the repairs to the strip mall vandalism, Jake had actually drifted off. He hadn't caught every word, and to his embarrassment, had been forced to ask Gary to repeat everything twice. Gary had stared at him as if he had lost his mind completely—and maybe he had.

Even a conversation with Detective Marsh couldn't keep his attention, though the detective's theory that the perpetrator was someone who had been within Talbot's employ had set no better with Jake than his original one where he had blamed errant teenagers. Detective Marsh had asked for a list of employees who had been fired over the last six months, and Jake had managed to pull one together before he left the office.

But now he was on his way to Kate's. It was strange how focused he was on this forthcoming evening with her. She was making dinner, and it was the first time she had invited him to her house. It seemed like a major step, but looking back on things, he had to concede that their relationship had truly lasted less than *one week* so far.

Okay, that wasn't completely true. Long ago and far away they had been lovers; they had even pretended they were spouses. But it was such ancient history that even in this new, not entirely welcome, giddy state, Jake recognized that counting those days in the past was beyond sanity. He was a completely different person now; so was Kate. Attraction and sexual chemistry, however, appeared to remain intact throughout a person's lifetime. He believed he had read something to that effect once, which explained why so many people who had once been lovers, then married other for years and years, tended to return to their first loves after they were divorced or their first spouse died.

Which didn't mean he shouldn't be careful with Kate. Once burned, twice shy, and all that. So now, as he searched the street signs for the road that led to her house,

Jake asked himself what, if anything, he expected of this evening. Kate's daughter April would be there, and that didn't leave much room for privacy. Searching his feelings, he realized he didn't care all that much. Yes, he would love to pull Katie into bed and make love to her—that hadn't diminished! But he also recognized that at some deeper level he was anxious to get to know April better, to become familiar to her, to infiltrate their home, their life, everything . . .

And that sounded very much like he had made some kind of commitment, though not a word had been spoken as such between them.

It's too soon, he rationalized as he slid the Bronco to a stop in front of the small cottage at the end of the curved drive. Rhododendron bushes flanked the front walk, their leaves thick and glossy this time of year while their blossoms were long gone, their last hurrah the previous spring.

He rang the bell and was rewarded with galloping footsteps inside, though April was the picture of decorum when she pulled open the door.

"Hi!" she greeted him, her eyes a sparkle of dusty blue, her teeth a shining curve of white. For a second he felt a strange déjà vu. She reminded him of someone.

"Thank you so much for the job," she said with heartfelt gratitude.

"You earned it on your own," he assured her, handing her the bouquet of yellow roses.

"For me?" The gesture tickled her, and if possible, her grin widened. "Come in, come in," she urged, leading him down the short hallway to the kitchen. Kate stood near the sink, a bottle of wine in one hand, corkscrew in the other.

Sight of her hit Jake like a hammer. No wonder he thought April reminded him of someone. She was Kate's likeness, Kate's daughter.

Kate's eyes fell to the red roses. "Oh, Jake," she said, as if he had brought her the stars from the heavens.

"I'll find some vases," April said, already digging through a nearby sideboard.

"You look great," Jake murmured to Kate, the words springing right from his heart. There was a lushness to her that couldn't be denied. She wore jeans and a soft taupe cotton sweater that buttoned to a collar at her throat. Her breasts were softly defined beneath the fabric, swaying ever so gently in an unconscious, seductive manner that drew Jake so completely he had to fight not to ogle at them like some lecher.

"You look pretty good yourself," she said lightly, clearly a bit embarrassed as she shot a look toward her daughter.

April took the two bouquets of roses and, after several attempts to arrange them separately, snorted her disgust before gathering all the roses in one vase. She set her creation in the center of the table and flanked it by two tall white candles.

"Vanilla," she said. "It just all smells so good together."

Musk and vanilla. He could remember scents way too well, Jake decided, eyeing Kate, who also seemed mesmerized by the artful display April was working on so feverishly. Did she recall that long-ago wedding as sharply as he did? When her eyes met his, the message in them said she did.

They ate chicken piccata and Caesar salad and drank wine. April pulled out a mud pie she had purchased from a gourmet ice cream store, and though Jake wasn't that much of a dessert eater, he managed a small piece, amused at the way April, who was as slim and muscular as a filly, tucked into her wedge of ice cream.

"So, what are the commercials like?" April asked.

"They're mostly industrial, made for other companies that do business with us. But we have one we want to air on television."

"Cool." April was enthralled.

"You'll appear to be an employee of Talbot Industries. We refurbished a downtown Portland hotel. You walk us through the lobby and talk about what's been restored and what's been added. The hotel staff's in the background, and they'll interject about how fantastic staying at the West Bank Hotel is. That kind of thing."

"Your company did the West Bank refurbishing?" Kate asked. To Jake's nod, she said enthusiastically, "It's fabulous inside now."

"We restored all the wood paneling in the lobby area, completely redid the kitchen, and we're still working on the guest suites. The top floor is the Presidential Suite on the river side; across the hall are two other minisuites which face the city. There are fireplaces and gas lighting and the works. You should see it," he told Kate, whose lovely face grew more and more animated as she listened.

"I would love to!"

"Do you mind if I tag along? Or, would you rather be alone," murmured April, fighting a smile.

"She's way too precocious," Kate complained, but Jake could see the affection in her golden eyes when she regarded her daughter.

"Let's go tomorrow night," Jake suggested. "We can have dinner and then coffee in the lobby bar."

"Great idea!" April was excited.

Kate just smiled. Neither of them seemed to remember that she had a date on Friday.

With dinner over, April grilled Jake on a few more aspects of the coming rehearsals; then she disappeared to her room. Moments later music throbbed from the end of the hallway, muted by her closed door.

"I don't know what's come over me," Kate said. "I can't concentrate when I'm with you."

Jake sent her a lazy smile. "You, too? I'm glad to hear

it. I'd hate to think I was the only one who was acting like this."

"Like what?" Kate asked.

She was seated on the edge of the couch. Jake, who had found the bottle of brandy Kate admitted to buying just for him, swirled the amber fluid as he stood beside her. Because they were past the preliminaries, he sank next to her on the cushions, crowding her to one end of the seat.

"You're in my space," she whispered, her lips curving expectantly.

"Am I?"

"Uh huh."

Jake set down his snifter on the sofa table behind the couch, cupped her face in one hand and kissed her lightly on the lips.

"Now, you're really in my space."

"I've been thinking about you all day."

Kate's lashes drifted closed, and the corners of her mouth quirked sensually. "Really."

"You just want to hear how crazy I am about you."

"Mmmhmm. Tell me more."

"You're beautiful. And—I don't want to talk anymore."

His mouth slanted down on hers, firm and slightly impatient. His ears were tuned to the muffled music down the hall. Kate met his kiss eagerly, but she, too, seemed to be listening.

"We're crazy," she whispered. "What if April comes out?"

"We're just kissing."

"Oh, sure."

"Well, we are. We'd just like to be doing something more. Tomorrow night," he assured her, his voice deepening as his mind moved ahead to what that meant. "After we drop April off."

Kate sighed. "I can't go tomorrow. I promised Jillian we'd go out."

Jake sucked air between his teeth. "I forgot."

"But maybe, if you and April go, I could meet you later?"

"Okay," he agreed, then added, "What is it that Jillian wants you to do?"

Kate hesitated. She hadn't quite explained about the "date" idea. "I feel stupid saying this, but I'm set up to go out with a friend of Jillian's boyfriend. I've never even met him."

"You're going out with a man?" Jake couldn't help himself from asking. The spurt of jealousy that shot through him surprised him.

Kate saw his expression harden and hastened to explain. "I don't want to go. It's one night. She's been after me for months since Ben's death, and believe it or not, it was only after I'd seen you again and didn't know what to do about it that I accepted. Of course, that was before last weekend. It scared me to see you again. All those feelings. I wanted to kill them, so they couldn't hurt me again; so I said yes to a date with Michael."

"You don't have to explain."

"Oh, right. I'd sure want you to, given the reverse situation."

"It's okay," he said quickly, annoyed that his reaction was so obvious. He wanted to strangle someone—this Michael person would be just fine. It was unfair and infantile, but he had to face his emotions for what they were.

"It *is* okay," Kate assured him, her soft lips moving forward to slide across his mouth. "I haven't exactly been hiding my feelings from you. A date with a stranger isn't going to change them if eighteen years and a marriage couldn't!"

"God, Katie." He buried his face in the fragrance of

her neck, and from some soul-deep emptiness he uttered the words that could only cement his fate, "I love you."

Her intake of breath was a tremulous gasp. "I love you more," she whispered fiercely in his ear.

The door to April's room flew open, shooting out a cacophony of blasting music. Kate and Jake broke apart like guilty teenagers, and when April appeared in the living room, she stopped short.

"I was just—getting something," she apologized.

"No problem." Kate was bright and cheerful.

Jake rubbed his nose to hide a smile. In all the women he had dated, he had rarely been involved with one who possessed a child. Maybe it was some failing on his part, or maybe he was generally attracted to unfettered females, but whatever the case, April was a new experience for him, and one he found, to his surprise, that he enjoyed immensely.

"Go on," April singsonged as she sashayed back to her room.

Jake and Kate stared at each other, their eyes filled with mirth. The moment spun out, and then the words spoken between them came back hauntingly, a memory of days long past and unfulfilled promises.

"I know it's crazy," Jake murmured, "but the gap since we were first in love seems really small right now. Maybe that's just wishful thinking on my part, because you know something? I want it all back!"

Kate nodded, searching his intense gaze eagerly. There were no hidden agendas. He wanted what she wanted! It was so perfect she couldn't help but distrust it, yet on the other hand, he was so easy to trust.

"I know you've only been a widow for six months, but would you think about marriage again?" he asked.

"Marriage! To—you?" she questioned, holding her breath.

"That was the idea, yes," admitted Jake, his mouth twisting into a smile.

Kate felt almost faint. She had dreamed of this so often she could scarcely believe she had heard right. Marriage to Jake Talbot, the only man she had ever truly loved.

"We haven't even been together a week," she voiced, airing the words she knew needed to be said.

"Does it really matter?"

She gazed at him helplessly. "I'm not sure."

"I just want to think that it's out there someday, you know?" Jake told her, picking through his thoughts. "I'm thirty-six. I'm tired of living alone, and I want to be with you. I want to marry you."

"I want to marry you, too," she whispered hoarsely, her throat hot and aching.

He swept her close, burying his face in her hair. Kate kissed his neck and beard-roughened cheeks. She was in a dream, playing a part that left her drifting limitlessly between reality and fantasy. "I love you!" she choked out.

A chuckle rumbled deep in his chest, and he dutifully answered, "I love you more."

And after that no more plans were made while they kissed and cuddled and generally chafed about April being their chaperone, whether she knew of her role or not.

Kate couldn't help dragging her feet as she finished getting ready for her evening with Jillian, Jeff and Michael. She pulled on a pair of black sandals and inspected her bruising. Not too bad. She wore loose, navy pants and a drapey matching blouse, and her expression, when she threw a glance at herself in the mirror, was mutinous. Spying the glowering lines between her eyes she wiggled her brows, then smiled at herself. Okay, so she wasn't excited about going on this date with Jillian *et al.* She could survive.

And let's face it, it kind of thrilled her that it needled Jake so much. Though he tried to act like it didn't matter, that it was one small hurdle before they got serious-serious, she knew her date with Michael bothered him. No amount of negating the evening on her part helped, either. In fact, the less she made of it, the more he tightened up.

Marriage! He had actually brought up the "m" word. Every thought, every uttered word and sweet touch, had echoed her own needs, wants and desires. It was uncanny. They were too in sync for her to believe.

When are you going to tell him about April?

This time when Kate gazed into her own eyes she saw the anxiety hovering in their gold depths. Marriage? Impossible without the truth! Yet, the truth would make marriage impossible in the first place. Some secret, selfish part of her wondered what would happen if she told him *after* the ceremony. To find out that April, whom he already cared about by his own admission, was his own flesh and blood? Shouldn't that be a blessing, not a terrible revelation to tear them asunder?

Kate's breaths came short and fast. Her chest tightened until it hurt. It was a betrayal already. It would be a breach of honor, a lie, a complete travesty of trust if she tricked him in that way. She couldn't marry Jake without telling him the truth. She couldn't.

Yet, how could she tell him? And then how could she tell April?

Realizing she was quaking with fear, Kate stepped back from the mirror. Her hair was a mess from raking her fingers through it. Brushing it with more vigor than finesse, the blond-brown strands flew around her face with static electricity. Drawing several soul-cleansing breaths Kate stepped away from the bathroom just as the doorbell rang.

A part of her realized she had hung on to this date because she was afraid of the future. Jake would leave her when the truth came out. She knew it. So, she was clinging to her life without him as if that would somehow save her from her own love for him.

Oh, god, she silently prayed as she put a false smile on her face and twisted the handle for the front door. What am I going to do?

Jake paced the confines of his living room with the restlessness of a caged panther. Kate had one silly date with this fellow, and that was it. One date. Dinner and a couple drinks, and then she was his. What could possibly be wrong with that?

Growling in frustration, he poured himself a brandy, then stared moodily into the amber fluid, less interested in consuming it than wanting to have something to do with his hands. Drink wasn't the answer.

He knew he was nuts. He understood that Kate's evening had been planned before last weekend. Still, he couldn't shake the feeling that somehow their relationship would never see that walk down the aisle.

Setting down his drink, Jake snatched up his keys and headed for the door. *Forget about it,* he told himself. He had a date with April ahead of him, and when Kate could politely get away, she was going to join them at the West Bank.

What could possibly go wrong?

The restaurant Jillian chose was an Italian chain from California which offered rich food, loud tables, painted archways, peach-colored tile and a window view of the street. If Kate had been with Jake, she might have thought it was heaven on earth. As it was, she couldn't wait to escape and walk the seven blocks to the West Bank.

Not that Michael wasn't a nice guy. He was sweet and attentive, and unfortunately, very interested in Kate. That much was obvious. Jillian's words to the wise apparently hadn't had any effect, so Kate was smiling her way through dessert, practicing how she would say goodbye, when a cluster of anxious people near the restaurant's front door caught her eye.

"What's going on?" she asked.

"I don't know." Jillian set down her napkin, never one to wonder for too long without asking. "I'll find out."

Five minutes later, she came back to the table, looking worried. "I don't exactly know," she told them with a frown. "Apparently there was some kind of explosion. The ambulances are on their way."

"Explosion?" Kate exclaimed. "Where?"

Jillian shook her head. "Up the street a ways. Looks like it could be the West Bank Hotel . . ."

Chapter Fifteen

"This is fabulous!" April enthused, glancing around the gleaming paneling of the West Bank's lobby. She looked this way and that, absorbing it all.

"It is," Jake agreed. There were several sets of couches crowded around glass-topped tables which were scattered around the lobby floor. People were drinking and talking quietly, the earlier, after-work crowd having already departed.

"Your company restored this?" She ran her hand over the lustrous wood.

Jake nodded. "It's the original."

April walked across the lobby in the direction of the underground walkway that led beneath the street to a car park. He could picture her doing much the same thing, sweeping an arm to encompass the lush appointments of the hotel, while the camera whirred away. She would be an excellent spokesperson for Talbot.

He came up behind, pointing past her shoulder to the two-story high windows that faced the street. Her gaze followed the direction of his fingers. "I understand they plan to film you from several angles. A nighttime shot will be with your back to those windows."

"Cool."

Her high school vernacular made him smile. Jake's back was to the underground walkway. He started to turn, to say something else. A loud, shrieking *bang* sounded. His ears rang. He glanced back. The door to the walkway was a surreal bullet, twisting toward him, blown off its hinges. Jake jerked around protectively. The door glanced off his shoulder, knocking him into April. They went down in a heap. Wood and Sheetrock and dust and fibers burst from deep inside the hotel, showering them, burying the lobby in rubble.

Glass shattered. People screamed. Jake's ears ached. It was deafening! Instinctively he covered April's body with his own. She quivered beneath him. He held her down. Something hit his leg. He felt no pain, but sudden warmth made him wonder if what he felt was blood. Choking dust filled his eyes and ears. He couldn't see. He couldn't *think!*

Time passed. Distantly he thought he heard a woman's voice.

"Mr. Talbot? Mr. Talbot? Jake?"

"April," he muttered, remembering that she was beneath him. With difficulty he shifted away; then darkness descended.

Kate raced past the gathering police officers into the destruction of the lobby. Someone yelled at her, and an officer tried to grab her arm. She shied away, her heart thundering with fear as she stepped over pieces of wood and glass and twisted metal.

"April!" she called. "Jake! Oh, God, *where are you?*"

"Mom!"

April's voice nearly sent her to her knees. A wave of weakness passed over her. Fear, in its worst form. Her legs quivered, and suddenly she couldn't move.

Out of the rubble and debris, April, her hair unnaturally whitened by the Sheetrock dust, her clothes torn and disheveled, practically ran through the mess to throw herself in her mother's arms.

"Are you hurt? Are you hurt?" Kate babbled.

"No, no, I'm fine. But, but," she choked on the words, tears filling her eyes.

"Oh, God," Kate murmured. "Jake . . ."

"I think he's okay. He's with the paramedics over there." She gestured to a cleared-out area of the lobby where the injured sat numbly in a cordoned-off grouping.

Kate's gaze swept the collapsible gurneys as she hurried forward, April's hand clasped firmly within her own. But Jake wasn't one of the bodies being attended to.

"Mom," April said, tugging on her frantic mother's hand. "He's right there." She pointed.

To Kate's relief and amazement he was actually standing, or leaning against the wall would be a more accurate description. He was in deep conversation with a man in a navy suit jacket and gray slacks who had "cop" written all over him.

Spying her, his face lost its grim concentration. He held out one hand, and with April still firmly in tow, Kate swept into the security of his embrace.

They stood that way for long moments, a family trio, if he had but known it. Jake buried his face in her hair for a tight instant, then turned back to the other man. "Detective Marsh, this is Kate Rose, April's mother."

"Were you here, too?" the detective asked with a frown.

"No, I was down the street. I just heard, and I knew Jake and April were here and I—" She drew a deep breath.

"Never mind," Jake told her in an unsteady voice.

She realized then that his pant leg had been split open and his thigh had been wrapped. "Are you all right?"

"A minor piece of shrapnel. I'm okay. It's the shoulder that's going to hurt tomorrow." He shrugged a bit stiffly.

"What happened?" she asked.

"Isn't that the sixty-four thousand dollar question?" he retorted, throwing a glance at the detective.

"We'll be done in a minute, ma'am," he dismissed her, and though Kate was reluctant to do so, she tore her arms from Jake and let him resume his conversation.

Kate huddled in a corner of the hotel lobby, away from the scene of destruction. Jake, his foreman Gary, and several hotel employees were with the police. They stood in a tight group near the worst of the vandalism. A section of the paneling that just a few nights earlier Jake had been so proud of had been ripped apart, blown to bits. It was repairable, possibly, but it meant hours and hours of painstaking effort to try to match it to the original.

It was a crying shame. Now that she was assured that April and Jake were all right, Kate had grown angry. Why? *Why?* The crime appeared to be pure vandalism, and she had never understood vandalism for vandalism's sake alone. A person who broke a window, or a door, or smashed a wall in order to burglarize a place was no less guilty, but Kate could at least understand the motivation. They were seeking gain.

But this . . .

From snippets of overheard conversation she learned that the explosion had taken place in the kitchen. A gas leak, the product of some criminal's hand, had blasted out half of the working area. Luckily, its power had been limited to that one section, though the force of it had blown out the door and shattered parts of the walls and windows nearest to the blast. The huge two-story lobby windows remained intact, but smaller ones had shot splinters of glass nearly across the room. Glass cuts appeared to be the worst of the injuries, with Jake taking a major slice to the back of his left thigh.

All in all, though, the consensus was that everyone was lucky: guests, hotel staff and the owners of the hotel of which Talbot Industries was one. It could have been much worse.

The kitchen was a disaster, but the kitchen staff had been reduced at this hour, slowing down after the dinner rush. No one had been directly in the path of the destruction. So, too, had the lobby area been nearly empty. Jake and April had unluckily been the people closest to the blast.

No one had seen anything. The perpetrator had managed to slip in unnoticed, do his deed and split. It was not a random crime. The hotel had been targeted, and Jake's refurbishing and remodeling had taken the brunt of the damage. So, what did that mean?

Jake detached himself from the group and came to check on her and April. "Looks like the kitchen's the worst of it. And the lobby will need work, of course." He grimaced.

"Why, Jake? Why you?"

"I don't know. It's a lot like the strip mall," he mused.

"It's like someone's trying to make a point," Kate observed, then added, "You need to rest."

"Did I thank you for saving me?" April asked in a small voice. "If not, thank you."

"I'm just sorry you were here when this happened."

"I'm okay," April assured him. "And Mom's right, you need to take care of yourself."

"Shouldn't you go to an Emergency Room?" Kate asked. "I can drive your car."

"Just take me home," he said, gazing at her soberly. His

intensity touched something deep inside her that responded to only him. "I'm glad I have you," he said. "I don't want anything to take you away from me."

"It won't," Kate responded, meaning it.

"Let's go," he said, throwing an arm over her shoulder and April's as they helped him out to the Bronco.

In the end, Kate drove April and Jake to the nearest hospital Emergency Room over both Jake's and April's protests. She sat in the waiting room and felt all her energy drain away. With an effort, she managed to ring through to Jillian and explain about her mad dash from the restaurant. She had been too upset to say anything at the time, but now she wearily related the events to Jillian, who asked too many questions, as far as Kate was concerned.

"I'll tell you all about it later," Kate finished. "They're okay, and that's what matters."

"You take care of yourself, too," Jillian warned her.

Kate sank into one of the faux-leather chairs which lined a small cubicle outside the Emergency Room. The arms were thin strips of chrome, not exactly conducive to comfort, but then Kate was anything but comfortable.

April appeared with a clean bill of health. She had suffered minor scrapes to her arms and legs. Jake took a bit longer, and when they pushed him out in a wheelchair, Kate caught his eye and hid a smile at his glower. Hospital policy had won this round, but as soon as they reached the sliding doors to the outside, he practically leaped out of the chair and into the heat of a late August night.

"I'm fine," he assured her. "A cut to the thigh, and a major bruise to the shoulder, that's all. They stitched me up and told me to rest. Good idea. I just want to fall into bed."

He didn't add, *with you*, but Kate got the message loud and clear.

"You can play nurse," he said, laying his head against the cushions of the passenger seat and closing his eyes.

"Can we stay at your place tonight?" April suddenly asked.

"Absolutely."

Kate was glad for April's suggestion because she wanted to keep an eye on both of them. At Jake's condo, she had to rouse him awake which worried her a bit. "You didn't get hit on the head, did you? You could have a concussion."

"I didn't get hit on the head," he assured her a bit testily.

"Just checking."

April yawned and said, "They practically turned me inside out. Mr. Talbot, too."

"I think you can call me Jake now, don't you?" Jake told her as Kate and April helped him off the elevator and to his front door.

"Okay, Jake." April grinned despite the soberness of their shared experience, and he grinned right back.

Inside the condo, April made appropriate noises about how lush and spacious it was, ripping off her shoes and burying her toes in the thick, cream carpet. Jake pointed to a short hallway across the room from, and opposite, the door to his master suite. "Make yourself at home in the guest room. Bedroom's on the right; bathroom's on the left."

"G'night," April called, lifting a hand at them as she departed to her space.

Kate helped Jake to his room, then said, "Just a minute. I want to check on her."

"I'll be waiting," he murmured, gingerly lying down on his back.

April was asleep on her feet. She had stripped off her

clothes, and Kate helped her wash up in the bathroom before she climbed into bed in her underwear.

"Save me a place," she told her, and April just yawned again and nodded.

When she let Jake know she planned to sleep with her daughter, he hauled her down on the bed beside him. "I know, I know. I'm all over you," he murmured, "but I don't want to let you go."

"I'm not leaving for a while," she assured him, stroking his forehead.

"I need a shower."

Kate slipped away and brought back a washcloth. He reached for it, but she did the honors herself, washing off the Sheetrock dust and grime.

"God, that feels good," he murmured. Then a second later, "How was your date?"

"My date." She half laughed. "Well, it was fine until I ran out of the restaurant in a panic. I had to call Jillian from the hospital and tell her what happened. 'My date' probably thinks I'm a hysteric."

Jake's lips curved, but his eyes didn't open. "What did you do?" he asked, keeping it light, trying not to sound jealous. It was ridiculous, really, that even with everything else going on, he didn't like thinking of Kate spending time with any other man.

"Oh, I don't know. Ate dinner . . . talked . . . had an Irish coffee for dessert . . ."

"So, what did you think of him?"

"He was just a guy. A nice guy." She hesitated, and Jake opened his eyes to see her face. "But all I could think about was—"

"Was?" he prodded.

"You. Us. I couldn't wait to get to the hotel and be with you and April. Last night you mentioned marriage, for pete's sake! It was on my mind all the while I was having dinner with Michael. I just wanted to be with you. Then when I heard about the explosion . . ." She shuddered.

"Come here." Jake dragged her close. Kate tried to be careful, and that amused him. "I won't break."

"I just don't want to hurt you."

"I'll let you know if it's too painful," he said dryly.

His hands tugged at the buttons of her blouse. Kate's own hands followed suit, pulling at his clothes until his bare, hair-roughened chest lay atop her breasts, his legs entangled with hers.

"You're sure this is all right," she murmured.

"Perfect . . ."

Desire-drugged, Kate determined she would tell him about April and everything else much later. Now was not the time. Their relationship was still far too tenuous, and Jake had been through hell and back tonight.

Jake's hot lips found the peak of one quivering breast. Kate arched, her lashes fluttering closed, her body taut with need. His hips fit perfectly against hers. She had grown used to him this past week, yet it was still a miracle how wonderful their love was.

"I love you," he whispered.

Kate sighed, and her mouth curved in amusement. Before she could respond in kind, however, he had trapped her beneath the weight of his body.

"Your leg," she protested.

"I'm not even feeling it right now," he pointed out, his lips tugging on her ear. She marveled, as she had so many times this past week, how his mouth could feel so tender when the rest of him was so hard and fit.

"Now, forget about my injuries and pay attention to the parts that are working," he advised.

Kate's answer was melodious laughter as she wrapped herself around the man she loved.

* * *

Blam! Blam! Blam! Kate opened one sleepy eye. Someone was pounding on Jake's door, and they weren't giving up. April stirred beside her at the noise but didn't awaken. Wondering if Jake were still fast asleep, too, she hastily threw on her blouse and navy slacks and headed to the door, finger-combing her hair on the way. She heard the shower going through Jake's door and understood how he had missed hearing the banging.

It was Phillip on the threshold. He didn't bother commenting on the fact that it was Kate who answered the door. "Where's Jake?" he demanded. "Is he all right? I heard about the explosion, and someone said he was there."

"He's fine. He's in the shower, I think."

"You think?" He eyed her tousled hair and clean face. Clearly she had stayed over.

"I haven't checked on him this morning," she said ironically. "My daughter's here, too. I slept with her last night."

"Oh." Phillip paced around the living room. "So, you were with him when it happened?"

"No, April was. She's okay, too," Kate hastily put in to Phillip's tortured look. "They're lucky. Everyone is."

"What happened?" Phillip asked, collapsing into a chair.

He looked thoroughly undone. His hair was uncombed, and his clothes appeared as hastily thrown on as Kate's were. He must have raced out of his place as soon as he had heard the news without bothering to pull himself together first.

Kate related what she knew about the accident, and Phillip seemed to shrink in upon himself. She realized that for all his sniping, Phillip really loved his brother.

"Detective Marsh was there?" Phillip murmured, shaking his head.

"There's some conjecture that this was another attack on Talbot Industries," Kate admitted, revealing what Jake had explained to her about the accident.

"It can't be! Why? It's coincidence."

Kate didn't respond. She only knew what Jake had told her, and like Jake, she tended to believe it was more than that. Clearly the detective felt so, too.

The door opened from Jake's master suite, and he hobbled his way into the room. He wore shorts, since his thigh was still tightly wrapped, and no shirt. Spying Phillip, he said, "What's going on?"

"Why don't you tell me, little brother? I hear you almost got yourself killed!"

"It wasn't quite that dramatic." He ran a hand through his wet hair. "Although I did have to balance half-in/half-out of the shower to keep from getting this wet." He tapped the bandage.

"How are you feeling today?" Kate asked. She wanted to rush to his arms, but with Phillip in the room, she contained herself.

"I'm okay." He shrugged, a spasm crossing his face at the effort.

"You're not okay," Kate declared, crossing the room to guide him to the loveseat. To hell with Phillip. She cuddled down beside him.

Phillip didn't care anyway. "How did it happen?" he asked.

"Someone tampered with the gas line to the kitchen. It could have been a lot worse. Marsh better find who's responsible soon, or someone's going to get killed!"

"It couldn't have been an accident?" Phillip was anxious.

Jake gave his brother a long look. "Apparently not." He

paused, then said, "Marsh thinks it's a disgruntled ex-employee, someone who's got a grudge against us."

"No way. I won't believe it." Phillip drew an unsteady breath. "God, Jake, you can't believe someone was after *you*."

Jake frowned. "Did I say that? No one's after me. I didn't have any set time to be at the West Bank. I just showed up when I showed up and happened to get unlucky. Marsh thinks the perp picked that time because there weren't many people around."

"Who has access to the kitchen?" Phillip asked, almost as if the words jumped out before he could stop them.

"They're compiling a list and hoping for a match."

"A match?" Kate asked.

"Between West Bank employees and ex-Talbot ones."

Silence pooled among them. Phillip got to his feet a bit unsteadily. "I don't like this."

"I've got to call our parents," Jake said slowly, as if this task were the most onerous to date, which maybe it was.

Phillip slid him an ironic look, showing a bit of his true nature once again. "Better you than me, little brother."

Jake snorted.

Phillip departed a few moments later, and Kate climbed to her feet. "Have you got anything to make for breakfast?"

"Pop-Tarts. The instructions are on the box."

"I was thinking more along the lines of eggs, bacon, toast and fresh fruit," Kate said dryly.

"You might find some of that in there, too." He slanted her a fond look, and Kate went about her chores with a light heart.

April appeared just as Kate was serving up the scrambled eggs, bacon and sourdough toast. "I feel like shi—" she started, then amended, "I feel like I was run over by a truck."

"I'm sure glad you're all right," Jake said soberly.

April smiled. "Same to you—Jake."

Kate's throat tightened. She would have never dreamed they would be in a situation like this. What would happen when the truth came out? What would Jake think? What would *April*?

"You okay, Mom?" she asked, witnessing the color leave Kate's expressive face.

"Never better."

Jake looked at her, too. Accosted by their twin expressions of concern, Kate's mouth dried at their resemblance—the same eyes, the same mouth, the same way of regarding her when they felt she wasn't being quite truthful with her feelings.

"Eat up," she admonished them brusquely, then turned away from their dual scrutiny.

Very, very soon she was going to have to tell the truth.

Chapter Sixteen

The rest of the weekend dragged by. Jake called, but he was embroiled in the West Bank Hotel affair and "other problems" at work, so Kate hung out with April and prepared for her daughter's commercial the following Monday. Luckily, her scrapes were minor and wouldn't show, and the ordeal had not dampened her enthusiasm. In fact, now more than ever April wanted to be a champion for Talbot Industries—Jake Talbot was her new hero.

On Sunday afternoon Jake stopped by—and made a proposal that filled her with cold fear.

"How would you like to come with me to visit my parents."

"Your parents!" Kate was instantly worked up. "Why?"

"I need to talk over the sabotage with my father, and he wants to see me in person to make sure I'm still in one piece. I thought it might be a good opportunity for them to meet you again."

"Oh, Jake!"

"I know how you feel, but let's get it over with. You may be surprised by their reaction."

"This I truly doubt," she murmured, but went to fetch her sweater as it was a cooler evening than it had been.

On the road to Lakehaven, Kate said very little. Of course this was bound to happen. She and Jake were planning a wedding, for crying out loud, so sooner or later she was going to have to see his parents again.

Gazing out the window, she watched the flashing landscape and passing miles with growing trepidation. The last time she met Phillip and Marilyn Talbot she had fainted dead away. She had believed she had told them she was pregnant, though the words had never actually formed and sounded.

Jake's hand caressed her knee as they neared the turnoff for Kate's hometown. She hadn't been here in years. Once, when April was around ten, she had taken her for an aimless country drive while Ben was at a meeting at Timberline Lodge on Mt. Hood, about a two hours' drive from Portland. Instead of heading to the east to meet her husband, she had turned west, as if she were heading to the coast, and when she had spied the turnoff for Lakehaven, she twisted the wheel without any previous intention.

The streets had seemed old and small and tired, an unfair evaluation because Lakehaven's central crossroads were a tidy, near trendy collection of shops. But on that date all Kate could see were the tattered remnants of her unhappy youth; the old hangouts that remained seemed worn and lackluster. Others had been replaced or refurbished or sold for some other business.

Now, she steeled herself for the same hit. They cruised into town, and Kate hazarded a look out the window. Bright blue awnings fluttered in the tiny breeze. Cafe tables clustered around a new ice cream parlor, cheek-to-jowl with a deli on one side and an espresso shop on the other.

"Wow," she said softly.

"It's changed a lot."

She glanced at Jake, whose terse assessment seemed out of sync with the unexpected happiness she was feeling. "What's wrong?"

He shrugged and didn't answer. He couldn't explain that coming back to Lakehaven was like revisiting the worst of his past. Every time he saw his parents, which wasn't often these days, he experienced the same sense of being smothered by a stifling, thick blanket. He hadn't spoken his feelings to Kate because he had really wanted her to join him today, but the truth was he hated coming home.

They pulled up in front of his parents' home, and Kate swallowed against a hot throat. This, at least, looked exactly the same in her memory: imposing and somehow hostile. Her gaze flicked to the section of brick-lined concrete that meandered from the curving drive on its way to the guest cottage at the south end of the property.

"We could go there instead," Jake suggested, his lips twisting. "Although this time we don't have blankets or a sleeping bag."

"I feel just the same way I did when I was a kid." Kate turned anxious eyes to him, and Jake sighed and clasped her chin between his thumb and forefinger, rubbing gently.

"It'll be all right," he assured her.

Kate wasn't even close to believing him. The Talbots had looked down at her as if she were dirt, and no amount of time and distance could make her forget how small and desperate she had felt that day.

They walked up the brick path together, Jake limping a bit from his tightly bound thigh. They stood tensely on the porch bathed by two lamps with wrought-iron lantern lights flanking the door. Jake pressed the bell which echoed dully in the depths of the house. Kate shivered.

"Come here," he murmured, dragging her into the circle of his arms. She wanted to burrow against him; but the sound of a heavy tread coming their way brought her to her senses, and she withdrew a foot away from him, tense and expectant.

Phillip Talbot, Sr., opened the door. He frowned at Kate blankly, then lightened a bit when he recognized his son. "Jacob, there you are. Your mother had about given up on you."

"I told her to expect me at seven," he responded a bit tightly.

"Well, you know how she is. Seven means five when it comes to you, son." He extended a hand to Kate and said, "I didn't expect Jacob to bring along such a lovely companion. I'm Phillip Talbot."

"Yes . . . nice to meet you." Kate shook his hand, glancing about a bit desperately for Jake.

"Father, this is Kate Rose. You've met her before," he pointed out softly.

"I have?" He examined Kate thoroughly.

"We went to high school together," said Jake tersely.

Phillip's brows arched, but he couldn't place her, which suited Kate just fine. Yet when the three of them entered the drawing room where long ago she had faced off with both Jake's parents, she could sense the sweat building on her skin until she felt clammy and slightly sick.

Marilyn Talbot had aged. Phillip, too, for that matter, Kate noticed as he stepped into the warm light bathing the room. But as Marilyn gazed over the top of half-moon glasses at her, Kate couldn't help seeing the wrinkles that plagued her lips and forehead, and the fact that her once dark brown hair was now blondish-silver.

Phillip had gone from gray to white, and his bulldog jaw had grown jowly. His waistline had suffered over the intervening years as well, but when he took up his place in front of the fire, Kate was thrown back in time unwillingly.

"Good evening," Marilyn said crisply, her eyes quick and seeking. Her sharp intake of break said it all, even before Phillip, Sr., remarked, "This is Kate Rose. Jacob says I've met her before, but for the life of me, I don't remember."

"We've both met her." Marilyn's smile was brittle, but she remembered her manners enough to stand up and offer Kate a limp handshake. "Would either of you like something to drink?" She walked straight for a side table that served as a bar and poured herself scotch, neat. *That's the second time in her life,* Jake thought inconsequentially. Phillip, Sr., asked for the same, and Jake followed after his mother, picking up another decanter and pouring two brandies into snifters.

When he handed one to Kate, he blocked her view of his parents momentarily and used the small bit of privacy to give her a wink of encouragement. Kate tried on a smile that felt wobbly and weak. She *had* to pull herself together.

"We heard about the explosion. Are you certain you're all right?" Marilyn asked Jake.

"Luckily, no one was hurt badly," Jake said by way of an answer. "But I don't know about next time."

"Next time?" Phillip, Sr., demanded.

Jake nodded. "I'll tell you all about it later."

"So, how have you been, Kate?" Marilyn asked after she had reseated herself. Her fingers were a death grip against her glass.

"I'm all right," Kate managed.

"When did we meet?" Phillip asked absently, his thoughts clearly still on Jake's disturbing comment about the accident.

Marilyn shot him a cold look, but it was Jake who answered. "Kate and I dated in high school. I went away

for the summer, and it ruined our plans for marriage."
His tone was light, not assigning blame, but Marilyn's lips
became a knife blade of repressed emotion nonetheless.

"Oh." Phillip's perpetual frown deepened.

"I understood you married," Marilyn said, probing.

"My husband died six months ago." Kate's mouth was
cotton, and she was afraid her sweating would stain her
blouse. Lord, she knew it would be bad, but she hadn't
realized how terribly uncomfortable this would be.

"So . . . ," Marilyn murmured.

Jake sighed. He almost pitied his mother for being so
locked in her own self-made prison of etiquette and expectation. "Kate and I are getting married," he said, shocking
everyone in the room, including Kate.

"Oh, my God!" Marilyn's face turned gray.

Phillip merely stared. He didn't remember Kate very
well, so his prejudices were less, but the announcement
had come out of the blue.

Kate, for her part, was light-headed. The whole scene
was surreal. She hadn't expected Jake to be so candid
and up front, when their own discussions of marriage had
seemed fuzzy and unformed, something to address in the
future.

Now Jake's arm came around her waist protectively. She
could see the small spasm of muscle in his jaw. A part of
her wondered if he were using her for some ongoing,
unspoken battle of wills with his parents.

"When—is the wedding?" Marilyn asked faintly.

"We don't know yet. As soon as possible, if I have anything to say about it."

This was news to Kate. She felt like a pawn, and yet she
didn't doubt Jake's love for her. Did she. . . ?

Phillip coughed into his fist. "Well, then, congratula-
tions are in order. Welcome to the family . . . Kate," he
said with an attempt at grace.

"Thank you," she murmured.

"Yes," Marilyn echoed. "Welcome."

Into the tense silence that ensued, Phillip said, "Jacob, let's go to the den. We've got a lot to discuss."

"Yeah," he agreed. "I'll be right back," he assured Kate, staring into her eyes as his father headed to a door at the back of the room that led to another, smaller retreat. "You'll be okay?"

"Right as rain," she answered with false brightness.

Left alone with Marilyn Talbot? A fate worse than death. As soon as the door closed behind Jake and his father, Kate wandered the appointments of the room, almost afraid to sit down. Marilyn seemed stunned by the events of the past few moments herself. But she surfaced eventually, and gestured for Kate to take a chair across from her.

Kate perched uncomfortably on the edge. She hadn't touched her brandy yet, but feeling Marilyn's probing stare, she took a fiery gulp.

"So, you found Jacob again, after all this time."

Kate nodded.

"I don't intend to apologize for what happened," she went on, somewhat distractedly, as if she were talking to herself rather than Kate. "I wanted the best for my son, but life is full of little surprises, most of them unpleasant."

"Oh, I don't know if that's true."

"Really? What about this—this sabotage?" She waved that away even before Kate could remark, returning to the other subject between them. "When Jacob was in Europe and I told you about his fiancée, you fainted dead away in our hallway. That was one of life's unpleasant surprises, wouldn't you say?"

"It was a shock." She swallowed. "And it turned out it wasn't true."

"What do you mean?" Marilyn's brows shot together.

"Jake wasn't actually engaged."

She dismissed that with a snort. "Both families had agreed. It just took Jake and Celia longer to accept the idea than either of us had anticipated." She hugged her drink. Glancing down, she seemed surprised to find her glass empty. Kate rose and refilled it without being asked, and that made Marilyn Talbot shake her head. "I can admit I made a mistake. Celia and Jake were a terrible match. I gave up after that. Jacob makes his own way, just like his brother."

The hint of derision in her voice wasn't lost on Kate. They both sipped in silence for several moments until Kate could feel the alcohol relaxing her own taut nerves. Marilyn must have felt a similar loosening, because she removed her glasses and shrugged her shoulders.

"I thought a small town girl from a—dysfunctional— family was the last thing a man like Jacob needed. I felt bad about it at the time, but there it was." She splayed her hands. "You didn't waste any time getting married, so I forgot about you. Do you have any children?"

Kate licked her lips. This was certainly tricky. "A daughter. April."

"How old is she?"

Was it her imagination, or was Jake's mother calculating already? "Seventeen."

"Seventeen. My God, a teenager. What year is she in school?"

"She'll be a senior. School starts in a week," Kate babbled on. "Right after Labor Day. It's hard for me to believe that my baby's grown up and near graduation."

"It happens fast, doesn't it?" Marilyn mused. "When will she be eighteen? That's when they're really adults, isn't it?"

"Yes," Kate agreed, her nerves screaming. Jake had never questioned her so thoroughly; he saw no reason to. But Marilyn was a woman with a clever, calculating mind, and whether she was on a fishing expedition, or whether she suspected something she wanted confirmed, Kate wasn't about to be truthful in this matter. If she told Marilyn that her daughter was born in January, she would realize April had been conceived in April. There was no way Kate's husband could have fathered her; the timing was wrong.

"April's birthday is June tenth," she lied, knowing she was digging her own grave. But it would be unfair, almost criminal, for Jake's mother to know the truth before he did.

Marilyn inclined her head, defeated. "Well, I'm glad you didn't name her June," she joked. "I had an aunt named June whom I couldn't stand."

It was an innocuous comment, but Kate's blood ran cold as she realized how close Marilyn was to the whole truth.

When Jake returned Kate literally leapt out of her chair to greet him. He seemed pleased that she and Marilyn had resorted to chit-chat, but Kate's head ached from the brandy and the strain.

"I'm going to take a look at the guest cottage before we go," Jake told his parents.

"It's unlocked," his father said.

They both said goodbye to Kate, and once Kate and Jake were outside in the fresh air, Kate gulped a deep breath.

Jake said, "See? It wasn't so bad."

"Hah. And you were dreading it, too. You know you were."

"I was," he admitted. "But, like I said, they see things differently now. In some ways both Phillip and I have been a disappointment to them. My mother would like to blame me for Celia, but it's all water under the bridge now."

Kate hoped he was right, but she had her doubts. Marilyn was somewhat less hostile, but it didn't mean that Kate had been accepted with open arms. No, judgment was still reserved.

What happens when they learn the truth?

"Did your father have any ideas on the sabotage?" Kate asked.

"Not really. He's just glad nothing worse has happened, yet."

The guest house had been nearly overrun by a wisteria whose trunk was as thick as a small oak and whose branches wound around the place in a choking embrace. Jake had to practically kick the front door open—not an easy task for him in his current state—as it was wedged shut from dampness swelling the wood.

Once inside, however, Kate's memories swirled. The air was warm and close as she glanced to where they had made love so long ago. Now brittle leaves covered the floor, but there was an old blanket rumpled in the corner.

"What do you know?" Jake whispered, amused. His mood was high. Unlike Kate, he felt the evening with his parents was a success, as far as their relationship was concerned.

"Don't think I'm going to cuddle up with you in that," she said repressively. "It's probably full of bugs and mildew."

"Where's your adventuresome side, my love?"

"Locked away until we get back to Portland."

He dragged her close, his lips against her crown, his breath tickling her hair. "Can I talk you into coming back to my place when we get there?"

"Mmmm . . ." She closed her eyes and rested her head on his shoulder. "Oh, I don't know. There's April, at home, and work tomorrow. If I were smart, I'd go straight to bed."

"That's the idea."

"My bed," she said, her lips curving into a smile.

"Your bed would be fine," he deadpanned.

"You know what I mean."

"I know exactly what you mean," he murmured hoarsely, his tongue rimming her ear. He drew her mouth to his, his tongue making a tight, insistent foray into the hot, moist cavern.

Kate let it happen. She wound her arms around his neck and sighed. August heat settled around them as Jake's taut body fit hers neatly against his. If Kate had any doubts about his intentions, the throbbing muscle pressing at the juncture of her thighs made the situation decadently clear.

"I am not lying down on that blanket," she murmured between small kisses he was planting on her mouth, cheeks and jawline.

"We can always stand."

Jake brushed aside her sweater and systematically began unbuttoning her sleeveless blouse. The release felt good, for Kate had been stuffy and hot and sticky inside his parents' house. Now, with her blouse open and Jake unsnapping the front clasp of her bra, she sighed with relief as her breasts spilled into his hands.

"God, Katie, you're beautiful," he whispered, his fingers massaging the bud of her nipple until she wanted to cry out from desire. Her own hands gripped his shoulders hard.

But a question loomed in and out of her conscience, and suddenly she knew she had to voice it. "Why did you blurt that out about marrying me?" she managed, even while her senses overheated. It had only been a few hours since they had made love, but it felt like a lifetime. And Jake's touch was driving her crazy, warming her blood and spiraling her emotions into a swirl of blinding need. She moaned in spite of herself, and Jake groaned, bending down to suckle one erect bud.

He staggered a bit unsteadily.

"Maybe we'd better sit on the floor," she suggested,

sliding downward. "Despite what you say, you're in no condition to stand."

The tiles were cold, but Jake's warm hands quickly made her forget her discomfort. When he resumed his hot perusal of her breast, she wound her fingers in his hair. "Jake!" Her body trembled violently as his hands cupped her buttocks, holding her against him hard.

"I wanted her to know we were getting married," he answered her with difficulty, desire making it hard to think. "I had to stop my mother from turning nasty."

"Why would she—be nasty? Oh, Jake . . ." Kate clung to him as he slid his mouth downward.

"It's her nature. Don't talk anymore," he pleaded. "Later . . ."

His fingers dug at the snap of her jeans. Kate was mindless. Weak and willing, she watched as if from a distant haze as he divested her of every scrap of clothing. His thumb hooked into her scant, lacey briefs, dragging them down her legs. Then his face was too near the center of her femininity for him to resist, and as his tongue hotly pleasured her, Kate arched her neck and cried out, "Please . . . please . . ."

When it seemed that Kate would die from wanting him, he tugged at her own hands, dragging them to where his manhood strained his zipper. Kate massaged him through his pants until he groaned and dropped his forehead on her bared shoulder.

Quickly Kate divested him of his pants and boxers, and then his body was hot and hard against hers. Her own body was on fire, and when he grasped her hips and positioned himself to take her, she eagerly clung to him, a moistness invading her insides as the tip of Jake's masculine shaft teased against her, back and forth, titillating to the extreme.

"Katie . . . ," he whispered again.

"You said don't talk!" she gulped.

"I love you."

"I love you mo—oh!" He thrust inside her so deeply that she cried out, not in pain, in pleasure. Then Jake was moving rhythmically, slowly at first, stabbing into Kate's hot sheath until Kate was squirming with need, hanging on to him for dear life, her hips rising and falling to meet his ever-increasing thrusting.

She cried out, climaxing faster than she ever had, her breath fast and uneven. Her mouth captured his, hard and demanding. Jake's sweat-dampened hair flopped over his forehead, his features strained. The spiraling, liquid pleasure went on and on, Kate's moans and soft pleas working a magic of their own.

"Oh, God." With his own hoarse cry, Jake spilled his seed into her, collapsing against her, so they were both pressed up against the tiles, gasping, their knees and thighs and bodies trembling in tandem.

"Next time—the blanket," he panted, and Kate laughed shakily above her thundering heartbeat.

He didn't pull away from her at once, and Kate wrapped her arms and legs around him, enjoying the moment. Eventually, he dragged himself back, and their glorious union ended.

"It wasn't like this when we were here eighteen years ago," she whispered.

"No." He smiled lazily, reaching for his clothes. "God, I missed you."

She gazed at him with all the love she felt shining from her eyes. Momentarily Jake was arrested by the beauty of her. Long, shapely legs joined together with a soft thatch of blondish hair. Slim waist, smooth, taut skin, breasts that just begged to be touched and caressed. Above that, the face of an angel. She was gorgeous, he conceded, though for years he wanted to forget her appearance and concentrate instead on her calculating, ambitious heart. Now, though, with all his love out in the open, he pleasured himself with the sight of her. Her lips were softly pink and right now swollen from his kisses. Her lashes drifted downward over eyes that glimmered with secrets and sensuality.

"I didn't bring you here to have my way with you," he admitted, "although I'm not complaining."

Kate began dressing as well, sliding on her jeans until painted pink toenails peeked through the end of one denim leg. Nothing had ever looked sexier to Jake. "Oh?" she asked.

"There's another reason."

When Kate finished snapping her jeans, pulling on her sleeveless blouse, and buttoning up, she gazed at him questioningly. Jake had slipped on his own jeans, but he was still shirtless. He was wondering just exactly how to do what he had planned when she suddenly slid her hands up his hair-dusted chest, caressing his pectoral muscles.

"What other reason, gorgeous?" she asked, her voice lilting.

"This," he said simply, withdrawing a small black case from his pocket.

Kate froze, her eyes widening. For a moment she seemed as if she wouldn't take the ring case. "Here," Jake whispered, pressing it into her palm.

With trembling fingers Kate opened the elegant case. Amidst black velvet sparkled a marquis diamond large enough to make her wince. "Oh, Jake."

"It's what I would have bought you years ago if I could've afforded it then." He chuckled. "Maybe it was good to wait."

Because she seemed completely undone, Jake took the engagement ring from its velvet sheath and gently slid it on to the third finger of her left hand. Light sparkled and glimmered, refracting off the marquis's facets. "I can't believe this," she choked out.

"Will you marry me?" he asked.

Kate couldn't find her voice. She nodded, laughing when Jake dragged her into his arms and kissed her all over her face and neck.

"Soon," he demanded. "Marry me soon."

"As soon as you want," she agreed, throwing caution to the wind.

"Then start making plans, because I want to start a family as soon as possible!"

Chapter Seventeen

Kate pulled back the covers of her bed, shivering in the heat. She was cold inside and out, and no amount of summer heat could dispel the chill that was soul-deep inside her. The marquis diamond mocked her. It was so beautiful, so incredibly exquisite, but it was given to her without benefit of all the facts.

I want to start a family as soon as possible . . .

Only she could no longer have any more children.

The headache building at her temples was a product of her own guilt. Unwittingly she had added another lie to compound the first, though this second one was a lie of omission. When Jake had blurted out his thoughts, she had thought she would pass out. She actually swayed on her feet, and he instantly wanted to know what was wrong. When she couldn't answer, he drew his own conclusions, blaming himself, though it had nothing to do with him at all.

"I should have said something before," he declared, alarmed at Kate's sudden weakness and mistaking its cause.

"I've always wanted children. A child. And I knew it wouldn't work with Celia. Never even considered it. In fact, I'd pretty much given the idea up because I'd never loved any woman but you.

"But now we're together and I just assumed you'd feel the same," he admitted, his gaze troubled.

"It's not—that," Kate whispered.

Jake's eyes searched hers. "You do want children? I mean, another child?"

"I would love another child," she choked out, aching inside. "But I never thought—it's just that—things have been moving so fast!"

"I know. I'm rushing."

"It's okay," she assured him quickly. "Really. I love you. I want to be with you."

"But . . . ?" he asked, waiting for the other shoe to drop.

Kate had struggled for what felt an eternity. The truth was so wickedly unfair. "I would love to have a child with you," she said again, fighting for each syllable. "I can't think of anything I'd want more."

"Then that's what we'll do!" He was relieved, a grin spreading from one corner of his mouth to the other. "As soon as possible. As soon as you're ready!"

She had been unable to burst his bubble, unable to tell the unpalatable truth. She had spent the trip back in a numb haze where her defense was a hearty smile—perhaps a bit too hearty and false—while Jake spun dozens of plans for them, his joy impossible to squelch.

But the truth was there would be no more children. Kate could no longer conceive. Ben had wished for a child of his own as well, and when it didn't happen right away, he'd had his sperm count tested and guess what? No problem there. Since no other children were ever conceived, Kate had accepted that she was no longer fertile. Once again, she realized how much of a blessing April was; without her, Kate would have never borne a child.

So now there was an added complication to their proposed marriage. Now Jake would learn he couldn't father a child in the future, but surprise, surprise! He already had one!

A knock on her bedroom door broke into Kate's tense thoughts. "Yes?"

"Can I talk to you?" April's voice was muffled through the panels.

"Sure."

She came inside, looking troubled and anxious herself. *Tomorrow's rehearsal!* Kate realized with a start, feeling guilty that she had been so absorbed with her own problems that she had completely forgotten about her daughter's. "You want to go over your lines again," she said, patting the spot beside her on the bed.

"Actually . . . no. I mean, yeah, I do. But there's something else."

"The explosion?"

"No, no . . . I'm fine with that."

"What?"

April's gaze fell on the diamond, and Kate sucked in a breath. She had shown April the engagement ring as soon as she had walked through the door, and April had acted as if she were thrilled to death. But maybe that had been an act. Maybe the truth was about to hit her square between the eyes.

"Jake kind of surprised me with it," Kate said to allay her fears. "We don't have to rush anything. I don't mind—"

"No, that's not it. I told you, I'm so happy for you I could almost cry!" A smile quivered on her young lips.

"Then, what is it?"

"Mom?"

"Yes?"

Her reluctance was a palpable thing. Kate's heart began to pound slow and hard. Oh, no. She braced herself. Ryan. April. She saw it coming at her so hard she actually flinched, waiting for her worst fears to hit like a freight train. "You're pregnant!" she whispered.

"What?" April's jaw dropped in outrage. "No way! Oh, my God! How could you think *that?"*

Kate had closed her eyes; now she squinched open one lid, afraid to believe her ears. April was the picture of affront. Her eyes snapped with disbelief and anger, and yet she seemed like she wanted to laugh, too.

"Hell, no," she swore, but Kate let it go since she was obviously poleaxed by her mother's attitude. "I just have something I need to discuss with you."

"Okay." Kate was growing more curious by the minute, and it was a welcome diversion from her own dire thoughts.

"Have you been sleeping with Mr. Talbot—Jake?"

"April!" Now it was Kate's turn to be affronted.

"Because you were married to Dad a long time, and it's a whole different world out there now," she rushed on. "I mean, there's AIDS and STDs, kinds you've maybe never even heard of. I'm not saying Mr. Talbot—Jake's—got any of those things. Pray to God not! But, you should at least demand an HIV test. You can't tell me there haven't been some women in his life, and he was married once, you said. Every time you have sex with someone, you have sex with every partner they've ever had and whoever they've had sex with and so on and so on. It isn't safe!"

Kate just stared, open-mouthed, at her daughter. Jake had explained that he had always used protection with any woman he was with, and that he had even taken an HIV test a few months back to assure himself on that score. She, of course, had only been with Ben. And though she and Jake had been a little lax on protection, it was because, she now knew, Jake had been half hoping for a child, while she hadn't had to worry about pregnancy because it wasn't an issue for her.

"I've paid attention in health class," April finished with a certain amount of pride. "And it's not wise to risk your health. You're my mom, and I love you." Her eyes were full of emotion. "I don't want anything bad to happen to you just because you've been out of the dating scene. AIDS isn't discriminatory."

"April, honey . . ." Kate was beyond speech.

"Promise me you'll be careful."

"Don't worry," Kate assured her, moved by her daughter's concern. "We've talked about this. I won't be making that mistake."

April's chest heaved in a sigh of relief. "Thank God!" she cried, flopping down beside her mother on the bed. "I'm glad that's over. I've been working myself up for hours to have this little talk."

"I appreciate it," Kate said with humor.

"Now, will you help me with my lines?"

"I thought you'd never ask," she said dryly, giving April a hug. If only her own secrets, worries, and shocking news could be dispensed with so easily. Kate couldn't help dreading the morrow when she would have to figure out how to break things to Jake—and April.

The following day Kate accompanied April to the commercial shoot, then abandoned her to her fate as she was needed at the talent agency. In fact, the pace of Rose Talent seemed to have increased a hundred fold, with she and Jillian rushing around like mad. At this rate, she would have to hire another assistant, which was comforting as she hadn't forgotten about the balloon payment she owed on the business.

Was it because word had gotten out that Talbot Industries had hired not just someone from Rose Talent, but Kate Rose's daughter herself? Possibly. Whatever the reason, Kate wasn't about to look a gift horse in the mouth; she was just glad she would be able to have a more positive talk with Billy Simonson, her accountant, next time he called.

As soon as she had a spare moment, Kate put a call into Jake, irritated to feel her heartbeat begin to accelerate just at the thought of the task ahead of her. It wasn't anticipation she was feeling; it was fear. Her palms sweated and her blood thundered in her ears. By the time Jake actually picked up the phone, Kate was a complete mess.

"Hi, there," he greeted her warmly. "I've been missing you."

"Have you?" Kate circled her mouth with her tongue. "You know, we've really got a lot to talk about. I can't even begin to start."

"Is this about cold feet?" he asked carefully.

"You know how I feel about you," she assured him in a rush. "I've just got to sort things out and make plans. I need some time with you—to talk about some things."

"I agree," he said. "I've got some business stuff we should discuss since we're getting married. Things you should know."

A business discussion was way down on Kate's list. She had more immediate concerns. "Maybe tonight we could meet at Geno's again? That restaurant near my place? Do you remember?"

"Sure."

"How about on the garden patio? We'll have dinner—and talk." She knew she was being a chicken. She should invite him to her house for such a powerful issue, but there was always the threat of April being around. Better to at least start her confession in public.

"I have one question to ask right now," Jake said.

"Oh?"

"Since we're officially engaged, I'm assuming it's all right to spread the word. I haven't told any employees yet. I wanted to talk to you first."

Kate's chest constricted. She knew he was being careful because he sensed her ambivalence. "Would it be all right to wait till tomorrow?"

Jake hesitated. "Is there some special reason? Because I have to confess, I've told my brother what my plans are. As far as he knows, I haven't asked you yet, but he knows I will."

"I just want to set things straight. Tonight," she insisted, bolstering her own courage.

"I'll see you then," he agreed, his tone a bit bewildered at her strained words.

April rotated her neck several times, driving the kinks out. She had been given the scripts for three commercials, and they were attempting to film the first one. The one for the West Bank Hotel was postponed indefinitely, but the other two, where she spoke about Talbot Industries' plans for development in and around Portland, were on schedule.

There was a lot of standing around time. Lighting was key, and she couldn't believe how many times she had been called back for a makeup redo. The advertising agency had brought in trays of fruit, cheese and breads if anyone worked up an appetite. April had been munching on grapes and half a bagel, then vigorously brushed her teeth before the next smiling moment.

Too bad Mom couldn't have stayed. She was the best. April had tons of friends who viewed their parents as the enemy, but she had never felt that way about Kate. Now, her dad, she hadn't been that close to; she could freely admit it. Not that she hadn't loved him and vice versa. But he was another generation older, and hey, he could have easily been April's grandfather. The generation gap was just too huge.

His death had caused April to grow up in ways she hadn't understood at first, but was beginning to notice in small ways now. Most of her friends bugged her these days. Their petty interest in rumor, and who was doing what with what cool guy, held no appeal for April. Ryan was the best, but even he could irk her sometimes. He had taken up smoking cigarettes, and it bothered April to no end. And though she had told her mother that he was college bound, she had seen no serious moves by him in that direction. He seemed content to sit around with his guitar and lazily thrum away.

Bogus. April had said as much to him, and Ryan had shrugged and asked, "Don't you ever want to just get away? See the world. Drive across the country and stand at the edge of the Atlantic."

"I'd like to do a lot of things," she had retorted with typical practicality. "But I've got to earn some money to do them, and I need college to get the right job and career."

"Man, you are so uptight." He had shaken his head along with another cigarette from his pack, sticking the smoke between his lips and holding it there while he strummed on.

It had started an uneasy feeling inside April's stomach. On their camping trip with friends, she had found herself alienated from most of the party when she showed no interest in smoking. She had joked to her mom about the screwdriver she had tasted at Ryan's dad's, but she hadn't revealed that most of her friends were steady beer drinkers, and that she had taken the sip more as a way to fit in.

She didn't get it. Whereas everyone she knew seemed to be floundering around, searching for themselves, she had always been on a clear path. Maybe it was being an only child. Maybe it was just her. Whatever the case, she was ambitious and she knew it. And she just wanted everyone to stay out of her way, Ryan included if he was going to act like a do-nothing.

This breakthrough with the commercial was a start. Not that she had seriously considered modeling as a career. Heck, no! She liked to eat way too much, and she didn't obsess over her looks. She was pragmatic enough to know she was odd that way. In fact, it really drove her crazy when her friends worried aloud about their hair, or weight, or zits. Good grief. It was so *high school.*

Speaking of, classes started in a week, April reminded herself, as she stood by the counter of food, contemplating her future. Senior year. She had always wanted to be a senior. It seemed so glamorous, so adult, when she had been a lowly freshman and sophomore. But now that it was upon her, she felt oddly let down. Like, is this all there is?

Yet, college loomed, and though she looked forward to it, she also felt unsure and adrift. Mom had told her that her feelings were normal, but Mom was a natural born cheerleader, always looking on the positive. Somehow April sensed she was at a crossroads. She supposed it was silly and fanciful, but she really felt that the path she picked now would seriously matter. As if there were good and evil just waiting out there, and she needed to be sharp to choose the right way.

Bogus again, probably, but she couldn't shake the feeling.

A couple of weeks ago she and a friend had rented that Tom Cruise movie, *Risky Business,* where he was a senior in high school chock-full of self-doubts. The hero's main goal was to get through high school without messing up his future. Unfortunately his choices—and, worse yet, his *friends'* choices—nearly made that impossible.

April saw herself in much the same position. Tiptoeing through this last year, so as not to ruin her future. She didn't want to be infected by the same insecurities that plagued her friends, but she knew, at some level, that she was. In fact, even though she constantly congratulated herself on being past all those petty worries her friends wallowed in, lately she had been feeling anxious and unsettled.

Grimacing, April munched on another sprig of grapes. Her father's death had started this, she knew. Oh, yeah, she'd had her worries before, but when she had realized that she and her mother were totally alone in the world, she had suffered nightly anxiety attacks until she had understood that Kate was going to be okay. It was incredible that Mom had reconnected with Mr. Talbot—Jake—and was actually going to marry him! She was pleased as punch, thrilled to her toes. And if she, April, achieved a little security out of the match, well, why not? She just wanted everything to go as planned.

Oh, please, she thought suddenly, knowing she shouldn't want it so badly. But Jacob Talbot was a catch, and so was Mom, come to that. April was quite aware of her mother's beauty, and it was more than skin deep.

Skin deep. That was the worry about this modeling thing. It really was only skin deep, and April already had doubts about measuring up.

Just be yourself, Mom always said, and let's face it, mother knew best.

"April?" The director motioned her back to the point where he wanted her to stand. "You ready."

"You bet." She flashed him her smile. Things were going perfectly. There was absolutely no reason to be feeling this

worry gnawing away at her insides . . . no reason at all.
Fighting off her plaguing doubts, April walked back in
front of the cameras where the floor had been crisscrossed
with tape to show her where to stand.

Nope, she reminded herself. Everything was going to be
just peachy. There was absolutely no reason to worry.

And that reminded her that she had Jake Talbot's money
tucked in the back pocket of the jeans she had worn to the
shoot. She had planned to hand it over to him today;
it had sat forgotten behind the kitchen telephone forever.
But then he hadn't been on the set like she had hoped.

Next time I see him, she told herself, smiling for the camera.

The people from Diamond Corp. were the epitome of
indecision. Jake glanced around the boardroom table at
the envoy of executives and lawyers and wondered what
the deal was. They had hemmed and hawed for the better
part of an hour, and his patience had worn to a nub.

"You either want to do a joint venture on the property
by the airport, or you don't," Jake pointed out reasonably.
"Talbot's putting up the land; you're investing the cash.
It's pretty straightforward."

Dennis Watley, from the law firm of Watley, Bishop,
Pettygrove and Darm, gave Jake a look meant to quell his
tongue. But Jake, unlike his father, liked to speak for himself whenever possible. He preferred not to have a lawyer
be his mouthpiece.

Diamond's lawyer, however, was the only voice at all
from the group of suited executives seated around the
table. He steepled his fingers and frowned down at them.
"There are some concerns."

"Such as?" Jake ignored a second, reproving look from
Dennis.

No one wanted to talk. Jake leveled his gaze at Marcus

Torrance, president of Diamond Corp. What was going on? The man pretended he didn't feel Jake's drilling gaze. He was content to let his lawyer field the questions.

"You've had a spot of trouble," the attorney revealed reluctantly. "We're worried that it could affect the profitability of the deal."

Jake listened in disbelief. "You're talking about the explosion at the West Bank."

"Among other things."

"We're building miniwarehouses. It's not like our customers are going to boycott us because there's been some vandalism," Jake pointed out, annoyed.

"We feel it's more than that. It looks as if you have a saboteur interested in destroying all Talbot properties." He lifted his hands apologetically. "It's not in our best interests to proceed right now."

Jake shot another glance at Marcus, who had pursed his lips and fastened his stare on the page in front of him. Although what Diamond's lawyer said was true, no one from their company should have had access to that information. The West Bank, okay. That was front page news. But the strip mall vandalism wasn't even common knowledge at Talbot yet, because Jake had asked Gary and Pam to keep it under wraps. So far, it had stayed out of the papers, and the saboteur theory hadn't been mentioned anywhere yet.

"Who told you we had a saboteur?" Jake demanded, jumping right to the heart of it.

"That's not the issue, Mr. Talbot."

"I disagree," Jake retorted. "It sounds like it's the issue exactly. Whoever gave you that information must have suspected it might affect our joint venture."

"I'm sure you understand why we can't move forward at this time." With that the attorney closed his folder and gazed at Jake steadily, ignoring his demands completely.

The rest of Diamond's entourage bustled around to put their things away as well, and they hurried out of the boardroom en masse.

When Jake was alone with Talbot's corporate attorney, he said, "What's going on, Dennis?"

"I'm not sure." Dennis was sober. "But whatever's happening, this deal is put on hold indefinitely. I suggest you call your commercial real estate agent immediately and get that piece of property back on the market."

Jake nodded tersely, boiling inside. But the analytical part of his brain was moving in new directions—and not liking what he was finding.

"There's a mole in the company," he said unhappily.

"A spy?" Dennis shrugged. "Sounds like a disgruntled employee with an attitude."

"It could be one and the same . . ."

As Jake ran on the treadmill later that afternoon, swiping a towel at the sweat that beaded again and again on his forehead, he came to some unpalatable conclusions. There were only a half dozen people who knew about the pending deal with Diamond Corporation and who also knew about the sabotage at the strip mall and West Bank Hotel.

Those people were the ones closest to Jake himself. Employees he had purposely culled from the company roster to work exclusively for Jake after Phillip, Sr., had turned over the reins to him. His personal secretary Pam was one of them. So was Gary, his foreman.

And then there was Phillip . . . his brother. . . .

Jake sighed. He had talked over the damage with his father the other night, and he had also tried to make some sense out of Phillip's desire to cut a piece of the company off for himself. Their father had seemed to think giving Phillip one of Talbot's properties and letting him make it or break it on his own was a good idea.

But Phillip, Sr., didn't know about the leak to Diamond

Corporation. Could that have been the younger Phillip's doing? As a means to make that particular piece of property available to him? He had to know that if the joint venture with Diamond was in place, Talbot would not be able to give the property to him. Could he have whispered the word "saboteur" in Marcus Torrance's ear and effectively squelched the deal once and for all, making way for Talbot to deed that property to Phillip Talbot, Jr., no questions asked?

Jake didn't like the path of his thoughts, but he couldn't help himself. And if that were true, was Phillip merely an opportunist, using the vandalism to Talbot as a means to his own ends? Or, could he have had some hand in the destruction himself?

No! Phillip would never take a chance on hurting someone like what could have happened at the West Bank.

But then Jake remembered how upset Phillip had been to learn he and April had been injured. It had seemed like a normal reaction at the time, but. . . .

With a sick feeling, Jake decided he really didn't want to know; but then, he was president of Talbot Industries now, and who else was there to dig to the truth? No one had a greater stake in the welfare of Talbot than he had. And brother, or no brother, if Phillip, Jr., were involved, he would have to face the authorities with his involvement.

Jake grimaced. He didn't like his choices at all.

Kate arrived at Geno's half an hour ahead of the appointed time. She had been strung so tight that April, who had been regaling her with the blow by blow of her filming, had finally complained at Kate's inattention.

"Hey, what gives? You're miles away!"

"Oh, I was just lost in thought," she murmured, feeling

almost ill. As soon as she told Jake the truth her world would shatter. She knew it. It couldn't be any other way.

Ryan was at the house, guitar resting on his thigh, humming a little as he idly strummed away. This appeared to irritate April, who threw him a speaking glance that he didn't see. Another day Kate might have wondered if the bloom was off the rose regarding their relationship, but today she was too tense.

April switched gears. "What did Jillian say about your ring?" she asked. "I mean, last Friday you were on a date with her friend."

"She didn't see the ring," Kate said repressively.

"Why not?"

"Because I wasn't wearing it."

"Why not?" April repeated, her eyes widening. "Mom, you didn't give it back, did you!"

"No, I'm just, taking my time," she muttered, inclining her head meaningfully in Ryan's direction, though he appeared completely oblivious. "I'm not ready to make announcements yet."

"What's the hold up? This is the man of your dreams. Your boyfriend from high school. It's—it's—well, it's romantic! I can't even believe it."

"Neither can I," Kate admitted. *And as soon as this evening's over, it may no longer be true.*

April gave up her inquisition, but she continued to dart looks in Kate's direction while Kate prepared to leave. Now, thinking back, Kate couldn't help feeling like a coward when she considered how she had told less than the truth to Jillian.

Apparently Michael had really liked Kate. Jillian had told her as much without overplaying it because she knew of Kate's interest in Jake. And though Jillian was glad that Kate had "fallen in love," a part of her really wanted to double again. So, while Kate and she had wrangled for the phone time and again, doing their best to keep some kind of control over the office, Jillian had kept up a constant barrage of quiet little suggestions.

"We could do brunch at my apartment," she posed as Kate caught the receiver on the fly.

Another time she said, "This is great barbecuing weather. How does a juicy burger sound, loaded with ketchup and onions?"

Later, she became even less subtle. "Let's go out again. I know Michael had a fabulous time."

"I ran out of the restaurant!" Kate declared.

"You were worried about Jake and your daughter. He knows that."

"Jillian . . ."

Jillian lifted her hands in surrender, but it just made Kate more uptight about seeing Jake again and getting to the truth. Jake's engagement ring was in her purse. Kate considered telling Jillian about it, but she didn't have the courage. She was afraid it might jinx everything if she spoke too soon. . . .

"Michael's a great guy, but I can't," Kate finally said in a regretful voice. "It's all timing. I'm with Jake, at least for the present."

Jillian nodded. "I guess I knew that. But, Kate, you sound so fatalistic about it."

"Do I?"

"Like a funeral dirge," Jillian admitted, her eyes searching Kate's as if to discover her secret.

It had unnerved Kate a bit. If she didn't get this thing settled soon, the whole world would be staring at her and trying to decipher what made her tick.

So, here she was. The waiter brought her a glass of Chianti, and she tried on several ways to broach the subject.

Jake, I can't get pregnant, but don't worry you've already got a child.

Jake, I know you care a great deal about April. If you found out she was your child, what would you do?

I was lonely and lost without you. And pregnant. I married Ben to have a father for April, but she's yours.

April's yours. Yours . . . yours. . . .

"Kate?" Jake's voice behind her head nearly rocketed her from her chair.

"You scared me!" she declared, a hand at her throat.

He sat down across from her, looking slightly amused. "I thought you were expecting me."

"Well, I was, but oh, I don't know. I've got a lot on my mind."

"Tell me yours and I'll tell you mine," he said, motioning for the waiter. He ordered a beer, and when the long-necked bottle appeared, he gazed at Kate expectantly.

She cleared her throat, watching condensation melt down the bottle's brown glass. "I've been meaning to talk to you about some things for a long time. Definitely since we started dating again, though there were so many feelings to sort through in the beginning it all just got pushed aside. Which is no excuse," she added, knowing she was rambling, but unable to stop herself. "I've been stalling. I've been afraid."

When she hesitated, Jake frowned reflectively, picking up his beer and downing a hearty swallow before wiping the back of his hand against his lips and asking, "Afraid?"

"Terrified. I never thought we'd have a chance again, and the thought of losing out a second time. It would be more than I could bear."

He reached across to cradle one of her trembling hands. "Then, I've been afraid, too. But we're together now."

"I know, but there are some things, some issues, we need to discuss."

"Tons of issues, I'm sure," he agreed distractedly, releasing her as he sat back in his chair. He couldn't see how desperate she was, and she sensed she was losing his attention in spite of her tension.

"Jake, please!"

"I'm listening."

But he wasn't. Not really. With frustration, she realized he was absorbed in his own problems, and her desperate cries to be heard were a waste of time right now. "What's wrong?" she asked him.

"You were telling me your problems," he reminded her.

"But you're miles away. What is it?"

"I'm sorry. You're right. I keep thinking about the West Bank thing and this meeting I had earlier."

Drawing a calming breath, Kate said, "Tell me about it. I think it'll help me talk to you about my problems. No, I'm serious," she added when he began to protest.

Jake threw her a sideways smile. He understood how difficult it was for Kate to be the one to wait; but she had made her stand, and he was onstage first. "Diamond Corporation is backing out of our joint venture because they were told we're being targeted by a saboteur."

"How did they learn that?" Kate protested.

"I wish I knew. It's certainly true that we've had some vandalism directed at Talbot Industries, but nobody knows that. The papers haven't reported it. They only know there was an 'accident' at the West Bank." He shook his head and made a sound of self-deprecation. "Remember when I didn't want to talk to you about my business?"

"At the beach." Kate nodded.

"It seems like years ago. Now I don't know what I'd do without you on my side."

Kate looked down at her hands, feeling so unworthy. He was making it impossible for her to confess, but she had to!

"But it gets worse," he went on. "Someone from Talbot specifically told Diamond Corp. about the saboteur theory.

Now Diamond thinks we're too risky to deal with right now. I had a meeting with them this afternoon. Our joint venture is dead. It was a multi-million dollar deal that a few careless—or maybe specifically mentioned—words crushed."

"Who told them?" Kate asked.

Jake stared down at his beer bottle. "It could only be one of a handful of people."

"An ex-employee?"

"Maybe a current one." Jake grimaced and gulped down the rest of his beer. Ever so gently he placed the bottle back on the tabletop. "Top of my list?" he asked her.

She nodded, already sensing she was not going to like the answer.

"My brother. Phillip."

"No!" Her reaction was instantaneous. "No! Why? Why would he hurt you like that?"

"He wants that airport property for himself, and my father thinks it's a dandy idea to break off a chunk of the company and give it to him!"

"I don't understand!" Kate blinked in bewilderment. "Your father would never want the company to fail!"

"Oh, that's true. He sees this as a way to divorce my brother from Talbot once and for all, *and* it keeps Phillip from being totally disinherited. It's great for Phillip, and in a way, for Talbot Industries. But Father never expected him to go for the airport property. He thought he'd take something smaller, I'm sure."

"I don't believe it! Phillip would never try to hurt you. He would never!" She shivered violently, hating the images of the West Bank's destruction, remembering how she felt when she wasn't sure whether Jake and April were safe. "What does Phillip say to this?" Kate asked, her mind racing. "And—and what about the vandalism? You can't think . . . ?"

"Can't I? Believe me, I've thought it all," Jake grated harshly, lifting a hand for the waiter. He ordered another beer. Kate shook her head when he raised inquiring brows at her. She had hardly touched her Chianti as yet.

Jake went on, "I haven't talked to Phillip yet. I haven't even asked him why he called Moss & Turner and wanted a new liaison to replace Sandra! Phillip hasn't been around since I saw him last Saturday morning when he checked in to see if I was still 'alive.'"

"Oh, Jake!"

The brand new bottle of beer came, and Jake took another long swallow, his mouth grim as he sat back in his chair. "He looks guilty as hell."

Kate absorbed all his news in shock. No wonder he had been unable to listen to her. Jake had been dealing with one crisis after another while she had been stewing about her lethal secret.

"God, I'm glad I have you," he admitted, his eyes a soft blue as he gazed at her with affection. "You're the only person I completely trust."

Kate's blood ran cold. "I'm—not perfect."

"Nobody is," he concurred. "But you're damn close."

"No, Jake, listen." This time it was Kate who reached for his hands across the table. She clasped them both within her own, staring at him, her lips trembling. She had his full attention now that he had unburdened himself.

Swallowing, she tried twice to speak, but the only sound that issued from her throat was a harsh croak.

"What is it?" he coaxed, his interest quickening. "Katie?" he whispered with growing alarm as she still couldn't speak. "Tell me!"

"I can't have another child, Jake," she fought through lips as cold as a glacier. "I can't get pregnant."

Chapter Eighteen

It was hot as a blast furnace even though the sun was setting, and April wanted nothing more than to take a shower. But she had set up this evening with Ryan, and now she was stuck. They had started at a friend's house, but everyone had been lying around listening to music, drinking, smoking and generally taking up space with nothing constructive to do. The girl's parents were gone overnight, so she had invited everybody over. Some of the kids had part-time jobs, but most were ending the summer by just hanging out. School was starting next Tuesday, the day after Labor Day, and everybody was just waiting for the inevitable.

Looking around, April shook her head and wondered if there was something wrong with her. What a bunch of losers! Yet, here she was, too. It was insane.

"Let's go back to my house," April suggested to Ryan, who was nursing a beer but basically sober. She'd had nothing to drink. She didn't want to stay here, and she had no intention of drinking and driving. Wouldn't that be just great? Drinking underage and a DUI to boot!

No, she hadn't taken complete leave of her senses, but getting Ryan motivated had taken all her powers of persuasion. So, now they were seated on opposing wooden benches on the back patio, staring at each other, with absolutely nothing to say.

The patio itself was sort of dilapidated, with an overhead trellis which once had been the training ground for some purple-petaled plant she couldn't name, but now was overrun by a voracious brand of ivy. Consequently, it was dark as pitch, and only a chance reflection of moonlight off Ryan's eyes now and again reassured her that he was even awake.

"So, have you signed up for your SAT's yet?" she asked, wincing a bit since she could almost predict the answer.

"No." He was terse.

"But you're taking them this November, right? I mean, you've got to pretty soon, or you can't apply. At the University of Oregon, I hear housing's really hard to get. As soon as you apply, you fill out a form and pay just to be put on a list. Then when they're good and ready to assign housing, it's first come, first served off that list."

Silence.

"So, you've got to start early," she finished lamely.

"I'm not going," he stated flatly.

Her worst fears were confirmed. She felt deflated and let down. And while she tried to pull herself together, Ryan lit up another cigarette, its tip glowing red in the darkness.

I want something to happen, April thought. *Something wonderful. Something to guide me to my destiny.*

"I get to miss some school right off the bat," she said, swallowing against an unaccustomed lump in her throat. "We're still filming some commercials, and I'll probably miss a couple days each week for a while."

"Do you want to quit seeing each other?" Ryan asked calmly.

She wished she could read his expression. Her heart hurt. It wasn't like they were having this mad love affair, or anything, not like Mom and Jake Talbot; but it mattered to her nonetheless, and it ached to think he could throw it away so casually. "Do you?" she asked.

"It just sounds like you're getting on my case."

"I'm just trying to find out what you're thinking."

"I don't know!" He sounded almost angry. "You always know, but it's not like that for me, okay? I want to just get in my car and drive. I don't want to think."

April's heart was heavy. "But that doesn't really work."

"My dad didn't go get a regular job. He kind of drifted through college. He's doing fine. We don't all have to be corporate executives!"

"I know that."

"That guy your mom's seeing?" Ryan made a sound of impatience. "He's not me, okay? So, if you think that's what's perfect, we might as well quit right now. I like you. You're smart. But I'm not going to change for you, so forget it."

April wasn't sure where that left her—except more confused than ever. Was she supposed to be the one to change? Was she giving up her youth for some impossible dream that the generation ahead of her was telling her she had to chase?

While she pondered her dilemma, the lights in the living room came on.

"Mom's home," she whispered.

Ryan chose that moment to move to her bench, draping his arm around her shoulder, cuddling her close. It was just the attention April craved, and they sat in silence while he ground out his cigarette, each absorbed in their own thoughts.

The living room window was directly above their heads, and it was slightly ajar. As April wondered if she should make her presence known, Mom's and Jake's voices filtered through the aperture.

Their words froze her motionless.

Jake's first reaction to Kate's news was relief. She had scared him so much with her fear, he hadn't known what to expect! His second reaction was disappointment. He would never have a child, something he had always suspected but hoped wouldn't come true.

But Katie had just voiced his worst fears, and now she looked as if she were expecting the axe to fall.

"It's okay," he told her. Her hands, holding his, were like ice.

"I'm sorry," she said in a voice choked with misery.

"It's all right," he assured her.

The tears that starred her eyes nearly broke his heart. He knew he had to get her out of the restaurant before she broke down completely. In retrospect he saw how much pressure he had inadvertently put on her when he had blurted out his heart's desire.

"Come on," Jake urged gently, slipping back his chair.

"No, I—I'll be fine," Kate murmured, swiping at tears that once started, seemed to rain down her fine cheekbones. "I haven't finished."

People were staring. Though Kate was too focused on internal thoughts to notice, Jake could see their curious faces turning one after another. He tossed some money on the table.

"Another outrageous tip?" she laughed, a bit hysterically.

"Probably," he conceded.

They left without ordering, but Kate stopped to collect

herself beneath Geno's grape arbor, hugging the corner of the building. "I know having a child is very important to you," she continued. "I know how much it means to me."

"Shhh." He didn't want her worrying anymore.

"And it should be important," she said urgently, raising tear-washed eyes to meet his own. "Maybe the most important, apart from loving someone."

"I can live without fatherhood. Don't talk about it anymore."

"I want to. I need to. You don't understand."

"Then I don't want to understand," Jake cut her off. "Katie, be quiet," he ordered, as she shifted to her feet, wiping her hands down her skirt from the dirt of the building.

"If you'd just let me explain."

She sounded as if she were about to break into out and out sobs, and it was more than Jake could take. Pressing a finger to her quivering lips, he pulled her into his arms and kissed her forehead. "I love you," he said fiercely. "I don't need a child to prove that."

"But Jake . . . ," she protested.

"Don't, Katie, for God's sake. Come on, we'll go to your place and flop down in front of the television or whatever, and we'll just let everything go for now. Can you do that?"

The sound from her lips was a combination of frustration and surrender. She bent her head and murmured something so softly that he couldn't quite catch it. When she looked up again, her expression seemed defeated, but when he questioned her about it, she merely closed her eyes and shook her head.

They drove around awhile because Kate hadn't wanted to go home immediately. Time passed. Hours drifting by while he periodically tried to tell her everything was all right, and she couldn't seem to listen.

Now they were inside her living room, and Kate was turning on lights one by one. Her movements were stiff and robotlike. But even so Jake's gaze feasted on this woman he wanted to make his wife.

She wore a tan shirtdress and sandals. Her ankle bruising was a faint reminder of how short a time had elapsed since they had begun seeing each other again. But it was a lifetime of emotion, as far as Jake was concerned. Since Kate had stepped across the pages of his life again, he couldn't wait for the next chapter.

He moved his shoulder which was sore as blazes. He had a few war wounds these days, too. Maybe they were unhealthy for each other after all, he thought with a twist of his lips. No, he knew they were made for each other.

Seeing her unhappiness, he blamed himself for being its cause. In time he would convince her that having a child was a distant second to having her. There was adoption, too, if they both felt strongly about the issue; but he wasn't ready to look at that yet, and if it never happened he could still be happy.

But for now, there was nothing more to be said on the subject. He had decreed to lighten Kate's blue mood, and he intended to stick by his guns.

However, he hadn't planned on Kate's fortitude and obsession in the matter until she said, "Having a child, your own child, is the most wondrous thing."

"Don't talk about it," he warned.

"You think you'll be giving that up, and I—"

"I don't care! Don't you hear me? I'm sorry I made such a big deal about it. It doesn't matter."

"It *does* matter!"

"Not as much as you think."

"Jake, I'm trying to tell you something, but you're not letting me!"

He expelled his breath in frustration. "I know what you're trying to say."

"No, you don't!"

"I pushed you. I made it impossible for you to believe I could marry you knowing you can't have any more children. I love you. I've always loved you," he admitted. "You know that."

Kate whimpered in protest, pushing back the curtain of hair that kept slipping over her face. "Oh, Jake. You make this so hard!"

"If you say you can't have children, I believe you. I don't care. I only want you."

"But I did have one child," she broke in. "April."

He didn't like being reminded that April was Ben's daughter. For all his protests to the contrary, it did hurt that he would never sire a child. He would never say as much to Kate because it would hurt her so badly, though it was clear she already sensed he was half lying to spare her.

"Ben wanted another child," she said, her voice shaking a bit. "But I couldn't have any more. He'd always loved April. From the moment he learned about her." She stood in front of the windows, staring into a black night lit only by a crescent moon.

"She was his daughter."

"He wanted another one," she stated, as if he were keeping her mind from staying on track, and she was struggling to remain focused. "April was—" She caught her lower lip between her teeth. "She was not—"

"A boy?" Jake cut in, suddenly thinking he knew where this was headed.

"No!"

"You don't have to go into all this, Katie. And don't try to talk me out of marrying you just because you can't have a baby."

"Jake, it's you who won't want to marry me! I've kept a secret from you. A terrible secret, but I didn't mean to. It just happened, and I let it happen because I was so—alone and helpless!"

Her face was full of anguish. Somewhere inside himself he felt a terrible fear. Nameless. A misery beyond bearing that broke his skin out in goose bumps and tortured Kate's beautiful face.

"What are you trying to say?" he rasped, throat dry.

"April's your daughter, Jake," she declared, closing her eyes and letting fresh tears squeeze between the lashes at her confession. "You left me pregnant that summer, and I married Ben to give our daughter a decent life . . ."

In the filtered moonlight of the ivy-choked trellis, April wondered if she had just lost her mind. Eavesdropping was a curse, one she never indulged in. It had just happened, and the comfort of Ryan's arms had made it so she was unwilling to move even when her mother's anguished voice and Jake Talbot's confused responses drifted down to her from above.

But she had never expected to hear something so soul-destroying. She didn't believe it. She had to have drifted off. She had been dreaming; because Mom was marrying Jake Talbot, she had made up a silly fantasy about them being a perfect, nuclear family.

However, Ryan had stiffened to stone beside her. His face swivelled in her direction. Moonlight slanted and bared his expression, and she saw reflected in his face her own unmitigated horror.

Jake Talbot is my father!

She whimpered, and Ryan clamped a hand over her mouth to hide the noise. She gazed at him through wide

eyes above his fingers. He blinked in bewilderment, as
undone as she was.

Mom lied. All these years. Mom lied!

Her head swam. She felt faint. She collapsed against
Ryan completely. Above her, deadly silence was the answer
to her mother's pronouncement. Was Jake as shocked as
she was? Undoubtedly!

Gently, Ryan got to his feet, pulling her with him. April
could scarcely stand. He pointed to the far end of the
trellis where black night and a path around the back of
the house awaited. Clearly he wanted to evaporate into the
stealth of the night, and April felt the same way. Cautiously,
wincing at each footfall that crackled a bit on drying leaves,
they made their way to the grass and footpath that wound
to the front of the house.

Once out of earshot, their footsteps quickened. And
then they were in the front of the house and staring with
the lust of thieves at Ryan's car. "You want to leave?" he
asked.

"Forever," she answered flatly. "I want to leave forever."

"Let's push it out of the drive so they don't hear us,"
he suggested.

April didn't ponder the wiseness of this choice. Her
whole world had been blasted to smithereens. There was
no hope. No going back. What was that phrase about a
"tissue of lies?" It had made no sense to her before, but
now she saw that a foundation based on lies was as flimsy
as tissue.

"Get me out of here," she told him. "I never want to
see her again!"

His silence was her undoing. His face had turned to
granite, the beloved curves and planes harsh and unforgiv-

ing. Beyond that he was too stunned to move; she could read that clear enough.

"Jake?" she whispered, afraid.

He staggered to his feet, slowly shook his head, then swayed unsteadily for several moments. But when Kate reached to help him he jerked away from her so fast he overbalanced, slamming his shin into the nearby end table so hard it must have hurt terribly. But Jake made no reaction. He simply moved out of Kate's range, as if she were as deadly and repulsive as a poisonous snake.

"Jake . . ." Her voice caught in sorrow.

"You're—lying," he rasped.

She couldn't answer. She didn't have to. He had accepted the truth or he wouldn't be so utterly destroyed. She didn't make the mistake of coming near him again. She just gazed at him unhappily and shook her head.

"You're a lying bitch," he added, though his words held no heat. It was as if he were trying to make himself hate her, and with time, Kate was afraid he would succeed.

"I couldn't tell you. You were gone! And I was pregnant and desperate, and when I went to see your parents, they told me you were engaged and that you weren't coming back to Lakehaven. You were going straight to Harvard!" Kate inhaled a shaky breath. "I passed out on their floor when I heard."

"You should have told them. You could have told them. They would have told me."

"Would they have?" Kate demanded through a screen of tears. "Would they have? And, if they did, what then? Would you have left your fiancée to *do the right thing!*"

"I wasn't—I wasn't engaged."

"But I didn't know that! I thought you'd left me as fast as you could. I thought it was all a sham. And that silly, fake marriage was just your way of getting me in bed."

"You knew better!" Jake roared.

"Did I? Well, you weren't here to ask!"

They glared at each other, and Kate couldn't help feeling indignation well up in her chest. She had suffered. Oh, how she had suffered all these years. And though a certain amount of guilt was deserved, and she understood his feelings of betrayal, it had not been an easy path for her. It had been the only choice available at the time.

"I don't believe it," he muttered, moving away to put the space of the room between them.

But he did believe it. The truth had ravaged his face. His cheeks were deep hollows, and his eyes were glazed with shock.

"Ben wanted April to be his," she went on doggedly.

"Don't . . ." He held up a hand to ward her off.

"He didn't want anyone to know he wasn't the father."

"Shut up," he begged, stumbling to the door.

"Don't leave. Don't drive away. Not yet." Kate was beside him in an instant, her hand on the knob, but Jake snatched at her fingers, prying them away as he threw open the door.

Kate gasped and pulled her hands to her chest, aching inside. She had known it would be bad. She didn't know it would be this bad. "I did what I had to do," she told him as he swerved toward his Bronco. "You shouldn't drive," she added, unable to help herself. "You're not thinking clearly."

With that he swivelled to regard her with such loathing that Kate shrank away. "I'm thinking very clearly," he stated coldly. "I'm thinking I've been so stupid and blind. I really wanted you to be something special. Something better than the rest. But you're a liar. And I hate liars."

Kate swept in her breath. His harsh words cut like a knife. "I'll take my share of the blame, but you're—you're a judgmental hypocrite! You don't know what you would have done if you were me! It's so easy to run off to Europe with Mom and Dad's money, but it's not so easy to be left behind, penniless and heartbroken!"

"Damn it," he warned through his teeth, shaking all over. She was getting to him in spite of himself.

She threw back her head, tears glimmering in her eyes, her hair falling around her like a sweet, soft cloak. There was hatred in her eyes now, and Jake could have cowered beneath its intensity, knowing he had produced it in such a normally gentle creature.

"I loathe you," she told him, digging at the ring on her finger as if it suddenly burned her flesh. "You don't deserve to be April's father! So, go away! Get out! Get out of my life."

She was crying full force now and quivering with pent-up rage. Jake knew it was reaction. Reaction to everything. But God, he was suffering from reaction as well. April. April was his. It was too much to take in.

His shoulder collapsed against the side of the Bronco. He felt used up, old, and wracked by such misery that if he could have, he would have broken down and wept himself. But he was unable to comfort Kate even though she needed comfort. Her betrayal loomed in front of him like a red cape, and he had to attack.

"You've had years to tell me," he hissed through his teeth. "Years!"

"Well, I finally did, didn't I?" Kate's lips quivered uncontrollably. Her whole body was a quaking mass. But her resolve was new, deep and solid as oak. She held up the ring which glittered hard and cold in the moonlight. Then she tossed it at his feet, turned on her heel and marched back inside. Jake braced himself for the slam, but with the restraint of pure hatred she softly closed the door behind her.

Then there was silence.

Slowly, he bent to pick up the ring. Slowly he climbed in the Bronco, and slowly he drove away to an empty, hollow future.

Chapter Nineteen

Kate sagged against the door. The tears that had plagued her off and on all evening turned into a raging torrent. She pressed the back of her hand to her mouth and fought back a hot flood that seemed to have no end. Her whole body hurt so badly she wanted to cry out in pain.

I hate him. I hate him! Oh, God, I hate him!

Kate hiccuped on a sob. It wasn't true. She knew she was lying to herself. But she wanted it to be true because loving him was so unfair.

"Oh, Jake," she whispered aloud, "what am I going to do?"

She heard his Bronco drive away, and then she sank down to the floor, her chin pressed to her shoulder, letting the misery just flow for there seemed no other answer. All her bravado had been just that, bravado, and though it had helped salvage a modicum of self-respect, it was an empty victory.

She felt like she had died.

Eventually, because there was nothing else to do, she

dragged herself to her feet again, glad April hadn't wandered in unawares and discovered her mother in such a state. How would she have explained that? she asked herself.

It was another twenty minutes before Kate roused herself from her self-involvement to wonder about April again. Ryan's car had been parked outside when they arrived; she remembered remarking on it. But with all the weighty discussions on her mind, she hadn't thought about it again, and now she realized it hadn't been there when she and Jake had had their fight at his car.

Which was why, she recognized now, she had behaved so rashly. Subliminally, at least, she had known they were alone. But when had Ryan, and she guessed April, too, left? It had to be sometime during her terrible discussion with Jake, and how had he—they—made their exit without passing by, or at least being heard?

Kate's head hurt from thinking so hard. She was just being overly anxious. A mother hen. Absorbed with so many worries of her own that she was making up problems when none existed.

But where is she?

After a few moments Kate checked the house, but April was nowhere to be found. And there was no note, which was unlike her. Kate drew a shaking breath and expelled it slowly. She wanted to call Jake and pour out this new worry. How ironic that their first conversation after she had dropped her bomb should be over the issue of parenting!

But no, she wouldn't call him. April would turn up any minute, and the best thing Kate could do for herself was take a couple of aspirin and head to bed. Just because her whole world had collapsed did not mean there wasn't work tomorrow.

As Scarlett O'Hara was wont to say, tomorrow was another day.

* * *

Jake didn't remember the drive home. He didn't remember the ride up the elevator or the fact that he had stripped off his tie and jacket and untucked his white shirt. Neither did he remember that he had been drinking himself into oblivion until he surfaced enough to catch sight of his swimming reflection in the mirror above the bar.

His first thought was how much he resembled his brother, and through the haze of his mind he instinctively knew it was because he was dead drunk, generally a malady of Phillip, Jr.'s, not Jacob Talbot's. He wasn't a happy drunk, either, he thought inconsequentially as he viewed his scowling face. He was downright enraged, yet he felt paralyzed, lost, unfocused.

Damn her. Damn her for making me fall in love with her.

When the phone rang, Jake realized distantly that it wasn't the first time someone had phoned. He had ignored the other calls. What time was it anyway? he wondered, attempting to push up his sleeve to examine his watch. After several futile tries, he gave up, only to have his blurred gaze encounter the kitchen clock. Midnight. A little after, actually.

It had to be Kate calling.

Growling beneath his breath, he lifted his drink, but with the glass to his lips, he lost interest. He barely managed to get the snifter of brandy on the counter. Not a smart idea. He shouldn't have wasted the good stuff on this binge. Cheap bourbon would have sufficed just fine, thank you very much.

Digging down through his anesthesia, Jake inadvertently stumbled on the source of his pain. *I'm a father!* he thought incredulously. *April Rose is really April Talbot!*

"I have a daughter," he said aloud.

Brrriinng. Brrriinng. Brrriinng.

The phone nagged on. In a sudden fury, Jake snatched up the receiver. "What the hell do you want?" he demanded coldly.

"Jake?" his brother's voice asked after a moment.

"Ahh, Phillip. Nice to hear from you."

"I've been calling and calling. Sandra's been looking for you, too," he admitted almost in a mutter, as if he didn't want to think about that one. "She's blaming me for getting her thrown off the account. It wasn't my fault."

Jake couldn't care less. "Fine," he said, turning away from the receiver.

"Jake? I can't hear you. Are you there?"

"Go away, Phillip. I'm going to bed."

"Okay, it might have been my fault. I don't think Sandra's right for the job."

Jake muttered something in response, or at least he hoped he did.

"Are you drunk?" Phillip asked after another moment of shocked assessment. "Little brother, are you *drunk*?"

That struck Jake funny. Feeling half-crazed, he said, "I prefer to call it liquor impaired." With that he doubled over, hooting with laughter, until he realized moments later he had accidentally hung up on his brother.

So what. Phillip was a liar and a cheat as well. *He* should have linked up with Katie. Now there was a match.

Pain ripped through him. It took him several tries to replace the receiver, and when he finally managed, the damn phone started trilling again. It almost hurt his ears. Snatching up the receiver, he growled, "I'm not home," then slammed it down again before Phillip could say anything else.

With that he went straight for the shower. He stayed under the needle-sharp spray for a millennium. At least that's what it felt like by the time he was staggering around the bedroom, nude. A pounding penetrated his fogged brain. Someone at his front door.

Thinking it might be Katie, Jake couldn't find a way to force himself to answer it. He couldn't see her. He had hurt her. God, she had hurt him! The pain was so intense it felt like his head was ready to explode.

"Jake!" Phillip's muffled voice sounded through the panels. "Open up!"

"Go 'way!" he yelled back, but the blasted pounding just kept right on beating until he yanked open the door to admit his brother.

"What the hell are you doing?" Phillip demanded, glaring at Jake, who had managed to throw on a robe. He glanced past him. "Is Kate here?"

"No!" Because there was nothing else he could do, Jake collapsed in a chair, bringing on a dizzying wave of nausea in the process. From the alcohol or his own internal misery, he neither knew nor cared.

"I've got a bone to pick with you, little brother," Phillip declared, towering over Jake. "Your friend from the police came to see me. Detective Marsh? Ring a bell?"

Jake didn't want to think about this. He rubbed his face with one hand and sighed. Detective Marsh . . . "What about him?"

"They think I'm the one responsible for the explosions!" Phillip declared angrily. "What have you been telling him?"

"Me? Nothing." That was the truth. He had only outlined his theories to Kate. *Kate!* Pain ripped through him at the memory.

"They fingerprinted an ex-employee of Talbot's who happened to work for me some of the time, when he was here. Don't you listen to your messages, man? They've got Nate Hefner detained on suspicion of breaking and entering, criminal mischief, robbery, and God knows what else. They think he did it at my authorization! Jake!'' he bit out angrily, grabbing his brother by the shoulders and dragging him out of the chair. "You've gotta help me. Now!''

"I can't think right now, Phillip.'' Jake wished he had his wits about him. Something was going on here. But he was too far gone to pull himself back.

Phillip swore several pungent words in sharp succession. "I need you to vouch for me. Say you were with me, so they don't try to pin this on me, too.''

"Let go of me. Tell them the truth.'' Jake tried to jerk away from his brother's grip, but Phillip hung on with near maniacal strength.

"I can't tell them the truth because I was somewhere I shouldn't have been,'' Phillip admitted.

"Where were you?''

"I was with a woman.''

Jake was getting his wish. He was growing more and more sober by the minute. He stared at Phillip. "What woman?'' When his brother hesitated, Jake asked again, harshly, "What woman, damn it!''

"Marcus Torrance's wife,'' Phillip admitted, slowly releasing his grip. "I told her about the vandalism at the strip mall, and she must have told her husband. After the West Bank explosion Diamond Corp. backed out. I'm sorry, Jake.''

Kate tossed and turned all night. She had thought she would pass out from sheer exhaustion, but she alternated between recalling every painful moment of her fight with Jake and the terrible fear that something had happened to April. Should she call the police? She had tried Ryan's dad, Tom, but there had been no answer and no answering machine. She had called two of April's friends and inadvertently discovered a party going on at a house where parents weren't home, bringing the whole thing to a crashing halt, but still no April.

The only information she had was that April was with Ryan. Had there been an accident? she wondered, checking the clock again. Should she call the police?

It was just breaking daylight when she finally dialed the number of the local police station, her fingers cold and shaking.

"My daughter is missing," she managed to get out before breaking down completely. Reaction to everything; she knew that. But she could hardly explain it all to the policewoman at the other end of the line, so she stuck with the facts as she knew them.

Of course, people weren't really missing until twenty-four hours had elapsed, and though April was a minor, the fact that she would be eighteen the following January, and she had been with her boyfriend when she had disappeared, certainly took the edge off it for the police; she could hear that in their kind but cautious way of dealing with her. But they would check all records of traffic accidents and get back to her.

Small comfort.

At seven o'clock she phoned Jillian at home. "I won't be able to come in today," Kate whispered. "April's missing."

"What?" Jillian demanded on a gasp, and Kate gave her the facts as she knew them.

By noon, Kate couldn't stand it any longer. She placed a call to Jake, steeling herself for what could only be an emotional exchange. But Jake was in a meeting, his secretary informed her. Would she like to leave a message?

"No, thank you," Kate murmured, hanging up. She couldn't pace around the house any longer without going completely berserk.

In the end she returned to work, burying herself in

the myriad of details that made up her life: scheduling auditions, soothing wounded egos, calling about overdue payments. Jillian eyed her with concern, and even she seemed subdued today, her bright red heels exchanged for a pair of dark blue, her generally hard to tame curly hair pulled into a discreet bun at the back of her neck.

Near quitting time she stepped into Kate's office and said sympathetically, "Kate, if there's anything I can do, just name it."

Kate tried on a smile which seemed to reach only some of the muscles of her mouth. "I'm just so scared," she admitted. "This isn't like April."

Jillian nodded. "Did anything happen? I mean, something to keep her from coming home?"

"No." Kate felt as if her head was mush, her bones liquified. She had no strength left, and it was an effort to think.

"Have you talked to Jake? Maybe that would make you feel better."

Kate couldn't speak. Her throat closed in on itself, hot and aching. Jillian didn't know about her broken engagement, but she understood her feelings. It was too much. Kate, who before her renewed acquaintance with one Jacob Talbot had rarely ever cried, felt her eyes burn once more. She inhaled a trembling breath, fighting, but it was no use.

"Hey . . ." Jillian came around her desk and put an arm over her shoulders.

"You wanted me to go out on another date with Michael," she said with an attempt at humor. "I'm available."

"What do you mean?"

"Jake and I—aren't seeing each other anymore." Swiping at her tearing eyes, she hoped she didn't sound as pathetic as she thought she did.

"What? Why not?"

"Because . . . because I . . . because I told him something unforgivable about myself."

"There is nothing unforgivable about you," Jillian said, squeezing her shoulders. "Come on, Kate. You're perfect. The perfect mother, the perfect wife, the perfect businessperson. The perfect *friend!* I don't care what he thinks, he's wrong."

Kate made a sound of protest. "I told him he was April's biological father," she whispered.

Jillian slowly withdrew her support, coming around Kate's desk to face her across its cluttered surface. She leaned on her forearms. "Oh, Kate. Why did you tell him that?"

"It's the truth. Jake and I were lovers in high school. He left me pregnant and I married Ben. He never knew about April."

Jillian sank into the customer chair, blinking rapidly, the stuffing knocked out of her. She tried to speak several times, but finally all she got out was, "Really."

"I don't know what's wrong with me. I should have told him long ago, but he wasn't a part of my life. Ben wanted everyone to think April was his. When he died, I should have come clean with Jake and April, but I didn't. Oh, Jillian, it hurts so bad," Kate murmured tremulously, "and I have no one to blame but myself."

"When did you tell him this?"

"Last night."

"Wait a minute. Wait a minute!" Jillian's hands covered her mouth. *"April* didn't know?"

"No, I kept my promise to Ben."

"And you didn't tell her the truth after he died?"

Kate sucked air between her teeth, gathering courage. "No," she admitted. "I should have. I hadn't got there yet."

"Where were you when you told Jake?"

"At my house, in the living room."

"Where was April?" Jillian practically shouted.

"Oh, no. No." Kate moved her hands dismissively. "She wasn't around. I know that. Do you think I would have mentioned it if she were?"

"No, of course you wouldn't," Jillian expelled.

But Jillian's words started wheels turning in Kate's brain, terrible little thoughts churning madly. "Oh, Jillian." She bit into her lower lip to stop its trembling. "Oh, Jillian."

"What?" Jillian's eyes were huge, scared.

"We were in the living room. There was no one there, but Ryan's car was out front at first. I know it was. I thought he and April left while we were talking because it wasn't there later. I thought it was strange that we never saw them."

"Could they have overheard you?" Jillian demanded, asking the question Kate didn't want to consider.

She moved her head negatively. "There's nowhere to hide in the house without us hearing them leave."

"How about an intercom system that was left on?"

"We don't have one. You can't hear—" Kate gasped, her eyes flying open wide. "You can't hear from inside the house, but if you were on the lower patio, beneath the windows."

"Were the windows open?"

Kate thought back. "I didn't open them, but April could've, and I was in such a state I wasn't looking."

They sat in silence. The office phone blasted, making them both jump. Neither moved to answer it.

"If she overheard . . ." Kate couldn't finish.

"Then that's why she left," Jillian did the deed for her. She climbed from her chair and headed back to her desk, picking up the receiver on the tenth insistent ring.

Now Kate had to tell Jake. They had to go to the police

and explain why their daughter was missing. On the positive side, it didn't look like her disappearance was based on some kind of unexpected accident; on the negative, her emotional state was at stake, and that could ultimately be just as devastating.

Signaling to Jillian, who appeared to be just as shattered as Kate and didn't seem to be hearing whoever was on the other end of the line, Kate whispered, "I'm going to Talbot Industries to see Jake."

Jillian nodded. To the voice on the phone she said without her usual bright cadence, "All the callbacks for Nike have been made. I would suspect they've already made their selections. There's another audition coming up later this month. We'll let you know . . ."

Jake appeared to laze in the conference room chair, his legs thrust out in front of him, his indolent slouch covering up the fact that he suffered a raging headache and was desperate for something non-alcoholic to drink. How did Phillip do it? he wondered with a pang of anger mixed with admiration. He, Jake, couldn't pound down a bottle of brandy without suffering serious aftereffects while Phillip seemed to spend most of his natural life under the influence, yet today, when they both needed to be sharp and clear, Jake was dense and fuzzy, and Phillip appeared remarkably alert and sober.

Sober. Well, at least he was that, now. Berating himself for his weakness the night before, Jake resolved never to turn to liquor for an answer. Oh, yes, he felt annihilated by Kate's confession, but he should have been able to handle it better than he had.

April's your daughter.

Shaking his head in amazement, he felt thunder roll around inside his skull, and wincing, he lay his head against the back of the chair, viewing the others in the room through narrowed eyes. Did they know he couldn't concentrate? Here, they were discussing one of the most devastating betrayals Talbot Industries had ever faced, yet he was absorbed with his own personal problems.

Some CEO and president you are, Jacob Talbot. You should have insisted Phillip be given the job.

He knew he was being ridiculous, but he was furious with himself and furious with Kate. How could she keep such a secret? How could she? He didn't doubt its authenticity. Sometimes the truth rang out like a bell on a clear night. He had been hit hard and true, and it still felt like he had been dealt a blow to the solar plexus.

"I don't know what you expect me to say," Phillip was arguing with Detective Marsh. "I told you. I had nothing to do with the vandalism at the strip mall or the West Bank. Jake, for God's sake, wake up and get your friend, here, off my neck!"

"I'm awake." Jake was terse. They had been at this all afternoon, and now evening had set in with its resultant noise of rush hour traffic. Phillip had opened a window, sweating in spite of the air conditioning, but all he had managed to accomplish was an invitation for more blasting heat, noise and urban dust.

"Hefner named you," Detective Marsh said for the umpteenth time. His patience must have been wearing thin, but he didn't show it. Jake supposed it came from dealing with criminals all his adult life. Phillip Talbot, Jr., was no match for his professionalism.

"I wasn't there," Phillip bit out through his teeth. He glared at Jake, demanding his corroboration.

Jake had had all he cared to stand. Phillip had dragged him down to the office last night and hammered at him from every angle, alternately bullying and pleading that Jake understand his position. Oh, Jake understood it, all right. Far better than Phillip had intended him to. He just wasn't sure what to do about it, and it would be a hell of a lot easier if he could forget the way Kate's amber eyes looked drenched in sorrowful tears, the way her lips quivered, pink and soft and defenseless, the way her legs lay crossed against each other, the skin taut, smooth and femininely curved.

"He was with a woman when the first sabotage occurred," Jake revealed. "He doesn't want her named because she's married."

Detective Marsh gazed blandly at Phillip, whose lips were tight. Jake couldn't tell if he was upset that he had finally revealed the truth, or not. "Will she vouch for you?" the detective asked.

"I don't want to drag her into this."

"Does it matter?" Jake asked, spreading his hands. "You say you've got this Nate Hefner fellow dead to rights. Phillip wasn't there."

"Hefner said he broke into the strip mall at your suggestion," Detective Marsh said to Phillip.

"Why would I do that?" Phillip retorted.

They had been round and round this issue. Jake grimaced, not liking any of it. When the detective refused to go through the whole set of rhetorical questions again, Phillip added, "It's Nate Hefner's word against mine." He was adamant. "I wasn't there. I'm not in the habit of damaging anyone's property, especially my own family's. You said Nate was an employee at the West Bank. He may have a gripe with them, and he wasn't happy when I fired him from Talbot. The man's got a screw loose, but it's not my fault."

Since this was the same defense Phillip had followed all day, there was nothing left to say. Detective Marsh glanced over at Jake and inclined his head. "We'll be in touch," he said as a goodbye; then Jake was left alone with Phillip.

"A fat lot of help you were!" Phillip declared.

"You encouraged Hefner," Jake said, meeting his brother's gaze coolly. So far he had kept his thoughts to himself, but the leash on his emotions was worn thin. "You've got a lot of resentment over my being head of the company. You want to get back at our father, and you want to get back at me."

"What are you talking about?" he blustered, taken aback.

"I mean, let's get to it, Phillip. I can't prove anything. I don't even think I want to. But Nate Hefner got the idea in his head that if he did some stuff, you'd look the other way. I talked to Ray Driscoll this morning while you were with Marsh. You remember Ray, don't you?" Jake didn't wait for an answer. "He worked with Nate when he was here, and he remembers how buddy-buddy you two were."

"Ray! There's a troublemaker!"

"You tried to fire him, too, when he complained about you and Nate drinking too much at lunch. Ray's supervisor came to me, and I didn't feel like having a lawsuit on my hands; so no, I refused to fire him. Then, a few months later. Bam! You let Nate go. He knew too much about you."

Phillip's face turned purple. He couldn't speak.

"But you patched things up, obviously," Jake went on. "So, now look what's happened. We're just damned lucky no one's been seriously hurt."

"It sounds like you're blaming me!"

"I'm not saying you're responsible for the sabotage, but I'd bet money Nate Hefner did it all to get back at you and me. So, what do you want, Phillip?" Jake demanded, cutting through the mess his brother had made.

"You're way off base," he growled; but his hand reached behind him for a chair, and he sank down heavily.

"You want the airport property? Is that why you told

Torrance's wife about it? You wanted to squelch the deal with Diamond Corp., so you started an affair with Marcus's wife, slipping her a little information during pillow-talk time?''

"I want my share," Phillip admitted tautly. "So, sue me."

"Well, guess what? Father wants you to have a piece of the company, too. So, if he okays it, the airport property's yours. Do with it what you want."

Phillip's jaw literally dropped open.

"But, in the meantime, if I find out you actually set up Nate Hefner to sabotage Talbot, I'm going straight to the old man, and you'd better hope you're in a different state by then because if he won't prosecute you, I will."

For once Phillip Talbot, Jr., was stunned into speechless contrition. His eyes reddened, and all his bluster was missing, unavailable to him. If Jake could have believed he knew how to feel sorry for his actions, he would have believed it now. But Jake didn't care. He was sick of the sight of Phillip. Sick of everything.

A soft knock sounded on the conference room door. Pam stuck her head inside. "Ummm. Detective Marsh is still here."

"He is?" Jake frowned.

"There's been some kind of misunderstanding. Kate Rose is outside and she thought—I don't know—that you'd found out her daughter was missing and called the police. She's talking to Detective Marsh now. Maybe you'd better come out here . . ."

Chapter Twenty

The door from the conference room clicked open, and Jake walked into the hallway. Kate fought the misery that turned her knees to water. There was an innate grace about Jake, some kind of masculine fluidity that never ceased to catch her attention, and seeing him now, his expression locked in granite, she wanted to throw herself into his arms and beg forgiveness.

"Detective Marsh?" he asked, by way of approaching the situation.

Marsh gazed sympathetically at Kate. "I don't know anything about the whereabouts of your daughter."

Kate nodded, realizing her error too late. She had hysterically assumed that the detective, who was accompanied by a junior officer in a patrolman's uniform, had been called in by Jake to help find April. Of course he was here for the sabotage. She had just been too distraught to think clearly, and when she had launched into her tale, his silent, blank regard had told her all she needed to know.

But it was too late. Pam, Jake's secretary, who had overheard Kate's terrified babbling, had waited only long enough for Kate to stop before she had murmured something about alerting Jake.

Luckily, the one thing Kate had managed to keep from blurting out was Jake's fatherhood. This was, however, a small victory since someone was sure to wonder why she had jumped to the conclusion about April at Jake's office. Right now, they apparently assumed it was because Kate was Jake's girlfriend.

It didn't matter anyway. She didn't care what anyone else thought. She only cared about Jake.

Jake threw Kate a swift glance. "April's missing?"

Kate swallowed and nodded. "I—already called the police. I just thought—I don't know. I made a mistake." Her voice was whispery thin. She couldn't put any strength behind it.

"How long's she been missing?" Jake asked.

"Since last night."

"I'll check with whoever's in charge," Detective Marsh assured them; then he and his junior officer left.

Kate gazed longingly at Jake's familiar face, and an ache filled her from top to bottom. She didn't hate him, but she hated loving him so much.

As she stood there, Phillip appeared in the doorway of the conference room. Her gaze flicked to his, which caught Jake's attention. If his face had been rock before, now it was petrified stone. "I'm leaving," he told his brother shortly.

"Will you be back today?" Pam asked.

"It's late. Let's all go home." With that Jake headed for the elevators, stabbing the down button.

Kate was too upset to just assume he wanted her to follow him. He was upset, too. As the elevator dinged to a stop, its doors sliding open, Jake glanced her way. Only his eyes betrayed any emotion, and the tired, aching worry she witnessed there convinced her to join him in the elevator for the trip down. He was in no mood to fight with her.

Silence pooled between them until they hit the lobby. Even then, Jake's terse, "Did you drive?" wasn't exactly an invitation to chat.

"My car's out front," she said, gesturing.

"Mine's in the downstairs garage. Meet me at my place. We'll talk," he said, and then he strode away.

Kate was too undone to do anything but comply, but as she was heading up the elevator to Jake's eleventh-story condominium, she began to wonder at herself. Just because she was half out of her mind about April didn't mean she could trust Jake to pick up the slack. After all, he had just learned he was April's father. She couldn't expect him to feel as she did.

Still, the door to the condo was propped open, Jake having arrived before her, and as she crossed the threshold she heard him on the phone.

"Call here as soon as you learn anything," he was finishing tersely. "Kate Rose, April's mother, is with me."

He hung up the receiver. "Missing persons," he explained. "I wanted to say, 'And make it fast,' but I guess that's understood." His jaw flexed several times. "You're sure she's run away."

"Yes."

"Why did she run away?" he demanded, gazing at her squarely for the first time.

She realized then that he wasn't just tired, he was completely exhausted. Beard shadow darkened his firm jaw, and his eyes drooped a bit. His mouth was tight and unhappy, and now, as he ran a hand around the back of his neck, she wondered if she looked as strained.

Kate drew a breath. "I think she overheard us," she admitted.

"What? Overheard us! Oh, God." His expression

changed to one of horror. "She overheard us talking about *her*?"

"I think so," Kate admitted unhappily. "Do you remember that Ryan's car was out front at first, and then it wasn't?"

Jake thought hard, his eyes darkening. For an answer he uttered a few swear words, directed more at himself than her, Kate realized, though she shrank inside herself anyway. She blamed herself, and so did Jake, obviously.

"He had a beat-up Chevy. Cream-colored. Late seventies, early eighties," he recalled.

Kate nodded. "I've given a description to the police. I've called Ryan's father, but there's no one there."

"They'll have checked that by now anyway." Jake prowled toward the kitchen. "Would you like something? I'm having orange juice."

"No, thanks."

"You can help yourself to the bar if you want."

He wasn't exactly the gracious host. She could scarcely blame him. All she wanted was to lie down and sleep forever, pushing all these worries away.

No, that wasn't all she wanted. She wanted the safe return of her daughter, and she wanted to fall into the haven of Jake's arms and listen to his even breathing and the familiar, sexy timber of his voice as it rumbled from his chest.

Her eyes burned. Unable to stand it any longer, she sank into a wide ivory, leather armchair, slipped off her sandals and tucked her feet beneath her. She wore a loose white cotton dress that gently hugged her curves. Her hair was down, straight, and she hadn't brushed it since morning. Now it hung in gold-streaked curls around her face, and Jake, though he fought it with every muscle he could muster, fell under the spell of her simple beauty.

Why did he have to love her? he mused to himself as he drank the juice. She was directly in his line of vision, though he struggled not to keep staring at her. Why couldn't her betrayal have made him truly hate her, instead of leaving him with this sick feeling of misery? And April . . . his brain simply shut down when he thought about his daughter. *His daughter!* He had barely accepted her new status when she had run off to God knew where!

Yet, now that he knew the reason, he didn't blame her. He had wanted to run away, too. But he wasn't seventeen.

"Who else knows that—April is my daughter?" Jake asked, his tone stern in an attempt to keep his emotions under strict rein.

"No one."

"You said something to Detective Marsh, didn't you?"

"No!" Kate straightened in the chair, her eyes huge. "No, I was upset, but I didn't even think about it. I just asked him if he'd found April. I wasn't thinking. I thought—that's why he was there." She swept in a breath. "Oh, wait. I told Jillian. She was the one who helped me realize why April took off."

Jake propped one shoulder against the wall, finishing his glass of orange juice and setting it on the counter. Kate's eyes ate up the sight of him. His sensual indolence, the smooth muscles of his throat as he swallowed the liquid. She was even entranced with his long fingers which were perpetually tanned, like the rest of him. Remembering how he looked naked sent spots of color to her cheeks, and she swallowed and looked away.

"Detective Marsh was at my office because of Phillip," Jake informed her laconically.

"Oh." Kate didn't know what to say.

"An ex-employee of Talbot's—a one-time friend of my brother's—is responsible for the sabotage. The police want to know how far Phillip's involved as well."

"You really think—Phillip could hurt you that way?"

"He's not wild about either my father or me."

Since this might be a fairer assessment than she could know, Kate simply demurred, "All I know is he honestly cared about having April as spokesperson for Talbot. He was excited about it. He thought she was perfect for the job. That doesn't sound like someone who would sabotage the company."

"Phillip did that because he wanted the edge on Sandra. He was angry at her. He wanted to usurp her power."

"Are you saying he picked April for other reasons?"

Jake hesitated. "No. He did think she was perfect. She is perfect."

Kate fought her reaction to that. What must April be feeling right now? Did she hate her mother for lying to her? What did she believe?

"Maybe Phillip isn't entirely to blame. From what I know of Nate Hefner, the guy's a loudmouth with a chip on his shoulder who liked to drink with my brother. When things got out of hand, Phillip fired him. Maybe it's a revenge against Phillip."

Jake sounded like he didn't believe that theory, but Kate was more than eager to accept that explanation. "I don't think Phillip's all bad, do you?"

"My father does." Jake slid Kate a look she couldn't read. "I don't know. When people disappoint you, you don't know how you'll react."

It was an opening of sorts, though hardly an auspicious one. Kate linked her fingers together and gazed at the man she loved. "I'm sorry," she whispered. "I didn't know how to tell you."

He was no proof against her candid emotions. Fighting her spell, Jake closed his eyes and counted to twenty. When he was under control once more, he said roughly, "Well, it doesn't matter now. Let's find April and see what she's thinking. That's our real problem."

* * *

It was twelve-thirty when the call came in. Jake had ordered take-out Chinese food, and they had stared at their food in relative silence since neither of them knew what to do. Jake had then turned on the news, and though images flickered across the television screen, Kate had taken no notice of anything except the slow tick, tick, ticking of the clock.

Her muscles were cramped, and her eyes burned from lack of sleep. She checked her own answering machine constantly, hoping for some word from her daughter. She even left a message, begging April to call her as soon as she got home.

Kate finally concluded she ought to go home and wait for her there, though the idea of staying in the house alone, waiting for God knew what kind of call or information, made her inwardly shudder. She had just uncramped her legs and was wondering if Jake was asleep with his eyes open, the way he stared at the screen, when the shrill telephone bell made them both snap to attention.

"Yes?" Jake demanded, snatching up the receiver. His shoulders slumped a moment later, and Kate's heart leapt to her throat. She wrung her hands, eyes huge, staring at Jake. "Okay. Thanks. We'll be right there."

"What?" she demanded anxiously as he hung up.

"She's fine. The Seaside police picked them up after a description of the car went out. They're bringing them back to Portland, and they'll be at the station in half an hour."

April could not believe she was being driven back to Portland in a police car like some common criminal. Ryan, clearly, felt the same way. They kept gazing at each other in disbelief while the officers, long-used to this kind of thing, engaged in conversation that had nothing to do with their two teenaged passengers.

It was humiliating and kind of frightening. April hated it. She wanted to cry, but she was too tough and too smart to head for tears. She was her own person. Independent and all on her own. She didn't need anyone's help or interference, and when these officers finally dumped her out, she was going to tell her mom much the same.

The thought of fighting with Mom broke something inside April. She couldn't bear it. Her bottom lip suddenly found a life of its own, quavering like some two-year-old's. April clamped it between her teeth, and then her nose started tingling and burning, and those blasted tears formed despite all her efforts.

She closed her eyes, but those wet betrayers drizzled down her cheeks and off her chin to land in tiny wet puddles on her cotton T-shirt. She was alarmed when her whole body began to shake as well.

"Are you crying?" Ryan whispered, and she gave him more of her shoulder. She was mad at him, too, because he had been almost glad when the police had picked them up. He was out of money and gas and had lost all interest in "going on the road." Wouldn't you know? April thought, angrily swiping at the tears.

With an effort she pulled herself together. She had to be ready for her battle with Mom.

And Dad, she reminded herself with another shudder. Jacob Talbot. *Her father!* The thought of facing them both filled her with cold dread, and as the patrol car swept into the outskirts of Portland she steeled herself for what was bound to be a nasty confrontation.

* * *

Kate cradled a white Styrofoam cup full of coffee between her hands. The cup was crippled from the pressure of her tense fingers, and the coffee threatened to slosh over the sides. Taking a tentative sip, Kate wasn't really surprised to find the liquid on the tepid side. She had been sitting with it like this for the better part of an hour. The half hour the police had said it would take to bring April back had stretched to twice that long, and with each passing minute Kate's nerves tightened a little more.

She and Jake had been shown a couple of chairs in a waiting-cum-interrogation room. At least that's how Kate would have described it. One thing about a police station, no one wasted a lot of money on decor. Her chair was black, durable plastic meant to resemble leather, the arms plastic designed to look like wood. The floor was polished linoleum, and the general odor was some kind of industrial cleaner.

Jake stood to one side of the room. He had scrupulously avoided sitting next to her, and though Kate would have enjoyed the comfort, she also understood his own tensions. Maybe it was best that they waited in silence.

She glanced at Jake, whose sleeves were now rolled up his arms. He had discarded his tie long ago, and several buttons were undone at his throat. His hair had grown overly long in the past few weeks, Kate realized in a detached part of her mind. She remembered burying her hands in its lush thickness. Dangerous thoughts. With an effort she dragged her gaze away from his lean body.

Distantly she heard a door open and the clomp of footsteps. She glanced at Jake, but he didn't react. They had been through this scenario a few times already, but until April appeared in the flesh, there was no need to work themselves up

Stress was digging its way through her whole system. Fighting its enervation, Kate climbed to her feet, pushing back her mane of hair and mentally girding herself for when she faced April. Just thinking about it made her wince internally, and she made some small sound of discomfort, for Jake threw her a sideways look.

"You should have told me," he said.

Kate, unable to battle any longer, simply replied, "Yes."

At that Jake swung around, his gray-blue eyes regarding her somberly. Her own gaze was half apology, half defiance, and when he inclined his head in a kind of acceptance, Kate's spirits rose a few notches. Her lips parted. She was about to say something, but it withered on her tongue, for at that moment a police officer pointed to where she stood and April rounded the corner to stop short in the doorway.

Behind her shoulder, Ryan glanced up, his head bent like a whipped puppy facing more expected abuse. But Kate saw only her daughter, who was far less cowed. Accusations hovered in April's blue-gray eyes, so much like her father's that when Jake's intake of breath sounded near her ear, Kate knew he had discovered the resemblance for himself.

"I'm glad you're all right," Kate said on a rush. Oh, God, she wanted this moment to be behind her!

April chose not answer. She dropped her gaze to the floor, tightened her jaw, then threw a hard look at Jake. Kate could only stand back helplessly and watch. If she'd had any doubts about whether April had overheard her, they were answered at that terrible moment.

"She called you?" April charged.

Jake lifted his brows and nodded.

Digging into her back pocket, she pulled out a crumpled stack of bills. She pressed it into his palm, and when Jake gazed at her blankly, she said, "You left it as a tip. I've been meaning to give it back to you. I don't want it."

Two officers entered the room. The elder one broke into a long account about how they had found the car and the two teenagers, and the litany seemed to go on and on. When Jake stepped forward and handled the official business, Kate gratefully let him. April, however, clearly resented it. From being Jake's champion, she had quickly become his adversary.

"It's not his fault," Kate told her in an aside as she was glaring daggers at her father's back.

"I know it's not. It's yours. *You lied to me!*" she spit out harshly. "How could you?"

"Ben wanted to be your father, and I—"

"You lied." April was having no excuses, and Kate didn't blame her.

"Yes," she said wearily, and it was her defeatism that seemed to penetrate the most because April subsided into hurt silence until they were on their way home.

Tom, Ryan's father, had been called to collect his son, and when he and Kate saw each other, Tom gave her a reassuring hug. He was with his girlfriend whose waist-length gray hair and artist's smock gown spoke volumes about her own artistic nature. They looked the epitome of what one would expect from a couple who craved a simpler, less commercial life. Just as she and Jake represented the perfect picture of the urban professionals of the world, she decided, her mind spinning out on tangents to keep from facing the reality of her own situation.

At the house, Jake cut the engine and opened his door.

"You're coming in?" April demanded belligerently.

Her daughter's turnaround was excruciating for Kate. April was blunt and liked to be outrageous, but never had she displayed such out and out hostility.

"Yes, I'm coming in," Jake answered right back, surprising both Kate and April. He eyed his daughter with a certain amount of challenge.

"Suit yourself." April strode away from them. "But I'm not interested in talking," she threw over her shoulder.

"Tough," Jake muttered under his breath, and Kate's mouth dropped open.

"Maybe it would be better if I handled this," she suggested uneasily.

"You've had seventeen years." He slammed the door to the Bronco. "It's my turn."

She didn't believe he was serious, but when he stepped across the threshold, she learned that he was. April, who had chosen to hide herself in her bedroom and close the door, soon found herself with a new, decidedly determined father, invading her space. In shock, Kate listened to the raised voices of a very vocal argument, though she couldn't actually hear the words since April had cranked up the volume on her stereo to ear-splitting decibels.

She couldn't decide how she felt about it. Ben had let her handle everything, sometimes to her annoyance since she could have used the support. Jake, who'd had a little over twenty-four hours to accept the fact that he was a father, had barreled into the job with more determination than Kate might have liked. Of course, April's disappearance had certainly upped the ante, so to speak, when it came to parental stakes. And Jake had decided to go for broke.

"What the hell," Kate muttered to herself. She couldn't remember the last time she had eaten, so she made herself a peanut butter sandwich and poured a glass of white wine and waited for the storm to subside.

If it hadn't been so tragic, it would have been funny.

Silence finally prevailed. Well, silence apart from the throbbing music. Even as the thought crossed Kate's mind, the stereo lowered in volume, and a few moments later April's door opened and Jake strode into the kitchen, his expression dark.

Kate eyed him warily. He'd had a lot to cope with, and she knew he was a long way from forgiving her. But a dose of parenthood from a strong-willed daughter had to have some effect. "So, how was it?" she dared to venture.

The sound he emitted could have meant anything. He gazed at her sandwich and wine. "Who's the gourmet?" he asked on a sigh, and Kate managed a faint smile.

"Would you like one?" She lifted the sandwich.

"Thanks. And I wouldn't mind a glass of wine, although after last night I thought I'd never drink again." He shook his head in bewilderment. "Was it only last night?"

"I don't recall you drinking too much," Kate said, slathering another piece of bread with peanut butter.

"Yeah, well, you weren't there . . ." He cleared his throat.

"Is she . . . really hurt and upset with me?" Kate asked, handing Jake the sandwich.

"What do you think?"

"I never wanted it to be like this."

"What did you want it to be like?" Jake demanded, biting into the sandwich as Kate poured him a glass of wine. "Did you ever think about what would happen when the truth came out?"

"All the time! It's been like a time bomb!"

"Why didn't you do something about it?"

"What?" Kate demanded, meeting his accusing gaze. "When? Good grief, Jake, it's not like there's any perfect moment, is there? Okay, I was wrong, terribly wrong. And I betrayed you, and hated you, and loved you. And I should have told April the truth. I'll take all the blame, but it doesn't change anything! I'm sorry. How many times can I say it? If I could change the past, I would! No," she corrected herself immediately. "That's a lie. I wouldn't."

"You wouldn't," he repeated tautly, clearly not liking what she had implied.

"No, because then I wouldn't have April. And I wouldn't have my memories of you."

Jake's eyes darkened. He hadn't expected her heartfelt honesty. Gazing into her anguished golden eyes, he couldn't stand it. He wanted to drag her warm body into his arms and bury himself inside her. He wanted to push all the dreadful realities away and forget for at least one moment, concentrating instead on his passion and love for her.

For he did still love her. He wished he could deny it, but he couldn't.

As if she read his mind, she suddenly said, "Jake, I love you. And I love my daughter. I'm not perfect, but it doesn't mean I don't love you both."

"Damn it, Kate, you ask too much," he muttered roughly.

"I know."

Long, dismal seconds stretched between them. Kate's nerves screamed. She gulped wine and fought treacherous emotions. She wanted to run to her daughter, and then fall into Jake's arms, but she couldn't do either.

"However, you do make a mean peanut butter sandwich," he said in a serious tone.

She glanced at him, searching his eyes for the humor she expected. For a heartbeat, she saw it—his mouth curved, and there was a flash of white—a smile as bright as Hollywood.

"Jake . . . ," she whispered.

The creak of a door opening froze Kate where she stood. Jake, too, tensed at the sound of April leaving her bedroom.

She came to stand in the doorway to the kitchen, looking rather pale for her and definitely on the serious side. Her gaze swept over their makeshift dinner. She snorted. "Good God," she said; then her eyes filled with tears, and she broke into heartbreaking sobs that nearly killed Kate.

"Oh, sweetheart," Kate choked out, holding her arms out to her daughter. April didn't move, and Kate crossed the room, dragging her daughter's resisting body into her embrace. She brushed back her hair, cooing reassuring love words, her own tears falling without heed. April turned her face into her mother's neck, and they stood together in the trembling comfort of each other.

The sight hit Jake in the gut. *My family,* he thought, dazed. *My family.*

"Mom," April murmured brokenly.

"I'm sorry. I love you. You know I love you. I'm so sorry . . ." Kate couldn't stop the words that tumbled like a waterfall from her lips. "I'm sorry. Oh, darling, I love you so much!"

April hiccupped, cried some more, then finally lifted her head and wiped her nose. On a half laugh, she asked, "Could I have one of those?" and she pointed to Jake's peanut butter sandwich.

Chapter Twenty-One

There was so much to be said, and nobody felt like talking. April merely curled up beside Kate on the couch, and Jake stood by the windows, staring into the dark night as if answers lingered in the shadows.

Kate was replete. Happy. The pain in her soul expunged. April had, if not forgiven her, started back on the road to forgiveness. Kate would have walked through fire for her daughter. She would give up her own life. And at some level April understood that as terrible as her mother's betrayal had seemed, it had been made to love, protect and provide for her child.

April's adult understanding was awesome. Kate had always known it, but it left her humbled and speechless tonight. And when April said, "I couldn't make the wrong decision now. Not really. Didn't you know that?" Kate understood that her disappearance had been an immediate reaction without any lasting consequences.

"Do you love him?" April whispered in Kate's ear, her gaze following Jake.

Kate nodded, not wanting him to hear.

"Does he love you?"

"He did," she said, picking her words.

"I don't know how I feel about him," she admitted just before disentangling from Kate's embrace and heading off to bed. Kate's gaze followed her, and April shrugged and frowned at Jake before disappearing.

"What did she say?" Jake asked, as soon as she was out of earshot.

"She's kind of unsure about things."

"Really," he said sarcastically.

"What did you say to her, when you were in the bedroom earlier?"

"You couldn't hear?"

"The music was too loud."

Jake smiled faintly. "I told her to turn down the music and she said no. We fought about it."

"That was it?" Kate couldn't believe it.

"Well, not quite. She finally screamed at me that I'd never be her father, and I told her that was okay because I didn't know the first thing about being a father. She said she was going to be eighteen in a few months, and I said fine, no child support."

"You didn't!"

"I did." Jake was unrepentant. "She almost laughed, caught herself, then turned down the music. That's all."

In truth, there was so much more. Jake had felt it, and he had seen an answering emotion in his daughter's eyes. But their relationship was too new, too fragile, to be anything but a fight for control. He had known it; so had she. And yet, he had suddenly wanted to hug her like a father, starved for the closeness he hadn't even known he had missed out on until two days ago.

She looked like him. The resemblance he had put down

to Kate was really a resemblance to him. The eyes. The chin. The smile . . .

But there was no smile in evidence tonight. She had stared at him with deep intensity, an intensity he also possessed. She was like Kate, too: her hair, her humor, her innate beauty.

"You would have been a great father," Kate said to him, drawing him back to the present.

"Yeah, well . . ." He didn't think he could hear it right now. With an effort, he said instead, "Should I take you back to your car?"

It seemed such a strange and cold response. Kate wanted so much more. She nodded her head jerkily, and she and Jake sped through the early morning in moody reflection until they reached her sports car.

But as she climbed from the Bronco his hand reached out to grab her wrist. "Don't go," he said simply.

She gazed at him, her heart in her eyes. "Don't go?"

Jake groaned. "I don't want to be alone yet."

Kate could see that even though he wanted her, he was fighting his own instincts. "It might be a mistake," she said.

"Then I want to make a mistake," he answered without smiling, his fingers releasing her wrist long enough to cup the back of her nape and draw her willing mouth to his.

She didn't recall the trip up the elevator to his condominium. All she could feel were his urgent hands and her own anxious fingers digging at him as they struggled through the front door, dragging clothes from each other, their mouths melded in a kiss while the rest of them fought for freedom from restriction. Once Kate laughed as Jake couldn't release his cuff, the shirt hanging on his arm like some offending, uninvited guest.

"Damn it," he muttered without heat, which sent her into gales of laughter.

For that he dragged her into the bedroom, sweeping off her clothes and his own until their hot, hungry bodies were tangled together. His mouth ravaged hers, and she reveled in the possession. Her hands slid down his sinewy back, clasping his hips until Jake groaned and pushed her legs apart with one knee.

She was starved for his possession. Mindless. Uncaring. She took his lack of control as a sign that he had half forgiven her. And she had forgiven him his callousness. She understood and she didn't care, and if Jake would only make love to her with some of the pleasure and abandonment he had before, their future could be sealed.

These were random thoughts. Unstable, and rooted in quicksand. But Kate had been so certain she had lost him and anything they could have together that she was feverish with desire and the need to put things right in the physical sense.

For his part, Jake was right with her. His tongue stabbed into her mouth, foreshadowing the possession she longed for from another part of his anatomy. He groaned his need, and as his mouth sought the hard nub of her breast, little moans of desire and frustration passed her lips in tiny squeaks.

She had never been so bold and needful. She twisted and writhed and practically demanded he thrust himself inside her, and though Jake sought to keep the rollicking pace under control, he gave in with a moan of pleasure of his own, driving inside her to the core of her femininity in a hot, sensual thrill that had Kate's body arching into a shooting climax within milliseconds.

"Jake!" she cried, her hands digging into the skin of his back.

"God . . . ," he rasped, his own pleasure spilling into her at the same moment.

Time seemed suspended. Hanging outside of her reality.

When Kate, sated and drugged with satisfaction, slowly opened her eyes, it was to find Jake collapsed atop her, their hearts still beating in rapid tandem.

"I never want to be without you," he admitted in a voice raw with need.

"Oh, Jake!"

"Marry me," he said, slowly disengaging himself from her. "Sometime in the next few months. Marry me and don't change your mind."

Her answer was an urgent nod of her head as she gazed deeply into his eyes and silently answered him with all the love she possessed.

"I'll take that as a yes," he said with a deep-throated chuckle, and as Kate kissed him all over his face, he added, "I've got an engagement ring, you know, slightly worse for wear. Tomorrow we start planning."

And drawing his mouth down to hers, Kate answered huskily, "Tomorrow . . ."

If Kate had envisioned a perfect future for herself, it couldn't have been any better than the one she had suddenly been given. Her engagement to Jacob Talbot was announced to the newspapers, and suddenly everything turned rosy. Even his reluctant and taciturn parents came around, and Kate was amazed at a quote from Marilyn Talbot citing that she "couldn't be happier with Jacob's choice" and how much happiness she wished for their future.

Of course, they still didn't know the truth about April. Jake, from years of experience, knew better than to hit them with too many blows all at once. The knowledge of April's parentage remained with only a select few individuals, and both Kate and Jake decided to let her make the choice about when, and how, she wanted that news to become public.

As for April herself, she threw herself into her senior year of school with a vengeance, sending out applications to dozens of colleges and working at her studies with renewed concentration. Kate could hardly credit it, and though she worried her daughter had given up her social life entirely—Ryan appeared to be out of the picture as well—Jake cautioned her not to interfere. It was April's way of finding herself, April's way of charting her own course, April's way of accepting.

Jake's brother, Phillip, had his suspicions when it came to April, however. She had been his find, his special choice for the Talbot spokesperson. While he and Jake worked through their problems, he spent most of his time on the set with April, bonding with her in a way neither Jake nor Kate quite understood. But Phillip's problems with Jake, and Talbot Industries, had taken an unexpected turn. As the investigation continued, it became more and more evident that Nate Hefner had executed his destruction and vandalism as a retaliation against Phillip rather than Talbot as a whole. He had been Phillip's friend while he was employed at Talbot, and when he had been fired over lazy work practices, he had been angered and infuriated that Phillip, because he was a Talbot, had gotten little more than a slap on the wrist for his liquid lunches while Nate had been ousted from a fairly cushy job, one he had not been able to replace. Nate consequently tried to renew an association with Phillip and, failing that, had let his drinking get away from him and had broken into the strip mall, then taken a job at the West Bank Hotel just to wreak havoc.

Throwing suspicion on Phillip had been a side benefit he had capitalized on.

Phillip, for his part, had suspected Nate from the start,

but had been unwilling to finger him to the brother whom he deeply resented. He had begun a relationship with Marcus Torrance's wife for no better reason than the woman had been willing, then had whispered about the sabotage just to cause problems for Jake and Talbot Industries as a whole.

Jake had gleaned most of this information from Phillip himself. "I offered him the airport property on a platter," Jake had explained to Kate. "And that apparently did it. As soon as I gave in and said, 'You're out of Talbot Industries once and for all,' he just stopped fighting."

"What happened?" Kate had asked.

"Detective Marsh was on to Nate Hefner. Phillip was straight with the police, and then he told me he was through causing problems for the company. I think, when I rolled over about the airport property, it forced Phillip to face his faults. He didn't really want to cut all ties with his family."

"Is he still seeing—Mrs. Torrance?" Kate hadn't been certain how to ask the question.

"No." Jake had been thoughtful. "She and her husband have separated, but apparently Phillip was a symptom of the problem, not the problem itself. The ironic thing is, Torrance wants the joint venture after all! He called Dennis Watley, our attorney, and wants another shot at it."

"That's great!"

At that point, Jake had gathered her in his arms and said, "Now, if April comes to realize how good everything is, it'll all be perfect."

Kate agreed. A part of her couldn't help regretting that Jake would never be able to go through all the steps of parenting, but that couldn't be helped. And the few times she had brought that up in recent weeks, he had shushed her instantly. "I have April," he reminded her, which was both a discouragement and a blessing since it was Kate's fault they had been separated for so many years.

Stop being so hard on yourself! she admonished now, as she reached for the phone on her desk. It was a set of circumstances that had built this scenario. Jake understood; so did April, come to that. It was Kate who wouldn't set the blame aside, and though she knew she must if she were ever to come to terms with everything, it was still difficult.

"Hey," she greeted Jake, as his secretary put her through to his office. "Are we still on for tonight?"

"Still trying to back out, huh?" he teased.

Kate's diamond winked at her in the light, almost as if it shared the joke. "Who me? Now, why would I want to back out of making wedding plans with your mother?"

"Give me a few hours and I'll list the reasons."

"I'm fine!" she chuckled. "I'll meet you at my house at six-thirty."

Kate had just replaced the receiver when Delilah, dressed in skin-tight black leather, whirled into her office. "I bet you're surprised to see me!" she declared.

"Well, yes I am." Kate actually had almost forgotten about her mercurial client. "How was L.A.?"

"Forget L.A. New York's the place to be. You know I had a callback for a soap?"

"Really? Which one?"

"Oh ..." She shrugged. "I was an extra on 'All My Children.'"

"Cool," Kate said, hiding a smile. An extra was hardly the same thing as getting a callback for a role, but hey, if Delilah's fantasies made her happy, who was she to argue? "Are you going back right away, or do you miss Portland?"

"Oh, I'm back home now. That was fun, but this is where I belong." She hesitated, smoothing her hair. "Do you have anything for me?"

"You mean, something to match the turkey commercial?" Kate asked, fighting to maintain a straight face.

Delilah gave her a swift look, then actually smiled. "I know I was bad, but will you forgive me?" For an answer Kate reached across the desk and shook Delilah's hand. Delilah's gaze, however, caught the glittering diamond on Kate's left ring finger. "Oh, my God!" she cried. "Who?"

"Jake Talbot."

"Of Talbot Industries!" Delilah shrieked. "You lucky girl! That does it! I'm never leaving here again. I could use a good man with a bankroll."

"Couldn't we all?" Jillian said dryly, ducking her head in the door. "Your daughter's on her way back."

"Thanks."

April was just finishing work on her second commercial. She had looked so incredibly grown up on her way to the shoot, her hair brushed back into a loose french braid, her slim legs encased in a pair of natural-shade nylons under a straight blue dress. They would pick out her apparel for the shoot when she arrived, but it was April's demeanor that arrested Kate. She seemed more like twenty-five than just shy of eighteen.

Kate finished up some paperwork while she waited for her daughter. She smiled to see the note from the bank stamped "Paid in full." As a means to solve her financial troubles, Jake had directed Talbot Industries to pay off her loan to the bank, so she was no longer under the guillotine of a balloon payment. Instead, she now owed Talbot the amount of the note, but there was no balloon payment looming. She had twenty years to pay the balance, and even with interest, the payments had been whittled down so that she was more than able to make them and still breathe easier. Also, business was increasing, thanks again to Talbot's association with Rose Talent Agency. She hated to think the business world was so political in its dealings, but she had to admit that being linked with Talbot Industries had helped her company enormously.

Still, Rose Talent Agency's health was way down the list of Kate's priorities these days. Call it selfish if you must, but all she cared about right now were her relationships with Jake and April.

Sliding her chair back, Kate climbed to her feet, adjusting her blouse as she stepped around her desk. A faint dizziness assailed her, but when she drew a deep breath it passed. Vaguely she realized she'd had a few other similar episodes. With a groan, she wondered if she was getting sick. It was now mid-October, and the flu season was just starting to get into full swing, even though the weather was still fairly mild and warm.

April breezed into the agency. She still worked a few hours in the afternoons, and Kate was glad to have her around. The truth was April was about to fly out of the nest, and Kate wasn't certain she was ready.

"How'd it go?" Kate asked.

"Pretty good, I think. By the way, have you seen the West Bank since they started fixing it? You can't even tell. It's almost done, so I guess we'll be filming soon."

"Great!"

"I saw Phillip at the shoot," April added. She had been told enough about Phillip's involvement with Nate Hefner to associate him with the sabotage.

"How was he?"

"Not bad. He seems—better," she struggled, in lieu of finding a more definitive word. "You know, he can really make people like him when he wants to." She glanced at Kate and Jillian, who were both noticeably mum. "When he's not drinking," she amended. "And he's been on the straight and narrow during this whole commercial shoot. I told him he should talk to Jake about taking over as liaison for the ad agency."

"He works for Talbot, not the agency," Jillian said.

"So? He's as good as that Sandra witch. Better really."

"How unkind of you," Kate said drolly.

"Yeah, I know." April was unrepentant. "Anyway, I think he's going to talk to Jake."

It was strange how things had turned out. Phillip's transformation was symmetrical with April's acceptance of Jake as her father. Kate didn't care how, or why, it had happened; she was just glad it had.

Later, as Kate prepared to leave work and drive back to the house, April said quietly, "Mom?"

"Yes?"

Jillian had already left, and for once the agency was quiet. Kate had just turned out the lights to her office, and April was finishing arranging items on the reception desk for the following day.

"I've been filling out all my college applications."

Kate nodded. "I've been signing checks and handing them to you to mail with those applications," she reminded her daughter with a smile.

"I changed some things on the applications," she said, frowning a little, as if she wasn't certain how her mother was going to react.

"Oh?"

"Just one thing, really."

"Okay," Kate said, waiting. It was odd, really, how April could draw out certain things that didn't seem to have any particular significance, while the really important stuff she just breezed through.

"My name. I added Talbot after Rose. April Rose Talbot," she confirmed, then quickly snatched up her lightweight jacket and headed out the door before Kate could react.

Kate didn't remember the drive home after that. She

wanted to shout with delight. She couldn't wait for Jake to come over, so she could tell him.

But later that night, while she was changing clothes to have dinner at Jake's parents' and discuss the upcoming wedding, Kate completely forgot about April's surprising statement. Spots swam before her eyes. Nausea followed the whirling dizziness. She ran to the bathroom and promptly threw up in the toilet.

Once she had finished retching, she rinsed out her mouth and splashed water on her face, then stared at her ashen pallor in the mirror. Her stomach still quivered. Cautiously, she climbed onto her bed, curling up to fight the debilitating feeling. Well, if she was going to have the flu, she reasoned, she might as well get it over with now before preparations for the wedding got into full swing.

For Marilyn Talbot wanted the whole nine yards. Jake and Celia had married in a quick ceremony, almost on the sly from their parents. Marilyn was having none of that this time, and her lavish ideas had appalled both Jake and Kate. Tonight's meeting was to try and calm her down. Kate would have loved to marry in front of a judge and then honeymoon at the beach; she wanted no lofty, overblown affair. Jake definitely leaned her way, but fighting his mother on this one was a losing battle that neither he nor Kate really wanted to fight in the first place.

Still, the woman had to be stopped—or at least stalled. With her stomach roiling, Kate seriously hoped Jake would take over and put a leash on Marilyn by himself. She just wanted to go to bed for the night.

When Jake arrived she was splashing water on her face again. "I don't feel well," she admitted.

"You just don't want to face my mother," he teased.

"True." Kate managed a wan smile.

"Let me take care of things," he told her. "Besides, my

brother's going to be there. He and my father are discussing his future."

"His future?"

"Phillip wants to stay with the company. I told him it was all right with me, but he's burned a lot of bridges with my father. You know what he said he wanted to do?"

"Be the liaison to Turner & Moss Advertising Agency?" Jake stared at her as if she were clairvoyant.

Kate grinned. "April talked to him about the idea. I think she put it in his head."

"Quite a girl, our April," he said. Taking Kate's hands in his, he examined the ring thoughtfully. "When do you think she'll be ready to tell the world that I'm her father?"

"I'd say she's already starting to." At Jake's swift look, she added softly, "She's signing her admissions forms, April Rose Talbot."

Jake took the news with a swelling of pride that made him feel slightly ridiculous. He'd had no part in April's development apart from scattering some genetics her way. It hardly seemed fair to bask in her accomplishments when it was April herself, and Kate, and possibly even Ben Rose— he had to admit, though it liked to kill him—who had fashioned the wonderful young adult she had become.

"Well, good," he said brusquely, his voice slightly rough. With a quick kiss for Kate, who looked all too aware of how he was feeling, he left for Lakehaven.

In the middle of the night Kate awoke with tears on her face, startled from a vague nightmare where everything she did and everywhere she turned, something horrible happened. Worse, she was the villain in every scene. April and Jake and Jake's parents and even Phillip all accused and blamed her for each and every misdeed.

Rising from the bed, Kate was glad to feel her stomach

under control once more. She walked to the window and gazed out at sharp, bright pinprick stars against a midnight sky. She should be deliriously happy. She *was* deliriously happy! But a strange, plaguing anxiety hung around her like a bad smell that she couldn't quite rid herself of.

Jake had called at about eleven to inform her that he had derailed his mother's eager attempts to take over the wedding—at least for the meantime. Phillip and his father had gotten along as well as could be expected, managing a civility sadly lacking in previous meetings. "Maybe things really are working out for the better," Jake had theorized with hope in his voice.

Now Kate winced, remembering her own dreams that seemed to suggest something else. She wanted to believe the best, like Jake, and why not? Even April was beginning to forgive and accept. What else was there?

Pushing her uneasy feelings aside with an effort, she climbed back into bed and fell into dreamless sleep.

At seven she rose from bed, beelined for the bathroom, and vomited up the remaining bit of food left in her stomach. Once again, she stared at her reflection. She felt horrible.

When she appeared in the kitchen she was still wearing her bathrobe, and as she fixed herself a piece of dry toast and cup of tea, April, who was busily shoveling in sugared corn flakes, lifted her brows. "Are you sick?"

"I think I've got the flu. That's why I didn't go with Jake to meet his parents last night."

"Mmmm . . ."

Kate nibbled her toast, concentrating on her uncertain stomach. She would have liked to take the opportunity to discuss with April her "about-to-be" relationship with Marilyn and Phillip Talbot. They were, after all, her grandparents, and as soon as they learned the truth, Kate imagined, knowing them, they would want an active role as such. But she couldn't manage it right now.

"Maybe you have food poisoning," April suggested. "I heard somewhere that there's really no such thing as the stomach flu. You might be sick with the whole respiratory thing, and then react to food, I guess. But it's not really the flu."

"I don't have a respiratory thing," Kate retorted, sipping tea.

"Touchy, touchy," April said, grabbing up her book bag and heading for the door. "See ya later."

Kate worked through half her piece of toast, and by the time she had finished her tea she felt a lot better. It was while she was rinsing out the cup that the shocking thought hit her: pregnancy!

The cup slipped from her hands, shattering in the sink. Instantly Kate was infuriated with herself. No. She couldn't get pregnant. She knew that. Just because April had slipped some doubts in her head didn't mean she had to start searching for some other answer.

A niggling thought kept at her. A memory. This was exactly how she had felt with April. It was, in fact, the reason she had begun to suspect she was pregnant.

"That was eighteen years ago!" she declared aloud. Too long to recall. It was all just a bunch of crazy little worries because she was feverish and sick and suffered a sleepless night.

Are you feverish?

With slightly unsteady hands, Kate searched through the medicine cabinet in the bathroom for the thermometer. Sticking it beneath her tongue, she went to stand at the window and think. She was grasping at straws. She was, what? Hoping for something that would bind her to Jake even tighter? Didn't she trust his feelings? He had survived the knowledge that she had kept April from him. Did she seriously think a baby would make things *better?*

No. A baby would make things worse. A baby would turn her into a liar once again, because she had sworn she could not get pregnant.

Jake wouldn't survive two lies—even if the second wasn't really a lie at all.

Kate's heart pounded as if she were in a race as she removed the thermometer from beneath her tongue. Ninety-eight point eight. Two-tenths higher than the norm. Not exactly a raging fever.

Inconclusive, she told herself, clamping her teeth together and shivering as if she suffered from palsy. With a moan of worry, she snatched up her lightweight jacket and headed for the nearest pharmacy.

It didn't open until eight-thirty and that was just for prescription drop-offs anyway. Kate called Jillian at work and explained that she wasn't feeling well and that she was just waiting for the pharmacy to open so she could get some over-the-counter flu medication. She thought she sounded moronic, but Jillian was too busy to notice. In fact, all she really said was that they were going to have to get some more help, something they had discussed off and on for the last month.

Kate drew a long breath as the proprietor unlocked the door, offering her a smile of greeting. More help? If she were pregnant, they would need to hire more than just one extra person.

If she were pregnant!

Kate dazedly shook her head as she purchased the home pregnancy test. She half expected to see someone she knew in line, but she managed to make the purchase and head home without running into anyone she recognized. Although the test warned her that the first urine of the morning held the highest concentration of the hormone for which the test registered positive, Kate wasn't interested in waiting. If the test was negative, she would just wait for her period to start. If it was positive, well, then. . . .

When was your last period? she asked herself with a jolt. With disbelieving eyes she watched the color of the test turn pink, a positive rosy glow, at the same moment she realized she had missed her last period.

Denial. She had been through such a roller coaster of emotion that she had been in denial. She still wanted to deny the results. It wasn't possible!

But why not? her reasoning mind answered. So, Ben had been proven an able sperm donor. So what? There were any number of reasons two people couldn't conceive together. It wasn't necessarily that one could and one couldn't. It was the combination that mattered.

So, why had she believed it was her fault, her body that was inadequate? Because Ben had wanted it that way. He had needed to believe it, and Kate had accepted the verdict without question because, truthfully, she hadn't really cared.

But she had been wrong. She had conceived once. She should have expected she might be able to again.

Especially with the same man!

"Oh, God," she murmured, sinking onto the floor as she considered all the ramifications. A pregnancy. A baby. Jake's child. Again.

He wants a child of his own. He said so!

But that was before he knew about April.

It makes no difference. He missed out on parenting. He'll grab this second chance like a lifeline.

He thinks you're a liar. He'll think you made it up, just to trap him.

He knows you better than that. He loves you.

His trust in you is paper thin. This will break it. It's over, Kate. Over.

Burying her face in her hands, Kate was consumed with fear. She was paralyzed for the space of a minute; then she jumped to her feet and ran to the phone. In the midst of calling her gynecologist she slammed down the receiver. There was an Immediate Care Center twenty minutes away. They could give her a pregnancy test. When she got those results, then she would call Jake and give him the good— *bad?*—news.

The streets of Lakehaven were fairly busy, even though it was an ordinary Thursday afternoon. Kate sat at an espresso bar and watched the world pass by outside her window. Her roiling stomach had been replaced by a low-grade collection of butterflies about to take flight at any second. She sipped another cup of tea, chamomile, but still couldn't bear the idea of any solid food.

She had come here because. . . . Her mind went blank. She couldn't recall. She had simply walked out of the Immediate Care Center after her blood test and said she would call sometime after two o'clock for the results. Then she had climbed into her sports car and driven straight to Lakehaven, as if she'd had it in mind all along, which she hadn't.

She had driven by the Talbots' and even cruised by the tiny home her parents had rented not far from the center of town. Not that there was anything to see there any longer. It was gone. Ripped down. Turned into a row of gray-painted shops trimmed in white.

Now, with the feeling that she had aged horribly in the past few hours, she walked to a nearby public phone and placed the call to the Immediate Care Center.

"Positive," the woman checking her file answered cheerily.

She had known the answer before she heard it. Thanking

her, Kate hung up, then stared through the walls of the phone booth, feeling as if she had somehow been dropped on another planet.

If she were brave, she would pick up the receiver once more and place a call to Jake right now. Her hand was still clenched about it already. But instead she loosed her grip and let herself out of the booth into a typical fall day where maple leaves drifted onto the sidewalk from the row of trees that lined the street, and the air smelled sharp and biting in her nostrils.

A watery sun still held sway in the heavens, but it wasn't enough to dispel the chill in Kate's soul. She climbed into the Mustang and drove aimlessly until she found herself on the outskirts of town and a very familiar knoll upon which sat the old church where she had once "married" Jake.

Someone had saved it. Window panes had been replaced, and the white paint looked spanking new. The walkway was concrete which ended in a set of curved steps to the porch. White rails flanked each side, and Kate, still in her self-imposed daze, ascended the steps and let herself in through the refinished double doors to the anteroom beyond.

Musk and vanilla and white candles. None of that greeted her as she walked between the pews to the altar. Gazing around, she realized that although everything was redone and well-loved rather than forgotten, it seemed small and insignificant to her somehow. She had built it up inside herself as some monumental ceremony to endless love, but in reality she and Jake had played a silly child's fantasy that had no bearing on real life.

"Can I be of help?" a male voice inquired, and Kate gasped in surprise as she saw the young man standing by a side door that led behind the altar to the rooms beyond.

"I didn't see you," she admitted.

"I didn't want to scare you," he said as he stepped forward.

He was somewhere in his twenties, Kate guessed. "Are you the minister here?" she asked. His casual clothes could have meant anything, but he possessed that easy aura of belonging that sent a clear message.

"I am. Did you want to see me?"

"No, I . . . was just passing through and . . . I remembered the church."

"It was vacant for a long time. Our congregation moved when we outgrew the space we'd started in. We've been here about five years."

"I came here once," Kate said, the words tumbling out, though she had no recollection of conceiving them before they fell from her tongue. "With my boyfriend. We 'married' each other, but it wasn't a real marriage. We wanted to be together, but we were too young and his parents . . ." She sighed. "It was a long time ago."

"It still matters to you," he said gently, reading her troubled thoughts with quiet certainty.

Kate uttered a sound that was half laugh, half sob. "You're good at what you do, aren't you?"

"Do you want to talk about it?" he asked.

Kate stared at him. She swallowed, expecting herself to deny it, but once again the words came from somewhere inside herself not connected solely to her brain. "Yes."

It was night by the time she left the church. A cold wind blew off her right shoulder as she climbed into her car and headed west toward Portland. She had been gone a long time without a note or explanation to anyone, and she knew both April and Jake would be concerned.

But she couldn't phone. She was in too much turmoil. The young minister had gently prodded and poked through her thoughts and forced her to face some truths she hadn't quite wanted to see.

She had told him about Jake. And April. And Ben. And then she had told him what she had learned today. Her anxiety was all too plain and raw, and when she was finally finished, the minister had asked the one question she hadn't even considered yet, "Do *you* want this baby?"

Now, as she turned into her own drive, it was with both trepidation and resolve. A black Bronco waited next to April's car. Jake was here.

Inhaling a deep breath, Kate pulled to a stop, levered herself from the seat and headed to the front door. It flew open on its own, and her daughter stood on the other side, eyes full of accusations.

"Where have you been? Did you forget how to use a phone? Geez, Mom, I leave you looking like death warmed over, and then you disappear without a trace. I'm not the only one who needs the police to drag them home! *Where were you?*"

"I went to Lakehaven," Kate admitted, her gaze searching past April to the depths of the living room beyond. Jake stood in silence, his deep frown an indication of his own worries where Kate was concerned.

"Lakehaven?" April repeated, closing the door behind them both and following Kate's faltering footsteps into the room. "Why?"

Kate's eyes were on Jake. He looked so strong and masculine and darkly virile in jeans and a black shirt. Or maybe it was just the harshness of his features. "Good question," he said.

"I just was—reconnecting, I guess," Kate answered. "Does anyone want something to drink? I could use a soda."

"You don't look sick anymore," April said, her gaze skating over Kate from head to toe.

"Don't I? I feel sick." She laughed a bit hysterically.

"Well, you're acting kind of sick," April declared to her mother's strange response.

"What do you mean by reconnecting?" Jake asked.

"I just had to go look around."

"But you couldn't go with me last night." The rebuke was implied.

"No," Kate admitted. She glanced a bit desperately from her daughter to Jake and back again. Sometimes they were so much alike it was scary! "I've got to tell you something," she added. "Both of you. I don't know if I should do it at the same time, or not."

"Just say it," Jake suggested in a lethally serious tone.

Kate felt frozen through and through. She drew a breath, exhaled it, drew another.

"I'll get that soda," April suggested, looking scared.

"I had to get my head straight," Kate apologized. "I had some things to think about. I remember how you said you hated liars."

It was Jake's turn to sweep in a sharp breath. April returned with the cola and placed it within Kate's shaking hands. "Mom, what is it?" she asked, deeply worried.

"I'm—I'm—" She gestured helplessly. "I'm pregnant."

Dead silence followed. The proverbial pin could have dropped and sounded like a cannon.

April gaped in wonder. "Really?"

Kate nodded, but her gaze turned to Jake. What she read on his face wasn't encouraging. His jaw was granite, his eyes an unforgiving arctic blue.

"You lied about being able to conceive?" he suggested softly.

"No! I didn't know. I thought—Ben said—it was my fault and I believed him."

"What was your fault?" April asked, frowning.

"I never could have another child after you," Kate

explained. "Ben checked out, so we assumed I was the one who couldn't conceive."

"That's why you thought you couldn't conceive? Good grief, Mom! That's dumb."

April's bald pronouncement brought a hysterical bubble of laughter from somewhere inside Kate's chest. "You're right!" she cried. "It is dumb. It's so dumb, I can't believe it. But you know what? I'm glad. I'm so glad. I want this baby so much. It's like a miracle, and I've spent the whole day just getting used to the idea."

"I'm glad, too," April agreed. "But you know something? You could really use a class in sex ed. I mean, it's Jake's baby." She pointed to herself with both hands. "Hey, you already proved you could have a child together, right? If they gave you a test on this, you'd flunk. Anybody else would worry that they could get pregnant again."

"You're right," Kate said. "You're right!" She swiped tiny tears of hilarity from the corners of her eyes. "It's just that it was eighteen years ago!"

April turned to Jake. "Didn't you think about it?" she accused. "Where were the condoms? I mean, I'm not saying it won't be great. I've always wanted to have a brother or sister. But hey, we're all supposed to act responsibly, aren't we?"

Jake was in a daze. He couldn't take it all in. He understood Kate's collapse into near hysteria, because he wasn't sure whether he wanted to laugh or cry himself. And then to have his teenage daughter remonstrate him on his sex life! He rubbed a hand across his face in disbelief.

"Well?" April demanded of him. A smile threatened the corners of her mouth as the whole situation fully penetrated her consciousness. "My God! I'm going to have a sibling."

Kate's gaze was fixed lovingly on Jake. "I didn't lie. I promise. I didn't lie."

"I know."

"You do?" she asked him anxiously.

"Yes." A baby. His baby. A child to raise from birth. With Kate. She was right. It was a miracle. He shook his head to destroy the lingering cobwebs. He could see the quandary she had been in. "I always wanted children," he said in a soft voice.

Kate gave a cry of joy and threw herself in his arms. For once April looked speechless. Her eyes grew round and suspiciously wet before she muttered an excuse and scurried from the room. Kate trembled in his arms. "You're happy? You're really happy? Tell me the truth!"

Burying his face in the glory of her sweetly scented hair, Jake squeezed her tight. "I'm really happy," he said, his throat catching. "Just don't ever do that to me again."

"What?"

"Leave without saying where you've gone. I had terrible visions. I thought you were sick and helpless, and—" He sucked air between his teeth. "I don't want to think about it anymore," he finished roughly.

"I promise. I promise." Kate kissed his neck and ran her fingers through the thick hair at his nape. "And Jake?"

"Hmmm."

"I know where I want to get married now. I was there today . . ."

Chapter Twenty-Two

Tomorrow . . .

The church was full of people. Wreaths of white roses festooned the altar and pews, and white satin ribbons draped and flowed over onto the bridal aisle where the scent from curling, ecru rose petals, strewn across the red carpet, drifted upward into the warm air. Music swelled from a piano, not an organ, and mingled with the scents to create a gala mood of expectation. Candelabra stood at attention on either side of the altar, each one displaying seven satiny candles. The scent of vanilla and musk wafted upward to blend with the rich aroma of the roses.

It was a sensual delight, made moreso by the elegantly dressed crowd and the scarlet, velvet wall hangings with their lush gold trim—a gift from Kate's soon to be in-laws. For a church that boasted plain roots, white clapboard and bare, though highly glossed, cherry pews, this touch of extravagance seemed like a sweet icing. Marilyn Talbot hadn't outgrown her love for Victorian excess, and any chance to spread the wealth was apparently welcomed whole-heartedly.

April wore a gown of palest blue, a color discerning members of the crowd murmured paid homage to her gray-blue eyes. She walked ahead of her mother, a soft smile curving her lips, as if she harbored a lovely secret, which in fact she did. Today was her birthday. She had insisted they choose it for their wedding, a last punctuation to the story that was her parents' love affair.

Members of the audience smiled at her in response. Marilyn Talbot herself, who had yet to realize April was her real granddaughter, was struck speechless by the solemnity of the occasion, her normally haughty chin quivering visibly. Pulling a handkerchief from her bag, she dabbed at the corners of very watery eyes. Her husband slid her a look, but for once there was indulgence in his gaze. In a rare gesture, he clasped one of his wife's hands, and they watched in silent joy as April ascended the stairs and turned to wait for Jake and Kate.

Jake was splendid in a black tuxedo and crisp white shirt. His brother, Phillip, stood beside him, a bit older, a bit rounder, and these days, a bit humbler. He knew that April was Jake's daughter because April herself had told him. And it was as if Jake, Kate and April's family ties had bound him tighter within his own. He had started to change his ways, and as he viewed his soon-to-be new sister-in-law coming down the aisle, he vowed that he would settle down and find a woman as wonderful for himself. It was past time. He wanted to fall in love.

Kate moved as if in a dream. The church was the same, except for the lavish touches added for this wedding. The weather was darned near the same: wild and cold, and threatening rain and lightning and thunder outside these protective walls. Her dress was the same. Tucked away in a closet all these years to be resurrected for this ceremony, its seed pearls danced in the flickering candlelight.

But most of all, the man was the same one she had married so long ago. Jacob Talbot. Her lover. Soon to be her husband.

Her throat grew hot and tight. She blinked behind a white veil. As she approached the altar Jake held out his hand to clasp her white-gloved one in the protection of his.

The young minister greeted them both. Kate felt a soft little wave inside her. Their baby, moving gently within her womb. "I love you," she mouthed to the man beside her.

He grinned. His trademark smile.

"I love you more," he mouthed back, while candlelight flickered in nodding satisfaction all around them.

AUTHOR'S NOTE

If you would like to receive a current Janelle Taylor newsletter, bookmark, and descriptive flyer of other books available with pictures of their covers, send a self-addressed stamped envelope (long size best) to:

Janelle Taylor Newsletter #31
P.O. Box 211646
Martinez, Georgia 30917-1646

Reading is fun and educational, so do it often!

Best Wishes from

Janelle Taylor

ROMANCE FROM FERN MICHAELS

DEAR EMILY   (0-8217-4952-8, $5.99)

WISH LIST   (0-8217-5228-6, $6.99)

AND IN HARDCOVER:

VEGAS RICH   (1-57566-057-1, $25.00)

YOU WON'T WANT TO READ
JUST ONE—KATHERINE STONE

ROOMMATES   (0-8217-5206-5, $6.99/$7.99)
No one could have prepared Carrie for the monumental
changes she would face when she met her new circle of friends
at Stanford University. Once their lives intertwined and became
woven into the tapestry of the times, they would never be the
same.

TWINS   (0-8217-5207-3, $6.99/$7.99)
Brook and Melanie Chandler were so different, it was hard to
believe they were sisters. One was a dark, serious, ambitious
New York attorney; the other, a golden, glamourous, sophisti-
cated supermodel. But they were more than sisters—they were
twins and more alike than even they knew . . .

THE CARLTON CLUB   (0-8217-5204-9, $6.99/$7.99)
It was the place to see and be seen, the only place to be. And
for those who frequented the playground of the very rich, it
was a way of life. Mark, Kathleen, Leslie and Janet—they
worked together, played together, and loved together, all behind
exclusive gates of the *Carlton Club*.

*Available wherever paperbacks are sold, or order direct from the
Publisher. Send cover price plus 50¢ per copy for mailing and
handling to Penguin USA, P.O. Box 999, c/o Dept. 17109,
Bergenfield, NJ 07621. Residents of New York and Tennessee
must include sales tax. DO NOT SEND CASH.*

ROMANCE FROM JO BEVERLY

DANGEROUS JOY   (0-8217-5129-8, $5.99)

FORBIDDEN   (0-8217-4488-7, $4.99)

THE SHATTERED ROSE   (0-8217-5310-X, $5.99)

TEMPTING FORTUNE   (0-8217-4858-0, $4.99)